READING
IN BED

SUE GEE

headline
review

First published in Great Britain in 2007
by HEADLINE REVIEW
An imprint of HEADLINE PUBLISHING GROUP

First published in paperback in Great Britain in 2008
by HEADLINE REVIEW
An imprint of HEADLINE PUBLISHING GROUP

6

Cataloguing in Publication Data is available from the British Library

ISBN 978 0 7553 0312 0

Typeset in Garamond by Avon DataSet Ltd,
Bidford on Avon, Warwickshire

Printed and bound in Great Britain by Clays Ltd, St Ives plc

HEADLINE PUBLISHING GROUP
An Hachette Livre UK Company
338 Euston Road
London NW1 3BH

www.headline.co.uk

In loving memory of Marek Mayer,
who was right about so many things

Part One

Part One

1

There they go, two clever women of sixty, making their way through the wet towards the car. They've been to a literary festival; now they are going home: Dido to York, and Jeffrey; Georgia to London, and an empty house. Clouds roll back over the hills: it's clearing.

– It's clearing, says Dido, avoiding a puddle.

– Just as we leave. Georgia shakes out and furls her umbrella, and they stand for a moment, both tall, each with a different kind of elegance, taking it all in: the soaking emerald fields beyond the car park, the scattered sheep, the forest, dense as legend, smothering the Brecon hills. The canvas of the festival marquees sits pleasingly amidst all this; postmodern flags, slashed strips of parchment white, flutter at the entrance as the last of the rain blows away and the afternoon sun breaks through. From inside a marquee comes a burst of welcoming applause.

– We've heard him before, says Georgia, as Dido all at once looks wistful. – We really don't need—

– I know. It's just—

– It's been lovely. If we stayed till the end we'd have to stay another night.

– I know.

– And I hate arriving home on a Monday. Georgia is getting her keys out as they reach the car. – It puts me out of sorts. I like the week to start properly: breakfast at my own table, and things in view.

3

– As if you were still working, in fact.

– Quite. There is much to be said for routine. Georgia unlocks the car, and puts her umbrella in the boot, where their bags are already resting, bulging with books, new and secondhand. The town is the kingdom of secondhand books. They settle themselves inside, the travel rug folded on the back seat. It is a mark of something, to buy a travel rug, and Georgia had felt it when she did so. She starts up, puts the wipers on, then off, looks in the mirror.

– Are we clear?

– There's a dog, says Dido, looking to the left.

– Is there an owner?

– No. Yes. It's all right, he's seen us.

– The dog?

– The owner. He's calling him. You're all right now.

– I say! says Georgia, backing slowly. – Call orf your dog!

They both smile, seeing approximately the same self-important figure striding across some middle-England field.

– I shall miss you, says Dido, as they turn, and drive towards the entrance. Wild barking follows them.

– Me, too. Now, then. Georgia scans the narrow hilltop street, thronged with shoppers and festival-goers. Everyone has a carrier bag of books. – OK, she says, seizing a moment between a Land Rover and an estate car, and they drive slowly down the hill. A sheepdog with mad pale eyes hangs out of the back of the Land Rover, panting.

– More dogs than people, says Dido.

They drive beneath the banner strung across the street: *People say that life is the thing, but I prefer reading.*

– And so say all of us, she adds, lowering the window a little. The sun is getting stronger. It's all at once quite warm. – I must look up Logan Pearsall Smith when we get home.

– Oh, don't you know him? Georgia slows by the clock tower.

People are having lunch at the pavement café where they themselves lunched yesterday. – He was a favourite of Henry's father. She looks to the right and left on the main road. – Essays, mostly. *There are few sorrows, however poignant, in which a good income is of no avail.*

Dido laughs. – I must tell Jeffrey.

– And also – Georgia pulls out, and turns down the hill – *Thank heavens the sun has gone in, and I don't have to go out and enjoy it.* Or was that Sydney Smith? She picks up speed. – I always think of Smith when I visit Maud: *In the country one has the feeling that creation is about to expire before teatime.*

– How is Maud these days?

– Worrying. I've only seen her once since the funeral.

They pass the garden of a gallery, planted with strange wooden carvings. – Something will have to be done, but I haven't the strength.

– I've never known you not have strength. Perhaps Chloe could help.

– Perhaps.

– They do have things in common.

– I'm afraid that's true.

They're out in open country now, spinning along on a good smooth road between black and white Tudor houses, dazzling fields of rape, young corn.

Dido puts her hand on Georgia's arm. – It's been perfect. I've loved every minute.

– Me, too, says Georgia again, and then, as the toll bridge approaches – Have you fifty pence?

Dido opens her bag. They rattle over the peaceful Wye. People are camping in a field beside it, gliding serenely in canoes. The river mirrors swans, fishermen, early summer sky. They pay for their ticket and succumb to ices, pulling up beneath a tree to lick away at chocolate and vanilla. Then they're properly off, looking out for the sign to Hereford, where Dido will catch the train to York, changing twice and arriving home at midnight. Jeffrey will be waiting at the station.

– How many books did you buy? asks Georgia.

– At least a dozen. At least. They're like drugs, those signing queues. And put me in Addyman's and I lose all reason.

They're on their way. They go through everyone they've heard. Enormous names fill the car.

– Just to look into Lessing's eyes.

– Benn was marvellous.

– He always is.

– Pinter was—

– Pinter. No more need be said.

– As he himself might have—

– Quite.

They drive on at one accord, as they have been since distant college days. There's not much traffic, out in open country: they've timed it well. Farmland stretches out beneath the hills, elaborate clouds are lit by the sun, the country air blows in.

– God, says Georgia. – London, after this.

– But it's lovely, where you are.

They slow at the approach to Credenhill, a charming village next to the headquarters of the SAS. Rolls of barbed wire top huge fences. Then they come to the Hereford road, and now the traffic thickens, full of Sunday outings. Georgia looks at the clock.

– We'll be fine, says Dido, and indeed they reach the station with a good fifteen minutes before the train to Crewe, and stand beneath hanging baskets filled with plastic flowers, watching the come and go of Sunday travellers, and a sweet young Labrador, being good as gold.

– Will you be all right? asks Dido. – All that long drive.

– I'll be fine. *Bookclub, Poetry Please.* I should be home by seven.

– Give the cats my love. Who's feeding them?

– Next door. They're very good.

The station announcement announces Dido's train. They gaze along the track.

– And Chloe, of course, says Dido. – Will you be seeing her this week?

– I expect so. And give my love to Jeffrey.

– I will. And he sends his.

Dido is painfully aware of Henry's absence from this exchange, but says only, again, as so often: – Will you be all right?

– I'll be fine, says Georgia, as she always does, and then the train comes in, and they settle Dido in her reserved corner seat, facing the engine, and heave up her bag on the rack. They kiss.

– Safe journey. We'll speak in the week.

– We will.

And Georgia climbs down, stands waiting, as the last door slams and then the whistle blows. They're off. Dido presses her hand to her lips; Georgia, always less demonstrative, nods and smiles as the blown kiss comes towards her. She stands there waving as the train pulls out, waits until it has rounded the bend, then makes her way out to the car park, following the joyous Labrador and his family, feeling a cloud of appalling loneliness settle upon her in moments.

– Stop it, she says aloud, but no one notices.

She reaches the car, unlocks it, has the radio on in a trice.

– Welcome to *Bookclub*, says James Naughtie kindly.

Georgia fastens her seat belt, and drives away.

London on a summer evening. *Pick of the Week* has taken her through the approaches: along the Westway and over Marylebone Flyover. Tower blocks glitter on either side: as always, returning, Georgia feels a pulse of excitement: this is the city, the splendid rush and throb. Everything starts here. But it's hard to sustain this feeling as litter blows along the Marylebone Road, and though her spirits rise a little at the glimpse of blossom in Regent's Park they sink again at Euston, and the clog of traffic crawling towards King's Cross, where the building of the Eurostar network has held everyone up for years. Well. One day perhaps she and Dido will use it to go to Paris. Perhaps Jeffrey will join them. She passes the British Library, and here her heart does lift, for the Library's airy spaces have nourished her for years, and she knows that by tomorrow she'll be back in the swim of life in London, refreshed by a week in the country and getting on with things. Well, pretty much. As much as anything is a swim these days.

Georgia leaves King's Cross behind her, drives to the Angel, Islington, a place she has known for over three decades but where she now feels adrift amidst a sea of youth: spilling out of pubs, crowding the pavements, talking for England on their mobiles.

Upper Street, with its rich mix of shops and cafés, as every estate agent describes it, is basking in the warmth. The Screen on the Green is showing something interesting and French. Outside the Marie Curie shop on Highbury roundabout stand clumps of black bags and a little rocking horse. Goodness. How could you give away a rocking horse? Would you not cherish it for ever? If Georgia had a grandchild she'd stop and take it, dropping in a donation next day, but she does not have a grandchild – will she ever? – and she drives past, taking a last look in the mirror at the horse's scarlet reins, and turns into Corsica Street, leaving the traffic behind. She's almost home.

Highbury Fields is enjoying the evening sun. Queues at the ice-cream vans, tennis, joggers, dog walkers; ball games and the end of a picnic in the dog-free enclosure at the top. Chloe took her first steps in there, light years ago. Well, thirty years ago. Chloe is thirty-one this week. Dear God, where have three decades gone? Swimmers stand talking outside the pool, children shriek in the playground, cyclists spin by. All this activity, all this vibrant life. Georgia drives slowly through it all, up a Georgian terrace and round, right round, into her own quiet street at last. Home again, home again, jiggety-jig, she hears her mother sing through the mists of time. There's a space outside her own front door: fantastic. She pulls up, turns off the engine.

For a moment she sits there, feeling she'll never move again. The sun is sinking over the rooftops, the Harrisons are walking up the street: she with the pushchair, he with their little boy on his shoulders. They wave and smile. Then they go into their house, and close the door. Georgia takes an enormous breath, and rallies. She gets out as stiffly as four hours' solid driving leaves you, stretches, heaves out her bag. Tomorrow she'd better have a swim. She points her keys at the car doors and hears the little beep as they lock. Modern times: so clever.

She walks through her front gate, brushing the lavender with her bag. The window-box geraniums have come on inches, just in a week. When she's settled in, she'll do the evening watering: comforting thought. And there are Tristan's ears, just visible behind the scarlet flowers. She unlocks the door, puts the bag down, stands there. The house smells shut up and feels as dead as a doornail.

– Come on, she says to the dusty air, and then: – Hello?

And the soft drop of cats from table and sofa to floorboards sounds at once. They're padding through sleepily; Isolde makes her little sound.

Fond embraces. – Thank God you're here.

Along past the stairs to the kitchen. Note on the table, a week's post, Saturday's milk in the fridge. Unlock the door to the garden. It's tiny, but they made it just right. Alchemilla and white forget-me-nots spill over the brickwork, the tulips are stunning. There are shrubs packed into every corner, a birdbath, a little pond. Last year a blackbird nested in the holly in the corner: in time for Henry to watch the male fly in and out to feed his mate, though not to see the fledgelings fly. Nor did he see the little bluetits emerge from the box on the wall: four, though one fell two weeks earlier, smack on to the brick path. It died as only a nestling dies: naked, blind and tragic. Georgia, when she found it, had (unusually) sobbed her heart out.

Now she stands there, looking at it all. Entrancing cream sprays of love-lies-bleeding turn a flowerbed into a wedding. Gentle moss covers the plinth on which Athene rests, her lovely stone head placed perfectly in that corner, ivy trailing down. Just in a week, everything's clumped up. Here are the cats, asking for supper. Tristan twines round her ankles. Isolde drinks from the pond. Birds sing from gardens all around, the traffic is a distant hum.

– OK, says Georgia. – Here we are again. And she turns decisively, goes in to shake cat food into dishes, read the neighbourly note, go to the loo and return to pour a drink, opening the bottle put in the fridge when she left, all ready for her return. She takes the glass into the garden, sips, rests it on the birdbath. She turns on the hose. Here comes the magical pattering fall of water on to earth and leaf and brick. The sinking sun just catches it all. She's home.

2

— How was it? asks Jeffrey, over breakfast. — Give me the highlights.

Dido, still in her dressing gown, shocking on a Monday morning, but what the hell, pours coffee for them both. Last night she'd been almost too tired to speak. Sunday service on two different rail companies, each as hopeless as the other. *We apologise for the late arrival . . .* Give me strength, she'd said to Jeffrey, giving him her bag. — Poor you. She kissed him. — I'm sorry.

— Not your fault. Let's get you home.

She'd fallen asleep as soon as her head hit the pillow.

— Well, she says now, reaching for the toast. — Benn was the star, I suppose. Benn and Lessing. Put all the young things in the shade.

— And Pinter?

— Pinter was Pinter, as Georgia would say. Looking better.

Jeffrey passes the marmalade: last jar but one of the batch she'd made in January. — And Georgia? he asks her. — Coping?

— When has Georgia not coped? We enjoyed every minute. Dido yawns. — But I'm shattered.

— You have a nice quiet day. Jeffrey takes a look at the clock, and opens the paper.

— I shall, says Dido. Oh, the bliss of retirement, and nice quiet days. Not that she often has many. — Pass me the other bit, she says, and Jeffrey passes a supplement full of media chitchat. She gazes at the cover of a new magazine devoted to cosmetic surgery. A glance

11

in the mirror. God, she looks a wreck. A face should be lived in, Georgia has always said firmly. A face should be real. Botox is for bimbos and has-beens. Dido turns the pages. Massive cuts at the Beeb. They don't know anyone there now.

– And the B & B? asks Jeffrey, from behind the headlines.

– Heavenly.

Jeffrey gives a sudden snort.

– What?

He reads out Hoggart on Blair. They giggle. – Bremner was brilliant last night, he says, then looks at the clock again. – I must be off.

– What are you up to today?

– It's Monday, it must be America. The Civil War. He folds the paper, swallows the last of his coffee. – Then a couple of meetings and a tutorial.

– Only one?

– Someone who couldn't get out of bed for the last.

– Tut-tut. And you're fitting him in?

– Her. Out of the kindness of my heart.

Dido shakes her head. – I haven't heard a thing about your week, she says, as he pushes his chair back. – How was it?

– Pretty much like this one. He drops a hand on her head as he passes. – I should be home by six.

– I'll have something nice in the oven. I'll be up to speed by then.

– Jolly good.

And he's gone, taking briefcase from the study, jacket and safety helmet from the hall. She gets up to watch him unlock the garage and wheel the bike out down the path. Sixty-two and – at least in summer – he cycles off to work as if he were a student still. He looks up at the gate, gives a wave. A helmet does nothing for a man, especially with glasses, but no matter: Jeffrey's tall, he's well-made, he can carry it off.

– Bye, calls Dido as he wheels away, and returns to the breakfast table. She must make a list.

Not quite yet, perhaps.

Bathed, dressed and in her right mind; unpacked, the books piled up beside the bed, the washing turning, Dido consults the calendar. This nice quiet day is just as well, as the week looks rather busy. Tomorrow the Centre, Wednesday the book group, and supper for everyone here. She can tell them all about the festival. Thursday the Centre again; Friday – what does that say? Buttock? Surely not. She tries it again, with and without her glasses. She should know Jeffrey's angular hand by now. Sturrock. Sturrock? Who he? Sturrock drinks. Oh, well, she'll find out tonight. Saturday's free, so they might go to a film; Sunday the children are coming to lunch.

She washes up the breakfast things, looks through the post. A week away has brought her mailings from the Early Music Centre and the open-air theatre in Rowntree Park. There's a couple of postcards, a request for a reference from an old pupil, a reminder from the dentist. Life's gentle tapestry resumes. Nothing that can't wait. She reheats the last of the coffee and makes her list. Jeffrey is far from incapable, but the cupboard is largely bare. Sustained all yesterday by a B & B breakfast (very good) and railway sandwiches (dismal) she's in need of something nourishing tonight. No doubt he is too. And what is she to give everyone on Wednesday?

The clock ticks, Marr questions meaningfully from the kitchen, the sun comes in at the open window. Dido loves this room: a breakfast room, a morning room, light, well-proportioned and facing on to the garden. She loves the whole house, always has done, knew when they found it, thirty years ago, that it would see them through, and it has: two careers in two small studies, one doubling as guest room; two (almost three) children, lots of friends; student lodgers, everyone mucking in: busy, busy years.

There's still a lot going on now, and Jeffrey is three years off retirement (when the mortgage will finally be paid, extra loans and all) but the children are more or less settled – Kate more, Nick rather less. And she – she has her time to herself at last. That she has chosen to fill it with many things is as it should be: she still has plenty to give. But she doesn't have to. After thirty years' teaching, fifteen as head of department; after all those courses, adding on experience and qualifications for her retirement years – Relate, the Samaritans, the Diploma in Counselling – Dido, when she so chooses, can go to a literary festival with her oldest friend, soak up literature and country air for an entire week, and still – bliss – have the next day off to potter. She's lucky. She knows that apart from that long sad time with the lost baby – oh, those dreadful days – she's been pretty fortunate all her life. Nobody's life can be without its sadness, and that distant time was hers. But she's worked very hard, she's done her stuff, she's allowed to enjoy it all now.

She finishes the list, drains the coffee, gets up and sees herself once again in the mirror. She's fit, she's tall and lean, she's active; she feels – on the whole – so young. Catch her back view in the street – good jeans, good navy sweater – and she could probably pass for forty. It's always a bit of a surprise to see the grey in the well-cut head of dark hair, the lines. She goes over, looks in the glass more closely. Does she imagine it, or is there, already, that telltale circle round the iris that shows you are getting old? Not older: old. She takes off her glasses, puts them on again. There's just a thin thin line, a milky pale circle.

Perhaps a little rest after lunch, a little feet-up. But now: shopping. Action. Where are the keys?

It's a bright and beautiful morning. Dido spends a happy hour or so prowling round the shops. Out on the Welsh borders, the approach of high summer had been borne on every gust of air, rich with heavy soil and cowpat, blowing over the forested hills, new crops and glossy grass. Here – here, it's summer in the city. A lesser thing? A different kind of thing. The breeze from the river rustles the trees, clouds sail over the Minster and the pale stone of the city walls is washed with sunlight. Everything is fuller, feels as if it will last for ever: the creamy candles on the chestnut trees, the pink-splashed magnolia on the corner of their street.

She crosses the main road. Cyclists spin past as she walks down Peasholme Green and makes her way to the pedestrianised streets of the Quarter. Here she is again, and it's as if she's never been away, the clock of Holy Trinity striking eleven, tourists queuing at the Roman Bathhouse, the market stalls piled high with summer veg. She can smell cheese and geraniums.

It's good to be back.

Now then. She gets out her list. A contented hour goes by.

Dido lunches on tomato and lentil soup from the health-food shop, and oatcakes and cheese from the deli. She listens to *The World at One*, finishes the paper, dispatches with firm kindness two Jehovah's Witnesses. She rings Georgia, but Georgia is out. Crisp tones invite her to leave a message. This she does. What is Georgia doing this lunch time, she wonders, climbing the stairs. Which is worse, in widowhood: to stay in an empty house or to return to it? How different – she knows this instinctively – is the emptiness she has all around her now, a steady quietude she can fill in any way she chooses, knowing that its hours are limited to Jeffrey's working day; that his key will sound in the lock; that he'll give her the campus gossip over a drink in the garden, that she'll fill him in properly over supper with details of her week away; that they'll watch the news together, read in bed together, fall asleep without having to give anything a thought.

Oh dear.

Poor Georgia.

They went back such a long way, the four of them. Taking her shoes off now, sinking on to the bed, Dido sees images come and go from the past: the punting, the parties, the cycling to lecture and seminar, the intensity of it all. She and Georgia had missed each other in the first year, clicked in the second and never looked back. That the men they both liked, then fell in love with, should also be friends was – well, that was what Oxford was like, when it went well, as it had for all of them. Finals. Moving to London: Henry to the civil service, Jeffrey to UCL, she and Georgia both to the Institute for the post-grad teaching diploma everyone did when they didn't get jobs in publishing, or didn't know what to do. Or even – good gracious – wanted to teach. Solid working lives began.

All around them, girls in Laura Ashley frocks got pregnant, wept at the British Pregnancy Advisory Service, never told their parents. Clouds of dope filled the air at every party. People went to India, to the Rent Tribunal, found squats in Brixton and occupied Grosvenor Square. Dido, Jeffrey, Henry and Georgia did some of these things, but not many. They did not drop out: indeed, they held on tenaciously to the lives for which everything – professional parents, good schools, and good examples – had prepared them. They married in their early twenties: Dido and Jeffrey at Finsbury Register Office, Georgia and Henry in Islington Town Hall.

Then Jeffrey, after years as a 0.5 at UCL, doing his Ph.D. the whilst, leafed through *The Times Higher* one more time, and saw the post at Fountains. He applied. He got it. Dido bought champagne.

Jeffrey's grandparents had come from Yorkshire: in moving back there, he was returning to his roots. But – how exciting – he was looking to the future in a brand-new university, full of sixties promise. Mist, the moors, the ruined abbey, all linked the place to the past: Fountains had depth, it came out of tradition. But its spacious campus, brick and gleaming glass, its stunning lecture halls and airy teaching rooms all proclaimed a vision of the future: radical, pioneering, unequivocally modern.

It was, of course, right in the middle of nowhere. You couldn't actually live there, not as a member of staff. Brand-new students caught filthy colds making a dash for brand-new halls of residence across the windswept grounds, but staff would have to commute. There was no railway station. Jeffrey, young and fit, decided to remain so by cycling out there, at least in spring and summer. His parents lent him and Dido enough for a deposit on a wreck of a house in a run-down suburb – now one of the most desirable districts in York. They moved; they settled down.

And Georgia and Henry likewise, in London. Combined incomes (excellent civil service, shocking teaching) bought them a Highbury flat. Promotions bought them a house.

The babies came: Kate for Dido and Jeffrey, Chloe for Georgia. That birth was natural and hellish: Georgia wanted no more. Dido and Jeffrey did, and Nick arrived. One of each! How fortunate they were.

Years passed. Settled, interesting, enviable lives took shape. Sometimes Dido thought: we're too lucky; this can't go on. Then came tragedy, with baby number three. A little girl, unplanned, and all the more beloved: a gift, a blessing, a darling new member of the family.

– Can I hold her?

– Can I?

Ella. Even now, she thinks of her.

Sometimes Georgia said on the phone, or at Easter in the Lakes: When Henry and I retire – it seemed donkey's years away – we're going to do VSO. Make ourselves useful.

– You're useful now, said Dido.

– Yes, but one must never give up.

Over the years this idea came and went. The women, in any case, would retire five years before the men, unless they took early retirement. Neither wanted to. Everyone was fit.

Georgia said on the phone that last autumn, after their holiday in France, all four together again: – Henry's a bit off colour.

Unheard of, except for things like flu.

– He's feeling a bit ropey, still, she said a week or two later. – I've told him to go for a check-up.

He went. He was sent for a blood test.

That was it.

Dido has intended to listen to the afternoon play, but drifts off with *The Archers*. A summery breeze blows in at the open window; so does the scent of the syringa at the garden gate. Footsteps go past. She sleeps.

3

Chloe is washing a lettuce in a beaded jacket. Edmund comes in. Rain is falling, soaking the window box and splashing off the black-painted fire escape, where pots of geraniums stand. Chloe shakes out the lettuce and a shower of water mirrors the rain in a flurry. Edmund switches the light on.

– That's better. He sets down the shopping. – How are we doing?

– Fine. I'm going to ice the cake in a minute. Did you get soaked?

– I made a dash for it.

– Well done. Have we got everything now?

– I think so. Coffee?

– I've been drinking coffee all morning; I'm wired. Let's have lunch.

– Soup and cheese?

– Soup and cheese. And a bit of salad.

Chloe tears a few leaves into a bowl, Edmund puts things away, Chloe opens a carton of country garden soup. They move round one another as companionably as only a couple with no sexual interest in one another can do. Edmund is an actor, currently appearing in China & Glass at Heal's. Previous productions have included Bedlinen and Christmas Lights. His extra-curricular interests are male, and at present unsettled. Chloe is hoping someone interesting might pitch up at the party: someone she's never met before, who will be – she'll know at once – The One. At thirty-one, this very week, she has faith that such a thing can happen, though since her father's death she has had little energy left over from the huge emotions of grieving. It's getting a little bit easier. She no longer cries every day, indeed has not cried for some weeks. She's giving a party, the first for eighteen months. She must be getting better.

She and Edmund sit eating Saturday lunch at the kitchen table. The kitchen is also the dining room, and indeed the sitting room. It has a double aspect, with three sash windows: one overlooking the fire escape at the back, beyond sink, stove, fridge, cupboards, and two at the front, looking on to Charlotte Street, several floors below. A sofa slumps beneath these front windows, between more cupboards, shelves, etc. A little yellow lamp, which Chloe found in a junk shop on a visit to York, perches on a cupboard heaped with this and that. The telly is shoved in a corner. The walls are a very dark antique green, nicely setting off window-box daffodils in spring and geraniums in summer. There are one or two posters in frames. This is not the age of the poster – such as it had been for their parents' generation, where no room was complete without Lautrec's *Jane Avril*, or Che Guevara, or Liv Ullmann's mournful gaze – but Chloe and Edmund have settled on Matisse and Hopper, both from Tate Modern shows. Chloe is sick of the Hopper now: that woman gazing out at nothing from an empty room – too many postcards have dulled its effect. No matter: she's part of the furniture.

The room, in short, is comfortable, has atmosphere, and though it's pretty small for a party, better too crowded than too empty, and there's always the fire escape. This is reached through a door at the back of the landing, and those without vertigo will be fine out there, so long as it stops raining.

It stops raining. Black-painted ironwork gleams. Edmund cuts another slice of walnut bread and offers it to Chloe, who declines.

He takes it himself and adds the last of the Brie. Geraniums sparkle at the window in the emerging sun. A happy afternoon of preparations lies ahead.

The party is making up for the fact that last year, Chloe's momentous Thirtieth, there had been only drinks and cake with Georgia in the garden at home. Neither of them could face more. Georgia had wanted to make an effort. Please don't, said Chloe. This is just how it has to be. It was six and a half weeks after the funeral. They sat in the summer evening, listening to the radiant cruelty of the blackbird's song.

— I'm so sorry, said Georgia, for the hundredth time, as if Chloe's fatherless state were all her fault.

— Stop it. Let's cut the cake.

Georgia did so, biting her lip.

— He loved you so much.

— I know. Me too. You too. Poor Mum.

The cats came out to join them. Isolde made her way to the pond, where the frogs were enjoying the deepening sun. She sat very close to the edge.

— Don't even think about it, Chloe told her. The cake was delicious, lemony, creamy, light as a feather. She let her mother pour another glass of fizz.

— Thanks. Cheers again. They chinked their glasses. Tristan sat washing by Georgia's wrought-iron seat.

— Do you think they know Dad's gone?

— I'm sure they do. Isolde sleeps in his chair all the time.

Chloe burst into tears.

One or two neighbours came over for supper. Dido phoned. Edmund kept his distance: today was a mother-daughter thing. Chloe stayed the night, sleeping in the room of her childhood with Tristan beside her: waiting on the bed while she had her bath, starting to purr as soon as she switched the light off. He came up to the bed and settled himself right next to her on the pillow, almost smothering her.

– Darling puss. What would I do without you?

In the morning, she and Georgia left the house together after breakfast: Chloe to go to the office and Georgia to Birkbeck, where she had classes until the end of term. Then she'd retire. Then what would she do? Life without Henry yawned ahead.

They walked down Highbury Fields with all the other people heading for the tube. Dogs raced about. Early swimmers left the pool with wet hair, unlocking their bikes from the rack, checking their watches. Chloe checked hers.

– What time's the shoot? asked Georgia, as they overtook a pushchair.

– Not till eleven, but I have to pick up all the stuff first. It's OK, I'll make it.

Beggars were waiting outside Barclays Bank. Georgia and Chloe walked briskly past, and stood waiting at the lights. Already the Holloway Road was roaring.

– Henry often used to give to them, said Georgia, using his name for the first time that day, and the last. People at work didn't want you to keep going on.

– He was a soppy date, said Chloe. – I never do. Well, I do sometimes, if they're busking. Not if they just sit there with those poor dogs. OK, let's cross.

Inside the station, they kissed goodbyes, Chloe keeping an ear out for the Silverlink train to Camden Road.

– Thanks, Mum. I'll phone you tonight.

– You don't have to.

– I might want to talk to you.

Georgia smiled. They went their separate ways.

That was then, this is now. Chloe, in celibate cohabitation with Edmund since answering an ad in *Loot* in 1999 (so they saw in the

Millennium together) is preparing for her birthday party. Behind this energetic day lies her birth, thirty-one years and three days ago, in the maternity unit of University College Hospital, smack bang between this flat and Birkbeck College, as it happens. Behind her lies primary school, where no one, in the late seventies, had wondered why, at seven, Chloe was still struggling to read. She was bright, she had a wide vocabulary, she was just taking her time. Georgia should stop fussing. Behind her lie the endless after-school extra sessions from the age of eight, once Georgia and Henry had taken matters into their own hands, taken her to an educational psychologist, and had his verdict.

Dyslexic? Chloe?

– Better to have a proper diagnosis than watch her struggle on.

– But she can't be. There's no one in the family—

– Maud, said Henry.

– Oh, God.

Behind Chloe now, icing her cake in childhood's pink and white, listening to the cricket, as Henry used to do, lies the transfer to secondary school: first the comprehensive behind the Holloway Road where no one minded about her dyslexia, lots of other people couldn't read or spell, and then the rapid transfer to a soppy independent school for girls where you didn't have to pass the Common Entrance if you didn't want to.

The whole thing was a nightmare. It went on and on.

– Not going to university? But Chloe, you must. You're so clever, you must. They'll give you lots of support—

– I don't want any more fucking support, OK?

It was dreadful. Slammed doors, white faces, nobody speaking. Georgia was worse than kindly Henry.

That's enough now. Chloe licks icing off the knife, feeling her head begin to spin as she lets all these memories come back. At thirty, you review the past: you have to. She hadn't last year, because the present had been so all-consuming. Now she is doing

it, twelve months and three days late, as the sound of the traffic
floats up and in through the open windows, the sun shines,
showing the dust up, and England declare for three hundred and
fifty-six for six.

– I'm not going, and that's that.

– Then what are you going to do?

– Go to art school. What's wrong with that?

– You can't draw. Sorry, but it's true.

– You don't have to *draw*.

Georgia, not for the first time, put her head in her hands.

Behind Chloe, finishing her icing, setting the cake to dry on the
bread board, lie four years of installations, mixed media, video
workshops, computer graphics. Byam Shaw off the Holloway Road
for Foundation, Central St Martin's for the Dip. She left in 1995.
Now what? She went to work in Liberty, where she had temped for
two summers. She moved from kelims to curtains to fabrics.
People bought bolts of Liberty-printed cotton, understated linen,
swathes of William Morris, over the counter, and often, as she
unfolded these fabrics and cut off lengths with fabulous sharp
scissors, Chloe experienced pure pleasure. What had begun as a
pleasant summer job became a passion.

After a while, she realised:

– I should have done *textile* design.

– Never too late, said Henry. – I'm sure we could—

– No, no, it's OK. Forget it. I don't want to drag on being a
student.

– It wouldn't be a drag if you—

– I said forget it.

But what could she do? Spend her life in Liberty, rise to being
a buyer? That might take for ever, and her dyslexia might really
matter if she had to order stuff, and write to people. And the pay
was—

Then it happened, lying on the sofa with Georgia's *Vogue* one

Sunday afternoon. Home for lunch, everyone in a good mood. Chloe, coffee cup resting precariously on her midriff, leafed through shots of sulky young women wearing lingerie in barns, boots in the desert, a silken slip of nothing in a rocking chair. Every interior shot (so not the desert, where only a camel loomed) was bestrewn with beautiful objects: antique cup and saucer, a green glass jar crammed with lily of the valley, an open book (old) whereon a pair of glasses rested (new, Dolce & Gabbana). Chloe noticed them all. After a while she picked up a Laura Ashley catalogue Georgia had left on the coffee table. Not the fashions, the furnishings one. She settled down with it.

A chalk-pink armchair (deep, deep), with mahogany feet and gleaming castors, rested on scrubbed floorboards. Books and a candelabra (cream candles in rosebud holders) stood on a chest, before an old gilt mirror. French doors led to the garden; there was just a bit of an easel. Chloe found herself thinking she could look at this chalk-pink chair for a long time, and would have much pleasure in choosing, herself, that candelabra. She turned to bedlinen: heaps of quilts and cotton lace, waffle pillow cases (Oxford) were flung across a four-poster. A spray of blossom stood on the bedside table, a dressmaker's dummy was hung with a little fur wrap the colour of *café au lait*.

Chloe lay on the sofa, thinking. Someone must compose all these shots. Someone – who? – must have decided on that little fur, realised how subtly it set off all that cotton. Someone must have spent days scouring junk shops for that green glass jar (or dug it out of her grandmother's cupboard). Chloe had a good eye: everyone said so. Really good. She could do that.

– I could do that.

– What? Georgia was deep in the reviews.

– Be a stylist.

– A what?

– Never mind.

25

* * *

Chloe went to interviews dressed to kill. She played up her art school training like hell. At last she was taken on: as a junior in a company called Dot & Carrie, the names of the two women who founded it, whose stylish logo involved a dot and a bag. The bag was crammed with marvellous things and accompanied Chloe to studios all over London.

She loved it. She was very good at it. After a while, she was made Senior Stylist.

She had never looked back.

To hell with dyslexia. Who cared?

Chloe began the best years of her life. Along the way she made many friends and went to bed with men, as you did. Quite a few men liked the look of her. And yet. Life was busy, life was full. And yet.

– What I want, Chloe said to Edmund one evening in the spring of 2004, drinking wine after work in a bar in Primrose Hill, – what I want is to love someone as much as my parents love one another.

– They do? You're lucky.

– No, they do. They really get on. When I was little, I could hear them laughing in bed.

– You really are lucky.

– How can I ever hope to find something like that?

– I have no idea. My parents divorced when I was three. Shall we talk about me now?

So it went on. That summer, Chloe and a group of people went on holiday to Spain while her parents and Dido and Jeffrey went reading in France.

– Dad isn't feeling too good, Georgia said on the phone a few weeks later.

– He looked brilliant when you all came back.

– I know. It's probably nothing.
So it all began.

It can't be true. It can't be.

Now, a year and a half after her father had sat his wife and daughter down, and told them what he must, Chloe is choosing what to wear for her party. Then, the nights had drawn in, and Georgia had drawn the curtains against the autumnal garden and dark street. They listened to Henry's quiet voice. Now – now, in the heart of London, the early summer rain has blown away and far below people are sitting outside pavement cafés. Greek music, lively chatter, the sizzle of Greek cooking, all waft upwards and through the open windows; taxis tick and high heels hurry – to her door? Please not yet, please don't be uncool and early, I'm not ready yet.

– Edmund? How long are you going to be in there? Edmund!
The shower is turned low; he'll be out in two ticks.
Chloe, in her kimono dressing gown, all silk and birds, goes back to her bedroom and surveys the heap. The only thing she's sure of are the shoes.

For her thirty-first birthday party, just about to begin, Chloe – five foot eight, inheriting some of her parents' height; size twelve; short dark hair in a feathery elfin cut round her elfin, unjaded face, marvellous eyes (everyone says so) – wears her beloved beaded jacket, even though she's worn it to death. Beneath is a dead plain little black thing just on the knee, fishnet tights and the shoes, which are just fantastic: black and white leopard print with scarlet heels (two-inch) and scarlet toes.

– Yes?
– Yes, says Edmund, in faded green velvet. – Very yes.
– Audrey Hepburn? She raises an endless and invisible cigarette holder to a scarlet pout. – It has been said.

27

– Not by me. Hepburn was a size eight. He sees her face. – Dear Chloe. Hepburn to the life.

– What time is it?

– Time I gave you this.

A little flat box, wrapped in gold tissue paper and tied with golden thread.

– Oooh . . .

Inside, the finest, slenderest, most understated yet extravagant—

– Oh, *Edmund!*

– Put it on?

She puts it on, taking off the jacket, turning to the mirror, hardly daring to breathe in case she breaks the clasp, or the thread, even though it's been hand-knotted by mice. There.

– Gosh. Yes?

– Perfect.

– Everyone will ask if they're real.

– The certificate is in the box.

– So it is. *The finest selected black seed pearls* . . . Oh, Edmund, thank you. She kisses him. – Thank you, thank you! Let's have a drink.

They have one, listening to Billie Holiday. The room is full of pre-party cleanliness and order: heavy bowls of olives, sparkling glasses, tealights everywhere.

– Cheers. Happy Birthday.

– Cheers. Chloe is suddenly full of nerves. – Just tell me that tonight I'm going to meet—

– We know everyone who's coming.

– Someone might bring a friend.

– I hope they don't all do that.

– But someone might.

– The only person I can *really* see you with, said Edmund – to tell you the truth, is Jez.

– *Jez?*

– Isn't that his name? Your photographer? I think he has his eye on you. I think you'd look pretty good together.

– Looks aren't everything.

– Since when?

– Jez is married, Edmund.

– I know.

– And has a daughter.

– I know.

– Well, that's the end of that, then. Chloe reaches for the bottle, and jumps as the doorbell rings.

– Anyway, she says, going to the window, glass in hand, to see if she can see who it is down there – my mother thinks photographers aren't real people.

4

Dido, far away in one of the choicest parts of York, is, on the morning after Chloe's party, listening to the radio and preparing Sunday lunch. The joint rests, stuffed with rosemary and garlic; a spinach quiche, made yesterday before they went to the cinema, sits upon a worktop. This is for Paula, Nick's partner, and perhaps for Nick himself, if refusal of roast lamb can help things along between them. Dido snips mint from the garden into a little blue jug and hears a sigh. It's hers. Oh dear. Oh, well.

The Archers comes to an end, and the kitchen, after a few moments, is filled with the sounds of violins and seagulls. Then: Katharine Whitehorn is on *Desert Island Discs*. How marvellous, what a marvellous woman she is: the real thing through and through. And listening to that distinguished, low-register voice, framing the account of such a well-lived life, Dido recalls student days lived out of *Cooking in a Bedsitter*, and feels proud to be a part of Whitehorn's generation. Here is someone she has read and heeded for decades, speaking now of that rare combination, a truly happy marriage and a rich and enduring working life; a woman who now, at eighty – eighty? Katharine Whitehorn? – offers a role model still. Someone who, furthermore, has resisted the temptation that comes to every female journalist: to write a novel.

Thus Dido, snipping and chopping and musing, listens to how widowhood, for Whitehorn, is becoming more bearable than she had imagined. 'There's a lot going on in London' – terrific, to be saying that at her age. And thus Dido, distracted from unease at the prospect of possible tension over lunch, wonders, as Whitehorn chooses her book and luxury item, if Georgia is listening too, and how she's getting on, on Sunday in London, with lunch, perhaps, alone.

She should phone her. She hears herself asking: – Did you hear Katharine Whitehorn? Wasn't she marvellous?

– Very good, Georgia responds, and in that little phrase encapsulates one of the differences between them. Dido enthuses; Georgia is restrained. Their voices are different, too, Dido's much lighter; and she is swifter of speech, on the whole. Georgia is generally measured. Dido wonders sometimes if it's something to do with having an only child – you never have to turn from one to the other, or intervene. Things can take their time, perhaps are calmer. Is that true? Certainly there have been flashpoints in Chloe's development, rows and crises, even. Now there are just the two of them, with Chloe still unsettled, do they comfort or distress one another?

– Comfort, on the whole, Georgia had said, over supper at the literary festival. – But of course I worry.

Of course she does. How can one have children and not worry? All the while they're growing up, you look ahead to the milestones and see beyond them the shining light of Adulthood. And then, when it comes, all the worries are larger. As now, for instance, waiting to welcome everyone for Sunday lunch, and dreading that look on Nick's sweet face: that fleeting mixture of anger, sorrow and restraint which breaks her heart. Why can they not be happy? Why can't Paula—

She takes down the phone from the wall.

– Going somewhere nice? she asks Georgia, when they have finished discussing Whitehorn. No, Georgia isn't going to be alone today.

– Lunch with Graham and Tessa.

Dido tries to think.

– The Milners, says Georgia. – Remember them? He worked with Henry, she's in publishing. He gave a reading at the memorial service – the sonnet.

– Oh, yes! Yes, of course. Sweet chap.

– They're rather good at Sunday lunch, usually one or two nice people there. And you? Are the children coming?

– They are. In fact I'd better get a move on. Dido looks at the clock. Whatever is Jeffrey doing, shut away in his study on a Sunday morning? He should be checking the wine, laying the table, even, though she'll do the flowers herself. – Have a lovely time, she says to Georgia. – Have you had a party report from Chloe?

– It's only half-past twelve. Georgia is dry. – She'll phone tonight, I expect.

– I do hope it all went well. Give her my love.

They say their goodbyes. Dido replaces the phone on the wall – God, kitchen phones get filthy – and goes to the doorway.

– Jeffrey? Jeffrey!

Lunch, despite best efforts, is not quite right. Quite wrong, in fact. Oh, why does it have to be like this? Why, on a perfect early summer day, the garden brimming, everyone needing to unwind after a hectic week, before they must wind up again – why, amidst easy family chitchat, must there be this little dart, little dig; this taking offence, taking something quite innocent quite the wrong way? It makes Dido long to give a swift sharp smack on the wrist. There. Over and done with. I don't want to hear another word. Now, then, where were we?

But she can't, of course, do a thing.

And while Jeffrey is at his most attentive, carving first and second helpings, refilling glasses; and when Dido has finished passing things – the market veg, more quiche, the fresh mint sauce

– she sits and surveys her family, trying to let Paula's barbs of discord and dissent wash over her, and failing.

Jeffrey is at the far end of the table, his back to the garden, from whence, through the open doors, come the sweet flute and trill, etc. Their daughter, Kate, is on his right, her husband, Leo, on his left: a solid, well-matched couple if ever there was one, two doctors as through-and-through the children of the intelligentsia as she and Jeffrey, Georgia and Henry, and so on. And happy, thank God, as they all had been. Yes? They were happy with one another, were they not? Dido, through instinct, experience and training, thinks herself skilled enough in human relations to know when the appearance of contentment reflects the truth.

She watches Kate listening to her father and Leo turn over the question of stem cell research, intervening with a word about one of her own patients, finishing her last potato and sitting, even now, as she had done as a child: elbow on the table, chin in cupped hand, a finger playing with that thick dark hair – inherited, though Dido says it herself, from her good mother. Just as well there's a strong gene there, for Jeffrey's hair has never been anything to write home about, and Leo, at thirty-four, is already balding. Not that it matters a jot: thinning hair only goes to emphasis good bones. What a fine, appealing face he has.

Next come their children, Izzy and Sam, bright sparks seated across from one another, with a certain amount of kicking beneath the table, the surreptitious flicking of a minted pea.

– Sam! Kate is part amused, part stern.

– Sorry. He doesn't look sorry at all, but––

– You're not in your high chair now, says Paula, and he flushes to the roots.

– Sorry. This time it's a mutter.

– Better luck next time, says Nick, flashing him a smile across the table. – Next time make sure you hit the target. He lifts his hand and points a doom-laden finger down at Izzy's head.

– Ha-ha, says Paula coolly, as everyone laughs and Izzy looks about her. – Don't let them make fun of you, Izzy.

– Who? asks Izzy, catching sight of the finger and giggling.

– Your brother. Your uncle. Men.

– Oh, come, come, says Leo mildly.

And Kate puts in: – I think Izzy can take a joke.

– Pardon me. Paula shrugs, and returns to her quiche, lifting the fork to her lips. – I'm not a parent, of course.

No one responds to this. No one says: Why? or, It's your choice, or, Have you never wanted . . . ?

Sam mutters something.

– What?

– I said, can we get down? Before pudding?

– Of course, says Dido, as Jeffrey reaches for the wine. – Go and play in the garden.

But what should be a happy little moment of release, two high-spirited children scrambling down and making a dash for it, is instead a muted withdrawal, trailing towards birdbath and compost heap, neither of which look much fun.

– What sort of a week have you had? Jeffrey asks Nick. He rests a hand briefly on his son's shoulder as he stands beside him, pouring glass number three.

– Oh, you know. Pretty ordinary. Nick's laughing moment with Izzy is gone; like Sam, he is muted, though endeavouring, Dido can see, to sound his usual good-humoured self.

– Progress? Begun a new chapter? Jeffrey moves round the table, refills Dido's glass, offers the bottle to Paula, who shakes her head.

– Nothing so ambitious. Nick raises his glass. – Cheers. It's Paula who's forging ahead. He flashes her a smile. Paula puts down her fork.

– It's not a race, she tells him.

– I didn't say it was.

And there it comes: that look on Nick's face, which hurts Dido to the quick: wounded, rebuffed, trying at once to disguise both feelings. Disguise or repress? Does he allow himself to feel what he can't express?

– It really must be quite a thing, she says, stepping into the breach. – Two people doing Ph.D.s at the same time. Under the same roof.

– So you keep saying, says Paula, wiping her mouth with her napkin.

– Do I? How silly of me, it must be an age thing. I just remember what Jeffrey was like, writing his thesis – simply buried, weren't you, Jeffrey? I used to come home from work, and if you'd had a bad day . . .

– What? asks Kate easily, as Dido trails away. – You're telling us Dad threw things?

– Hardly. She gives a little laugh. What had Jeffrey done? Moaned a bit. Been a bit quiet, recovered enough to cook supper. Memories of the two of them, out on their little balcony, raising a glass as the London dusk descended, take Dido quite away for a moment or two. Jeffrey's thesis – *The Peasants' War: The influence of the Lutheran Reformation on the defence of agrarian rights in the Rhineland 1524–5* – has stood unopened in the bookcase in his study for almost three decades, dusty black spine a reminder of the achievement from those distant, early married days. No children. Lots of sex. Lots of reading and lots and lots of sex.

– Well, says Paula – I haven't thrown anything yet.

– Nor me, says Nick, and for a moment this joint achievement unites them as a couple, against all who hurl, or shout, or slam a door.

So what do they do, wonders Dido, when clearly things are so difficult between them? She tries, and fails, to imagine.

Do they still . . . ?

Is that why . . . ?

– Oh dear, she says aloud, and everyone laughs.

– Penny for your thoughts, says Leo, down at the other end of the table, looking at her with the easy affection they have always felt for one another.

– Nothing, says Dido, pulling herself together, gathering plates. – Time for pud.

Nick is tall, like his father, and has his father's hair, which in youth is floppy. He has his father's loose-limbed grace, and kindness, and where Dido has always had for Kate, the elder, a loving respect, she has for Nick a tenderness that springs from the knowledge that he's less resilient: just as clever but less capable. Kate's progress through life has been an arrow: knowing she wanted to read medicine, knowing that Leo was the man for her – so that Leo, almost at once, knew this too – wanting, and having, two children, a boy and a girl. She knows what she can do, and she does it well: running an orderly life in which children are dropped off at school on the way to the surgery, cover is arranged two days a week so that she can do the evening shift, piano and football and friends to tea are balanced with homework, and people come to dinner once a month. All this, and the theatre and the concert too; all this and walks on the Wolds at weekends. Kate, like her mother, can pretty well do it all, and like her mother has a contented marriage within which to do it.

But Nick . . .

Nick's hamster died and he sobbed until he was sick. Nick made it to the Second, not the First Eleven, and told no one for a whole term, though no one would have minded, or even, in a busy week, have noticed. (Oh, those busy weeks. Sometimes Dido lies awake and wonders: by the time Nick came along, was I trying to do too much? Did he never get quite enough from me? But mostly, of course, there was Ella. My little ghost, my baby gone. I was a wreck. I went back to work, but I was a wreck. How can that not have affected all of us?)

Nick, like Kate, might have read arts or sciences, but found the choosing painful.

– I'd be more useful in science, wouldn't I?

– Are you saying I'm not useful? Jeffrey, ten years ago, sat at the kitchen table on a summer evening and listened, trying to lighten Nick's intensity.

– Nor me? asked Dido, a long evening's marking ahead of her. Year Twelve on *Hamlet*, Year Ten on the war poets.

Wilfred Owen was probably gay, but in those days it was banned . . .

Keep to the text, wrote Dido in the margin, a Leavisite to her bones. *Tell us about the poem itself.*

– Do I not have my uses? she asked her troubled son.

Nick's brow furrowed. – Of course. You're both fantastic.

– We jest, dear boy. Jeffrey covered his son's thin suntanned hand with his own.

– You must give yourself to what you really love, said Dido.

– Well, I suppose – I suppose it's History, really.

– Good man. Jeffrey patted the long brown fingers.

– You don't mind, do you, Mum?

– Darling, for heaven's sake.

Kate knew what she must do, Nick wondered what he should. Kate knew there was a job to be done, Nick worried about hurting people. On that summer evening, at sixteen and a half, he was as anxious to please as he had been at four, dropping teaspoons of raspberry jam into each pastry circle with heartbreaking care and precision, wiping off every drop and trail.

It was the kind of thing which could drive you mad, of course.

Lunch is over. People have gone outside, Sam and Izzy batting a Woolworths shuttlecock back and forth over the net put up between the apple trees, grown-ups drinking coffee at the garden table and reading the papers.

– Here he is, says Dido, gazing at a young novelist's soulful photograph. – We heard him at the festival.

– Any good? Leo glances across as she holds the page aloft.

– Rather too pleased with himself. I didn't buy the novel. Mind you, I bought up most of the town, so one more or less hardly counted. She takes her specs off, looks about her. – Where are the others?

– Nick was loading the dishwasher, says Kate, and then: – Well done, Izzy! as the shuttlecock sails in a perfect arc over Sam's curly head.

– I told him not to bother. Dido turns, and calls into the house, – Nick? Coffee's getting cold.

No answer comes.

– Leave them, says Jeffrey, from behind the cricket. – They'll come out when they're ready.

– I know, but—

– Stop fretting.

Dido, outwardly, stops. She returns to the reviews, but cannot concentrate. There's a new life of Woolf – another? A tiny publishing house has a book on a longlist, good for them. Titles come and go beneath her gaze, but those which occupy her mind are not in print. Not yet.

Madwoman on the Couch: Phallocentric discourse and the politics of desire. We all know who's writing that one. Dido can hear its author's level tones from the kitchen, she's sure she can. Does she imagine that cool insistence, as Nick loads plates and glasses, bends to cram in spoons and forks so no one can see his face? *Phallocentric discourse* . . . hasn't it had its day, all that stuff? Whatever would Chloe make of such a thing?

– *Where did you find that brilliant couch?*

– What are you laughing at, Granny? Sam is beside her, laughing too.

– Nothing.

– *Fallowcentric?*

– Granny!

Dyslexia leads Dido, as it were, to a grassy field, or perhaps a crop circle. Whatever happened to them? She turns the page, and lets her eyes close for a moment. That pleasant field leads, in its way, to *Patterns of Settlement and Cultivation in North-Eastern England, 1200–1380*. This is the subtitle of the other thesis under production in the scholarly household that is Nick and Paula's rented flat across the city. A sexy overall title has yet to be found; Dido is doing her best. Even without it, medieval agriculture, on the page and in Nick's conversation, has its own appeal. It conjures ancient nouns and places: farmstead, furrow, moat and mill, monastery and manor. All are elemental associative words which make Dido feel interested and happy: earth and wind and rain and sky; oak, swan, herb garden, breviary. These nouns connote order, purpose, solidity and timelessness.

Someone more radical would locate in it all poverty and disease, exploitation, revolt. Nick is of course aware of these things (as who could not be) but his interest is in the land, and in what is discernible in the landscape now, from those distant workings. He is becoming, in fact, an agricultural historian, something which no one, on that evening in the kitchen all those years ago, would ever have predicted. Something that might, indeed, be considered useful, if not in the immediately recognisable way that Being a Doctor offers. Nick, if he succeeds, and why should he not, will be Dr Nicholas Sullivan and on the strength of this, please God, will next summer, or perhaps the next, up his teaching status and income from the lowly part-time hours which now engage him.

She sees him, in York's glorious doctoral colours, striding across the platform at the graduation ceremony to receive his honour from some celeb scholar – Schama, perhaps, or Starkey, if they're lucky – while they all clap madly. The children must come – so good to have a role model of achievement after years of work. She would wear – what? Might there be, at long last, the chance to buy a hat? No. No, definitely not. Hats were for weddings and nothing else at all, ever, though with Ascot at York last year, if she and Jeffrey were Ascot people, which they aren't . . . Dido feels herself begin to gather wool. She yawns, trying and failing to picture Paula beside them on this happy day.

– Granny's falling asleep, says Sam, flopping down at his parents' feet.

So she is.

Georgia's Sunday lunch is rather different. No children. No discord. Very N1. She has driven from her own quiet street to another, up towards the Angel: sleeker, deeper, dripping with wisteria and backing on to the canal. Not a front door without a bay tree in a pot, or even two; end-to-end Farrow & Ball at their most matt and chalky; wrought-iron railings in the most solid black; gleaming brass. Just streets away sprawls an estate of crack dens and prostitution, but you'd never know that, lifting the heaviest knocker that money and good taste can buy, waiting on the flagstoned step for that warm—

– Ah, Georgia. Good to see you.

The kiss on both cheeks, the entry into a spacious hall, the rugs and flowers and polish, the glimpse of garden. Graham closes the front door with a heavy click, and the outside world is banished: the crowds of pierced youth spilling out of the pubs on Upper Street, the cruising cars throbbing with hiphop, the grim estates stretching out towards the fabled East. Georgia does, in truth, know all about those concrete walkways and kicked-in doors, having in her time taught many of those who live there; and Henry knew about them too, involved as he was – with Graham – in framing social policy under successive governments. Others here today also know, for this is not a lunch party for Islington bankers, but the professional and concerned: a therapist, a radical lawyer approaching retirement, two doctors whose surgery is filled with the hollow-eyed and wasted. Everyone, sitting on weathered garden chairs beneath the trees, soothed by the passage of barges on the canal below, knows all about what goes on over there. None the less, as that deep blue front door closes behind her, and Graham ushers her through, Georgia and everyone here today is shielded, for now, from all of it. It's Sunday. It's time for a drink.

– Georgia. How lovely to see you.

Tessa approaches, takes the proffered bottle with a kiss. – How kind. How are you?

– I'm very well, says Georgia, as she has said all her life, and then, her guard dropping for just a moment, adds: – Well. You know.

– I know, says Tessa, though she doesn't, only in theory, and Georgia at once regrets her slip. She has not come here to be pitied – and, after all, she's coping, she's just come back from a literary festival. They can talk of this.

– Come and have a drink. I think you know everyone.

She does. They rise, they kiss. They are also all very well, though none, as yet, has lost a lifetime love, so their quality of wellness is unstrained – although shot through, she knows it, with that inescapable mixture of curiosity, dread and relief that surrounds all widows. *How is she really? How would I . . . ? Thank God it's not . . .*

– Lovely to see you. Come and sit down.

She sits. She takes her sparkling glass. Here are the olives, Gallo Nero's best. She is the last to arrive, and now they can all settle down. Blackbirds sing in the trees, as blackbirds will. A dog runs along the towpath far below, and a barge puffs out a plume of petrol-blue.

– How are you?

– How are you?

– I'm fine, says Georgia. – I've just come back from Wales.

* * *

Dido wakes with pins and needles. No, really. Her foot has entirely gone to sleep, and as she waves it from side to side myriad bright sparks of pain shoot everywhere. Heavens. She bends to rub it, hard, cannot restrain a wincing and a little sound of distress.

– Mum? You OK?

– My foot's gone to sleep, that's all. Gosh, it's really quite . . . Give it a rub, would you, darling?

Kate gets up from her chair, comes over. Dido's stockinged foot is expertly held and massaged between long fingers.

– Marvellous. What it is to have a doctor in the family. Dido smiles up at her, feels everything begin to settle down.

– Better?

– Much.

– Can I rub it? Izzy is at her side.

– Of course, the more the merrier. Oh, that's wonderful, Izzy, thank you so much.

– I thought she said, Can I rabbit? says Sam, and everyone laughs.

– She does rabbit on, says Leo, and Kate groans.

With this pleasing little piece of family nonsense Dido quite recovers, withdraws her foot from public view and slips her shoe on. There. Now, then.

– Have I been asleep for long?

– Hours, says Sam. – You were *snoring*.

– Sam!

– I wasn't. Oh, how horrid.

– You were snoring sweetly, says Izzy.

What a dear child she is. Look at her, in that second-hand sundress, as steady and good as her dear parents, and no wonder. Dido gives her a kiss. How lucky they are.

– Where's Grandpa?

Extraordinary, to speak of Jeffrey thus. Grandpa? The man is not yet retired. He cycles (usually) to work. Yet this is what happens if you marry young, and your children follow suit. One of them, at least. She looks about her. Jeffrey is – where is he?

– He went inside. I think he's in the study.

Still? Again? Has she missed something? It's early June, and everyone's deep in marking, but surely—

– Can I text him? asks Sam of his father. – Dad? Dad. Can I? Please?

Leo says, Oh all right then. He fishes his mobile out of his pocket. Sam is upon it in a trice, and his fingers race over the keys. While his parents, who've seen it all a million times, bury their heads in the papers once again, Dido watches with some awe.

– Gosh, Sam, you're a whiz.

– Texting's cool.

– What have you said?

– *Hi, Grandpa, what are you doing?* But I'm doing the text, see? He comes over, shows her the tiny screen. *Hi, Gpa, wot U do?*

Dido laughs. – Show me how.

Sam shows her, at some length. Izzy interrupts. The mobile makes a little sound.

– He's answering, see? Now you just press the Yes button, to get the message. He presses it. Up comes Jeffrey.

– *Marking papers. Boring. Gpa.*

– Poor Gpa. I'm going to send him a joke. What's long and thin and—

Sam, left to his own devices, would continue this all afternoon, but:

– We must be making a move, says Leo, folding the paper.

– Oh, must you really? Dido gets up, moves the funny foot about a bit on the ground. The sun seems to be going in, and though it's June you need to have your cardigan to hand. She pulls it round her shoulders. Where are Nick and Paula?

– Where's Nick?

– I'm afraid they've gone. Kate is kneeling, letting Sam lean on her while he shakes a stone out of a trainer.

Gone?

– What do you mean, gone? Without saying goodbye?

To her astonishment, Dido feels tears well up. Was she really asleep such an age? What's been going on? And why the hell is Jeffrey . . . ?

Kate gets up, comes over, gives her a pat. – They didn't want to wake you, that's all.

– How ridiculous. Please don't pat me. Dido wipes her eyes, and looks at her. – Was something wrong? Did they quarrel?

– I don't know.

– Yes, you do.

– Well, you know what they're like. Kate starts picking things up: Sam's sweatshirt, Izzy's cardigan. The battledores lie on the grass by the net like two dead creatures, and where's the shuttlecock?

– Go and find the shuttlecock, says Kate to her children.

– Sam hit it into the bushes.

– Go and find it.

Leo goes with them; there's a lot of bending and peering and bashing about.

– *I* can't see it anywhere.

– It must be *somewhere*.

– Stay and have a cup of tea, says Dido to her daughter, hearing Jill Archer speak. – I'll put the kettle on. I've made a cake.

– Cake? After all that lunch? How lovely. Kate puts her arm round her mother; Dido leans briefly against her. – Are you OK?

– Just a bit out of sorts. I hate to think of Nick being miserable.

– He's a grown-up, Mum. He can sort things out.

– I know. I just ache for him sometimes, that's all.

They go into the kitchen. It's spotless, everything in the machine and every worktop wiped. Dido supposes she should be pleased, but finds it rather chilling. She fills the kettle through the spout; water flies everywhere.

– Damn. She spins the tap to turn it off, but it sticks. The washer must have gone. – Kate? Turn this thing off, will you?

Kate does so. Everything subsides.

– Thanks. Can't even turn a tap off today. Dido plugs in the kettle, with a sudden vivid memory of a Monica Dickens novel, read in childhood, in which a pregnant woman does just this, resting her hand on the lid as it comes to the boil. Her hand gets stuck, she's electrocuted—

– Mum? Sit down, you've gone all—

Dido sits at the kitchen table, and puts her head in her hands. A cry of triumph comes through the open window from the garden:

– *There* it is!

– Mum? Kate's arm is round her again. Dido leans against her again.

– Dear, oh dear. Whatever's the matter with me?

What is Georgia going to do, now she's retired? She's asked this twice, over a delicious lunch in an eau-de-Nil dining room washed by watery light from the canal. Sun plays over the walls, the pictures, the mahogany china cabinet whose dark polished wood hangs so perfectly upon that palest green. The tablecloth is softly glazed in strawberry and mint, the china old, potatoes new, and the salmon melts in the mouth.

– Well, says Georgia, helping herself to buttered mangetout and courgettes from the dish her neighbour proffers. – Well, there are various possibilities.

– Viz.? A playful smile. Michael, one half of the Community Practice (supportive doctors in T-shirts, addressed by their first names; posters about drug dependency), takes the dish, helps himself, passes it across the table.

– I shan't give up teaching entirely. But on a part-time basis.

– None of the ghastly admin.

– Less, certainly. A little silver boat of mayonnaise is making the rounds; Georgia takes it. – Mind you, she says, spooning a creamy mound on to her plate – you can hardly walk into Birkbeck or City Lit these days without being asked to fill in a form about Learning Outcomes.

There ensues general talk about the stranglehold of bureaucracy with which New Labour is throttling the country's greatest professions. Medicine. Teaching. Targets, targets, targets. – All rather phallocentric, says the therapist with a dry smile, and they agree. Nothing New about it.

– Anyway, says Georgia, when pressed by Michael to pick up where she left off – I shall teach a day or two a week, and take my students on trips and outings.

– That sounds fun.

– Yes. I hope so. Sometimes I think about becoming a guide: Wren and Hawksmoor, Literary London, that sort of thing.

– You'd be brilliant.

– Do you think so? I understand there's fearful competition, but I thought I might apply.

– I wish you'd join our reading group, says Ruth, the other half of the surgery (posters of happy women breastfeeding their toddlers, going through the menopause, offering support).

– I'm honoured, says Georgia, spearing a potato speckled with fresh dill. Her own surgery, where she and Henry went for thirty years (or in truth hardly ever went, until tragedy befell him) is more down to earth: on a main road, run by doctors whom you address as Doctor. The men wear ties. She likes it, trusts them, has wept there once or twice. – Isn't your reading group very select?

– Oh, very. That's why we'd be honoured to have *you*. I'm serious – we've just lost a member. Ruth takes a sip of wine. – It was all rather difficult, really.

– Because?

– She didn't do the reading.

A pleasantly ironic laugh engulfs the table; ironic little tut-tut-tuts ensue. But there's a seriousness too, as Ruth continues, for everyone here understands what's what: you commit, you do your stuff. You read. No one wants flaky people making excuses – about anything.

– Anyway, she says – in the end I lost my cool and told her it wasn't on. I mean, everyone's really busy, and yet we all managed it. It's only a book a month.

– I've answered the door to our group finishing the last page, discloses Tessa, and everyone laughs again.

– She took umbrage? Graham asks Ruth.

– She did. Out of all proportion. Then she joined a choir. Anyway, it's over. And there's this gap. Would you consider, Georgia . . . ?

Georgia says she would, and thank you. How kind. What is the book for July?

– It's Margaret Atwood, but not a novel. A sort of memoir about writing, asking what the role of the writer is.

– That sounds interesting. Georgia feels in her bag for a pen. – I must make a note of the title.

– It's called *Negotiating with the Dead*, says Ruth, and an infinitesimal chill falls upon the table, like the shadow of an angel's wing. There's an infinitesimal silence. Then Georgia, well-bred and considerate as she is, comes to the rescue.

– How intriguing. I shall look forward to that. And when's the next meeting?

The date is given – always the second Monday. No meeting in August, since everyone's away, but they generally read a classic, then, and discuss it in September. This year it's *The Brothers Karamazov*.

Ah.

– One of Henry's great books, Georgia says lightly.

And so it had been, occupying a whole summer in a rented house in Spain. Chloe was six? Seven? The sun beat down, the sea was turquoise, but Henry (my love, my own) took himself to a shady patch in their courtyard garden, and from thence to a darkened village street, the murder of a father, courtroom drama.

– It asks all the great questions, he told her, reading in bed on the last night of the holiday. Across the little landing, Chloe was fast asleep.

– Which are?

– You know what they are. What is justice. Who decides. Is there a God. If not, how do we live . . .

He put the book down, turned the lamp off, took her hand. They lay there, listening to the sea.

– Henry's relationship to modern fiction was always rather dutiful, Georgia tells the lunch table, lifting herself from reverie, and everyone laughs. Then (she senses they don't want to linger on this) they move on: to a play about Dostoevsky with John Hurt, surely born to play him; to a book launch hosted by a local publisher of classics in translation; to raspberries, snowy with the finest drift of sugar, and a jug of organic cream. They eat, they talk. Graham and Tessa's spaniel yawns from his place on the rug. A dog in a pool of afternoon sun; old friends here for a long lunch: how good life is. Over coffee, taken in the garden, they talk about their children: successful, every one.

And Georgia, quite genuinely, enjoys it all, even if that small brush with death, and memory, made for a difficult moment. Difficult for them, not her: she, not they, knew how to smooth it over. No one wants to talk about death over Sunday lunch, and though there is no one here, from the therapist to the civil servant, who is not educated in the stages of grief, no one, really, wants to talk about Henry now. It's a year: they've talked about him a lot.

Graham misses him, she knows he does, and he always, always, has something good to say about him, some little reminiscence. Henry hasn't been banished – but he's not around much any more. It's time – oh, what did people do before this phrase, this mode of being held them all? Time to move on.

What will she do in retirement? She's given acceptable answers. (What will she do in her empty bed? Read Margaret Atwood. Or Dostoevsky, thinking of Spain, and the great – still unanswered – questions.)

Has she plans to go away? Not yet – she's just been away. Henry's mad cousin Maud is due for a visit. Down in deepest Sussex. She and Chloe might go for a long weekend.

And how is Chloe? (Successful, yes, but not quite in N1's top drawer. A stylist. Not a lawyer, nor a medic, not an aid worker in the Sudan; not a seller of the rights to modern fiction at the Frankfurt Book Fair. A stylist.)

Georgia tells them that Chloe had her thirty-first birthday party last night, and now she must go and phone her, hear all about it. It's been lovely – a simply lovely lunch.

They rise. They kiss. They say goodbye. Graham sees her to the blue front door. It closes most solidly behind her.

Then Georgia is out in the street again, now barred with shadow from the descending sun, and very quiet.

She unlocks the car, and turns the radio on. Proust has been adapted, in six instalments. Someone else Henry admired. And she falls into the middle, driving home on a wave of haunting voices, dreamy violins. In truth, it's very beautiful and sad. She reaches home just as it comes to a close, sits spellbound listening to the credits, the violin rising and falling still. *The Remembrance of Things Past* . . .

– Oh, Henry, says Georgia, sitting in her car. She turns off the engine. People come and go along the street: back from tennis, off for a swim. She gazes at the wheel. Then she takes herself, quickly, out, and up the path to the front door. Lavender fills the summer air. She unlocks, she enters, she closes the door behind her.

Henry, Henry, Henry . . .

The cats appear; they twine around her ankles.

– Henry? Her voice fills the empty hall. – Darling? Are you there?

– Darling heart.

Jeffrey is rubbing Dido's neck. Everyone's gone, the house is quiet, it's just them and the soothing tick of the clock, the prospect of supper *à deux* – something simple and comforting, like scrambled eggs on toast, yes, exactly that – and then bed. A hot bath and an early night: when did this ever fail anyone overtired, or overwrought?

Why is she overtired? She's just had a holiday, for God's sake. OK, the Centre was busy on her return, but she's never found it too much before. And it's only two days a week.

Why is she overwrought? Nothing very dreadful happened between Nick and Paula: it's always tricky, nothing new there. And you could say they had been considerate, tiptoeing away so as not to wake her.

– How does that feel? Bit better? Jeffrey's fingers caress shoulder blades, vertebrae, knead all the muscles. Dido moves her head from side to side, round in a circle, feeling everything ease up. It's as good as her yoga class, and she hasn't even had to leave the house. How marvellous to have a loving husband who can do this so well. She leans back into him as he stops at last; his arms go round her.

– There, there.

He's as gentle as if talking to one of the children, or a poorly animal. All those animals, loved here down the years. Strange not to have one now, and the house is free of them just at the point where most people feel they must have a cat or a dog about the place. Yet it's rather peaceful, not. No dishes, no letting in and out, no holiday arrangements. When Jeffrey retires, then perhaps they'll think again. A dog to walk on the Wolds: the children would love that. For now, it's Kate and Leo's turn to chivvy about fresh water, and cleaning out the cage.

– OK? Jeffrey kisses her, releases her.

– Fine. Thanks so much. What shall we have for supper?

They agree on the scrambled eggs; they eat in the kitchen, talking over the day.

– You seemed rather out of it, says Dido, passing the pepper.

– No, not really.

– Shut away in the study all morning, and after lunch. What was all that about?

– A HEFCE meeting tomorrow. I did tell you.

– Did you? Sorry.

– Convened by Sturrock. We talked about it at his drinks do. You probably weren't listening, and who can blame you?

– Sorry, says Dido again, recalling Friday's drinks on campus. Dr Donald Sturrock, just appointed, getting to know a few key people. Jeffrey used not to be quite so key, just a bloody good head of department, but times change and bureaucracy strangles. Now he sits on a Higher Education Funding steering committee and co-ordinates all the research returns. Dido – he's right – had not been listening properly, being preoccupied with preventing cramp by shifting from one foot to another. In the end, a walk along the lake with their old friends Alan and Hester Watt had done the trick. So many of these welcome drinks dos over the years; so many committees. She glazed; she knew it; she is glazing now.

– Sorry, darling. What did you say?

– Never mind. I'm going to watch Bremner. Coming?

They watch, they laugh, they clear away the supper, the papers, fold the garden chairs. It's dusky now, the air cool. Bats flit about, and lights go on in neighbouring houses. Dido yawns.

– I'm going up. Coming?

– In a minute.

She leaves him, climbing the stairs, running a bath with the last of Kate's birthday bath oil: orange and geranium, just the thing to ease everything away. She lies there, soaking, hearing from Jeffrey's study the ting of the phone. Now who's he talking to? She reaches for the bathroom radio, lets Andrew Rawnsley tell her in his gravelly tones all about the week in Westminster.

Tomorrow she'll rally. Perhaps having Monday off had been a mistake: the psychological equivalent of softening of the bones. That's the thing about retirement: let up for a minute and you start going soft in the head.

Dido pads out of the bathroom in her summer dressing gown. She's about to go to the bedroom, but then, on the landing, she does something she hasn't done for years: goes to the door of what for a long time now has been a guest room, but which once held a cot, wherein, in succession, three dear babies lay. Kate. Nick. Ella. Why, especially, is she thinking of Ella now? To lose a baby – it's the worst thing that can happen to anyone, yet they'd come through. Twenty-one years ago – and no one, in those days, suggested that the mother might have been responsible. At least they'd been spared all that. But still . . .

She stands there, in the evening quiet, hearing as if from a very great distance Jeffrey come out of his study, lock up at the front and go to lock up at the back, stepping out to the garden for one last look at the bats, as the first stars prick the sky.

– Ella, says Dido, deep inside herself. – You'll always be part of me.

Then she pulls herself together, goes into the bedroom where she and Jeffrey have slept for thirty years, brushes her hair at the mirror and chooses a book from the pile beside her bed. She's finished Jennifer Johnston – so good, the real thing, always. Somehow couldn't finish the lesbian crime novel everyone was going on about. Now what? Justin Cartwright: *The Promise of Happiness*. Just what she needs.

She slips off her dressing gown, pulls back the covers.

She's tucked up, her specs on her nose, the pillows just right. She settles into chapter one, is turning page six by the time Jeffrey joins her, fresh from a shower – that boiler will never do more than one bath at a go.

– Hello, my darling.

– Hi. Jeffrey reaches for his own book, puts on his specs. They settle down.

Dido is restored. What sweet companionship is this, to read, to sleep, to lie night after night against the man you love – still love, after all these years.

Poor Georgia.

Her specs slip down, her novel falls to the quilt. Jeffrey is tenderly seeing to both.

– I'm so lucky to have you, she murmurs, as the light goes out.

5

White wine, red lipstick, the flare of a joint: the party is a great success. So Chloe and Edmund agree, over a very late Sunday breakfast, well, lunch, (coffee, leftovers, last morsels of pink and white cake) and so Chloe conveys to Georgia that evening, curled up on the sofa with her mobile. Edmund is out and the flat restored to pre-party order, just as her mother would like it: clean glasses draining on a red-checked tea towel, empties out in the recycling box on the landing, kitchen floor washed and sitting-room rug and carpet vacuumed. Chloe's birthday flowers stand about looking summery, and the fridge is full of little bowls covered in clingfilm.

Pleasing though all this is to behold, with a busy week ahead, much more happy-making are the ghosts of party guests, lingering like smoke in every corner. Maybe a dozen in here, a dozen more out on different levels of the fire escape, where tealights in jam jars shone softly as the sun went down. Those perched out there became shadowy, painterly creatures, offering glimpses of bare arms and halter neck (Annie), white throat ringed with fat jet-black beads (Dot), linen jackets slung round shoulders (several, including Matt and Will), a crimson camisole (who was that?). Had you nothing better to do, yesterday evening, you could have curled up as Chloe is doing now, watching it all out there against the darkening rooftops and the setting sun. But there were better things to do, for after a while a sweet old-fashioned kind of party went on in here: the rug rolled back and music playing, and people dancing, actually dancing in couples, like some old wartime scene in a cramped little flat, everyone drinking cheap gin and smoking a lot, and moving slowly in one another's arms two steps forward and two back, and the whole thing incredibly romantic, until the sirens came . . .

Chloe, dreaming away as usual, has called up Georgia's number and is on another planet by the time her mother answers.

– What? Oh, hi, Mum, I'd forgotten who I was ringing for a moment.

– That must mean it was a good party.

– Oh, it *was*.

But Chloe is not too tired and dreamy to edit her account. She describes the scene, the food, the flowers (masses) and Edmund's heavenly black seed pearls; she brings into view the friends whom Georgia knows or knows about: Matt and Sara back together again, Jessica doing a brilliant maternity cover on the *Standard* 'Homes and Property' pages, Dot and Carrie giving her the most amazing espresso thing (still in its box), Amber's fantastic powder puff, and people actually *dancing*, like in couples . . .

– Not raving but dancing, says Georgia drily.

– Is that a quote or something?

– Stevie Smith.

– Who's he?

– Oh, Chloe. Never mind. Go on. Who were you dancing with, if I may enquire?

– Lots of people. I was the birthday girl! Edmund, of course. Matt. Adam.

– Adam?

– The shop designer. He did that refit of Penny's place in the spring. I styled the shots for the fliers, remember?

– I think so.

Chloe can hear the familiar veiled disappointment in Georgia's voice. A shop designer. Another lightweight man, probably gay, certainly no one with whom Chloe might be about – at last – to move into a milieu (how do you spell *that*?) that her mother might understand. So Chloe edits out entirely the main event of the evening, which has left her (secretly, she's just brushed over it with Edmund) excited and confused, and which went as follows.

– Hi, Chloe. Happy Birthday!

– Hi, Jez. Gosh, are those for me? Aren't they *lovely*? Chloe takes the bouquet – purple tissue paper, Cellophane, raffia, delphiniums in every shade of blue, creamy stock with that fantastic scent – and buries her nose therein. – Heavenly. My favourite. Thank you!

Everything has been going for about an hour (no dancing yet, a lot of drinking, a crush in the micro hall).

– I'm late, I'm so sorry.

– Oh, please. It's not a *reception*. Come on through.

They squeeze past Dot's enormous personage (not yet out on the fire escape – Jez! How are *you*?) and into the kitchen. Jez has never been here. He looks about him, greets Edmund and takes the proffered glass. He raises it to Chloe. They chink.

– Love the jacket.

– Thanks, says Chloe happily. – And look what Edmund gave me.

Jez admires as he is bid (but genuinely, she can tell). The doorbell rings again. Someone in the hall can answer that. Someone does.

– Have an olive, says Chloe.

Jez takes one, oily and speckled with thyme. He is wearing black (crumpled linen, unironed T-shirt) with the hint of stubble he always has, and the usual flop of hair, which in the studio he is always having to push back, not in a poncy look-at-me fashion but just because it gets in the way. Chloe, over the years (two? three?) has watched him at work a lot. She supposes he's watched her, darting about in jeans and cardi, putting a spray of this and that here and there, or heaving in enormous carrier bags of props (you practically have to be a *weightlifter* in this job). – Here, let me. – It's OK, I can manage. – Sure? – Oh, well, all right then. Thanks. He's nice, she has always thought so. He's married, she has always known it.

– I'd better put these lovely flowers in water.

– Chloe!

Matt and Sara are pushing through, looking happy. And pregnant? My God, is Sara pregnant?

Nobody says so. Chloe introduces them. She goes to find a vase. When she comes back, Jez is talking to Sara as if he's always known her. It's because of the baby, Chloe thinks. He knows about babies. And she feels the merest thread of the strangest feeling run through her, just for a moment. Then the doorbell rings. Her turn to answer.

– Chloe!

And so it goes on.

Who begins the dancing? It's quite late: she's cut the cake and blown out all the candles (two breaths) and everyone, led by Edmund, has sung 'Happy Birthday' at top pitch. Chloe thinks of her father and begins to cry; lots of people kiss her. She has another drink. After a while, the place thins out a bit, people going on to a club where she said she might join them, though she knows she won't. She's recovered from the tears; she's happy here, giving the first party for ages, everyone being nice to her. Also, Jez is still here. Who then puts on that retro piece of romance? All at once, in the tiny kitchen crush, she's aware of something tender and sweet murmuring through the buzz, and turns to see the rug rolled back and Ben and Amber – yes, it's those two – move into one another's arms.

A haunting tune, a funny posh voice on a scratchy recording: lovers leaning over a bridge in some distant 1940s England . . .

Tealights and candles burn softly everywhere, dusk has fallen beyond the open windows. Chloe can see people in one or two lamplit flats across the street: the silhouetted end of a dinner party, someone at his computer. Pigeons are fluttering on to the ledge below. The chap at his desk out there makes her think of her father again, even though he was decades older: just that sense of someone quietly working late at night, as Henry used to do, right at the top of the house. She makes herself turn her mind away from him, comes back to the party. Amber is wearing a backless dress, her hair knotted up with strands escaping. An earring glitters; she rests her head on Ben's shoulder, and his hand presses into the small of her back.

They're watching the river, racing beneath that old stone bridge, and their love flows as constantly as water . . .

All these people in couples: Ben and Amber have been together ever since art school. Weird: a bit like her parents, and Dido and Jeffrey – meeting so young and never parting. Like Matt and Sara, now dancing with three or four others: OK, they'd split up a few months ago, but now they're back together again, and now Sara is *pregnant* . . .

While I, thinks Chloe, taking a joint from someone, have had my moments, had my flings, but never, ever met anyone I wanted to *stay* with. Or who wanted to stay with me, come to that. Perhaps I have singledom in my blood – perhaps people can tell. Chardonnay and the joint make her not care, not tonight, not exactly, anyway.

Time passes by like a dream . . .

– Let's dance, says Adam the interior designer (how many interior designers does she know?) and they move on to the floor, she rather feeling her way, wondering if she might just crumple elegantly to the carpet, so full is her head now of gently swirling things. Like thoughts: what had she been thinking?

– Steady.

– Oh, Adam.

She melts into his linen jacket (another) and closes her eyes.

Once, two lovers held hands on a bridge and gazed down and down . . .

This is the wrong you and the wrong I, she knows it. Adam is being kind. But, hey. She lets herself unwind (no choice, in truth), lets the funny old song float round her, through her, somebody's thirties favourite, calling from all those years ago.

After a while, as the music ends and slides into something else, Adam goes to get another drink.

– Back in a minute.

– Sure.

Then Edmund is there, and it's as easy as anything to dance with him, even though they've never done so before.

– Happy? Nice party?

– Lovely party.

Now it's Billie Holiday, sexy and sad.

– I'm really stoned, says Chloe. – Like, really.

And so it is that after a while she finds herself carefully deposited upon the sofa, where she sits watching the smoky silhouettes of people on the fire escape out there, and the dreamy sway of the dancers in here, moving like water, this way and that, taking her far far away from wherever she is (where is she?) to a languorously lovely shore, where the waves sweep in and sweep slowly out again, gosh how beautiful is that . . .

– Hi.

Jez is standing a million miles above her, holding out a hand. What an intensely elegant hand it is, like a – like a Michelangelo. And Chloe finds herself far far away from wherever it is she has been and walking in echoing marble halls.

– Will you dance with me?

– Mmm.

Jez helps her to her feet, quite an achievement, and she moves into his arms, as Amber had moved into Ben's, and Sara into Matt's, and so on, and so on, all these really fantastic friends whom she will always love and care for . . .

Billie's Sunday is the saddest in the world . . .

– And what, asks Jez, as they move back and forth in the crush – is that frivolous object?

– Which?

– On top of the telly.

Chloe looks. A bright pink box, tied with a bright pink organdie ribbon, comes woozily into view.

– Ah, that. Amber gave it to me.

– And what's inside?

– A black fur powder puff. And sparkly powder.

– Well, well. How imaginative.

Chloe smiles. Gosh, he's nice.

– And when you use it, she says recklessly – it makes you sparkle all over.

– How enchanting.

He draws her closer; she rests her head on his shoulder. Jez is taller than she, which you can't say of everyone, or even many. She shuts her eyes, feels him draw her close, hears through the open windows on to the street people laughing and talking far far below, the shout for a taxi, the slam of a door. Real sounds. Like, there is a real world out there.

– You know something? murmurs Jez.

– Mmm?

– You look like Audrey Hepburn.

– I wish, she says, into his crumpled linen. – She was *tiny*.

– I know, but you have a look.

– I do? She can feel herself returning from wherever she's been. Is that a good thing?

– You know something else? He slips his hand under her chin, tilts up her head. – I've always fancied you.

Tall as she is, Chloe has heard this line before. Not everyone thinks she looks like Audrey Hepburn, but she does have a look, an air. She has had her moments, even if they haven't lasted. And she's less stoned than – than whenever it was.

– You're married, she says. – Where's your wife?

– We don't live together, said Jez. – Not any more.

Chloe frowns. She's coming down to earth.

– How long?

– We've been separated for about a year. It wasn't working.

– And your daughter?

– She's OK, she lives with Madeleine. I see her. A Michelangelo finger runs down her cheek. – It's all right, Chloe, you don't have to worry about her. Or anything. Look at me.

Chloe looks. Jez's eyes are dark as sloes, and his expression is tender and true. His hair is flopping down, as it does. He is, in truth, very lovely to behold, and she has always thought so.

But gosh, what sorrow is in that song.

– May I kiss you?

This is a line which Chloe has not often heard. She has been kissed many times in the past, but rarely has anyone asked permission. In quite this way. This Jez way.

– OK, she says, and his mouth closes over hers.

The warmest, sweetest-tasting, most gentle and then most thrilling . . .

And thus, by the end of the evening, when (good girl) she sends Jez home, Chloe – susceptible, bereaved, and so longing to fall in love – has begun to do so. And thus she enters that tormented territory which no one in their right mind should ever enter, staked out as it is by those whose marriages aren't working. Hell awaits.

And of course she tells Georgia nothing.

– By the way, says Georgia, before they ring off. – Maud's due for a visit, you know.

– She's coming to stay?

– God forbid. But we must go and see her before too long.

– OK.

– Have a good week.

– I will.

Chloe ends the call and presses another number at once, as people with mobiles do. Georgia puts down the receiver, and hears silence all around her.

Sunday evening. The summer sun is sinking towards dusk. Out in the garden, one of the cats – Tristan – is sleeping in the shade. What a sweet phrase.

Sometimes Georgia feels she'd like to sleep in the shade for ever.

Sunday evening. Teachers all over the country dread it, heaving out the bag of marking or lesson plans from wherever they flung it on Friday night, settling down in a study, if they're lucky, or at a cleared space on the kitchen table if they're like most people; pulling out books with a sigh. Here we go again. Here we bloody go.

Georgia has been lucky. The house has three good-sized bedrooms, one of which she and Henry shared for years as a study. Such companionability: sitting down, getting on with it, looking up now and then at one another, carrying on. A sign of a good marriage, being able to share working space in this way: not everyone can do it. She has one or two writer friends who can't share the house, never mind the study. They go to the British Library, or borrow rooms in other people's places. Mind you, writers: a precious, self-regarding lot, if the festival was anything to go by. Of course, Henry and she had both worked full-time, so their sharing was limited to weekends and evenings. Sunday evenings: tricky when Chloe was small and unhappy.

– I don't *want* to go to school . . .

– Oh, darling . . .

All that listening, all those evenings trying to comfort and reassure while heaps of marking waited. Then Chloe grew up, and went to art school. Then there were two spare rooms. Georgia and Henry, after some discussion, moved one of the desks in their shared workspace down into Chloe's room, making marks on the wallpaper as they did so.

– Careful.

– Sorry.

Now Georgia had her own space – sort of; she did her marking and preparation surrounded by the objects of her daughter's youth and childhood: the bear she had taken with her, but two precious dolls remained, gazing glassily from the shelves whose books Chloe had found such a struggle. Vintage necklaces hung from the cupboard doors, scarves were strung across the bedhead, rock stars stared sullenly from peeling posters. Georgia, in this alien environment, tried to concentrate.

By now, with mixed feelings of regret and relief (approximate ratio 10:90) she had stopped teaching in the violent spaces of the secondary school, and taken a post in the calmer pastures of further education. Here, from time to time, she met old, excluded pupils, last seen smashing someone smaller up against a wall in the heaving hell of stairs or corridor, hurling a chair across a classroom or gazing, miserable and wasted, at something in the clouds above the playground which no one else could see, and wouldn't want to. Now they were being paid thirty pounds a week to brush up (ha) on literacy and maths. Or study literature. Georgia and they greeted each other (mostly) like old friends, drew breath and tried again.

Meanwhile, Henry was managing – just – to carve out time from policy papers and briefings to work on something personal. A great-great-uncle had once governed an African province which no longer existed. Henry had come upon his diaries while helping Maud with a clear-out, something to be attempted only once. At home, he dusted the diaries down and read them. He thought there was something there: he might well examine the era through the life. Privately, Georgia thought this project unlikely to find a publisher – the empire was writing back, and no one, in these post-colonial times, wanted to know about Henry and Maud's great-uncle – but good marriages endure on things withheld, and she made encouraging noises.

That was quite a few years ago now.

When Henry died – the book completed, and indeed unpublished – Georgia left everything in his study exactly as it was. She tidied up, brushed away cat hairs and dusted, but she did not change a thing. His specs were on the left of the computer, his mug on the right. His jacket hung on the door. The heaps of paper illuminating long-gone colonial days – notes, drafts one and two – lay in their labelled folders. The last book Henry had read up there was still on the desk, marked by a slip of paper. Georgia, mournfully tidying, picked it up: a Penguin Classic from the seventies, the black spine cracked from rereading, the pages yellowed. Left to himself, away from the review pages, and her own urgings, Henry chose to spend what reading time he had in the company of the masters. Often – as in Spain, as on countless holidays – the Russians.

And in illness?

Tolstoy had accompanied him into hospital, and come home again. Wordsworth had been who he wanted near the end. Somewhere in between: this.

Gorky. *My Childhood*. Georgia opened it, at the page with the slip of paper.

I came to in a corner of the front room, near the icons. Grandfather had me on his knees, and he rocked me, and muttered:
   'None of us will be forgiven, no one . . .'
   An icon lamp burned brightly above his head and a candle burnt on the table in the middle of the room. The dull winter morning was already looking in through the window . . .

* * *

Georgia, for a while, lost herself in that Russian winter, and a brutal childhood. Then she closed the book, and kissed it, and put it down. If Henry came back, everything would be ready for him: he could just settle down and pick up where he had left off.

Georgia – rational, secular, intelligent – has for some time been intermittently sustained by the thought that this will happen. On the one hand she knows perfectly well that the dead are gone for ever. On the other, she knows that while this is the case with most people, Henry's case is different. When people offer their deepest sympathy, early on and even now (occasionally); when they wonder at her calm, her coping, part of her thinks: ah, but you don't know. You think Henry's died, but I know better. He's gone – but he'll be back. Another, longer life awaits him, a life with me, our retirement years, the life he should have been allowed to have – all the time he wanted, to read and travel, and see his grandchildren, if cancer hadn't . . .

The life that God had planned for him. Sometimes Georgia, secular and sceptical, even finds herself thinking that.

These are not things she ever says to anyone. She keeps her secret, waiting.

Sunday evening: what should she do? No marking, no preparation, no class tomorrow. Georgia, three months after losing her husband, had resigned from her post at Birkbeck College, surely one of the happiest and most purposeful places in London. She'd been fortunate to work there: to walk through Bloomsbury's tree-lined streets and swing her briefcase through those plate-glass doors; to talk about Keats and Coleridge, Auden and Plath, with people who also had their poetry coursing through their blood, or who longed to learn it. To go for a drink with them afterwards, or arrange a theatre trip; to give them, on a diploma course, a new qualification, as well as new life, new interests: all this had been deeply satisfying.

Now it isn't there.

No meetings, no classes, no marks moderation. No coffee in the canteen, no drinks in the pub with students or colleagues, no timetable to pin up above her desk at home, no handouts to copy with her own copying card. How these little things add up. No sight of the last smokers in the world having a quick one out on the pavement, no greeting Reception, no laughs with the admin lot—

No work.

One might have thought that Georgia, organised to a fault, never one to let the grass grow beneath her feet, nor fail to plan every single thing – every blessed thing, thinks Chloe, every last bloody whisker – would have had her retirement sorted. And so she might have done, so she would have done, had Henry not had his future taken so cruelly away.

Anything can happen to any one of us, at any time. This is one of the things which Georgia has always known in theory but which she now knows in her heart. Now she knows that she herself might live a much shorter life than one might expect, given her general health and wellbeing. Fit and energetic as she has always been, there's nothing – nothing – to say she won't wake up one morning and find a lump. Or go into town one day and get blown to bits on a bus. It happens. It's happened to people better than she. Henry was better than she – she often thinks this. He was kinder, more patient, more open to things. Why should he die and she live on? This is a question – one of the great questions – which takes her into the realms of religion or philosophy, and is one to which there cannot be an answer. She has learned, good and proper, that life is not governed by the imponderables of religion or philosophy (whatever her secret thoughts about death and return) but by biology and chance. All she knows now with certainty is that she herself must not fall ill, or fall off a ladder in an empty house,

SUE GEE

because she has Chloe, and Chloe is still single, and has no one to watch over her. This is Georgia's role: performed at the required distance but there, always.

Meanwhile, there are days to get through.

Sunday evening. No Henry to have supper with. Chloe has given a party and is happy.

Now what?

Georgia, looking out at the dusky garden from the kitchen, opens a bottle of wine. That's one thing to do, and one thing she'd better keep an eye on. A glass or two on your own is one thing; more than that not such a good idea. Well – she's not having more than that. Cheers. Oh, that's better. Where are the nuts?

For a moment, having found them, Georgia's hand hovers above the kitchen telephone. She could give Dido a ring: she can think of nothing more comforting. But she's seen her so recently, they've spoken just this morning: she can't be forever turning to Dido. Who, then? She runs through any number of people in her mind, and her mind shies away from each one. What is she to say? I'm feeling ghastly. No. Never. Saying this will only make it worse. Say: I thought I'd just ring for a chat? It's not her style. Too many people chat too much, these days. Say: Would you like to go to . . . ? Well, that's better, but she hasn't thought what to go to.

To hell with it. She'll rustle up the cats.

Actually, no. There's someone she really should speak to, even though you need a stiff drink to do so. Stiffer than a glass of wine. Oh, come on, just do it. You haven't spoken to her for months. Henry was so good, keeping in touch. Well, he was her cousin. Her only living relative, in fact.

Oh, go on, do it. Do it for him.

Georgia checks her address book and dials.

Down in deepest Sussex, the telephone rings and rings.

68

6

Maud is out. Maud, as so often, is tramping along a lane. Her square, uncompromising body is made for gumboots, and it is gumboots she wears now, though summer is well established: you never know when the weather will turn. Besides, the boots are comfortable. Round about July, it is possible that they will become too hot, and Maud will then exchange them for trainers, bought at a bargain price from a basket outside Cutprice Clothing. If it gets really hot: flip-flops, but this is rare.

Inland Sussex, on the whole, does not go in for cut-price clothing. It's rich. It's posh. Maud's tastes and general appearance and lifestyle put her outside the run of things – the commuting to town, the four-wheel-drive school run, lunch in the garden, bridge (though in fact she once played well) drinks and dinner parties, trips to the Chichester theatre, church, private views in converted barns, Hospital Friends. Maud's appearance and lifestyle once put her inside a hospital, and briefly inside a locked ward, but that was a long time ago, and is not something she ever thinks of. Besides, such places are almost non-existent now, their rambling corridors and wards long since converted into flats for the rich retired (how do they not go mad in there?). Stretches of the endless grounds have been sold off for development. It's all care in the community. Maud, uncared for and outside most of the community, tramps o'er hill and dale.

Inland Sussex is rich and posh. If you heard Maud's voice on the phone, you'd know she is very posh indeed. Those tones boom out from centuries of landowning, commanding ships, governing the colonies. Hear Maud enquire about the price of fencing and you'd see a great hall hung with oils and antlers, gundogs flopped before the fire, a butler with a tray. All that. Meet her in the flesh (uncared for, unseen by anyone, ever) catch sight of her in the street, or in this lane; deliver a free newspaper or turn up to mend the roof, and you'd think: bag lady. Except that there aren't many bag ladies in the country, it's an urban thing. You'd think: poor old bat, and keep your distance. Then she opens her mouth, instructing you to close the gate, or accept a fifty-pound note in the newsagents, first thing on a Monday morning, and you'd think: blimey. You can never tell.

And then again, receive a letter – as from time to time Henry used to do – and your eyebrows would be in your hair. That Maud, who sounds as if she should have a seat in the House of Lords, should be incapable of putting together two words spelled correctly . . .

Georgia gazes at the pages passed across the marmalade.

– Good Lord.

She has seen better in Special Needs. Well, almost. And that this condition should have been visited upon her daughter . . .

Maud, uncaring, fires off letters about Council Tax, unmarried mothers (as she quaintly calls them), myxomatosis (coming back), tuberculosis (likewise) and Iraq. She tramps the lanes, as she is tramping now, and with an expert eye notes every hedgerow plant (what's left of them) and every bird.

Time was when Maud – in her prime, as perhaps one might say, looking back – farmed a hundred head of cattle. A hundred sheep. Centuries of landowning in her blood made this a natural occupation. But farming, even in the gently rolling pastures of

Sussex, can be a hazardous occupation, and so it proved. A beef herd of Charolais and Hereford, a dairy herd of Friesian: all require, as well as good grass, a steady market. Let BSE or foot-and-mouth put the country on red alert, and kill European export; let milk quotas drastically rise and fall, and you can be in real trouble. Raise a hundred short wool Suffolk ewes, treat them for liver fluke and scrapie, dip them, lamb them, shear them, and with foot-and-mouth, or the market price of lamb plummeting and the loss of subsidies, it's possible to go bust.

Maud, in 1989, went bust. She sold off a field, and then another. She sought Henry's advice about investment of the proceeds, and did not follow it. In this uncertain world, some things are safe for ever: paper, cat food, funeral parlours – not that Henry had suggested any of these. Maud, menopausal hormones raging, a lurking mad gene or two from the eighteenth century finally kicking in, sank tens of thousands in another farm, and lost the lot.

Now, she rents out her remaining acres, and watches other farmers' sheep graze safely. Let them have the worry: she still likes to see the lambs. She lives off the rent, and her state pension. She still has the house. What remains in the way of livestock consists of two or three ewes bought for old times' sake and kept for sentimental reasons. No more breeding, no more swinging a lantern out across freezing fields in February, just a few old girls living out their days in the little orchard, snoozing beneath the trees on summer days. Maud, on summer days, has been known to join them.

There are a couple of outdoor cats, and an indoor dog, now nosing about in the hedgerow as the sun gilds summer clouds. Kep is – was once – a working sheepdog, a very bright border collie, who on many farms would live outside, except in the depths of winter, when he might be granted a piece of sacking in the porch, an occasional lie-down before the fire. Kep is an exception to all this, like so much in Maud's life: a pensioned-off worker, he's the heart of everything, without whom she could not go for her walks, nor sleep without anxiety in her isolated house. Only a dog can settle companionably in his basket yet be alert in an instant to defend you to the death.

Maud is tough. She could do a pretty good job of defending if she had to, but even she is aware of the terrible things that can happen to women living alone: the sudden waking in the dark, the certainty that you've woken for a reason; the straining to hear, then the creak on the stair, the landing. The turning of the handle. Too horrible to contemplate. But with Kep in his basket she has no need to think of these things, and doesn't. He is her dearest friend, like Rex before him and Max before that. They're buried out in the orchard. There are stones to mark the spot. Spots.

And now it is summer again, the evenings long and light. Finches flit in and out of the hawthorn, the verges of the lane are thick with cow parsley, ragged robin, rosebay willowherb, hogweed. Maud, heedless of Georgia's attempt to phone her, strides out with her dog, as her ancestors have done for generations, if not in quite this way.

– Kep! Kep! Here, boy!

She's growing peckish: what's for supper? She casts her mind about the pantry, a word from the past, which no one uses now. She likes to keep it in circulation, even if she cannot spell it, and her inner eye now flits up and down the shelves of ancient cake tins, the last of a joint in a zinc-doored safe, a jug of something covered with beaded muslin. What's there? She cannot quite remember.

There are quite a few things Maud cannot remember now. Quite a few moments such as this. She's half aware of it, knows there are good days and bad. On good days she can shop without a list, on bad she can't remember what it is she can't remember. Is this the long-term effect of long-distant ECT, or the natural concomitant of ageing? She doesn't know, rarely, if ever, thinking of the former, though someone else will think of it, over the next few months, as she declines.

For now . . .

What is she going to eat this evening?

– Kep!

He's back in a flash. She turns and makes her way homewards, her dog at her heels.

It's Tuesday, and Dido is at the Centre. She's risen early, as befits a working day: properly, no slopping about in dressing gowns. Shower, breakfast with Jeffrey and the headlines, and off they both go, he wheeling his bicycle along at her side until they reach the junction with the main road. Then he swings a graceful leg across the bar, perches for a moment to kiss her goodbye, and rides away into the traffic.

Dido proceeds to the bus stop, shows her pass when boarding, and travels over Skeldergate Bridge. The day's first pleasure boats are out; the river's full; gulls wheel above. It's a bright, breezy day, and as she alights in Lower Priory Street she feels uplifted and purposeful, the weekend's strange little turmoil of emotion quite forgotten. Things to be done. She just checks, as she turns into a narrow side street, that the strap of her shoulder bag lies across her body: they're still within the city walls, but only just, and twenty-four-hour CCTV observes this neck of the woods, from a spot near the public toilets. Not many muggers prey upon middle-aged women first thing on a summer morning, but you never know. For all she's aware, there are muggers amongst some of the young people she calls her clients now. Young, old, lonely, adrift; miserably single, miserably married, drink-and-drug-dependent, longing for a baby or worn out by the kids – they all pitch up at the Centre in time, and Dido and her colleagues are there for every one.

73

She's almost there. She walks past the ancient street's contemporary mix – the boutique (droopy skirts, candles, incense, essential oils), fish-and-chip shop (very good) bookshop (Mind, Body, Spirit) and newsagent. The atmosphere is what she and Georgia would once have called bohemian, a word you don't hear so often now. And there is the sign hanging out above the green-painted door: two clasped hands. Comfort and consolation await the sad and brave. Dido presses the buzzer beside the half-curtained window, and is admitted.

– Morning, Alex.

– Hi, there.

Alex, who has buzzed the buzzer, looks across from her place at the reception desk and smiles brightly. Oh, the young, the young. Look at her, so fresh and clean, that long hair falling over the vintage cardigan, that stud in her lower lip, those rings through her left nostril. That smile. Alex is – so far – one of life's sorted individuals. She can cope, she has emotional energy to spare. She's sympathetic to those who come here, but she has her boundaries, as must we all. Hers involve a proper lunch hour and leaving on the dot. But while here: efficient to the tips of those black-painted nails. Fresh skin, clean hair, nose rings, vintage and Goth – they all meet confidently in Alex and everyone loves her.

Now why couldn't Nick . . .? Someone like Alex would make him so much happier.

Not necessarily. Dido puts the thought away, hanging up her jacket. Nick is seriously clever: he needs a marriage of minds, he's always said so. Alex, marvellous though she may be, is a trainee herbalist. It wouldn't do.

– Beautiful morning, says Dido, picking up her bag again. – How do things look today?

Alex's appointment book is open on the desk; Dido's column is almost full. She is handed an efficient sheet, with all the names and times recorded, to take up to her consulting room. Consulting box, to be accurate: the house is tall and narrow with a number of microscopic rooms, just enough space for the lonely and adrift and damaged to sob their hearts out. Sometimes they do this by appointment, sometimes they drop in. Dido and her colleagues take turns: today is full of scheduled clients – marginally less in crisis than those who just turn up. If you can make and keep an appointment, there's hope. On Thursday, she'll be on drop-in duty, seeing those who've stormed out in despair from desperate situations, who've seen the two clasped hands, taken a deep breath and decided to seek help at last.

OK. Now, then. Dido looks at her list. Time for a coffee: no one until ten. The phone is ringing. Alex picks it up.

– Hand in Need. Can I help you?

They'd all thought long and hard about this greeting, when founding the place. In the age of the call centre, the first point of contact must be a human being. Must, said Caroline, sound like a human being. She herself had recently bought a car from a company whose greeting consisted of *Hello, Murray Motors, good people to deal with, my name's Tracey, how may I help you today?*

– Every time, said Caroline. – Every single time she picks up the phone, that poor young woman has to reel that off.

They all shook their heads. They'd been given millennium funding by the council: two years' start-up money, enough to pay a good receptionist, all the running costs and counsellors' travel expenses. Such grants were like gold dust: they had to make a go of it.

– Just keep it simple, said Dido, at this particular meeting. – Simple and warm. Our name and the offer to help.

– But not How may I help you today?

– Absolutely not.

– That's what they say before they tell you they're Just Going to Pop You on Hold.

So here is Alex, listening carefully, and here is Dido, crossing the reception area to go to the loo and put the kettle on in the tiny galley kitchen. She's the first to arrive, as so often. Waiting for the kettle to boil, she comes out of the kitchen and pads about. The reception area is softly lit, thanks to the cream half-curtains running on tabs across the window on to the street. They say: you can be assured of privacy, but also: it's nice in here. From the street you can see the tops of posters, calming pictures. When you come in, you see – always – fresh flowers on the desk. There's a map of the city, a rack of leaflets: information on sexual health (a euphemism if ever there was one) drug abuse, alcohol dependency, abortion, anorexia, Relate, the Gay and Lesbian Helpline, HIV, the Samaritans, debt counselling, Help the Aged. Everything you could think of. Some things are kept locked away: the address of the women's refuge, for example.

– But what do you actually do? Georgia had asked her, hearing about it all in the early days. – You just refer people to all these places?

– We don't 'just refer', said Dido, fresh from her counselling diploma. – Referral is an art in itself. We listen, and we offer support.

Georgia shuddered. – Please don't use that word.

– What's wrong with it?

– I don't know. It's just over-used these days.

– Thank you for your support; I shall wear it always.

Georgia conceded a smile.

Dido knew what Georgia meant, but she couldn't think of a better term for what she and colleagues did. They weren't psychotherapists, but they weren't just any old listener, either. They were trained, they had their antennae out. Sometimes their clients came for just one or two sessions; sometimes they were with them for ages.

– You don't think you're contributing to the culture of dependence?

– No, said Dido. – I don't. Georgia could sound so cool. This was before – three years before – Henry died. – We see them in six-week cycles, she said. – At the end of every six weeks we review where they are. How does that sound?

– Very wise, said Georgia. – Very sensible.

– So nice to have your approval.

– In truth, I take my hat off. Jolly well done.

– As you might say.

– As I just have.

They kissed one another with their old affection.

The kettle is boiling; Alex is still on the phone; the buzzer buzzes. Alex, with a practised hand, reaches for the button beneath the desk, and the door is pushed open. Here's Caro – Caroline as once she was, Caro since the divorce. Large (very large) and dressed in a bold print cotton. Making the best of it all.

– Hi, Dido. Nice holiday?

– Lovely, thanks.

Caro herself had been away when Dido returned last week.

– And you? she asks her.

Caro is taking off an enormous linen jacket.

– Well, you know. My mother's almost ninety. Still, it was pretty good.

Dido makes coffee for three, beneath the notice which reads NO ONE ELSE IS GOING TO WASH YOUR CUP. It can get pretty busy; there are another eight volunteer counsellors on the rota: M:F ratio 2:6, as so often. Lots of cups of tea for clients. What's now a calm and soothing place can get hectic.

She steps out past the bright red box of toys and books. She climbs the stairs to her room on the second floor, with her mug and her list. Caro, after a moment or two, follows with a heavy tread.

Poor old Caro. Such a brick. She hadn't deserved what she got.

* * *

Eight-thirty and Chloe is in a taxi on the Kilburn High Road. Enormous bulging carriers are at her feet, and one on the seat beside her, covered with a protective arm as the cab brakes suddenly and swerves. Glass tinkles from within the bag.

– Bleeding cyclists. The driver glances at her in the mirror. – Sorry about that.

– It's OK.

Chloe, a bag of nerves, gives him a confident little smile. Her sympathies are entirely with the cyclist, so brave and free, hurtling along amidst the fearful traffic. She used to bike everywhere herself when she was a student. Now she has an expense account. Not huge, it's true, but enough to get her about town with all the stuff for shoots. Enough for lunch, and/or a little happy hour moment.

They're almost there.

– We're almost there, she tells the driver, and he nods. He knows. Soon, they're off the High Road; turning into a purpose-built collection of low-rise buildings centred on a car park. Horrible notices about fines and clamping are bolted to the brick. Chloe, a nippy London driver but unlikely to be able, ever, to afford a car, doesn't have to think about clamps. Truth to tell, she can't really think about anything much at the moment anyway, except her insides, which are liquid with anticipation. They pull up; she clambers out, heaves out the carriers.

– Want a hand?

– No, no, it's fine, thanks. She fumbles for her purse, a nifty little number with a cheering lining in red check. What can money matter when it comes from such a place? Anyway, it's not her money. She pays, she glances at the door to the studios. He's not there, waiting to help.

Yes he is.

Oh, Christmas.

She gazes at the taxi driver, counting change elaborately.

– Keep it, she says, quite unable to work out what she is owed and what a sensible tip might be.

– You sure?

And he's off, swinging round as other cabs pull in. She watches him go, as if it's really important to see a black cab safely through the gates.

– Hi.

She can't put it off any longer: she turns, he's there beside her.

– Oh. Hi.

Jez smiles down at her; he kisses her on both cheeks. He's against the early morning sun, so she can't really see him properly out here, is just sort of aware of the stubble, the flopping hair, clouds sailing by.

– Good to see you. He touches her face.

– And you.

Clouds sail, doors slam, an aeroplane heads west. Or is it east?

– We'd better get going, she says.

He picks up three of the four bags, nods towards the one at her side.

– You can manage that?

– Of course. This is the fragile one, anyway; it's better I carry it on my own. Is everyone here?

– Pretty much.

He tugs at the door. A vast white container lorry is pulling into the yard. Chloe glances at it. Television cameras? Asylum seekers? Jez is propping open the door with his foot. She goes inside.

– Hi, there!

A skinny ash-blonde woman well into her forties greets them with a radiant smile. She's wearing a miniskirt, boots and bare legs. A weighty glass vase filled with flowers in primary colours stands on the desk. Gerbera, those great big daisy things. They're the flowers of Chloe's generation, but she doesn't like them: scentless, somehow meaningless. Never mind: this morning is charged with meaning. She smiles back, follows Jez along the corridor through black rubber swing doors, which he holds aside. She's been here a million times: these studios are used by everyone, booked up months ahead. When she first started at Dot & Carrie she used to do the bookings herself. And work on reception. Now she's a stylist, and can make demands. She had a credit in *Dazed & Confused* last month.

Another set of doors, and then they're there; the door to the studio is propped open with a brick. Inside, she can see Dot, feet up, with a fag, naughty, trestle tables and a backdrop being set up by a studio hand and someone on work experience. The model is nowhere to be seen.

– ?

– On her way, says Dot. She stubs out the ciggie, rises from the director's chair.

They're shooting for a mid-market catalogue, which in lesser hands would look just that. The company has come to Dot & Carrie to shift up into a different league: to make pretty ordinary jeans, trousers, sweaters look the business. There's going to be a pull-out in the *Mail* in the autumn. Ideally, the shoot would be done on location – a Scottish castle, some Irish ruin – but they can't quite run to that.

– Not to worry, Dot tells them. – Leave it to me.

It's Chloe's task to transform Studio Three into ancient splendour. Bolts of old velvet cram the carriers. There's a chandelier, and many candlesticks.

– Right, then, says Dot, as all this is set down. – Let's get started.

The trestles are draped with old linen, the backdrop window hung with chocolate velvet. The chandelier – two people up a ladder needed to hang that from a beam – sparkles in the spotlight; candles drip. Seated at the table in Dot's Windsor chair, before some glorious teapot; drinking from an antique green and white cup; gazing thoughtfully out of the window, etc., etc., the model (size eight, highlights, late twenties) transforms routine T-shirts, cardis, camisoles, gilets, etc. into classic chic. Actually it's not a bad collection. Chloe, her work done save for darts here and there to remove or rearrange, wouldn't mind the coffee cardi sprinkled with minute glass beads, or that lacy camisole in cream and white. They've got a new designer.

Somewhere in a corner of her mind, as she sits in the darkness watching Jez behind the camera, she hears her mother tell her that those beads were sewn on by child labour, the slender ribbons threaded through that camisole by tiny Third World fingers.

One day, Chloe will give up all this frippery and do something useful with her life. She's been thinking this for a while.

But for now—

Now she's doing something she loves and is good at, and which pays the rent. What more do you want?

Now – she's watching someone she's been watching on and off for years, has always liked and always quietly fancied. He's declared himself. Interested. Separated.

She still hasn't told a soul.

– OK, now look at me again, look at me as if you really mean it . . .

The model produces a long cold gaze. Jez bends to the camera. He's tall, he's straight, one black-clad leg just bent at the knee, the other stretched out behind him. He has style and presence: he could be an actor. Would Georgia think an actor more real than a fashion photographer?

– Perfect.

There are plenty of shoots where the model never smiles. Smiling is so uncool, so naff. The look is straight, uncaring, even cruel. You can look, but you can't touch. Until today, this catalogue has always had happy smiles and healthy people. Healthy is cool now, but not that kind. Now they want youth – not nasty, but not so nice.

– Now look away, turn your head, you're never going to speak to me again . . .

Not an actor, a director. Chloe, perched on a folding chair next to Dot, the catalogue picture editor on her other side, wonders if she could move from fashion to theatre, if that would be more meaningful. Just a different lot of egos? Probably. She's getting hungry.

– OK, says Dot to everyone. – One more change and we'll have lunch.

Will he sit next to her, on one of those low black sofas? Should she save him a place or ignore the whole thing and sit with the studio guys? She bites her lip. She and Jez used to be so easy around one another – not close, like she and Edmund, but chatting away. Now it all feels tense and nervy.

Chloe, when tense and nervy in the past (often) would seek out her father. Now she can't. No more Come and tell me all about it. No more Why don't we go for a walk/have lunch one day/see you at home for supper. No more of any of that. She shuts her eyes.

Lunch is, in truth, a little fraught at first. Ash-Blonde Streaks brings along vast trays of sandwiches, jugs of juice and, as always, too much fruit. There's the usual sorting all this out, settling down in the anteroom with glass and cardboard plate, the disappearance of Dot and the studio hand to smoke outside. But usually Chloe doesn't have to think about a thing: she chats away to everyone she knows, is nice to the model, perches on a sofa arm if there's no room anywhere else, tucks in.

But now—

Now she finds herself wondering if she's heaped her plate too high. She's starving, had hardly any breakfast; surely two or three sandwiches and a banana are OK? She glances at the model's lunch, and sees the usual crumb. And Jez, who has directed her so well, is talking to her, not Chloe. OK, it's his job, he always does this, keeps the energy between them strong and communicative; these days are long, and models must not wilt. In the past (like last week) she'd never have noticed who he was talking to, at least not in the way she notices today, wondering: Has he changed his mind? What happens now? And: Should I be doing this anyway?

Doing what?

– Hi, Chloe.

The lighting guy sits down beside her.

– Oh, hi. God, she can't remember his name. – How are you?

– I'm good.

Now *his* plate is heaped up like Vesuvius. Sandwiches, samosas, crisps . . . He's overweight, he sits in here all day, goes home to – what? She finds herself glancing at The Finger. There's no ring, but that doesn't necessarily mean anything. She glances at Jez, who's made the model laugh. No ring. Did he wear one before? Of course he did, that's how she knew he was married, that was why she never gave him a thought. Not that kind of thought.

Not for long, anyway.

The lighting guy is saying something. She gives him a radiant smile.

– Go on.

And he does, for a bit, about the shoot and things. She doesn't have to listen very hard. Let's face it, if you're stuck in a studio all day you don't have a huge amount to talk about, not unless you have a life outside. This is perhaps one reason why Georgia doesn't rate her world: it's busy busy (like, frantic) but self-absorbed. Trivial. Not that Georgia's not interested in clothes: she's always dressed well, perhaps that's even where Chloe got it from. But Georgia's dressed well and done serious work. Valuable stuff, struggling with hellish school-refusing kids—

Like me.

So how come she didn't understand *me*?

– Hi, Chloe.

It's him. She drops a sandwich. He picks it up.

– Thanks. Left to her own devices, she'd probably dust it down and eat it. Now she sets it delicately aside. The lighting guy – God, what's he called? – gets heavily to his feet. Flakes of samosa fall. He's going outside for a bit, breath of fresh air.

– Sure. See you back in there, Mike.

And Jez sits down next to her, drapes an arm along the soft black leather against which, if she chose, she could softly lean. All around them there's the buzz of lunch-time talk.

– Mike, she says. – I couldn't remember his name.

– Nice guy. What are you doing after this?

His long black-clad legs are stretched out beneath the glass-topped coffee table, he's just inches away from her. He's gorgeous: deep down she's always thought so. She hesitates. Should she invent some fascinating new interest which makes her totally unavailable, tonight or ever?

She who hesitates is lost.

– I don't know, says Chloe, turning to look at him. – You tell me.

It's been a long, worthwhile day. Dido, her last client seen from her consulting room to the top of the stairs, seen through the front door by bright kind Alex, yawns and shuts the window. The catch is stiffer than she remembers: she fumbles, then it's done. Through glass which could do with a clean she looks down on to the gardens at the back: lit by late afternoon sun, and filled with birdsong, little walled squares of domestic space in varying degrees of care and neglect – like her clients. No one has time to tend their own patch here, though Alex does water the pots. The fish-and-chip shop has a wasteland of weeds and empty oil cans; next door there's a young family with climbing frame and slide. The children are home from school, and out there; their cries have punctuated the stream of talk from Didio's last client, perhaps distractingly, but the room's too small and hot up here to keep the window closed.

– When do you think you first felt like this?

– All my bloody life.

Dido listens, does not try to fill a silence, from time to time reflects and amplifies.

– You've felt like this all your life? Ever since . . .

A long pause. Tears well up.

– Since . . .

Sobs and incoherence.

– I've never told anyone.

– You don't have to tell me.

Out it all comes.

Dido, at the dusty window, her notes all written up, looks absently down upon walled gardens in this run-down part of the city, and reflects upon varieties of pain. On things kept hidden from all who know you, things that no one would ever guess at. Sometimes her clients' faces are transparent with years of pushing strain and suffering away – drink, drugs, insomnia, self-harm; too much ghastly sex, years without sex at all. More often, you would never dream what lay beneath that smile, that easy manner.

Dido picks up her notes from the table and her mug; she picks up her bag from the floor by her chair: one of a pair of low and comfortable chairs, nicely covered, not some dismal brown moquette. The low table is set against the wall between them. These tables in each room hold a plant – a nice plant, no ancient cactus here – and the regulation box of tissues. A print or two on the walls: they'd spent a long time choosing those. Not so bright they made a mockery of distress, not too much pastel-coloured sky lighting the horizon of a pastel sea. None of that.

– It says hope, said Maggie, at another meeting.

– No, it doesn't, said Caroline (as she was then). – It says death and the vicarage.

She should know.

Dido meets her in the reception area, where Alex is putting files away. She and Caro give her their own heap, and wash up their mugs in the kitchen.

– What sort of day?

– A bit grim, says Caro brightly.

The buzzer buzzes, the evening shift arrives in ones and twos: Maggie, Kathy, Andrew. The phone goes. Soon, Alex's opposite number on the evening shift will be here: Paul, camp as a row of tents and as cheering. There's a chorus of greetings and goodbyes. Alex goes to the loo. Then Dido and Caro are out on the street, in the deepening light. They walk along together; children run past.

– I'm sorry it was grim, says Dido. – Why?

– Oh. Caro shrugs. – Just one too many abandoned women. She waves her hand. – Never mind, let's not talk about it until we have to.

They had to in weekly supervision.

– Of course, says Dido. Her long tall stride is too much for Caro, bearing so much weight. She senses this and slows down.

– What are you doing this evening?

– It's my choir night, says Caro. – Vivaldi's *Gloria*, end of June. I'll give you a flyer.

– Lovely. We'll be there.

At the corner of the street they part, Dido to walk to the bus stop – or perhaps walk home across the river, it's such a lovely evening – and Caro, living right across the city, to the car park. Dido watches her go, large and square and lonely. Keeping her end up: the choir, Hand in Need, the garden; taking her mother on holiday, babysitting for her grown-up children, never letting down a soul.

But still . . .

Deep down, hurt and lonely.

Better by far to live alone than live with the wrong person. Dido knows this: from everything her clients tell her, all her experience of school parents down the years. The single life can be fulfilling, happy, stable and good.

But still . . .

For Caro, after the divorce: not much fun.

Dido gives a last friendly wave, then strides down Newton Terrace. Pigeons are fluttering above the city wall, murmuring from ledges in the stone as the light grows deeper. A companionable supper with Jeffrey lies ahead; her book awaits. They're doing Justin Cartwright in the book group; also she's travelling in Southern Turkey with Duncan Grant. She picked it up one browsing afternoon between festival events: it's bliss. And as she reaches the river the day's tears and sadness all slip away, like the water under the bridge.

The magnolia is over, the petals on the pavement swept away. Now it's the first roses, rambling over an old stone porch or standing tall in well-kept gardens – the bush, the hybrid tea. There's a scented Duc d'Ambrey two doors along at the Murrays', deepest pink and most perfectly formed in bud, opening to a sculpted bloom . . . Dido adores it. Perhaps, now she's retired, she can really get into roses. Grow one into the apple tree, something proper gardeners do. And she stops to drink in the scent, to say hello to the cat who comes strolling down the path: Mimi, a sweet-faced tabby who is, she knows, a killer. The number of times she's shooed her away from their own bird table. But today – today she's a softly purring thing, inclining her pretty head for a caress. Georgia has said quite openly that the cats keep her going; perhaps it would be nice to have one again, after all. And Dido gives Mimi a last little fluff-up round the ears and straightens up. Rather stiffly: she's tireder than she thinks. And her head's a bit swimmy – no, it's gone. But just for a moment, as she moves away, there's the strangest sensation of weakness in her legs, as if she could collapse, there and then in the street. She puts out a hand; she grasps the Murrays' gate. Then it's gone, as quick as it came: she feels fine again.

She walks on, opens her gate, gets her keys out. Already, that strange flood of weakness is forgotten: she's home, a blackbird singing his heart out behind the house.

Inside the cool of the hall she hangs up her things, picks the post up, goes into the kitchen, pours a drink, opens the doors to the garden. The grass needs cutting. That blackbird! She looks at the post: a junk mail announcement that you, Mrs Sullivan, have won a prize in our Special Draw, a couple of letters for Jeffrey, a card from Georgia. Ah.

Visiting a rather peculiar exhibition at Tate Modern, which I felt I ought to see. Thought I'd send you this.

Dido turns over the card. A blank-faced young woman, naked but for stiletto boots, is draped across a fifties armchair. A goldfish bowl and standard lamp with tasselled fringe stand about.

What's that supposed to mean? She turns the card over again.

All well here: Chloe's party a success, I gather. She says you sent a marvellous present. (Has she written to thank you?) Love, G.

Dido sips her drink. Chloe hasn't written, and she probably won't: it's a struggle, Georgia knows that. She'll phone, when she's got a minute. Dido yawns, looks at her watch. Jeffrey will be about half an hour: there's time for a little kip before supper. She shuts her eyes, sees Georgia's elegant tall figure wandering through the spaces of modern art. Had she gone to that show alone, or with a friend? *All well here . . .* How was it really?

She yawns again, drifts into slumber.

* * *

When she wakes, the sun has slipped down a little, and shadows stretch across the lawn. She gives a shiver. Should have put something on. And she gathers things up and goes indoors. The kitchen clock ticks comfortably; she opens the freezer, pulls out a couple of chops, goes into the hall, taking Jeffrey's letters. He'll be home any minute.

She takes the post – a letter with the university postmark, another from his publisher in London – into his study, drops it on the desk. It's warm in here, without an outside door, and the sun is slanting in painterly fashion across worn green carpet, rug, wastepaper basket. A lovely room to work in, prints from his father's study on the walls, pictures of the children and grandchildren on the mantelpiece, the top shelves of the bookcase lined with everything he's ever edited, contributed to, written or reviewed. He's had a good career, no doubt about it; he deserves a good retirement. All the admin he has to do now, all the heading-up Research, chasing people for their returns, sitting on funding committees, validating new programmes to attract overseas students – he rarely complains, but it's not really Jeffrey.

Three more years.

Dido sits down in the swivel chair and swivels. She swivels back. The mantelpiece clock shows almost seven: he's late. She hasn't forgotten a meeting, has she? She glances at the papers on his desk. There are minutes from something last week.

> *A supportive developmental culture . . . a carefully articulated strategy of growth and development . . . a distinctively different mode of education . . .*

God, how does he stand it? Even school stuff was getting like this by the time she left, but she avoided it like the plague.

Is it possible to formulate programmes with a strong subject area core with specialised options?

– I don't know, Dido says aloud. – You tell me.

She's about to get up and go back to the kitchen when Jeffrey's mobile, left behind on the desk in his hurry to be in time for this morning's meeting, makes a little texting sound. That'll be Sam, expecting Jeffrey to be home, as she is. *Hi Gpa, how RU? Luv Sam.*

– *You just press Yes*, she hears Sam say, out in the garden after Sunday lunch. – *Press Yes, to get the message.*

Should she?

Dido was brought up to think that reading other people's mail was to sink lower than the low. She's brought the children up to think the same. Is texting any different?

Oh, come on: it's only going to be Sam.

She presses the button, and the tiny screen lights up.

Hi Gpa—

No.

That's not what it says.

It says *Can U get away tonite?*

It isn't signed.

Dido gazes at it.

Who is this from?

A colleague?

But a colleague, wanting to meet up for a drink after work, would text Jeffrey: *RU free?* That's ordinary, that's everyday, it happens all the time. Are you free, let's go to—

Can U get away is different. Isn't it?

Get away from what?

From her. Who else?

The slanting sun falls on the desk. It's so quiet in here. Jeffrey should be home. He isn't.

Dido, in the swivel chair, sits very very still.

7

There are no absolutes.

There is no reason why.

There is (most assuredly) no God.

Nothing matters.

In this uplifting frame of mind, Georgia sits in Henry's study, in the chair at Henry's desk. His spectacles are on her left, his mug to her right, by the phone; she is facing his computer screen: switched off, and as grey as the clouds piling up beyond the window. Summer rain: let it come, the garden needs it, she needs it – anything to break the blankness, the emptiness, which seems both to reside within her and stretch to the limits of human experience.

Up here, with the desk occupying the whole breadth of the window, she can see only clouds and rooftops, the tops of trees. The well-tended walled squares of north London garden, thirsting for rain below, are hidden from view; so is the private road which runs beyond them, on to which each garden has a door, set in its wall. On the other side of this unmade road are the purpose-built blocks of flats occupied by the young and rich – the brokers and bankers who are now the only people who can afford to buy round here. Those big square picture windows offer in the evenings glimpses of coupledom: the jacket taken off, the kiss, the bottle uncorked and salad tossed, the endless conversations on the mobile, even while eating together. Even in bed? Georgia used to wonder, coming up here in the evenings from time to time, to stand next to Henry as he tapped away. His hair was thinning, his nose a little bonier, his forehead lined – but she could still stand here, watching that intent tap-tap, that gentle cleverness brought to bear on Whitehall briefing paper or colonial Africa and feel pleased by what she saw. She could watch the mews blinds pulled down, as it grew late, speculate idly and perhaps aloud on bankers in bed, and still, after all these years, look forward to going to bed with Henry.

Middle-aged love. Late middle-aged love. If you've lasted that long, it's all known and familiar: the chat from the bathroom, the sinking into your side of the bed, the reaching for book and specs, companionable talk of this and that, reading side by side, book dropping to the quilt, the lights switched off. And then? So focused is the world upon the young, their relations to one another, that these days you'd think no other kind of relationship existed. But she and Henry knew better – still reached for one another in the dark, wrapped round one another; more often fell asleep than not, but still, from time to time, made love. With interest, even.

Sitting up here, amidst all that is loved and familiar and empty of the man who gave it meaning, Georgia closes her eyes and is taken to an afternoon in France: the heat intense, the shutters closed, Dido and Jeffrey having time to themselves away from their jointly rented gîte, lunching in the medieval town nearby. Now she and Henry have time to themselves. Cicadas make their music in the olive trees, time stretches into hazy infinity. Then a bell rings out three slow deep notes across the valley; in here, within this shadowed space, these narrow chinks of brightness, Georgia and Henry awaken from a siesta, kiss, and murmur things. They kiss again, more deeply, and then the room and the hour are given over to sex of a Tantric intensity. Their need, and longing, surprise them both.

Later, when Henry gets up to go along the sunny landing for a pee, she lies there in a rare state of complete contentment, listening to the endless rasp of the cicadas, and the arrival of the swifts. Henry returns, opens shutters, comes back to lie beside her. They hold hands, watching the celestial ballet of the birds.

– That was wonderful.

Suntanned fingers entwine once more; they fall asleep again.

That was the last time. Affection, yes; sex no. The holiday came peacefully to an end: lunch on the shaded terrace of the town's best restaurant; a last evening walk down to the river, all four of them; a good flight home. Fond goodbyes at Gatwick; home to the cats, and phoning Chloe.

Then—

– It's just a check-up. I'm sure it's nothing.

Then—

Summer rain is falling: Georgia opens her eyes, watches it patter on the pane, and slant against the blank unpopulated windows of the flats across the garden. Everyone's at work. And she, who has worked all her life, is sitting up here in the middle of a weekday morning, more than a year after her husband's death, well over a year after her retirement, fighting off the void.

She should have prepared for this: these days without routine, hers to fill as she chose. She would have prepared for this, was gearing up to think about retirement on their return from France: six months to go, then freedom! But the prospect of retirement spent in interesting activities until Henry, too, was free, was very different from retirement spent alone. Georgia has been active and independent all her life: she should be able to do this, but she can't, not really. She paces about Tate Modern, lunches with friends in the Members' Room, gazing at St Paul's across the river; she goes to see Chekhov at the Almeida and afterwards to supper at Le Mercury; she goes out to Sunday lunch, talks to Chloe, reads in bed. She's deep in Volume Two of

The Brothers Karamazov, listening for Henry's quiet tones in every line.

> *As for everything else around me, all these worlds, God and even Satan himself – all that hasn't been proved to me. Does it all exist of itself or is it only an emanation of myself . . .*

She puts the book down, says his name aloud.

When all this becomes too painful, she looks for light (but intelligent) relief. Thank God for Alan Bennett.

So. Things get done. Get read. Yet lapping at the edges of all this, like the Thames against its wall, is the dead sense of marking time. No more than that. Getting things done to tick the days away. Thinking about the future, when the past is all that matters. The closest Georgia has come to losing herself in any activity was in those happy days at the festival with Dido. Daily companion-ship – how sweet that sounds. That was what they shared. But then Dido returned to York, and companionship with Jeffrey.

She should get a lodger, but she doesn't want to. Perhaps she should do it anyway. She should be working again; she should be teaching. Application forms for part-time tutoring jobs are on the desk beside her, but she knows the score: they're like gold dust, these jobs, and at sixty there's not much point in chasing them. Besides, she's not sure if she has the energy. The oomph. Teaching requires considerable psychic strength: on days like this she has none of it. She sits up here, and tries to work things out.

It's raining harder, splashing on the ivy-covered garden wall below, dripping down the green-painted door set within it. When Georgia was a child, she went through a little spate of painting just such walls, and it gave her enormous, undefined happiness. She kept changing her mind about what lay on the other side of that carefully painted brick, those watery splodges of greenery and trees, that rounded door with its satisfactory brown doorknob, painted last of all, but whether old orchard, meadow, or a kitchen garden, it was filled with enchantment. No doubt this came from childhood reading – *Narnia*, *The Secret Garden* – but for Georgia, at eight or nine, there was never anyone else walking through these sunlit places, just great warmth going on for ever. And when she and Henry found this house, decades ago, it wasn't the fact that it was a proper, good-sized and just affordable family house which sold it to her, nor the light which its east-west position gave all day, but the sight of that garden door in the wall. She belonged here: she was rooted, even before they'd moved in.

Sitting up here now, Georgia, not generally given to sentimentality, thinks: heaven was what I used to think was on the other side. I'm sure I never said so, perhaps I never even thought it consciously, but deep down that was what I believed, that was why it made me so happy. Silence, afternoon sun, the smell of grass – they were translated into eternal peace and safety.

It is a very long time since Georgia has believed in heaven.

She has learned that nothing is permanent or safe.

When Henry died, amongst the shoals of letters she received was one which hoped she would find the meaning in his death. And where might that be, she wondered then, and wonders now, in the middle of a morning whose loneliness is tipping towards despair. There is no door to the garden, no door to heaven through which my love might pass: no hand of God to hold him, no everlasting arms to bear him. There is no reason for his death; no meaning in that suffering except to show that cancer is still unconquered. All the meaning of our lives is here; there is no sunlit space beyond.

But if life leads nowhere, when all the human impulse is to move forward – what's the point? What the hell is the point? To live – and then to stop.

Meanwhile, I have (probably) years and years to get through – and without my life's companion where is the purpose for me now?

The rain is blowing away. Something else is happening. Sunk so low in grief and reverie, Georgia comes to with some confusion. It's the phone: she lurches towards it.

– Hello?

– Who's there?

– I beg your pardon?

– To whom am I speaking?

Someone is calling from the poop deck of a vessel in full sail. Commanding tones ring out across the seas.

– This is Maud Hannaway here.

How could she not have known that voice? Georgia is restored to the present with some urgency.

– Somebody rang me, says Maud. – I dialled that number one can dial. Fourteen seventy-one. She intones it as a date from the reign of Henry VI. – Then, she continues regally – I dialled this one. And you are . . . ?

– It's me, Georgia, says Georgia.

– Who?

Oh, bloody hell.

– Georgia, she says again. – Henry's wife.

There is a silence. Georgia tries to cast her mind back. When has she last rung Maud? Days ago. Last Sunday evening, and no answer came. Has no one else rung that crumbling ruin in all this time? If Maud had decided to check her calls on 1471 and found Georgia's number as the last, then, yes, this must be the case. No one phones her, she speaks to no one except sheep, she's lost the plot. She doesn't even know Georgia and Henry's number. Or Georgia's name.

With a flash of her old spirit and determination firing up her veins, Georgia thinks with awful clarity: I must never let this happen to me.

Now, then.

– Maud, she says, clearly and calmly. – This is Georgia Hannaway. You remember me.

– Georgia! How nice of you to phone.

Georgia prepares for a long haul.

– How are you? says Maud warmly, as if striding across the room at some drinks do. (Has she ever gone to such a thing? In youth? Surely in youth.)

– I'm very well, says Georgia. – How are you, Maud?

– Me? Oh, I'm in the pink. And Henry?

Georgia, seated at Henry's desk, with his books and notes and things all round her, takes a long deep breath. Easier to go along with it all. Easier by far to tell his cousin that he's fine, working hard as usual, will be so glad to know she's called.

She can't possibly do that.

– Henry died, she says carefully. – You remember.

– *Henry?* There's a pause. – He's died? But this is terrible.

– Yes, says Georgia.

– When did this happen?

– Over a year ago. You came to the funeral, remember?

What a time *that* had been, the hearse moving slowly along the Finchley Road and Maud, dressed in ancient skirt and anorak, sitting next to Chloe in the family limousine, remarking on London traffic as if she were on a shopping expedition. Still, at least she'd known she was in London. Clearly, in the months that have passed since the last (difficult) visit to Sussex, she's really gone down hill. There is a silence now. Georgia waits, watching the last of the clouds roll away, and a patch of summer blue appear.

– Poor Henry, says Maud at last. – I didn't know he'd died.

They talk for perhaps another ten minutes, during which Georgia learns nothing reliable. Maud is keeping well, the weather's been glorious, the garden a picture, any number of lambs have gone to market. Surely those ancient ewes aren't breeding still. Of course, they could be any old lambs, sighted by Maud on a walk. She's been watching a rather good wildlife programme, where famous people brave dreadful creatures in the tropics. After a moment, Georgia realises that this is *I'm a Celebrity Get Me Out of Here*. Unimaginable. By the time they say goodbye, a complicated business, her head is reeling.

She puts the phone down.

Something must be done.

Jez lives in Willesden. This is not good news. There are parts of Willesden which are coming up (or there already) and there are the parts where Jez lives: close to the railway, with a skyline dominated by power station, tower blocks and superstore. It's handy for Kilburn and the Dot & Carrie studio – not that Jez is always there, he works in studios all over London – and, like Kilburn, it thunders with traffic heading out towards the North Circular. The High Road is full of betting and kebab shops, as high roads tend to be. Wormwood Scrubs is not a million miles away. Chloe, spoiled by an upbringing in the tranquil purlieus of Highbury, and by her own little rented flat on Charlotte Street (so clever), tells herself that this is much more real. At some distance from the High Road there are, as in Kilburn, gentrified streets populated by the professional classes, including successful actors and rich photographers, but Jez, since the break-up with his wife, is not rich, and renting what he can afford, while Madeleine and Ellie stay (partly supported by him) in the family home. This is in Tufnell Park.

Chloe learns all this over supper in a cheap and cheerful Italian place near the Grand Union Canal. This waterway leads all the way through north London, to become, in Islington, the Regent's Canal, running past the kind of well-heeled streets where her parents have friends, and Sunday lunch. The Italian isn't on that kind of street. Trains whistle past, and clouds of steam drift from the power station through the summer evening sky. But all this has its own romance: everything this evening is charged with brink-of-something atmosphere and nerves. Here they are, on their first date (if hitherto unarranged supper after a long day at work counts as such), twirling their tagliatelle and finding out about each other.

Jez had not suggested going straight back to his rented flat, and Chloe counts this as a good thing: a sign of serious intent. Or perhaps it means he's as nervous as she is – hard to imagine, but a possibility. Is she – will she be – his first lover since the split? If not, who has preceded her, and is this person still on the scene? This is not something she can ask, not yet. But she can wonder.

– How long is it since you broke up?

– About a year.

All that time, and she hadn't realised. There must have been someone else, surely. Men like Jez wouldn't be on their own for long. Or perhaps they broke up because he already had someone else. Not good. But then maybe his wife – Madeleine – maybe she's met someone else, and Jez has had to go. She wants to ask about all this, but cannot bring herself to do so; she wants to ask if this break-up is really permanent (but ditto).

Instead, as he pours her another glass, she says: – Tell me about Ellie.

Why does she do this? Why does she bring a daughter into the spaces of seduction – someone who should be kept far away from such a place, for her own sake and perhaps for Chloe's. But she's curious (and already anxious) and it's easier to ask about a child than a wife.

– Tell me a bit more about her. What's she like?

– She's lovely, says Jez, and he reaches into his wallet. Chloe finds herself gazing at a primary-school photograph of a little girl smiling against that background of synthetic sky which graces all such portraits, whether taken of an infant or graduate. It's a background which offers a dreadful poignancy when child or student goes missing: there in the press is this gap-toothed boy or smiling young woman in her graduation gown, set against eternity in the shape of misty clouds, which tell you: this life is ended now. Something terrible has happened.

All this flashes in scrambled fashion through Chloe's mind as she looks at Ellie, eight years old (as Jez has told her) and bright and pretty. She has dark hair in a fringe and (of course) a gap-toothed smile. She's wearing a green sweatshirt with the school logo printed on in sunny yellow, over a white school shirt. There is nothing to indicate that her life so far has not been calm and happy (or as calm and happy as is the life of any child now).

– When was this taken?

– At Easter, I think. Last term, anyway.

So Ellie's parents had already separated. Nothing in that clear-eyed smile suggests that this is anything other than perfectly OK. Perhaps it is.

– How often do you see her?

Jez hesitates, just for a moment. Then: – Most weekends. And once during the week. I pick her up from school, and on Saturdays I pick her up from dance class. She comes to stay – not always, but quite often.

So her things will be in his rented flat. If there's going to be a love affair – is there? – it will be conducted around the arrangements with a little girl. A daughter with her own needs and (no doubt) demands. Chloe passes back the photograph. Jez tucks it into his wallet.

– You've gone very quiet.

– Have I?

– Yes. He reaches across the table, he takes her hand. It's the first time they've touched since that kiss on both cheeks outside the studio this morning. All that kissing at her birthday party, and then a greeting such as everyone gives everyone now. His arm had draped across the back of the sofa at lunch time, but that was all. Well, almost. He'd touched her shoulder as they made their date, and a current of desire had electrified her bloodstream. It does so now. Jez strokes her thumb with his. She shuts her eyes.

— You mustn't worry, he tells her, as a train goes hooting past. The restaurant is filling up, everything smells warm and Italian and delicious.

— Shall we go?

Dido and Jeffrey are having supper. It's warm enough – just – to eat outside, and they're at the garden table, a piece of furniture weathered by sun and rain whose pleasing paleness says quietly: this old thing has been here for ever. There is no counting the number of family meals down the years which have been eaten here, as Dido and Jeffrey are eating now.

This one is different. Dido cannot eat. Jeffrey's mobile is now on the table out here, next to his glass.

— More salad?

— No, thanks.

— You OK?

— Fine.

— Long day?

— We've both had long days, says Dido, gazing out across the garden. Everything is summery and full: late-June perfection. The grass needs cutting.

— The grass needs cutting.

— I know. I'll do it after supper.

— If you're not too tired.

— No, no. Jeffrey cuts another slice of bread. – Sure you won't have half?

— No, thanks. Tell me a bit more about today. What have you been up to? She asks this in very lightest tone. Too light? Noticeably so? Is it possible for him to guess how utterly unreal she feels?

Jeffrey arrived home perhaps an hour later than usual – an hour whose duration was as long and difficult as any Dido can remember. Well, she can't remember: in thirty-five years of marriage she has never experienced the kind of doubt and anxiety which assail her now. Then she's been very fortunate. She knows this from everything she has seen around her, down the years; the bitter break-ups amongst the parents of her pupils, one or two in particular; her clients, weeping and enraged; poor Caro's stoicism. Split up when the children are young and you're faced with endless fatigue, worries about money, access arrangements, Christmas – everything. Split when your children are grown and have lives of their own, and loneliness darkens all the years ahead.

For heaven's sake, Dido has told herself, trying to concentrate her mind on preparing supper, who is talking about divorce, or anything approaching such a thing? What would you say to a client who came to you in this ridiculous state, after a single little text? *What makes you afraid to ask about this? Have you any real reason to doubt?* She asks herself these questions. It is no help at all.

When at last she hears the click of the gate, the tick of the bike up the path, the key – oh, thank God – in the lock, she just calls out – Hello? You're late, as if it were any evening, with one of them held up at work, as has happened over and over again in the past, as it does to everyone.

– I know. Sorry.

He drops his cycle helmet on the shoe rack, comes to the kitchen door with his briefcase, smiles.

– Meeting overran. I'll be with you in a tick.

And he goes into his study, shuts the door. Does he check his mobile for messages? Surely yes. Does he not usually leave the door open when he comes home? Does the next step in this frame of mind find her listening outside it?

Dido turns on the radio, deliberately, to blank the very idea of such low behaviour. It's the middle of *Front Row*: Francine Stock is talking to Siri Hustvedt, a woman with a golden marriage if ever there was one. Or so it seems. She's talking about a new collection of essays: perhaps this is something for the book group. Dido tries to concentrate. Siri H. thinks that *Girl with a Pearl Earring* is, in truth, the picture of an annunciation. This is such an original thought that Dido is for a few moments genuinely distracted from distress. She must look at the painting again.

– What have I done today? Jeffrey is yawning at the table now, breaking his bread in two. – Management meeting this morning, supervision tutorials this afternoon, marks moderation at four. That was what went on and on.

And he describes the convening of the School Management Team in the morning: budgets, applications for a junior lectureship, arrangements for sabbaticals, budgets, work programmes for next semester, all the usual stuff. Dido listens, can find nothing remotely anxious-making. A few doors down, they're having a barbecue, the first of the season. Jeffrey remarks on this. The phone rings in the kitchen.

– I'll get it.

And she goes inside, knowing that it must be someone safe and familiar, that no one by whom she might be threatened would ever use – or have? – this number. Even so, her breathing quickens as she crosses the kitchen.

– Hello?

– Hi, Mum.

It's Kate, confirming babysitting arrangements. Dido confirms them. They sound faintly complicated. Kate sounds faintly fraught.

– You OK?

The family question, all down the busy years, everyone rushing off to the next thing, just checking.

– Fine, just a bit tired. How are you, Mum?

– Fine, says Dido. – Dad and I are having supper in the garden.

– It's been such a beautiful day.

– Hasn't it? See you on Thursday, then. Bye, darling.

As she puts the phone down Dido finds she's almost trembling with relief. Is this what things could be like – anxiety about every phone call, wondering about every hour spent cloistered with email? Then she lets her relief – it was only Kate – take the upper hand. Everything's in place, she tells herself; I've let something become nothing. Now, then . . .

And she returns to the dusky garden. Jeffrey is reading the paper, finishing salad.

– That was Kate.

– So I gathered.

As she sits down, his mobile, left on the table between them, gives a little ting. A text is coming through. Dido's stomach turns over. Jeffrey looks up, frowning.

– God, can't they leave me in peace?

– Do you want to see who it is?

– No, I don't. I've had it.

He turns the pages, miles away. The mobile, with its secrets, glows on faded wood. Why has he brought it out here? Dido starts to stack up the supper things, asks if he wants coffee. He doesn't. A bat flits across the garden, as every summer. It must live somewhere in the roofspace: their own bat, now revisiting. She points it out: Jeffrey looks up, interested.

– I must tell Sam, she says. – When I babysit on Thursday. He's a good bat watcher.

Jeffrey murmurs agreement, returns to the paper, yawning again. She rises, picks up the tray of plates and glasses. It's heavy – heavier than it should be? Is this the effect of anxiety, or—

As she turns with it, her head begins to swim. The tray is all at once like lead. She puts it down again, clumsily, and everything rattles about. Jeffrey looks up.

– Dido?

– I don't feel well.

The dusk is becoming darkness. She sinks to her seat, puts her head on the table. Little sparks of light dance behind her eyes, and everything is tingly and strange.

– Dido.

He's by her side.

In bed, on a long summer evening: it's like being a child again. And now she's here, she feels perfectly all right. Jeffrey has helped her up the stairs, laid her down, covered her with the quilt. He's listened, as she tells him, her head quite clear, about that strange little moment on the way home, the swimminess, the weakness in her legs, no sooner felt than all over and done with.

– I suppose it's what they used to call a funny turn. She smiles up at him, hovering at the bedside.

– Two funny turns, he says, frowning again. – Two in one day?

– Summer flu?

– Is there such a thing? Why don't I give Kate a quick ring?

– Oh, no, don't, says Dido. – She sounded frazzled; she's got so much to think about. I'm fine now I'm here.

– Are you sure?

– Certain. She pats the quilt. – Sit down.

He sits, he takes the hand she offers. She shuts her eyes. She wants to say: I read a text to you: I'm so sorry. Please tell me it's nothing. Please tell me I'm being a fool.

But it's so lovely just being quiet up here together, hand in hand, so long since she has been able to give in to needing an early night, to being looked after. Why disturb it all?

She lies there. The light at the lace curtains of their bedroom window is dusky and soft. She yawns.

– Tuck down, says Jeffrey gently. – I'll cut the grass and come up soon.

– Lovely.

And he's gone, out and down the stairs, just as the phone in his study begins to ring.

Chloe is in bed with Jez. The blind is drawn down; there's a thin border of fading light all round, in which dust dances, as dust tends to do. This evening, that seems fantastically romantic.

The double bed is low, pine-slatted, standard issue. Apart from her proper sprung divan at home, Chloe has rarely slept on anything else. Sex with Jez, however, has not been standard issue. She lies there, gazing at him.

– Gosh.

He laughs. – What a sweet old-fashioned girl you are.

– Not too old-fashioned, I hope.

– Not where it matters, certainly. A hand runs over her again. – Bold comes to mind. Not to say brazen.

– That's because of you.

– I'm glad to hear it.

They kiss, in sated fashion. Trains go past.

– I need to pee.

– Go on, then.

While he's in the bathroom, Chloe looks about her. It's like being a student again: a rented flat with a cheap carpet, vile wallpaper emulsioned over but showing a pattern beneath. This bed, that cheap pine chest of drawers. Her stylist's eye notes everything, more calmly now than when they first arrived, coming up unvacuumed stairs past a heap of junk mail in the hall, taken into a tiny kitchen overlooking the street, and untidy living room next door. There's a varnished table, chairs, MDF bookshelves, a telly. There's another photo of Ellie on a narrow mantelpiece, a sofa covered with a throw. When Ellie comes to stay, that must be where she sleeps – or does Jez give her this double bed and doss down there himself? There's nothing in the bedroom to say a child stays here. Perhaps, now she knows him (quite a bit) better, she can ask him.

Sounds of rushing water come from the windowless bathroom,

where, when she used it on arrival, Chloe took in Pears soap, boxers hung to dry, two toothbrushes, one small and very pink.

– Chloe.

He's standing in the bedroom doorway now, towel wrapped round him, looking gorgeous. – Can I get you anything?

– What sort of thing?

– Crack? Herbal tea?

She smiles. – A tea would be nice.

– Camomile?

– Great. Shall I get up?

– Certainly not.

But she does, to go to the bathroom herself. It's not fantastically clean, and she checks an impulse to look beneath the sink for Ajax. She goes out, naked, stands in the kitchen doorway watching Jez watch the kettle come to the boil. He turns, sees her.

– Forget the tea.

Then it's grown dark.

– Am I staying the night?

– Would you like to?

She would.

– I'd better phone Edmund. He'll worry, otherwise.

– How touching. You do that. Now I will make tea. He turns on the Anglepoise lamp by the bed. The room is filled with shadow beyond its cone of light. She fishes her mobile out of her bag, dropped to the floor with her clothes. Edmund's phone is on voicemail.

– Hi. It's me. I'm staying out tonight. She can see a blond eyebrow rise with interest. – I'll have to come back at the crack of dawn to change, so don't worry if you hear me banging about. Hope you're OK. Lots of love.

Jez is back, with two gently steaming mugs. He climbs back in; they snuggle up. They talk.

– Two huge things have happened to both of us in the last year or so, says Chloe. – Without either of us knowing about the other.

– What were they?

She sips her tea. – You split up from your wife. And – she hesitates – and my father died.

– Actually, I did know that, says Jez. He strokes her arm. – You didn't turn up for a shoot one day. Dot told me about your dad.

– You never said anything.

– Should I have done?

– Yes.

– There's always loads of people about. In the studio. At your party. I didn't like to intrude. I didn't know what to say.

– You should always say something, said Chloe. – I've learned that. It's much worse when people just gloss over it, as if nothing's happened. It makes you . . . it makes it all seem invisible. You don't have to say much. Just: I'm sorry.

He draws her to him.

– I'm sorry.

– Thanks.

– Tell me about him. Were you close?

– Yes, says Chloe. – We were. He was . . . easier than my mother. Easier on me. He was lovely . . .

It's a long time since Chloe has been to bed with anyone. She's full of emotion. She begins to cry.

Jez is very sweet to her. He strokes her hair, murmurs nice things. He gets her a handkerchief.

– Thanks. I'm so sorry. She blows her nose.

– This is why I didn't like to ask you about it on a shoot. He kisses her. – We can't have tears at work.

– I suppose not. Chloe reaches for her camomile tea. It's going cold. – Still, might make life a bit more real. What a bloody shallow world it all is.

– Thanks.

She kisses his neck. Rap is throbbing somewhere in the building.

– Not you, she says, though in truth she doesn't really know if Jez has depth. – I just mean, in comparison to everything that's happened. My father . . .

She shuts her eyes. Henry is lying upstairs in bed at home, a week or so before his death. It's Sunday. The cats are on the end of the bed, the window is open at the top to bright spring weather. Henry can't take the weight of the cats on his feet, so they have to be watched. He can't take the weight of his book, so it lies open at his side. He's reading – was reading – Wordsworth. Georgia has been reading aloud to him. Now she's downstairs, talking to the Marie Curie nurse, who has a daffodil in her lapel. Chloe gazes at her father's thin thin face. She holds his weightless hand. – I love you, Dad. A finger lifts, taps hers. He loves her too: she knows it.

– Tell me about him, says Jez, beside her.

She cannot speak.

– Tell me about him, he says again. It's late, the sun sunk low, and shadows move this way and that against the blind.

Where to begin? It's hard to imagine two more different men, and often hard to remember her father except in illness: aged, ashen, always in pyjamas, trying to smile.

Jez is so lithe, so fit, so sexy. He moves amongst models and stylists and magazines: his whole working life depends on what things look like. So does hers. But behind her stands someone who—

– He read all the time. He was very clever. So's my mother. I'm the big disappointment.

He strokes her hair again. – Never.

She shrugs. – It's true. I didn't go to uni.

– So?

– It matters to them. Especially to my mother.

– So why didn't you?

– I'm dyslexic. Like, really dyslexic.

And she tells him, because it's easier than talking about her father, what that's been like: the tests, the extra lessons after school, the being told all the time that you're bright, but still getting dreadful grades; her mother reading up all the research, suggesting specs with orange lenses (America) or BIG BIG PRINT (Sweden) until she was SICK OF IT ALL.

Jez listens. – Well, he says, stroking away her fury – you seem pretty clever to me. And you look fucking gorgeous. I've fancied you for ever.

– Really? She turns in his arms, looks up at him. That flopping hair is all messed up (by her) and those sloe-dark eyes look down at her, darkening still further with desire.

Again.

She tries to imagine taking him home. Surely Georgia would see how lovely he was. But who needs all those questions, all that wondering about The Future, all reined in, but there. She tries to imagine what Henry would have made of him. Two more different men, etc.

Furthermore: Jez is living apart from his wife and daughter. It is unimaginable that her father could ever have done this. She tries to picture herself, at Ellie's age, living with Georgia and visited by Henry. Going to stay with Henry at a different place. Some flat somewhere, where she keeps some of her things.

There are a million children who live like this. They probably manage fine. Perhaps they even like it: two parents telling you you're the most special thing in the world.

Two parents not speaking to each other, as you're picked up/dropped off?

Is this what it's like?

– Jez?

Now it's really late, and they're both really really sleepy. She can hear the rap, she can hear trains, traffic, a yowling cat out somewhere.

– Jez?

– Mmm?

– Can I ask you something?

– Mmm.

She plucks up her courage, lies dead flat on her front next to him on the pillow. Their breath mingles, their feet cross companionably.

– Why have you split up?

There's a silence.

– Do you mind me asking?

He says: – No. And then: – We're just not getting on. We need a break.

– Oh.

Not: We weren't getting on. We had to split up, for Ellie's sake.

It's still in the present tense. She might be dyslexic, but she can hear.

Darkness has fallen. Dido has got up. She's very tired, undresses properly, goes into the bathroom in her dressing gown. This room too has lace at the open window, a half-curtain, but it overlooks the garden at the back. While her bath is running, she stands looking out, on to the light spilling on to the patio, the mighty silhouettes of the trees, the broad stretch of lawn, which Jeffrey, her husband of thirty-five years, has mown in the gathering dusk. The scent of cut grass comes up: a scent like no other, with the power, always, to tug you back to endless summers past. The sky is pricked with stars.

Looking out, as so often, on this deep and quiet space, Dido recalls a distant time when she stood gazing blankly out from a different window. It's a spare room now, but once it held a baby. Then it didn't. Ella, says Dido, deep within, and all the sadness of

111

that desolate time wells up, and meets her anxious sadness now.

– Ella?

The bath is foaming behind her. She can hear nothing but running water, though downstairs Jeffrey must be . . .

What must he be doing?

A new moon is rising, a fingernail of white.

Let there be nothing really wrong with me.

Let everything – please, please – let everything be as it was.

Part Two

8

What did you do in your summer holidays?

Dido, before packing for the house they've rented (again) in the Lakes, attends York District Hospital for tests. The results have not come through by the time she, Jeffrey, Kate, Leo and the children all set forth. She counts this as a good sign, and refuses to think about it, or anything else unpleasant. She has had tests because Kate thinks she ought to, just to be sure. Most of the time, she feels completely well. She's hoping Nick (without Paula) might join them all for a week, but he's not been definite. She suggests that Georgia comes up too, and stays in the nearby B & B.

Georgia knows that she must not expect Chloe to want to come on holiday with her. She's right: she doesn't. Chloe is preoccupied and unavailable: Georgia senses that a new man may be on the scene, but isn't told this. She bides her time, hoping he's suitable, as her own mother might have said. The older she gets, the more she connects with her parents' generation. No doubt this will one day happen to Chloe, but it's a long way off. She tries to talk to her about visiting Maud. Chloe – Sorry, Mum, I really can't – doesn't want to know. It's understandable. Georgia will go down by herself.

She keeps putting this off.

In the meantime, she accepts a (very) kind invitation from their old friends Robert and Maggie Cartwright, to join them for two of their three weeks in the Dordogne.

There's also this possibility of going up to the Lakes, to see Dido and everyone, as they used to do. She should, Dido tells her on the phone, book the B & B pretty quickly: she knows what summer in the Lakes is like, even in their less popular bit, away from Windemere, Dove Cottage and all that. Georgia books three nights. Is it possible that Chloe might like to join her, just for this? She books two rooms, recklessly, just in case.

She flies out to France from Gatwick. Staying with the Cartwrights was something she and Henry had done quite often, over the years. Now she's doing it alone. Retired couples mingle with the family hordes. Georgia observes them helping one another with luggage, fetching a couple of coffees, reading the papers as they wait for their flight to be called. One or two people are short with one another, but on the whole they look happy and harmonious.

Her longing for Henry is intense.

Chloe has got involved with Jez just a few weeks before school breaks up for the summer. She has not been introduced to Ellie by the time this happens, and senses that it's still too early. She drops a hint or three about a long weekend somewhere, at a time when Jez does not have Ellie with him. He says he's broke; she suggests a fantastically cheap lastminute.com. He says last minute might be difficult/tricky: he doesn't know Madeleine's arrangements yet.

When will he know?

He's not sure.

Chloe books two weeks in Spain, with Edmund, Sara and Matt. Like last year, except that this is the last time Sara can fly before they have The Baby.

Oh God.

Maud doesn't do summer holidays.

9

Maud is reading in bed. Old habits die hard, and Maud, in her seventies, her farming days behind her, is in the comfort zone of Livestock in the local paper. Her eye runs down columns of Limousin, Charolais, Simmental and Belgian Blue bulls; over smallholder ewes (speckle, with good lambs), Pure Breed hatching eggs and chicks, Aylesbury ducklings; chick brooders (old-fashioned wood and metal, approx. 2 ft square); Bantams, sheds and equipment; young cow with calf (cow has been running with bull); bee-keeping equipment (phone for details) and Free Range Woodland Weaners.

What is a Free Range Woodland Weaner? Here, unusually, Maud is stumped.

Her eye wanders back to the Belgian Blue bulls. They are full pedigree, eighteen to twenty-four months old and ready to work. They come in a choice of white, and blue and white. Maud is put briefly in mind of something, and after a moment or two recalls her kitchen tiles (faux Delft, with windmills). She returns to the bulls, such handsome beasts. She pictures a new arrival in Parry's Meadow, three fields away from the house, and on a rise. A two-year-old Belgian Blue takes possession, ambles to the top of the incline, looks about him. Sussex clouds roll past. Magnificent.

– Magnificent, says Maud aloud.

A herd of cows is introduced. The grass grows long and lush. Calves follow, in the spring. Maud is out with her bucket in the calf-pens. Long trembling legs and dark eyes wet with fear and longing greet her. Clang of the pail, the sweet rich smell of the milk, her fingers dipped, and licked, and suckled on.

'Comfort zone' is not a term which Maud would recognise or understand, but she is happy, thinking of all this. Outside, in the summer evening (unless there's something good on the Television, Maud retires at eight) pigeons are murmuring somewhere, and other people's cattle graze on distant fields. Today has been a good day, as far as she can remember. Or was that yesterday? Someone has died, but these things happen. She turns the pages. Something falls out. It is a two-for-one offer at Lo-Cost. Maud gazes at cans of beans and packs of streaky bacon. How can two be one? How can they? She struggles with this for a short time, then skims the leaflet across the room. Dust rises gently to greet it.

Her eye settles upon new notices. Under the Insolvency Act of 1986 (she detours into a little tussle here: was that before or after the war?) Bankruptcy Orders have been made against the under-mentioned. These are a painter and decorator (lately carrying on business as Mats Decorating Services), an antiques dealer (lately a company director and trading from 5 Willow Court as Cathedral Antiques) and a lorry driver (lately carrying on business under the style of T. G. P. Haulage Contractors from 1 Bridge Street).

Carrying on business under the style of. What a nerve. No wonder they went bust. Maud knows 1 Bridge Street, if she's not mistaken. If she's not mistaken it's near the petrol pump. He had a shady look, that T. G. P. She gazes now at Applications for Planning Permission (proposed change of use to create a Car Park at Field adjacent to St Mark's Church, disgraceful); adorable baby rabbits; an unused Whirlpool gas double built-in oven (incomprehensible), a body sculpture inversion table brand-new in box (likewise), bottled gas, sunbeds, holiday gîtes in France, scrap dealers, tree surgeons, plastic dog beds (vile).

Kep is sleeping contentedly in his basket of ancient wicker. It creaks as he shifts and stirs. He does so now. The basket is set between door and window, a position deliberately chosen by Maud long ago, reminding her of a funny song.

Shut the door, they're coming through the window.
Shut the window, they're coming through the door . . .

She sang it then, and she briefly sings it now, looking across the heaped-up eiderdowns (even in summer, it can be cold up here) to where her love lies sleeping. At door or window, he would stop them, and he may well need to. Dreadful crimes are on the increase everywhere: she read about them over supper, such as it was.

What was it?

Almost done with the paper now. Tractors and trailers and pregnancy tests. What a fuss. Surely a girl would know. Mitsubishi HS-C20E Camcorder in case, pair of speaker stands, spiked bottoms (?). Puppy Group Obedience Classes (quite right). Adult Fantasies. Maud has no idea what these might be, but they cost 45p a minute. Rabbit hutches. Rest Homes.

Courtney Hall. Visit us on the Web at www. courtney hall.co.uk. Let us explain how you can afford 'Care and Kindness without Compromise' whatever your finances!

Maud has only the haziest idea of what this Web might be, though everyone is talking about it, even on *The Archers*. How can you visit someone on a web? She does know it has nothing whatsoever to do with spiders, because someone once explained this. None the less, it's hard not to imagine, as you grow drowsy, the hairy dark beckoning into a parlour. Horrid. And since she does grow drowsy, at half-past eight on a summer evening, this creature locates itself within a rest home, and Maud gives a little shake. Thoughts bang about in her head. Unpleasant.

– Here, boy.

He's by her side in an instant, tail beating slowly, nose in her outstretched hand. That's better.

– Good boy. Good boy.

She lets the paper fall. What it is to have a dog. One thing she can be sure of, in increasingly uncertain days: with Kep to watch over her she'll never have to think about a rest home. Well, thank the Good Lord for that.

– Basket.

And he returns, claws clicking over the lino, broken wicker creaking as he gets in once again, and settles with a sigh upon his blanket.

Maud prepares to settle down herself. Her horn-rimmed specs (same frames, different lenses down the years) go back in their case with a snap. Her teeth are already soaking in their jar. She pats an eiderdown around her. Very old feathers fly up. By nine, she is, as her mother used to put it, away in the Land of Nod.

And now it is morning. Another sunny day: she can see this through the faded curtains.

– Here, boy.

And here he is, as always. Her hand runs over his head, his dear old ears.

– Good boy, good boy. Sun's up. Now, then.

Teeth. Glasses. Slippers. Feathers float everywhere, as Maud gets out of bed. Kep observes them like a hungry hunter, snaps at one or two. Maud shuffles off to the bathroom. Getting slow, no denying it. Mornings are not what they were. The lino in the bathroom is almost gone, bare patches revealing floorboards, gnawed. Cobwebs droop from the cistern. These are not fresh new creations, populated by strong, purposeful spiders, but old old skeiny things, thick with dust and long abandoned. Rust stains mark the bath, and crusts of Vim, from the days when Maud used Vim, cling to the taps in the basin.

She pulls the chain, and the cistern shakes. Gallons of water fall, not all of it into the lavatory. Vast damp patches testify to this. She washes, after a fashion. Back in the bedroom, she pulls on the things she wore yesterday, and the day before that, and the day before, and so on, into the mists of time. She does change now and then, but not so as you'd notice. There is, of course, no one to notice, which is how she's always liked it. Her skirts have elasticated waists, her knickers have holes in, her bras are secured with safety pins. Maud is a stranger to tights, though someone once gave her some very good pull-up stocking things. Perhaps one Christmas. These she has worn to death.

Kep is waiting patiently. She drags a nylon jumper over her head and pulls it neatly down. It's mauve, very nice. She spends a moment smoothing it over the greenish skirt. Slippers to start the day, and . . .

– Breakfast!

He's up, he's bright-eyed, he's ready to go. Together, they make their way downstairs. Through to the kitchen, unbolt the back door, and off he runs, into the sun, the dew, the orchard. The ewes back away beneath the apple trees; Maud gives a shout.

– Kep! Leave them!

To hear her, you'd think you were in the presence of a judge at the County Show. White coat, megaphone, decades of experience, the lot. Well, she does have decades of experience, and Kep obeys at once. They go through this every morning. Now he's off in the hedgerow, as if he's never seen it before, waiting for the rattle of the biscuits in his bowl.

There is nothing like a big paper sack of dog biscuits to give a house a heart. Maud has always thought this, never fails to gain pleasure from the mealy smell, the lovely shapes and colours: ovals, bone shapes, round ones, all in a mix of dusty pink, sage green, wheaten yellow, black. She scoops out a handful, rattles the tin bowl and sets it down at the door. He's there before

121

you can say jack rabbit. She fills up his water bowl, puts the kettle on.

Very few people visit Maud. Almost no one. If they did, and came into the kitchen, down the very darkest passage from the hall, this is what they would see. There's a very nice schoolroom clock on the wall, which Maud winds every Friday. (What day is it today?) It belonged to her grandparents, and its Roman numerals are worn and faded. One day she'll have it restored.

Newspapers, dating back perhaps ten years, stand in heaps in every corner. A distressed old kitchen table – truly distressed, not some rip-off modern thing – bears bills (generally paid), any other letters (not many), carrier bags and general bits and bobs. These might be screwdrivers, gun cartridges (she sometimes shoots a rabbit for the pot), prescriptions, plant ties and garden twine, sheep dip (not recently), jam jars, mouse traps, clothes pegs, advertisements torn from the paper, train timetables, Stop the War leaflets, bus timetables, seed packets . . .

It goes on and on. It's a big table.

In other rooms of the house are places where Maud might keep some of all this: a desk, for instance, inherited from her father, and a lovely thing, mahogany and tooled green leather. This is in the sitting room, as it once was called, but it's a long time since Maud has been in there. The Television is now in the kitchen, perched in a corner on a shelf so she can watch it while she has her supper. In the mornings, Maud listens to the wireless, which she now puts on. It's her father's: it has a wooden case and a super wooden sunburst across the torn webbing on the front. Maud has always kept it tuned to the Home Service, as her father did. Recently, however, something has happened to the tuning. It has become unreliable. Sometimes she can listen to *Today*, but sometimes a local thing breaks, in, playing dreadful music and telling her about the traffic. This happens now. She turns it off at once. What else? There are dear old prints of cottage scenes – hollyhocks, girls in bonnets, sunshine. They've been with her all her life. There's a cream-coloured Rayburn, dating from about 1953, into which Maud shovels scuttleloads of coke morning and evening. It's her greatest expense. She shovels some in now, waiting for the kettle on the hob to boil. Worn and holey tea towels droop from the rail; she pushes them aside and lifts the scuttle. Almost empty: there's a job to be done. She does it, in the coal house round the back, bringing in coke dust on her slippers. She sees this, looks down, looks at her Wellington boots by the door. Getting forgetful. This won't do. Now, then.

There's an enormous saucepan of porridge standing on the side of the Rayburn, something Maud adds to over and over again. When was it last put to soak and given a good scrub? Who knows? She shakes in Quaker Oats from the box on the shelf by the sink, adds a good slosh of water, and a good slosh of milk from the fridge.

The milk is no longer delivered: she must walk to the village, and bring it home in plastic bottles. The country is going to the dogs. The paper comes every evening, and every morning comes the post. It's generally junk. The time of its arrival has become more and more erratic but this morning, as the kettle begins to sing, the letterbox bangs in the hall.

Maud shuffles out down the passage, past the mildewed mirror and the water-stained hall table, whereon reside heaps of junk mail, and (inexplicably) the toaster. A letter! Even at this distance she can tell. Not a bill, not a Special Offer, not a Prize Draw (once she sent off for these things, but now she has their measure) but a letter in a nice cream envelope.

What a good start to the day.

She picks it up, she calls her thanks, she takes it back to the kitchen. The kettle is boiling. Everything's going well.

With her tea in the metal pot, and her porridge in a bowl, Maud settles down, clears a space at the table, and searches for a knife. She finds one in the kitchen drawer: a carving knife, as it happens, but no matter. She slides in along the seal, pulls out two good cream pages.

Dear Maud,

Who's this from? She turns the pages over.

With love from Georgia.

Georgia.

Who she?

Dear Maud,

I do hope you are well. It was so nice to talk to you on the phone a couple of weeks ago, and I'm sorry not to have been down to visit you for such a long time. There does seem to have been a lot to organise since Henry's death, and of course I am trying to readjust, and work out my new life. Chloe has been very busy too: she has one of those jobs which takes up every minute (rather like farming, as you will remember). She's always off on a fashion shoot, or to some new shop or restaurant: it's hard work, with glamorous moments, and she loves it.

We're both off on holiday now: she's going to Spain with friends, and I'm going to France, to the Dordogne, where our old friends Robert and Maggie Cartwright have a house. Then I'm hoping that Chloe will join me for two or three days in the Lakes, where Dido and Jeffrey have taken a house for all the family. Do you remember them? We were all at Oxford together, and since Henry's death Dido has really kept me going. Anyway—

I'm afraid I won't to able to get down to see you just yet. However, I am writing to suggest

THURSDAY 24th AUGUST

Would that suit you? Could you

PUT IT IN YOUR DIARY?

I will TELEPHONE YOU ON MY RETURN FROM THE LAKES.

Much looking forward to seeing you then. (And Kep, of course.)
With love from Georgia

Why has Georgia written thus? Does she really expect that Maud can take it all in? After their last phone call?

The truth is that (a) old habits die hard, and Georgia is really incapable of writing to an elderly member of the family except in such polite and conversational terms and (b) in the writing, she found a lingering affection for the old bat. Georgia and Henry's family is not large. Their parents are all long dead. Henry has a younger brother in Canada, a professor of mathematics at the University of Ontario, whom they last visited some ten years ago. George has his own Canadian life, and wife, and children (both doing marvellous clever things). He was shocked to hear of Henry's death; he flew over for the funeral. Then he flew back. A single letter followed. Not much, in the scheme of things. Georgia herself is an only child. She has an only daughter.

In sum, Maud is the closest thing to family she has left. She *is* family, albeit by marriage. She's related by blood to Chloe. Though Georgia has often in the past lamented this, now – well, blood is thicker than you think.

And she feels guilty. Poor old Maud. It's been clear for a long time that she needs a hand into the next stage, whatever this might be, and if Henry were here he'd be keeping an eye. Making arrangements. (What? What is to be done with her?) His illness prevented anyone doing anything, but now – now she has no excuse. She'll have a holiday, then she'll swing into action. Really.

So here is the letter, on good cream paper, and here is Maud, trying to get to grips.

Who is Georgia? She gazes at the address. London: it's a long time since she's been there. Over her porridge, she struggles to remember. She reads the letter again. *Henry's death . . .*

But this is terrible!

Henry has died, and she never knew. Why has no one told her?

Then, as she puts her bowl and teacup in the sink (on top of many other bowls and teacups) it comes to her.

Georgia. Ah, yes. She must be Henry's sister. The other names in the letter are a mystery, but this now shines forth clearly. And she's coming for a visit. Well, that will be nice.

— Visitors, Kep, she tells him, as she goes outside.

He gets to his feet, he follows her on her rounds. Rusting cans and ancient feed bags lie about the yard. In the woodshed Maud scoops corn from a sack into a pre-war saucepan. Something scurries away.

— Kep!

He's there in a flash.

Out to the orchard, where small green apples are thick along the boughs. Up past the ewes to the henhouse. Interested sounds come from within.

— Come on, girls.

She unbolts the door, and out they come, stepping daintily down the ramp on their scaly yellow toes.

— Breakfast!

Corn and corn dust are flung across the grass.

— Tuk tuk tuk. Tuk tuk tuk tuk.

A lifetime of such mornings, and she has their sounds so well you'd be hard put to it, if you came past, to know if they were made by hen or human. She peers into the dimness of the hut. What a glorious smell. Anyone left in here?

— Come along, Hilda. No skulking.

Out she comes, old and moulting.

— That's a good girl.

The sun is climbing, the sky is bird's-egg blue, the smell of silage drifts across the fields. Everything's tiptop.

* * *

Lunch is accompanied by *The World at One* (without musical interference) and the local paper. It is ever thus. Maud, eating her tinned soup, Edam cheese and apple, takes in with half an ear a suicide bombing in Baghdad, a missing child in Glasgow, a missing box of GCSE papers and the axing of three hundred jobs in a Primary Care Trust. What is that? What is a Health Care Service Provider? No matter: the moment has passed and they're off to Northern Ireland. She turns the pages of the *Gazette*, takes in with half an eye an outbreak of measles in a primary school, plans for a rock concert, the opening of a leisure centre and the death of a dog in a hit-and-run accident. This last claims her undivided attention. There is a picture of the family, holding a picture of the dog: a lovely old labrador-collie cross. Maud feels her temperature rising. She can see it all: the swerve, the shout, the sickening thud, the shriek of pain and then the wicked roar into the distance.

– Ought to be shot, she says aloud to Kep, now stretched out in the sun at the open door. – Ought to be shot in the back.

She'll write a letter. People who let their dogs run loose. Hit-and-run drivers. Drivers generally. Where's the pen and paper?

By the time *Round Britain Quiz* has come to an end, the Letter to the Editor is complete, some pages long. She looks for an envelope amongst the table's heap, and comes upon Georgia's flowing hand. Ah, yes, the sister. She must have a reply. By the time *The Archers* has finished and *The Afternoon Play* got into full swing, Maud has penned one.

Dear Georgia,
  How very kind of you to right. I was so glad to here from you.
  A lot has been going On.

In spelling it would be unkind to reproduce, she writes of measles, and parents who will not vaccinate. Of the dreadful wars in the world, and the dreadful death of dogs. Of unmarked exams and six eggs yesterday. Of Kep, who is very well, and how lucky she is to have him. She signs the letter with affection, with the courtesy and grace with which she has been born and bred, then adds a PS, to the effect that Georgia is welcome here at any time.

This letter would have been waiting for Georgia on her return from the Dordogne, had it not been for the fact that Maud, taking her post to the hall, to await her next trip to the village shop for stamps, dropped it into the toaster.

She has been using it as a letter rack for some time, and very useful it has proved to be. On this occasion, however, some instinctive thought, some atavistic knowledge of toasters, kicks in: she presses down the lever at the side. The thing is plugged in, who knows why? The dial is set to Frozen, perhaps for some long-distant hot cross bun, and so the letters, and a number of pizza leaflets dropped in for good measure, have quite a long time to set alight.

While this is happening, Maud goes to put the kettle on. Toast for tea! She hears a triumphant cackle from the henhouse and goes out to see what's what. Boiled egg and toast! What could be nicer? But one of the ewes is limping: Agnes, poor old stick. Egg in hand, she stops to have a look.

By the time she gets back to the house, the flaming letters and pizza leaflets have set light to two winter scarves, drooping from the hat stand. The scarves have set light to a hat, and a shard of peeling wallpaper. The front door being open on this lovely day, the flames are nicely fanned by a summer breeze, and begin to roar.

Kep, who has followed Maud out to the henhouse, is shooed away from fluttering birds and returns to the house. He begins to bark wildly. By the time Maud has come back to see why, there is conflagration. She smells it, she hears it, she strides from the kitchen and gives an enormous, aristocratic shout of horror.

Then: – Kep! Out of the way!

Fortunately, a passing motorist sees the smoke.

– Have you family? he asks her, when the fire brigade has gone. Maud struggles to think. Water and foam are everywhere.

– Who keeps an eye on you? the kindly motorist asks her. He had been on his way to visit his old father in Petworth. There are still some good people in the world.

– No one, says Maud, at her most regal – I have no need of that.

10

Surely, thinks Georgia, as she flies home from France, surely, if I wait long enough, Henry will come back.

By anyone's standards, she's had a lovely holiday. Robert and Maggie, now seated across the aircraft aisle, are kind and considerate old friends who could not have been kinder nor more considerate. Their house in the Dordogne, bought for fifteen hundred pounds in 1972, is meltingly beautiful and French: old, tiled, tranquil, with thick stone walls and shutters of faded blue. There is an orchard, and a river not far away; they are half a mile out of the village, where they walk each morning for fresh bread. Georgia has read in the shade, rested in the afternoons, eaten and drunk abundantly, swum in the river and seen a kingfisher. Robert and Maggie's children (she in publishing, he with Save the Children) have come to stay for one of the weeks and been charming company, as have the local friends, French and English, made over the years and making up a number of lunches or supper parties held beneath the trees. Butterflies (Swallowtail and Clouded Yellow), fireflies, cicadas, lizards, frogs and shooting stars have all featured, as they have in the past, when Henry has been here too.

Now he isn't.

The holiday has been like all the other Cartwright holidays: seamlessly well arranged and relaxed, with, this year, a fault line running through the whole, which from time to time has left

Georgia feeling as if the cracked French earth beneath her feet will yawn open at any moment and receive her, plunging in hideous freefall, into its endless depths.

How can Henry not be here?

Where is he?

Georgia, rational and secular, no believer in lingering presence or spirit, asks this question of every baking rock and stone; of an old old tree in the fragrant pine woods across the river where she and Henry walked three years ago; of the espaliered peach and pear trees on the orchard wall; of the swift-running river where they used to bathe.

– Look, Henry, quick!

That miraculous flash of blue.

What of it, now? Who cares about it, now?

Part of her does still care: she catches her breath as the kingfisher skims the glittering water, strains to see it again when it disappears, tells everyone about it when she goes back to the house. Deep down, it serves only to underline her loneliness and sorrow: for herself and for Henry – such a radiant thing, and he not here to see it.

In the hot hot stillness of the afternoon, she closes her bedroom door, closes the shutters, lies down. This is the room they had three years ago.

– Is this OK? Maggie has asked her, showing her up there. – Do you mind, Georgia, having this room? It's just that when the children come—

– It's fine, says Georgia, Henry's absence ringing in her ears. – It's absolutely fine.

Now, she shuts her eyes, and wills herself to hear her beloved sit down on the creaking bed and slip his shoes off, take off his specs and put them on top of his book, swing round and lie beside her, take her hand.

– Henry?

How can he not be here?

Every room, every corner of the garden, each place and each occasion – the swimming, the meals, the farmers' market and the mountain walk – all are filled with his absence. Georgia smiles and laughs and talks to everyone; there are moments, hours, even, when she truly does enjoy herself, and is more than grateful for it. But deep deep down . . .

– You're making such a good recovery, Maggie and Robert tell her, on their last night together.

– Thanks to friends like you.

They raise their glasses, out beneath the trees. Candles glow on the table, the Milky Way is flung across the sky, and look—

– Look!

That fragile fall to earth, that arc, now here, now gone.

Now they are flying home.

Georgia looks down at heaped-up clouds, a landscape of chemistry and light and water, whereon surely one could walk safely for a while. All children think this, when they fly, and she, at sixty, thinks it now, eating her British Airways sandwich, drinking her glass of wine. Behold those hills and valleys, Elysian fields of white.

Where is Henry now?

Could he be, might he be (please, please let him be) walking in the sunlit halls of heaven?

Across the aisle, Robert and Maggie are talking companionably. Georgia pours another glass, and gazes out.

They kiss goodbye at Gatwick. The Cartwrights are spending a night with Maggie's aunt in Reigate: they'll catch a different Surrey train.

– Henry's cousin lives in Sussex, says Georgia, as they wheel their wheelie cases down towards the platform. – I've told you about her.

– Mad Maud?

– Mad Maud. I'm going to see her in a couple of weeks. Poor old thing. Well, now . . .

Trains are hurtling in and out, and whistles blow.

– It's been lovely.

– Thank you *so* much. Thank you for everything.

– Thank *you* for coming. See you when you get back. Love to Jeffrey and Dido.

Doors slam, people run and wave. The Gatwick Express to Victoria will leave in fifteen minutes. Georgia catches it. She listens to a hundred mobile phones go off and hears about a hundred holidays. Fields flash past.

She rings Chloe from Victoria, just to say she's back. *Hi, this is Chloe, leave me a message . . .* – Hello, darling. Ring me tonight?

She catches the tube to Highbury, gets stuck in a tunnel, reads the same paragraph of Anita Brookner twenty times while waiting to move on again. It's very very hot down here. At last they move, at last she's out in the air. Lorries thunder down the Holloway Road. Everything looks dusty and August-in-London dead.

As she wheels her wheelie suitcase up Highbury Fields, past the pool and ice-cream vans, and up towards the tennis, Georgia catches sight of herself in the wing mirror of a parked car. She's suntanned; she's also going grey. Where all her life she has felt, and been, fit and strong and essentially youthful, now, no question about it, she is tipping towards another stage. Get a grip, she tells herself, walking briskly on.

And surely, after this long two weeks, surely, when she reaches home, Henry will be there.

The street is quiet and empty. Everyone's away. She unlocks the front door, falls shamelessly upon the cats.

– Here I am, here I am.

Well fed and watered by catsonhols.com, they are largely

indifferent to all this, and spring from her arms. She feels almost sick with disappointment.

– Henry?

The house is silent. She opens every door and window. Late summer: few birds sing. She sits out in the garden, going through her post. A card from Chloe in Spain, from Dido in the Lakes, from Graham and Tessa in Croatia – any number of friends on their hols. Not a peep from Maud.

Later that evening, she rings her. There is no reply. Oh, well: she'll be down there in a fortnight. She does get through to Chloe, who doesn't sound quite herself. Yes, she might come to the Lakes. She'll come to supper tomorrow. Perhaps.

Georgia showers, has a scratch supper, goes to bed early, with her book.

– Henry, Henry, Henry.

Brookner speaks like no one else to faded London women trying to live alone. This is why Georgia sought her out; this is why, all at once, she can read no more of her. Pages remain unturned. She's had a good holiday, but she's tired. It's always tiring, travelling home to the city's August-dreary desert, unpacking and sorting out – but this is different. Her spirit is tired – exhausted, even – just with the effort of keeping going. And the truth, of course, is that her loneliness is beginning to overpower her.

For someone whose life since her schooldays has been filled with activity; who has worked at the coalface of human interaction for over three decades, and been (generally) contentedly married for longer; who has been (generally) accomplished at balancing work, family life and friendship all these years, this is a new experience.

As Chloe and her friends would put it: she doesn't do lonely.

She's doing it now.

She has (more or less) kept it at bay: through little trips, and longer holidays; through joining the book group (rather intense);

lunches, galleries, walks with friends on Hampstead Heath; out for drinks, in for drinks, people for supper, Chloe for anything she has time for.

Now . . .

Unlike Dido, who has always cried often and easily, Georgia is not much given to tears. She wept over that fallen fledgeling, but in the year and a half since Henry's death she has mostly been numb and dry-eyed. Now, all at once:

– I miss you. I miss you. What am I going to do?

It's still light outside, the last of the sun showing here and there behind the curtains. Dreadful, to be in bed alone on a summer evening. The house and the street are deadly quiet, the cats have turned away from her; beyond this little corner of the world, London on holiday stretches away to an eternity of nights like this.

– Come back, come back!

Georgia is sobbing into her pillow, reaching for Henry's pillow, cradling it in her arms.

It is death, not sex, which is the greatest intimacy. Over and over (and over) again, she has replayed Henry's last days, last hours, last moments. To trust someone so much you will let them watch you die . . .

– Henry, sobs Georgia. – Why did you die, and not me? Why am I here, and not you? I love you. I love you. I'm so so sorry . . .

At last she can cry no more.

It's dark. The beam of headlights shines through the curtains; somebody's car door slams. Not everyone has gone away, then. Georgia sits up, and puts the light on. A little sound comes at the bedroom door; it brushes open.

– Tristan!

He springs up, licks her face, allows her to caress him. She buries her face in his Abyssinian fur.

– Did you miss me?

He missed her, and then he withdrew, into a private and independent cat place. Now he's returning; so is Isolde, whose smaller, sweeter face comes round the door.

– Up you come.

Alone with the cats on a summer night. Well, this is how it is. This is just how it is, and she's going to have to face it, as plenty of others have to.

Something of Georgia's toughness and briskness stirs within her, as her cats – so beloved of Henry, too – purr, turn round and round, and settle. She gets up, goes to the bathroom, washes away her tears. A woman much older than she has always thought herself to be looks back at her in the mirror.

You'll just have to get on with it.

She goes downstairs, makes hot chocolate in the prettiest cup and saucer in the house (this makes her think of Chloe) and takes it back up to bed. She reaches for her book, and finds her place.

And as she eventually settles down to sleep, the cats at her feet, she reminds herself that she's not going to be in empty London for more than a few days. Thank God for Dido and the Lakes.

11

Sheep speckle the fells, and the waters of Buttermere sparkle in the sun. Boats come and go – the yacht, the motor launch – and everywhere are walkers: up there, following a path of scree on to springy turf, tiny figures in shorts and shirts just visible; or down here, making their way round the lake in good strong boots and Tilley hats, binoculars, maps and Wainwright at the ready. Jeffrey is one such figure, striding forth as always; Dido (not every day) another. When they're not out walking – gazing up at the lovely line of hills, out at the outline of the Isle of Man, or down from their grassy picnic place at the lake and winding river; when they're not lifting binoculars at every passing bird – A chough! I'll swear that's a chough! – they're resting and reading in their shady garden.

The house is shady too; it's bliss. They've been coming here for years, ever since Kate and Nick were small: how lovely that now Sam and Izzy can enjoy it too: a hideaway house at the foot of the fell, tucked away in a quiet stretch of woodland by the river, the perfect place for bathing, sailing little boats, looking for water creatures to bring home in jars. The house has no television, but a cupboard of worn old board games: when it rains there's Scrabble and Cluedo and Ludo and Snatch, a good game found by Georgia in the British Library shop a couple of years ago, and given to them all for Christmas. (Henry's last Christmas, come to think of it, as Dido does, clearing up one evening.)

In short, it's a proper family holiday.

With all that that implies.

It's morning; they've been here just over a week. Jeffrey has marshalled everyone for a major expedition: the children's first climb up all three thousand and fifty-three feet of Skiddaw, accompanied by their parents and their uncle Nick. Paula hasn't joined them, though she might. Nick has finished a chapter. Paula hasn't. She's chosen to stay in York until she's nailed it (Dido's expression, not hers) and though Nick rings her almost every evening it is impossible for Dido not to notice his changed demeanour, on holiday with his family and without his partner. He's laughing a lot. He's open and relaxed and fun with the children; he's walked for miles and miles with Jeffrey in companionable father/son bonding such as neither of them ever has time for in York; he kisses Dido when he comes in to the kitchen, stirs things, pours drinks. In short, he seems happy. Not radiant, but perfectly content. Of course, this might simply be the result of knocking the chapter on the head, being able to come away with a clear conscience, instead of (as last year) bringing heaps of books and laptop with him. Somehow, she knows that it isn't. And God, he looks gorgeous, tall and loose-limbed, hair lightened and skin darkened by the sun, bright-eyed with plenty of sleep and fresh air.

They all look better, including her, though she says so herself – the others have said it too. And she feels better: only one little turn, two days ago, about which she said nothing, and will not allow herself to dwell upon. Her inner self is calmer too, watching Jeffrey unwind, feeling his arm around her now and then, as they come back from their walks, being kissed by him now and then, as she falls asleep with her book. Quite often, he stays up reading late. Sometimes she wonders, feeling so much stronger: will we, tonight? It's been an age. (An *age* – she can't remember the last time.) But it doesn't matter: there's over a fortnight to go, and often, with all this walking, she's too tired anyway.

And will she, in a quiet, companionable moment, take a deep breath and ask him about that horrid little text thing? She will not. She has pushed its very existence to the very back of her mind, said nothing to no one. Though Dido might spend her professional life urging her clients to disburden themselves of sorrow and anxiety, now, in this particular situation of her own, she follows Georgia's rule: keep mum. It's a very good rule: with no one to question her further, ask how she's feeling, or offer Support, she has almost (if not quite) forgotten the nasty little thing entirely.

It's nine o'clock. At half-past seven she has waved them all off at the gate, setting out in the car with their picnic and the windows down, catching the cool of the day to begin walking; expected home for supper. Dido would not, at the moment, think of climbing three thousand and fifty-three feet, though she has often done so in her time. No one, at present, expects her to. No one talks about the tests, the turns, the gnawing anxiety which no one (including her) can help but feel now and then. But they do encourage her to rest and take it easy and she's happy to do so – to reach for the glass Nick hands her while she reads, to let Kate and Leo wash up or even cook (though they both arrived so weary that she's only too happy to cook most evenings). And today . . .

Today Georgia is arriving. How lovely. She's booked into the B & B a couple of miles away, and Chloe is, almost certainly, going to join her in a day or two. They haven't seen Chloe for ages, just had a phone call after her birthday to thank them for the earrings (always fun, choosing things for Chloe). A New Man, Georgia has intoned down the line, at her driest and most pessimistic. Is he making her happy? They'll see. Such lot of catching-up to do.

Now, then. Dido is out in the garden, drinking in the dew, the birds, the distant cries of Islington at Sail. Something burbling and bubbling and intricately exquisite sounds through the summery air. The curlew. Perfect. She stands, she listens, she drinks in being alive.

* * *

Georgia is driving steadily up the M6. Rising long before dawn, she seems to have been on it for ever. But the weather is glorious, the traffic not too bad, and *Composer of the Week* is telling her all about Rachmaninov. Soothing and smooth as always, Donald Macleod (whom she and Henry once met at a party) describes the artist's life: the flight from Russia in 1918, the new life in America, the banning of his work by Stalin, the great mourning at his death. When Georgia was young, and falling in love with Henry, Rachmaninov's sweeping romanticism meant a lot; in later life her tastes, like Henry's, have become more austere: Bartok, Beethoven's late quartets, Bach in all his guises. Today, listening and half listening, as you do, she's poignantly reminded of Oxford days, taken back to when they all were young, she and Dido becoming friends and then, so gratifyingly, finding Henry and Jeffrey, good friends too. They'd made a good quartet, had they not? Read a lot, worked a lot, gone to all those films and plays and concerts. Who would have imagined, then—

A cot death?

Henry dying?

Surely such things could not be meant for them.

And once again, as *Rhapsody on a Theme of Paganini* soars into the car and out through the open window, she finds herself thinking: but there is no meaning, there is no determinism, there is no Being Meant. Why one person and not another? Foolish to ask: life is a lottery, and all things show it.

Georgia's grown used, over the last eighteen months or so, to moving continually between the great questions and the everyday business of living (even if the great questions take the greater part). Now, as violins rise and fall, she summons the courage to overtake the vast container lorry whose rear doors she has been gazing at too long. (Am I a good driver? Call 0800 . . .) Checking the mirror, then looking not to right nor left, she holds her breath as she passes its endless length, then moves perhaps a shade too quickly back into the left-hand lane as a speeding BMW roars past them both.

Phew. She's almost shaking. Perhaps she should take a break, as various road signs have been urging her to do. It's not such a good idea, driving for hours by yourself. Of course, if Chloe were with her . . .

Why is Chloe not with her? Why? Why is she coming up by train in (probably) two days' time, needing to be fetched from Penrith, or Keswick, or wherever it is, instead of driving companionably with her mother, with a chance to talk, for once? Why can she not be sensible for once?

Georgia knows very well why. Chloe has fallen for someone and – as Chloe, not she, would put it – he's taking up all her headspace. And her time. She'd love to come for supper, but. She'd love to meet Georgia for lunch, but. She's working late, she's working through the lunch hour, she's working through the night.

Oh, yes?

Though Georgia has long experience of Chloe's truly hectic schedule, she knows, instinctively, that at present the schedule is A Man.

Georgia can only hope that this time it won't end as so often in the past: in tears, in boredom, in five minutes, in disarray. This time, might it end in happiness? Why is it, she wonders, noting a sparrowhawk hover above the grassy verge, that she and Dido had found the right people so easily, so young? Why is Chloe, in her thirties, single still, and searching? And why can she and her mother not discuss all this? Why can they not be as other mothers and daughters: easy with one another, doing things together, sitting up late and talking? Something broke through between them with Henry's death, because it had to. For quite a long time they were loving and careful with one another. But now, the shutters have come down once more, and she doesn't know how to prise them open.

Donald Macleod is announcing the last of Rachmaninov for today. Georgia is yawning. She glances at the clock. She'll turn off at the next A road and have a coffee. Never one to waste money at hideous service stations, she's brought her flask, her sandwiches and fruit. And behold: a junction. She signals left and turns. Soon, she's away from the dizzying infinities of the motorway and on a peaceful road winding past farmland, where the harvest has begun. A distant combine crawls through swathes of corn; the mid-morning sky is a deep and dazzling blue; old farm buildings nestle in a fold of hills. And unifying all of this is the music flooding the car: the opening of the Second Piano Concerto, something which, no matter how often you hear it (and she's heard it many times) will always stop you in your tracks. Filled with emotion, she slows, she rounds a corner.

What she sees next will stay with her all her life.

On the brow of a hill, a dapple-grey horse is grazing. The grass and late buttercups are so tall, and the hill at such an angle, that she cannot see his head, plunged deeply into lushness, greenness. There is only the dappled coat, the long long graceful neck, the entire intentness upon a task. And it seems to Georgia then, as the great music of her youth fills every part of her, that this is a vision: that this beautiful animal's remoteness, intentness, partial invisibility are offering a glimpse of another realm, a place of complete contentment.

I am in another place.

I need nothing else but this.

You cannot reach me. I have no need of you. But look —

All is well and all this lasts for ever.

No grass could be greener, no buttercups brighter, no sky more endless or more blue, than all are now. Rachmaninov is taking her, as he took her in her youth, into a sunken summer garden, and the morning has brought her to the foot of this hill, this sloping field, this vision of (perhaps) a life beyond.

She stops the car. Flooded with joy and pain, she sobs as if her heart must break.

Then she drives on.

– Georgia!

Dido is waiting at the gate. What sweet, old-fashioned thing is this. As Georgia draws up, and parks at the side of the lane, she's waving and calling, hugely welcoming. Georgia, always less demonstrative, turns off the engine and raises her hand with a smile. Mixed feelings fill her: relief and a flood of affection at seeing her closest friend again; a sliver of anxiety and caution: will she, on her own, be able to rise to the occasion – extended family life, lots of talk and chatter, hugs and kisses. Then she gets out, locks the car (even in the Lakes you can never be too careful) and walks the few yards to the gate.

It's late afternoon, the late summer sun bathing the wooded lane, the sheep-strewn fells. Everything feels welcoming and warm, and she herself travel-weary, stiff from all that driving; drained, after her vision, of all emotion.

– You're here! You've made it! Well done!

They embrace: two tall, good-looking women, dark head and fair head both going grey, each in good old clothes for the Lakes: getting that, as so much else, just right.

– Come on in.

As Georgia follows Dido up the front path – flagstone, well-planted borders now fading with the end of summer – she's told that everyone's out on a major climb and they have the house to themselves until suppertime. Tea in the garden awaits. So it does. She can see the table beneath the trees.

– I'll put the kettle on.

The kitchen is cool and dim at the back, windows open on to the prospect of the woods, the glimpse of river. How clever Dido and Jeffrey were, to rent this house all that long time ago and go on renting: Georgia, Henry and Chloe have often joined them over the years, staying in the B & B nearby or once or twice taking a cottage themselves. So good for Chloe to have Kate and Nick as holiday companions, though it's been a while since Chloe came. The last time Georgia was here was in 2001, with Henry. It seemed (as indeed in France in 2004) that such companionable times might go on for ever: walking, talking, eating out, splitting off to be just the two of them for a couple of days, then meeting up in the pub for lunch or supper.

Well. Those days have gone.

– How are you? asks Dido, filling the kettle.

– Fine. A bit weary. Just going to the loo.

– You've checked in with Mrs Whatsit?

– No. I'll do that after tea. She knows I'm on my way.

– And Chloe?

– Wednesday or Thursday. We've yet to finalise.

They raise their eyes companionably to the heavens. Children. Chloe. Even at her age. Oh, well.

– See you in the garden.

– Lovely.

In the downstairs loo (white-painted tongue-and-groove door with a pleasing black latch, like all the doors in the house) Georgia trips over a small pair of sandals and a small Playmobil person flat on his back. He's a farmer, with a plastic yellow kerchief and plastic pitchfork. One or two tiny hay bales lie about. She gathers them up and puts them on the sill. Grandchildren. She hears herself give a sigh. There is, she reminds herself, plenty of time. She must not, she reminds herself, go on at Chloe.

– Well, now, says Dido, out in the garden with the tea things. – Where shall we begin?

There's Assam tea, and a sponge cake made yesterday by Sam and Izzy, oozing jam everywhere. Georgia leans back in her dark green deckchair with her (local) pottery mug and plate and gives, once again, a long deep sigh, though this time of an unwinding nature.

– You start, she says to Dido, licking jam off her fingers. – What have you all been doing?

Will Dido, with her oldest and dearest friend, confide what has troubled her since they spent that book-lined, Welsh-borders week together? Will she tell her about the turns, the giddiness and momentary absence from the world, the dropping things (she broke a glass this morning), the difficulty with keys in locks, getting splinters out (Izzy, a couple of days ago, soon handed over to her doctor parents) or plugging in the Hoover? Something in her is off the true, something is not as it should be, and though no one can expect, at sixty, to thread a needle with the ease of youth, this is not just about advancing years. She's been for Tests. How can she not tell Georgia this?

Part of her longs to. Part of her really doesn't. She's following Georgia's line: say nothing, and the thing is manageable. Say nothing, and it might even go away. And also: Georgia's had enough illness to think about, enough to last her a lifetime. She's here to relax, to be cosseted, if she will ever allow it. Beneath the French tan, she looks strained: has she, in fact, been crying? Poor Georgia: she shouldn't have to think about hospitals on holiday. Besides, if anything were seriously wrong, their GP would have been in touch. She gave him (at Kate's quiet insistence) Jeffrey's mobile number. Each time it rings, she wonders what's to come, but it's always just a call from work, taken by Jeffrey with irritable briskness. Why can't they leave him alone? OK, he's heading up this and that, steering this and that committee, but surely, in August . . . She's watched him take the phone to the end of the garden, answer questions curtly, come back, turn off the wretched thing, pour another drink. Once or twice she's wondered: is it just work? Is it—Then she clamps down. Leave it, leave it, leave it be.

All this runs through her, an undercurrent, as she describes to

Georgia the walks, the children's growing expertise with birds and binoculars, Kate and Leo's exhausted arrival: two hard-working parents with two small lively children: how do they manage?

– We did.

– It all seems more fraught these days. They're brilliant, so organised, but working in the NHS . . . Dear God, it's tough.

Georgia, picking up on this, recounts an anecdote from a London friend: a referral letter lost between hospital departments, precious time lost as a result.

Dido thinks: that won't, will it, happen to me? She hears herself say lightly, pouring second mugs for each of them:

– I went for a couple of tests, before we came away.

– Did you? Georgia's voice, always lower than Dido's, and always measured, indicates at once her full attention. – What kind of tests?

– Oh, nothing much. Dido settles back in her chair. – I've had a few dizzy spells. Felt a bit under the weather. I've been much better since we got here. But gosh – having a doctor daughter . . . She leaves no stone unturned.

– Very wise.

Georgia drinks her tea and listens. She lets her gaze rest upon Dido, whose face she has known all her adult life, whose gradual slipping from youth to middle age is almost as familiar as her own. Now, they both stand on the threshold of another stage. No one, in the twenty-first century, could ever call sixty old, and no two women could have had more active lives. And yet . . .

Unusually, she reaches out a hand, gives Dido's arm a squeeze.

– Dear Georgia. Dido squeezes back. – Not to worry. They'd have phoned if it was anything serious. Now tell me how you are. How was France?

And so an hour passes. The sun sinks down, and shadows deepen; tea turns (as it were) into a glass of wine. They cover most things: the children's school accomplishments (quite a few), Nick's completed chapter and Paula's pleasing absence, everyone's overload at work –

Jeffrey, Kate and Leo in their different and demanding spheres, even
Dido hardly able to draw breath between her clients; Chloe's man,
as yet unseen, Maud's silence, France, the kind Cartwrights and their
clever children, the books they're reading now.

Georgia has abandoned Brookner, rather too close to home.
She's still with Alan Bennett; she's deep in Volume Two of *The
Brothers Karamazov*.

Dido has now read three Cartwright novels, and thinks the
whole country should read him. Such a mind, and such humanity.
Inspired by the festival, and that awesome hour with Lessing, she's
rereading *The Grass is Singing*. Still her best book. Georgia takes
issue: *The Golden Notebook* defined a generation. It didn't define
me, says Dido.

So it goes on. Neither touches on the big things: possible illness,
possible betrayal ... (surely not, surely not Jeffrey), loneliness
threatening to become despair, a horse on a hillside and a flood of
tears. There's plenty of time in the days ahead for this, or some of
this, if each decides to tell.

At length: – I must do something about supper. They'll be back
any minute. Do you want to go and settle in with Mrs Whatsit? Or
why not stay on, and go there afterwards?

Even as Georgia's setting down her glass, considering her
options, there's the sound of a car pulling up in the lane. Doors
open; children clamber out.

– We did it! We did it! We got to the top!

Family supper. Family expedition.

– We could see for *miles*!

– You were on Nick's shoulders half the time.

– So? So? Dad was almost *carrying you*.

– Ssh, ssh, ssh. You were both fantastic.

– I could never have climbed so far at your age. Who wants
more potatoes?

– Me!

– Georgia?

– Lovely. Thank you.

– Can I top you up?

– Better not, Jeffrey, thanks. I'm driving after this.

– Not very far.

– But not worth risking it.

Georgia spears another new potato, flecked with parsley, and lets it all wash over her: everyone talking and yawning at the kitchen table, candles down the middle, local pottery dishes heaped with couscous, peppers, potatoes, quiche, glazed ham, heaps of salad and a vast brown home-made loaf – healthy food for healthy walkers, lots and lots of wine. Since Henry's funeral, she's seen only Dido out of all of them: now she observes how much taller and more confident are the children (who did not, of course, attend the service); how kind Kate and Leo are with one another; how relaxed and good-looking is Nick these days; how Jeffrey (this is painful) looks so fit and strong; how Dido (who has prepared all this much earlier in the day) is basking in having her family around her, the focal point of their return. For what is an expedition without someone waiting at home to hear every detail?

– I saw a snake.

– A slowworm.

– Not *that* snake.

– We put stones on the cairn.

– How was the picnic?

– Yummy.

Rucksacks and walking boots stand about, unwashed plastic boxes are heaped up by the sink.

– We saw an eagle.

– You didn't!

– We did, he was *massive*.

Listening to it all, almost as tired as if she had herself climbed

Skiddaw, Georgia wonders: would easy-going, affectionate Dido have made a better mother for Chloe? Would Chloe not have been happier with all this all around her: siblings, niece and nephew, endless coming and going, endless talk? How difficult was it to be an only child? She herself had been one, and her memories were not unhappy, but then she'd always been so focused, so together, worked so hard at school. In Chloe's miserable struggle with the written word, wouldn't it have been easier to have a brother or sister to take the heat off? And now – now she doesn't even have a father, and the two of them must find a way to be: a mother and daughter who have, in truth, not so very much in common.

Dido is laughing at something. Leo is clearing plates.

– What's for pudding?

– Treacle tart, if anyone has room. Or fruit, of course.

– Treacle tart for me, says Nick, poking about in the last of the salad. – Is there cream?

– There is.

– Fantastic.

He gets up, picks up the salad bowl, catches Georgia's eye. The smile he gives her turns her heart right over – and how long is it since *that* is how she felt? She smiles back, filled with warm feelings. What a nice young man he's turned out to be, after all that shyness, over-anxiety about every little thing – she can remember how Dido used to worry.

Izzy is almost asleep at the table. Georgia knows how she feels, and she hasn't an inch of room for treacle tart. Not even a grape.

– Dido? Would you think me very rude if I took off, now?

– Of course not. You must be shattered.

– Just a bit.

She rises; there's a general turning of heads.

– Are you off? Jeffrey sets down his glass.

– I am. I'll see you all after breakfast.

– No rush. We won't be going far.

General laughter, yawning, getting up to say goodbye.

– Please, stay where you are.

– Good night, Georgia. Good to see you again.

Jeffrey sees her to the door, and out to her car, in the darkened lane. A couple of bats flit past.

– Lovely to have you with us.

– Thanks, Jeffrey. It's good to be here.

She gets her keys out. He's a good man, is he not, and he must miss Henry too.

– You remember how to get there? I hope it's all comfortable.

– I'm sure it will be. Well, good night.

The moon is rising behind the trees; they kiss, good old friends, once and then twice on the cheek: as everyone does, as they've done for years. Since Henry's death, Georgia has greeted or said goodbye to countless friends in this way, male and female, everyone being loyal and kind. She has not, however, kissed a man alone in a dusky, moonlit lane, his family all having supper together, and not a soul about. For a split second, as their lips brush one another's cheeks, she's aware of him, this man she has known all her adult life, as purely male, and she as purely female. For a split second only, she finds herself thinking: if we were to go to bed—

Then he's patting her arm, watching her unlock the car, get in and drop her bag beside her. He's raising his hand in farewell, and she knows, as she nods and smiles and turns on the ignition, that no such thought has crossed his mind, that he's as deeply married to Dido as Henry was to her. It's over, that moment, and she's glad.

– Night!

– Good night.

Her headlights flood the grassy verge, the hedgerow. Within their beam, Jeffrey walks away, turning to wave, and then she's out on the lane and past him, past the lit-up family house, and off to her B & B, widowed and unsexed once more.

12

Chloe is here! Chloe, trailing chic little clouds of urgency and disarray, has made it to the Lakes! Everyone perks up. Not that they were unperked, just weary from the climb, but who could not feel cheered by the sight of someone so pretty and alive, so stylish, yet so scatterbrained? (If you think 'chic' and 'disarray' constitute an oxymoron – not a word which would mean a huge amount to Chloe – then you haven't met her.)

– Chloe!

– Hi, everyone.

Georgia has collected her from Penrith, later than expected. (– Hi, Mum, I'm still on the train, I missed the connection, sorry.) The weather, as if in anticipation of this new arrival, has become unsettled: it's cold, pacing up and down on the platform, and when they come out to the car park there's a flurry of rain.

– It's freezing! I thought you said it was sunny.

Chloe is wearing a green and white cotton ra-ra skirt, a tiny green top and vintage black cotton jacket, suntanned bare legs and cream peep-toed cotton mules. The peeping toes are pillar-box red, her eyes rimmed duskily with kohl; feathery hair and enormous black and silver earrings blow madly about in the rain.

Georgia, in jeans, walking shoes, two warm layers and a navy fleece (a nice one) swings her daughter's bag into the boot.

– You know it can be like this up here. I hope you've brought *some* warm things.

Chloe's teeth are chattering. She scrambles in to the passenger seat and takes a long deep breath. Don't rise to it. Do-Not-Rise-To-It. She straps herself in, sets the heating on High, has a vision of Jez, warm and naked beside her this morning. As Georgia gets in and turns on the ignition, she gives her a dazzling smile.

– Hi, Mum.

– Hello, darling.

They start again.

– How was France?

– Beautiful.

– I bet you missed Dad.

– I did. And Spain? How did you all get on?

– Fine. It was so *hot*. Sara had to stay in the shade all the time.

– Sara?

– You remember, Sara and Matt. They're having a baby. They're getting married.

– How lovely, says Georgia carefully, changing down at traffic lights. She's not quite sure how to follow this announcement. – Whereabouts were you exactly?

– Santa de Segura. Same place as last year.

– Near Valencia?

– I think so.

Chloe hasn't a clue where it's near, she just flew there. She got out her bikini, gave herself up to the sun and spent two weeks missing Jez with every cell in her body. Why couldn't he have come? Just for a few days. Of course he couldn't come up *now*, do the whole mother and family friends bit. No one would expect him to do *that*. But Spain . . . It rankles still.

– Sorry, babes. Just can't manage it.

Something of her mother stirred within her.

– Please don't call me babes.

Georgia is burbling on about Moorish architecture and the

Prado. Her Spain – the one she once shared with Henry – is different from Chloe's. Velathqueth. Give me a break.

– Watch out, Mum, there's a cyclist. A pause. – Or should I thay thyclitht?

They both laugh so much that Georgia almost kills him. By the time they arrive at the B & B (a place Chloe remembers fondly from childhood) the rain has blown away.

– The thun'th come out!

– Chloe!

– Hi, everyone.

Tea in the kitchen, because the garden's still a bit wet. It's snug in here, (local) pottery teapot in an ancient cosy, fruit cake, tea towels drying on the Rayburn rail.

One day, she wants a family just like this.

– Lovely to see you again.

– You too.

Here they all are again, the people of her childhood: Kate (still a bit frightening) and her family: nice Leo, even balder, the kids grown suddenly enormous. Dido, whom she's always loved; Jeffrey, tall and kind as ever. (Why is he here, and not Dad?) Nick. He's looking pretty good these days.

– Hi, Nick.

– Hi, Chloe, good to see you.

Where's Paula?

– Is Paula here?

– Paula's deep in a chapter, says Nick, pulling out a chair. – She might come up in a day or two.

– Oh. Right.

All these clever people. Doctors and chapters and God knows what. Bloody terrifying, if she hadn't known them all her life.

– Tea?

– Please.

Even the children are brainy, you can tell just by looking at them.

Everyone starts chatting away. Jeffrey goes to take a phone call. Leo asks her about her journey, and Kate about London. The children listen, especially Izzy.

– I like your earrings.

– Thanks. Your granny gave them to me. She flashes a smile at Dido. – They're great. She takes one off. – Want to try it, Izzy?

– I haven't got pierced ears. Izzy holds a moon-sized black and silver disc against her cheek.

– Pretty.

Chloe gets out her mirror and shows her. Sam starts fiddling with bits of Lego. Nick helps. Dido and Georgia are talking about supper.

Family hols.

Why isn't her father here?

Why isn't Jez?

Family hols. Something is brewing, and has been for some time. Will it come to a head now, or back in York? Dido knows only that Jeffrey, in this second week, is perceptibly withdrawn. It's not just the phone calls, which take him from the room, to the end of the garden, to (it feels like) the moon. There aren't so very many, not really; before The Text she would barely have noticed them, much too busy with meals, plans, chitchat with the children. But now, knowing him inside out, she notices everything: that although he's kind and considerate as always, looking after everyone with drinks, doing all the usual household stuff – the logs, the fires, the endless washing up – he talks less than usual, doesn't listen as well as usual (– Dad! What did I just say?) and is apt to take himself off: for an afternoon nap (unheard of), for a walk by himself (unusual) or a breath of fresh air after supper (quite a lot of those).

And she's always in bed before him. Always.

– Jeffrey?

– Shan't be long.

But he is, he is. Is he hoping she'll be asleep before he comes up? If so, he's successful: what with the walks, the air, the endless meals, the children (Leo and Kate need time to themselves; Dido is happy to play games, supervise splashing about in the river, look for lost bits and pieces) not to mention, now, making sure that Georgia and Chloe are enjoying themselves on their first holiday up here without poor Henry – what with all this, she's asleep as soon as her head hits the pillow. Her books lie unopened beside her – a page or two with her morning tea, and that's it. And though Jeffrey, as always, brings up her morning tea, it's hers, not theirs. He doesn't climb back into bed beside her.

– Jeffrey?

– Back in a minute.

But he isn't, he isn't. He's downstairs with the children, so Leo and Kate can have a lie-in (or sex, even, something which, with the lives they lead, must be in short supply); he's taking the children out to look for mushrooms, frying them up for breakfast. It's kind, it's the sort of thing he often does up here, but every day? And as for sex (their sex) – forget it. Clearly, it's just not going to happen.

If Dido were listening to one of her clients pouring all this out, she'd be waiting for this unhappy person to start facing facts. There is a crisis. There is surely an affair. Possibly a breakdown on the way. And when all these anxieties and dreadful truths are bravely faced for what they are, what advice would she give?

She's not in the business of giving advice. That's not what Hand in Need is there for. It's there to help people find their own solutions, come to their own decisions, meanwhile (she hears Georgia snorting) offering support. Phrases from her training float into view, as she lies there with her book and her mug of tea, and contemplates the day, their long long life together. Avoidance Strategies. Passive Aggressive. Psychic Disintegration.

No. Not Jeffrey. He's much too solid to disintegrate.

But all the rest?

He's certainly avoiding her. You could call that an act of quiet aggression.

But surely . . .

Surely she and Jeffrey, after all these years, could never reach an impasse, not be able (oh, cliché, cliché) to talk things through, work things out, renew their love for one another?

Has he stopped loving her? Could this really happen?

Dido has a sudden sight of Caro trailing bravely off to choir, in that outsize linen jacket. Abandoned, after thirty years. It happens.

But surely not to them.

She puts down the pottery mug with a thump. Tea splashes on to the book. She swings herself quickly out of bed and stands up. At once, she's so swimmy that she has to sit down again.

She's on the edge of the mattress, her head in her hands.

Oh, bloody hell.

Days pass. Well, one or two. Georgia and Chloe are here for three or four, depending on nothing very much except Chloe's need to get back to work (already had two weeks in Spain) to London (and all her friends) and to Jez. The first two she discusses with her mother, the third is invisible. And if passive can become aggressive, then invisible, to a mother with her antennae out, can be as visible as if the man has just walked right into the room and is taking her daughter's clothes off.

It's breakfast time in the B & B. Cold but bright outside, the morning sun lighting willow-pattern coffee pot, orange juice, three kinds of cereal including porridge, bacon, new-laid egg, sausage, tomato, field mushrooms, toast and marmalade. None of those mingy little foil-wrapped portions of butter or Non-Dairy Alternative, but a proper china butter dish with a china cow on top. No metal teapots in the bedroom with a saucer of carefully counted teabags, but a knock on the door at eight, and a tray. There's even a tray cloth.

This is a proper B & B, such as these days you find only in novels, which is why Henry and Georgia came back year after year bringing Chloe with them. As a child, she thought these breakfast just fantastic (– We never have *anything* like this at home!).

Now: – I can't possibly eat all that.

But she does, every morning. Georgia doesn't. Tall and lean as she is, she's put on weight in France and must get it off again. Why? Who cares? Who's going to see? She is, and she has her self-respect. She drinks her coffee, spoons a moderate amount of homemade marmalade on to two slices of wholemeal toast, and looks at the paper. Another good thing about Mrs Whatsit: you can order the papers on arrival and they'll be here every morning, brought in from the village by her son on his motorbike. Chloe tucks in and reads the tabloid bit. It's peaceful, the other guests, a retired couple and two young teachers, having long since left for the fells. A tractor bumps past the window en route for the farm from whence come their eggs, milk and cream. Chloe can, as in childhood, hear the triumphant cackle of a hen who has laid an egg. When she was little, she used to go up there with her father and watch the milking. Sometimes the farmer let her look for eggs in the hedgerow, and sometimes she found one. What she wants now, skimming over an interview with last week's outcast from The House, is a little girl of her very own to take up there and do all these things with all over again. She knows just what kind of basket she'd buy her for the eggs: a little wicker one with a gingham lining.

Will it be her very own daughter, or might it – could it – be Ellie?

Will it be both? (She wants lots and lots.)

Sara's baby is due on 15 November. She and Matt are getting married on 1 September. Both these dates are in Chloe's diary, and every time she comes upon them, writing in studio bookings and all that stuff, her stomach does a little nosedive. Or flip-flop. Whatever. She certainly feels it.

– What are you reading?

– Oh, just some *Big Brother* thing.

– In the *Guardian*? They're writing about *Big Brother* in the *Guardian*?

– Oh, Mum, for God's sake. It's popular culture, innit? She folds it up. – You're seriously out of touch, you know. It's time you got back to work.

– I've only just given up.

– Yeah, I know. But what are you going to do?

– I wish I knew. Georgia speaks lightly, but Chloe has touched a nerve. What is she going to do? How is she going to live out the rest of her life? And 'live out' is how it feels: time to be got through, time to be endured.

– More coffee?

– No, thanks. What're you going to do when we get back to London?

– Visit Maud. I've told you. I don't suppose—

– I'll see. And then what?

– Oh, Chloe. Georgia finishes her cup. – Don't go on at me. She takes a breath, carefully using the moment. – What are *you* going to do, come to that?

– How do you mean?

– What does the autumn hold for you?

– Oh, the usual stuff. She launches into a list of shoots, openings, promotions. Busy busy busy.

– And apart from work?

Chloe picks up the paper again. – Edmund's in a new play, I think. Yup, he is. Something at the Tricycle. Some political thing. (Her mother's sigh is inaudible, but she hears it all right. What political thing? Why has she not taken it in? Why doesn't she take an interest in the wider world?) – And there's Matt and Sara's wedding, that'll be good. And then the baby. Yup – quite a lot going on.

She leafs through, settles on the Health page. 'Female fertility: Can we stop worrying, now?' Yes, please. Tell me thirty-one is nothing. The feature, hooked as it is on a beaming psychoanalyst of fifty-six, does exactly that. But *fifty-six* – is she mad, or what?

– And what about you, Chloe?

– Mmm?

– What about you? Georgia's tone across the table is quietly insistent.

– Oh, Mum. Don't start.

– I'm not starting. I'm just taking an interest. As mothers do. How are you, Chloe?

– Fine. Fine. Don't go on at me.

– Darling. (Chloe feels a lump in her throat begin to form.) – Darling, if you were fine, you'd be telling me all about it. Georgia, feeling her way, knows at once she has gone too far. But how else to convey concern? How else to offer the chance to open up?

– Stop it! Chloe is suddenly crimson. Tears brim, then spill. – Stop it! How would you like it if I went on at you about getting over Dad? How are you feeling now? And now? Is it getting better? Is it getting worse? You wouldn't like it, Mum. Now leave me alone!

And she's gone, just restraining herself from slamming the door, and running upstairs to her room. Just like when she was little. Just like when she was a teenager. Just like most of her life, in fact – it all comes flooding back – until she found the right career, and was so so much happier. And now – Georgia is shaking – she's ruined all the good relationship they've built up since those years, all the closeness they'd found through Henry's illness and death.

If he were here . . .

If only he were here . . .

She's on the brink of tears herself now, and here is Mrs Whatsit, with a tray.

– Everything all right?

– Fine, says Georgia. – A really lovely breakfast.

Upstairs, Chloe sobs into her lovely old-fashioned Lake District eiderdown, as quietly as she can. Everything pours out upon its feathery mound: every anxiety about the future, every sorrow about her father, all her need of him, her longing for Jez, which seem, as she weeps, to be one and the same. She needs a man. It's 2006, and women are not, not, not supposed to be like this, but she is, she is.

She wants her father. Would she have told him about Jez? She tries to imagine it: up in Henry's study, him taking his glasses off, swivelling round to look at her. Just being quiet, until she was ready. Yes – she probably would. She could tell him anything. He wouldn't have liked it, though.

Oh, what is she to do?

– Chloe?

Georgia is knocking at the door, very quietly. Poor old Mum. She didn't deserve all that. But please, please, go away. Just leave it.

Georgia leaves it. Chloe hears her walk slowly along the landing to her own room, and shut the door.

After a while, she recovers. Sort of. She gets up, blows her nose, washes her face in cold water at the basin. God, what a sight. How's she going to face everyone up at the house? Oh, why did she come at all? Just to keep her mother happy, but they're both on edge without Henry, and it just doesn't work, the two of them.

It's got to work.

Chloe breathes deeply, looks for her makeup, realises she's left it downstairs in her bag, goes to the open window. Field and fell stretch away, old farm buildings look just right. Bringing her up here was her parents' gesture at a country childhood. When she has her own family she'll move to the country for keeps. Definitely. Look at it all. A combine harvester is crawling through a golden field, clouds drift slowly above the fells, the sheep look so pretty on the slopes, and that hen has laid another egg. Listen to that. Perhaps she and Georgia can have a soothing walk down there, before they drive up to the house. She leans out, letting the morning air do its stuff, blowing away (she hopes) all trace of tears.

OK. Now, then.

She goes along the landing, knocks at the door.

– Mum?

– Come in.

What a brave tired voice.

– I'm sorry.

– *I'm* sorry, says Georgia, rising from the chair. She's been crying too. Oh, God. – My fault.

– No. Mine.

They kiss, they hug. It's a long long time since they've had a scene like this, and the hug does them both a lot of good.

– I brought your bag up.

– Thanks.

Chloe perches on the edge of the bed and repairs the damage. Then they go for the soothing walk. She still doesn't tell her mother that she's sleeping with a married man. Georgia guesses. She keeps it to herself.

13

There's one good thing about it all: at least, for the first time, she can put her hand on her heart and say that she's in love. She must be. Why else would she feel like this?

– I'm deeply in love, she tells Nick, out in the garden that evening. – I mean, like really. Properly.

– Gosh. That's – that's good. He twirls his glass in his hand. – Another one?

– Why not? Thanks.

She watches as he heaves himself out of the deckchair and crosses to the table. He's a good-looking bloke, no doubt about it. Who'd have thought that skinny little worrier would turn into this? Not as gorgeous as Jez – well, different. Fair, for a start, must get that from Jeffrey. Tall, like Jez, but not as lithe, not as light on his feet. For all that, he does move nicely: like Jez, he is pleasing to watch. Jez, always in black – black jeans, black shirt, black leather jacket – wouldn't be seen dead in those scruffy old shorts and ancient shirt, but that faded blue really suits him, and the walking has given him a tan. Not like hers, of course, but then she's been to Spain.

He brings back the bottle, refills her glass, sets it down in the grass between them. This is nice. She's always been fond of Nick. Mind you, after the drama over breakfast, the whole day's been pretty nice, really. She and Izzy spent the morning trying on earrings, painting nails, doing different hairstyles. Now Izzy has pearly pink nails on one hand and witchy green on the other. She has a coil of plaits round her head, woven in with ribbon. Chloe has Goth-black fingernails and funny little plaits sticking out here and there in the feathery haircut. Both of them have been hugely admired over lunch, though Kate isn't keen on nail polish for children, not really; Chloe can tell. She thinks it's sexualised and vulgar, and in a way she's right, but they're on holiday, for God's sake, it's just dressing up, that's all.

After lunch, they all (except Dido, who had a lie-down) went for a walk in the woods. Nick and Sam and Leo made a den. Georgia and Kate talked about clever things – or perhaps they weren't so clever, just ordinary stuff, family life stuff: they just made it all sound so intelligent. Jeffrey – where did Jeffrey go? She can't remember. She and Izzy swam in the river, and how could you not feel better after that? Only two more days, and she'll be back with Jez. Meanwhile . . .

– What about you and Paula? she asks, as Nick settles back into his dark green deck chair. (Nothing but the best, up here.) – Are you happy?

– Oh, yes. He fishes an insect out of his glass. – We've been together for ages, now.

That's not the same as being happy. Still, she doesn't press it.

– What's this chapter she's writing? Would I understand it?

Funny how easy it is to ask him that. If she were talking to Kate she'd have to be all polite, pretending to be clever too, when they both knew they were chalk and cheese.

He smiles. – I'm not sure if I understand it myself.

– What's it about?

He clears his throat. – Affirming and Questioning Sexual Identities: Woman as Castrated Other.

Blimey.

What on earth do you say to that?

Nick laughs. – Not quite your thing? Tell me about this chap you've fallen for. Is he someone at work?

– Sort of.

But Chloe, after baring her soul in response to a simple How's life? is drawing her horns in. First, fashion photography seems a million miles away, up here: how can she make it sound interesting and real? Second, the chief thing about Jez is that he has a daughter, and isn't yet divorced, and she doesn't want to tell Nick all this now. If she can't – won't – tell Georgia, why tell someone she hardly ever sees?

– More of him another time, she says. – As my mother would put it.

– She's doing awfully well, your mother. So are you. He reaches out a hand, lets it rest for a moment on her bare arm. – I'm so sorry about your father. We all are.

– Thanks. Chloe raises her glass to her lips, drinks, smiles at him. – Thanks, Nick.

– He was such a nice man.

– He was. I expect your parents miss him too.

– I'm sure they do. They all go back such a long way, don't they?

For a while, they reminisce companionably about childhood summers up here. The sounds of supper preparations come from the house: Dido and Georgia are cooking together. Jeffrey has gone for an evening stroll along the lake with Kate and Leo, the children are mucking about somewhere. Just as she and Nick used to do: it's not only their parents who go back a long way.

– Tell me about your Ph.D. thing, she says, after a while. – Would I understand that?

– *Patterns of Settlement and Cultivation in North-Eastern England, 1200–1380.* At the moment, I'm writing about the Black Death.

Chloe tries to hold it all in her mind.

– Well, at least I've heard of the Black Death. Couldn't tell you when it was, mind you, but I've definitely heard of it.

– Fourteenth century. In 1348–9 it killed a third to a half of the population, up and down the country. Everyone had to start again:

all sorts of things changed. There was a redistribution of land from manorial lord to yeoman . . .

He's off, and pretty soon she's stopped listening, though she does try.

– My mother says my title is a subtitle. She says I need something strong and sexy to catch the eye.

Chloe wakes up. – To pull in the punters, you mean.

– Exactly. Not that there are many punters swarming round a Ph.D. But still, it's got to sound good.

– What's Paula's title again?

– *Madwoman on the Couch*, he reminds her. – *Phallocentric discourse and the politics of desire.*

– Gordon Bennett.

She gets the giggles. So does he.

– The thing is, she says, when they've pulled themselves together, and poured another glass. – The thing is, I keep thinking that there must be something in your stuff that I'd find interesting.

– Thanks.

– No, but I mean like really. I mean, if you're writing about fields and stuff, you must be writing about farms.

– True.

– Well, I'm interested in farms.

– You are?

– Stop it. You know me, I'm interested in *things*, real things. If I wanted to posh it up, I could give you a Ph.D. title about interiors.

– Are you sure?

– Stop it! You know what I'm saying. Tell me about – oh, I don't know – milking, or kitchens, or something.

Well. After that, there's no stopping him. And it's lovely, lovely stuff. Drunk as she is becoming, Chloe takes in – properly – endless facts and details. She hears about moats, which after the B.D. were used, apparently, not just as defence things, but as fish stores for all the new fishponds. Carp, pike, tench, bream and roach. (– What does a tench look like?) She learns about deer parks and dovecotes (– They *ate* the doves?) and how when people kept more cattle they kept more pigs, feeding them on whey. Nick tells her about eighteenth-century kitchens (– Out of my period, but you might like this) and plain strong words hang in the evening air: saltbox, skillet, hog pot, rush light, hundred-eyes lantern (– full of holes). As they both grow drunker, and hungrier (– WHEN is supper?) he describes the eighteenth-century things that shepherds used: the yoke and bell, the leg crook, dip hook, drench horn, turnip crook. There's a mention of mole traps.

– Poor moles. What about clothes?

– Mole clothes?

– Don't be silly.

But of course they're both helpless.

Then he's off again. Agricultural labourers wearing sacks split down the side to make rainproof hoods. Smocks of unbleached linen. How Thomas Hardy (she's heard of him) described all the different smockings in *Under the Greenwood Tree*. (– That's a good title. Why can't you find a title like that?)

He's telling her how to make a haystack (more to it than you might think) when Dido calls from the house:

– Supper time!

Thank God for that. But gosh, this is fun.

And then his phone goes off in his pocket. He fumbles drunkenly.

– Hello? Paula? Paula, hi. How are you getting on?

Chloe watches him listen. Pissed as a parrot.

– You're coming up tomorrow? Well done. That's great. I'll meet the train.

Dusk is gathering. She follows him rather unsteadily into the house.

* * *

Supper is over. It's been very convivial (– Lovely to hear you two laughing out in the garden like that.) The children have been bathed and put to bed. Chloe goes up to say good night. She walks along the landing, past half-open doors revealing all the muddle of family hols, past the bathroom, strewn with wet towels and sweetly scented with bubble bath. She's still a bit drunk.

– Where are you?

– In here!

Light spills out on to the landing. This is Nick and Kate's old room, she can remember, from all those years ago. She puts her head round the door.

– Hi.

– Hi, Chloe.

They're reading in bed. They're – what are they? – six and eight, and they're tucked up in bed with their books as good as gold. The curtains are drawn, but it's not quite dark, and shadows from the garden trees play against a pattern of pandas and giraffes. The window's open, letting in all that good fresh country air. She can hear sheep. She can hear an owl.

– Whooo! He's scary, that owl.

– Only if you're a mouse.

Giggles. Chloe looks around the room, in whose twin beds, over the years, dozens of children have snuggled down. There's a battered old chest of drawers, cheap and cheerful, as Georgia would put it, a clothes rail in an alcove and a ladder-backed chair with a rope seat coming to bits. T-shirts, shorts and sunfrocks are piled upon it. There are two pictures, one of Grace Darling, rowing away in her lifeboat, (Henry told Chloe that story) and one called *Spring in the Fells*. She has known them all her life.

– Your mummy used to sleep in here.

– With Nick, we know.

– Must be great to know everything. Whose bed shall I sit on?

– Mine!

– Mine!

She perches on Izzy's.

– You first. What are you reading?

– *Little Grey Rabbit Makes Lace.* It was Mummy's book.

– You're reading it all by yourself?

– Some of it. Mostly I'm looking at the pictures.

Phew.

– Let's have a look.

Together they turn the pages. Sunlit village streets, cosy kitchens, cottage gardens all make a darling background to cushions on a rabbit lap, bobbins (bobbins!), birds helping with their beaks.

> . . . *they all watched her paws.*
> *A tiny strip of lace appeared, and it took the shape of a bee. On she went, and a flower came, and then another bee. She made a row of bees and flowers, with a wavy edge to the sheep's wool lace like flowing water.*

Heaven, as Dido would say. Chloe notices that Izzy's nails are no longer pink and green: Kate, at bath time, must have got out the remover. Oh, well.

Sam, in his bed, is quietly turning a page of his own.

– What are *you* reading?

– *Little House on the Prairie.*

– I remember that. My dad used to read that to me.

– *My* dad's reading it to me. But we're allowed to read on by ourselves, if we want, before lights out.

Chloe looks at them both. Do you have to live in York to have children like these? Do children like these really still exist? Apparently so, as her mother would put it.

– You're both such brilliant readers.

– Were you a brilliant reader? When you were my age?

– Ah, says Chloe. – Thereby hangs a tale.

– What kind of tail?

– A tale told by an idiot, she says, a line from long-forgotten Shakespeare (what kind of hell was *that*?) making a rare appearance. – Never mind. I'd better say good night.

– Night, Chloe.

Izzy's lips on her cheek are just the sweetest thing.

– What about you, Sam? Can I kiss you good night?

– Sure.

Dark curly head: she rests her lips upon it. Gosh, how nice.

Would it be as good to have a son as have a daughter? Can you make sure you have both, now? Surely you can. If you can get pregnant at fifty-six (!!!) you could give birth to a giraffe, if you wanted.

– What are you laughing at?

– Nothing. Good night. See you tomorrow.

For a moment she stands in the doorway, pretending they are hers. There they are, heads upon the pillows, lamplight keeping everything warm and safe. They're hers, and she'll have them for ever: what a fantastic feeling.

Then footsteps come along the landing. Kate is here, to tuck them in and turn the light out. They smile at one another: nicely, but they're on different planets, really.

Chloe leaves her to it.

Paula is here. Not quite so much perking, now. Not that they don't give her a welcome.

– Paula. So glad you could make it.

– Hi, Dido.

– Well done, Paula. Let me get you a drink.

– Thanks.

She looks about her. Everyone feels slightly chilled. They all make valiant efforts. Soon, she and Georgia (rescuing Dido, who has confided her apprehensions about this visit, even if so much else has been concealed) are ensconced with their glasses on either side of the fire. (It's cold again, and has rained in the night.) They talk about feminist literature. Nick hovers. Chloe, with face paints and a box of this and that, turns Sam and Izzy into pirates. Kate and Leo join Georgia and Paula, and talk about doctorates and academic life. Paula isn't terribly forthcoming, but she is, she tells them, immensely relieved to have finished the chapter. Dido is getting the supper (again). Jeffrey is . . .

– Where's Dad?

Nobody seems to know.

He's back for supper, which perhaps would have been rather muted and polite, were it not for the sudden appearance of people with cutlasses, eye patches and blacked-out teeth.

Dido cowers behind a tea towel. – Terrifying! You're terrifying!

– We're going to make you walk the *plank*.

Jeffrey bundles his fist into his jumper and grabs a fork. – Think you can terrify *me*? Captain Fork the Terrible?

Everyone shrieks.

– You people certainly know how to enjoy yourselves.

Guess who says that.

Eventually, it's bedtime. Georgia and Chloe drive away down the lane; Kate and Leo, their over-excited children tucked up and read to, go out for a quiet drink in the pub. (What do they have to say to one another?) Dido and Jeffrey climb the stairs. An owl hoots from the garden; then comes the soft sound of rain once more.

– Lovely to see you so relaxed again, my darling.

– It was a lot of fun.

When she comes out of the bathroom, he's gone downstairs again.

– Jeffrey?

– Think I'll read for a bit.

– You can read up here.

– I'll be up soon.

Stonewalled. Not a damn thing she can do.

She could blow her top, of course. She could shout and stamp and yell down the stairs that she's had more than enough of all this, and what the bloody hell does he think he's playing at. But Dido is no shouter or stamper, their marriage has not been that kind of marriage, and besides, there are the children. She takes herself wearily to bed.

And what of Nick and Paula?

Nick has already carried Paula's bag, briefcase and laptop up to their room. Now they too go up the stairs to bed.

And then what?

He takes her in his arms. She gives a thin little smile, then draws away.

Is this it?

Is this how their life together is always going to be?

– Paula?

– I'm really tired.

Paula is gay. This is something which has been suspected by several people over the years except for Kate and Leo, doctors with a good sixteen years' experience between them; Jeffrey, a senior academic (with problems of his own); Dido, a trained counsellor, and Nick, who lives with her. Sometimes, even the most sensitive and intelligent people, even in the twenty-first century, find it easier not to see things. The other person who has, all her life, chosen not to face the fact, is Paula herself: a brilliant, troubled woman who thinks unhappiness the norm. It has taken the summer vacation, and her supervisor's long long absence (a conference in Chicago, a holiday in Greece) to make her realise, once and for all, that the feelings she has for this (female) person are, in truth, such as she has never had for Nick.

Now what?

If you think that coming out, in the twenty-first century, is easy-peasy, the struggles of your twentieth-century sisters having long since paved the way, then you have never been in this situation, and you do not know Paula.

All other considerations aside, her supervisor (Emma) is married, with two children. There are, of course, any number of married women prepared to jump ship in order to find themselves, at last, in lesbian love, but Paula senses, deep in her bones, that Emma is not going to be one of them. She may have a doctorate in feminist studies, she may have given a mesmerising series of lectures on women's alterity in a patriarchal culture, on constructing sexualities and the myth of the vaginal orgasm, but she's as straight as a die.

Tears (in private). Sleepless nights. Avoidance strategies.

If she cannot have Emma (and oh, how she longs for this) then she must, must she not, settle down with Nick. He's nice, she's fond of him, she respects his work, they've been together for years. But to live such a lie, to have children, as Nick has said he wants to do, while living such a lie . . .

Can she do this? To him, or to herself?

Then she must tell him, and hurt him, and then what? A lonely life awaits. Why? If she can't have Emma, then perhaps she can find someone else. She doesn't want anyone else. It's Emma, Emma, Emma (that fringe, that voice, that mind, those frameless specs; those hands, pale and elegant as a Raphael Madonna) and no one else will do.

So she's not going to go out searching. She will settle to her work. Her work will save her.

A lot of the time, she simply wants to die.

Thus Paula, gazing up at the ceiling of the fourth bedroom in the Sullivans' rented house. Cumbrian rain patters prettily against the window. God, God, God Almighty: what is she going to do?

Thus Nick, lying beside her, certain she's awake, though she breathes so steadily; contemplating a life without sex. Without love: there, he's said it.

He'll have to end it.

He doesn't know how to. He's always hated scenes.

Rain falls faster, sinking deep into the earth. At last they sleep.

Georgia and Chloe's last day.

– Oh, please don't go!

It's warm again, warm enough to have lunch in the garden. Everyone pitches in, carrying out trays of plates, glasses, knives and forks, bowls of salad, the breadboard, the cold meats, the quiche (– Sorry, Paula, quiche again. – Oh, it's fine, I'm used to it). Here come the juice, the fruit, the chairs. Dido, Chloe and Izzy are in sunhats; the others, round the crowded table, seek places in the shade. Tinkle of ice and clink of glasses.

– Cheers.

– Cheers. It's been lovely. Thank you all so much.

– Well, now, says Jeffrey, as they all settle down. – What are you two going to get up to after this?

Plates are passed, and servings taken.

– Lots of work, says Chloe. – Once September starts, we're really busy.

– What *is* your work? asks Sam.

She tries to explain. How silly it sounds, amongst all these serious people. It's like having Georgia multiplied by six.

– I, like, arrange things. For photographs. Fashion stuff.

She feels Nick looking at her. Mole clothes. She bites her lip.

– So clever, says Dido. – I wish I had your eye.

– And you, Georgia? asks Jeffrey, passing her the salad. – What awaits you, in London?

His tone is light, but there's something oddly barbed about it.

Georgia feels a little frown come upon her. What do you think? she wants to say. An empty house. Filling up the days with nothing I give a damn about. How would you manage, on your own? She steadies herself.

– The first thing I've got to do is visit Maud. Things have gone awfully quiet down there, though I did have the maddest phone call.

She describes it. Everyone but Paula hoots. Paula has views about women and mental illness. She shares them with the table. Georgia knows she is right. She also wants to smack her on the nose. How does Dido stand it?

– And when you've sorted out Maud? Jeffrey is refilling her glass. (Does she imagine it, or does he drink too much?) – What are your plans?

God, will he let it rest?

– I'm not sure I have many plans, she says carefully. – Not yet. I'm just getting the measure of things, if you know what I mean.

– Of course we do, says Dido. If she were sitting beside Jeffrey now, she'd be putting a hand on his arm: that's enough, darling, just let it go. What's got into him, all of a sudden? One minute he's nowhere to be seen, the next he's being utterly insensitive.

Kate and Leo are nodding at Georgia in doctorly understanding. (Does she imagine it, or could their perfection get upon your nerves? Is she, in widowhood, becoming sour?)

– All I'm saying, says Jeffrey, with a smile, – is that you're a bright woman, Georgia. All that energy. I can't imagine you letting all your talents go to waste. He lifts his glass, takes a considering sip. – Retirement without an occupation: it's not right for someone like you.

Georgia can feel her irritation begin to get the better of her. This is their last day, they've all been wonderful, the last thing she wants is to have a quarrel. A quarrel, with one of her oldest friends?

(Besides – she flushes – there was that moment in the lane.) But to be patronised like this . . .

– Of course, idleness isn't right for anyone.

She can't quite look at him. Everyone seems to be listening: it's like being in court. – I'm just trying to work out what I should do, now – now everything's different.

– Quite right. Of course, of course. He's drinking again. – And what sort of things have you considered?

Enough! She looks at him in fury.

– Hanging myself?

There is a ghastly silence.

Unheard of for Georgia to be anything but restrained, well-mannered, perfect company. Unheard of for Jeffrey to behave like such a boor. Aggressive: nothing passive about it. Chloe blushes crimson. Dido opens her mouth and shuts it again.

Then: – Well, good for you, Georgia, says Paula, putting down her napkin. – No one should let themselves be interrogated like that. Then she rises, and walks – almost runs – towards the house. Nick puts his head in his hands.

Dido rises, too: too quickly.

And everything goes black.

– Mum? It's OK, I'm here, just lie still.

She's on the grass. Kate is feeling her pulse. Anxious faces float a mile above them. Jeffrey is bringing a glass of water. He lifts her head – Careful, Dad, be very gentle – and she sips. Georgia brings a cushion, and slips it beneath her head.

– Don't try to get up, Mum.

She couldn't if she tried. She wants to lie here for ever. She smiles weakly, shuts her eyes. Something is happening – something terrible has happened. Tears trickle; she begins to sob.

– What's making her cry like that?

– It's the shock. Someone get a rug.

Chloe sprints off.

But it isn't the shock, not this shock, anyway. What's happened now (what did happen?) has flung her straight back to the past, and a day whose hideous impact has never left her. Going into that sunny bedroom, full once again of baby things. A mobile of bluebirds turning this way and that above the cot, in the breeze from the open window.

– Hello, my darling. Are you still asleep?

The stillness, the silence, the turning of the birds.

Ella, Ella, Ella . . .

She weeps unstoppably.

14

What a way to end a holiday.
— I'm so sorry, says Dido, over and over again.
— Dido, please.
— Stop it, Mum.
— The main thing is to get you better.

She's up in the bedroom, half-drawn curtains shading the room from the afternoon sun. After all the huge energy involved in creating this family holiday for everyone — the booking, the planning, the packing, the beds, the shopping, the cooking, the picking up and putting away, the games with the children, the so wanting to give Kate and Leo a proper break for once, to give grieving Georgia and Chloe a happy few days; after the quietly mounting anxiety about a husband who will no longer share a bed while both of them are conscious; after all this, and that great outpouring of sorrow — at last she is having a rest.

The shaded room could belong to another age: the age of the sickroom, straw put down in the street to muffle the horses' footsteps, of powder in a glass, and frightened children. (Had Sam and Izzy been frightened? Leo has taken them down to the village for ice cream.) Georgia is beside her. Cool, undemonstrative Georgia is holding her hand.

— Tell me, she says quietly.

Dido closes her eyes. — Ella. It all came back.

— I did wonder.

– Did you? That was clever. Or sensitive. Or something.

She opens her eyes. They smile at one another.

– What a good friend.

Georgia's eyes fill with tears. – What a good friend you've been to me.

– We all are. We all were. Oh dear. How sad life is.

Footsteps along the landing. Kate puts her head round the door. Georgia rises.

– You must sleep.

– Perhaps.

When they both have kissed her, and left her, she lies in the gentle shady light, and wonders. Why now, why today, should that long-lost baby girl, that darling, cherished little daughter, come back to haunt her?

After a while, she thinks she understands. Because, she thinks, today, just then, I was as vulnerable as she was. I'm so fit, I'm so strong, I'm so busy: I might have wept for Ella in the past, but I was still outside it all, in a way: I didn't know, deep down, what it really must have felt like for her – I didn't know, in my own body, what it was to be weak, to be trembling, to be on the very brink . . .

Now, somehow, I do. As Henry must have done.

Drifting up through the open window, on this late August afternoon, come sweet reassuring sounds of life: the drone of a plane in the summer sky; the putter of a motorboat, out on the lake; someone, out in the garden, setting down a tray. How precious is each and every one.

At last she falls asleep.

When she wakes, the room is full of dusk. Jeffrey is beside her. She looks at him, puts out her hand. He takes it, enfolds it in both of his. This feels as everything between them used to feel: known, safe, certain.

– How are you?

– OK. Better, thanks.

Even in this half-light she can see how pale he is, how drawn.

– What's going on? With everyone?

He leans over, kisses her, settles down.

– Everyone's fine. Georgia and Chloe have gone: they sent you all their love. Georgia will phone tomorrow.

She frowns. – I hope they didn't feel driven away.

– Not at all. Chloe has to get back to work, remember. They just didn't want to disturb you.

– And everyone else?

– They're fine. Kate's getting supper, Leo's about to bath the children, I think.

– Nick and Paula?

– She's gone for a walk.

– It's dark.

– I expect she'll be back soon. Nick says he'll come up later, if you feel up to people.

– I always feel up to Nick.

She moves on the pillows. She needs a pee, but it'll have to wait: she's not going to let this moment pass.

– What about you, my darling?

– I'm fine.

– No, you're not. Jeffrey? What's troubling you?

Silence.

– Jeffrey? Please tell me. Something's going on, isn't it? Tell me. Tell me.

Gently he releases her hand. He takes off his glasses, rubs his face. And now she wonders: do I want to know?

He says slowly: – You're not well. I really don't want to burden you now. Let's wait until we get home. Get you looked at properly, see what's what. It's really nothing serious.

– I don't believe you.

He doesn't answer.

Dusk is deepening into darkness.

– Shall I put the lamp on?

– No. He moves her hand from the switch.

– Tell me.

Sounds on the stairs: Leo and the children: bathtime. She can hear him shushing them, then shutting the bathroom door. Water begins to pour, another warm, reassuring domestic sound: someone is running a bath; everything's all right.

– Jeffrey.

He gets up, goes to the door and shuts it, comes slowly back. She has loved him all her life: his height, his walk, his cleverness and kindness, everything they've shared. Even the death of a baby. They survived it, even if today has shown her: not entirely. Now—

He sits down heavily, takes the deepest breath she's ever heard.

– I'm up on a charge of sexual harassment.

– What? She hears his voice, her own voice, as if in an echo chamber. – What?

He says it again. It's one of his students. A second-year. The date has been fixed for a disciplinary hearing. She's threatened to go to the papers.

Dido's mind is whirling.

– And is there . . . there can't be . . . is there – Jeffrey? Of course there's nothing in it—

He gets up again, as slowly as a much much older man, goes to the window, looks out through the gap in the curtains at the darkened sky.

– I wish I could tell you that.

184

Part Three

15

Meanwhile, down in deepest Sussex.

Maud wakes to a violent banging on the front door.

– Kep?

He's already beside her, ears up, nose thrust into her outstretched hand. She heaves herself out of bed. What time is it? What day? The clock, in need of a new battery, has shown 12.15 for some weeks. Its second hand ticks repeatedly, but is unable to make progress. Maud and Kep make their way to the window. It's morning: this much is clear. The hammering downstairs has given way to loud enquiry.

– Hello? Are you there, dear?

Maud, in her nightgown (best left undescribed) flings back the curtains, flings open the window, and looks out. Kep joins her. You can picture what they might look like, from below.

– Who's there? barks Maud.

The person beneath the window steps back, looks up, steps back further.

– Oh, you *are* there, dear. I'd almost given up!

A small neat car is parked in the lane. The woman shading her face with one hand as the morning sun beats down, is also small and neat. She's wearing a sensible summer dress, white cardigan and flat white shoes. She carries, in her other hand, a briefcase.

– What are you doing on my land?

– Social Services, dear. Joan Starkey.

Maud slams the window to.

– Just come for a little chat!

Maud draws the curtains, and settles down. One or two spiders hurry away. Kep yawns, stretches out on the dusty floor, and waits. Maud puts her arm around him, and does the same. At length, the letterbox bangs, footsteps go out to the gate and the small neat car drives away. But for the distant bleating of sheep, and a passing magpie, all is quiet.

In these days of budget constraints, cuts, redundancies and overstretched staffing resources, you might think it extraordinary that anyone has the time to drive out from a busy office just to check up on Maud. But these are also the days of performance-related targets and accountability. The kindly passing motorist who a few weeks ago saved the house, and perhaps Maud and Kep, from conflagration, did not stop there. He phoned Social Services. So did the Fire Brigade. Maud, for the Outreach Team, became a target, and quite right too. No one likes to think of vulnerable elderly people living alone, and dying alone, without anyone taking a blind bit of notice. You can see the headlines now. Maud, slipping into dementia, seeing no one for weeks on end, with (apparently) no family to call on, is unquestionably At Risk. Besides, it's a beautiful day, and a nice journey into the countryside. Joan Starkey, drowning in paperwork, has been only too glad to pop an Elderly Persons Care Pack into her briefcase and set forth.

The trouble is, of course, that Maud will have none of it.

What is to be done in such situations? Georgia, recently returned from the Lakes and (as it happens) setting out to visit Maud this very day, will have many occasions on which to ask this question.

* * *

For the first time in a long while, Georgia's return to her house, after the long journey down from Cumbria, has given her undiluted pleasure. Chloe was dropped at the tube and seen, in Georgia's rearview mirror, talking animatedly on her mobile within seconds of her cheery wave goodbye. Their journey down had been companionable, not to say close: anxiety about Dido opened up a long conversation about the past, such as neither could have had with anyone else: the old Oxford days (all that falling in love), the decades of friendship, Chloe's childhood affection for Dido and all the family, reminiscences about shared hols. They speculate about Jeffrey's tactless questioning of Georgia. (You were amazing, Mum, I've never seen you like that.) About poor Dido's health, about Kate and Leo (yes, a bit too good to be true, though terribly nice, of course. Especially Leo.) About Nick and Paula (are they really happy? What's her problem?)

Time flew by. It was late when they arrived in London, but Chloe insisted on going back to her flat, rather than coming home to stay the night. Work the next day, a shoot in the centre of town. All that. Georgia, watching her daughter stand chatting away outside Hendon station, suspected that she wasn't going back to Charlotte Street at all (and she was right). It was almost midnight: how could she not worry about Chloe's safety on the journey, not to mention her future happiness?

Someone was hooting behind her: she drove on through the traffic, reminding herself that Chloe was thirty-one and must be allowed to live her life as she chose (an idea peculiar to the West). Georgia would (please God) be around for quite a while yet to pick up the pieces if necessary. Meanwhile, her thoughts returned to Dido, whom she would phone tomorrow.

The house, when she reached it at last, was lit by the timeswitch in the hall and by one upstairs. The street was empty, and Georgia, stiff as she was from all that driving, could not help but walk quickly up to her front door, studiedly not looking over her shoulder. Women alone. Women returning alone to empty houses. Strong and independent as you may be, and Georgia has been so all her life, there will always be that shiver of anxiety.

But no one was lurking behind a hedge, or in a darkened doorway, and no one, in her absence, had broken in. The cats came sleepily out to greet her as she dropped her bag, and after affectionate greetings she took herself upstairs to a long, lavender-scented and most refreshing bath, and thence to a long deep sleep.

There is, of course, a great distinction between loneliness and solitude, and it is the pleasures of solitude (not a few) that Georgia, next morning, finds herself at last enjoying. In an ideal world (i.e., the past) she would have been up to the Lakes with Henry, returned with him, slept by his side. Or she would have gone up there alone and returned to tell him all about it. Since neither of these scenarios is any longer possible, it is, frankly, something of a relief, after all this Family Life, to sit quietly in the garden over a late breakfast, opening her post and looking at the headlines, with no one else's grandchildren, dear as they are, to race about or ask for things; no intra-couple tensions to disturb the air; no old friend (fond of him though she has been for years) to drink too much and tell her how to run her life. There is no daughter in floods of tears, no need to help feed the five thousand.

In sum, if she cannot have Henry (and she wants no one else) then she wants, today, nothing but what she has: peace and quiet.

The only thing which disturbs this tranquillity is her anxiety about Dido. Even this, after a long sleep, and at this distance, recedes a little. Dido has her family about her, and very strong and reliable they are too. Later, she will phone Jeffrey on his mobile and see how things are. For now, there is nothing she can do.

So a quiet morning passes. Things are snipped, dead-headed, watered. *The World at One* goes by. It's all perfectly pleasant. But listening and half listening to terrible events in Baghdad and Gaza;

hearing of paedophiles, vigilantes, ASBOs and another set of astonishing A-level results, Georgia feels restlessness begin to stir. It's not so very long since she was a part of the swim: is she to sit and listen for the rest of her days?

Taking her tray indoors, a tiny part of her mind on *Round Britain Quiz*, she thinks again of Jeffrey's insistent questioning. Insensitive, yes, but her furious reaction was because he'd touched a nerve. So had Chloe, in the B & B: *Time you got back to work, Mum.*

The questions on *Round Britain Quiz* are impossible. Chloe wouldn't give them the time of day. She turns it down, rings Jeffrey's mobile. It's switched off. But reception is never good in the Lakes, and they'll all be back in York by the end of tomorrow. She rings the house there, leaves a message on the answerphone.

– Just to welcome you back, and thank you all for everything. Do ring me, Dido, when you feel up to it. I'm going down to Sussex on Thursday, otherwise pretty much here.

And on Thursday, still with no word from York and by now a little anxious, Georgia gets in the car and goes down at last to visit Maud.

She has telephoned to confirm arrangements, and had no answer. This was not unexpected. But as she turns off the main road and begins the familiar progress along B roads and through pretty villages, she does wonder what kind of reception she'll have. Will Maud have any recollection of this date? Or even of her letter?

The pretty villages offer trim verges, well-kept gardens. Apple trees are fruiting up nicely, lawns bear climbing frames, Wendy houses, garden furniture. (White plastic. Even here.) It's midday, and mummies in jeans are waiting outside a village hall for the end of Playgroup. A church bell strikes; amazingly, a cuckoo calls. How very pleasant it all is, and should they perhaps have moved down here, given Chloe a gentler, country childhood, and kept an eye on Maud?

Too late now. And all that commuting. And the Tory party, dug right in. Forget it.

Georgia drives on, turns off the B road, follows nicely painted signs down winding lanes. The hedges grow tall, the lanes grow deeper, there are no more signs. She turns again. Now she can see the house.

Crikey.

As often in the past, Georgia is reminded at this point of *The Darling Buds of May*, a book she adored in childhood. But where the Larkin wilderness of nettles, hens, bluebells, rusting cars and dead machinery was animated by children (lots) and presided over by laughing Pop in shirtsleeves and the vast, dreamy, sexy presence of Ma in a flowery dress, Green Lane Farm, even in late summer, is an empty wreck. It sounds like something out of a Ladybird book; it does not look like one. It looks like Constable reworked by Hirst.

Georgia, pulling up at the broken gate, beholds the sinking roof, the weed-choked drive, the towering nettles. Hens squawk. Paint blisters off the front door, the windows are firmly closed and drawn with drooping curtains. All this she has seen before, except those deadly windows. But today there is something else: does she imagine it, or has there been a fire? The front-door frame is not just peeling but charred. Those downstairs curtains droop not just from missing hooks, but because – yes – they are scorched, in burned tatters.

Oh my God.

Georgia is suddenly sick with guilt and fear. All this time, while she's been in lovely France. All this time, chatting away to Dido up in the Lakes, laughing about Maud over lunch in the garden, thinking (endlessly) about herself and her own sorrow. Paula was right: it's not a laughing matter. Anything could have happened here, and it looks as if it has. Could Maud, inside that shut-up, rotting house, have died alone? Burned to death, even?

She's shaking. She gets out of the car, walks to the gate. It's almost off its hinges; carefully, she lifts it open, over sun-baked ruts of mud. At once, wild barking comes from behind the house: in moments, Kep is racing round, and down the drive towards her.

– It's all right, Kep, it's me, it's me!

Behind him strides a gaunt old figure in nightdress and Wellingtons, brandishing a stick.

– Maud!

– Who the hell are you?

– Maud, it's me! Georgia!

– Get off my land!

Georgia, after a long long time, is admitted to the house. Kep, within moments, has become the dear old dog he always has been. (Henry had loved him.) Once he gets to know you (unless you're a particular postman) it's all wag wag, lick lick, lie down to be scratched. Then he forgets all about you, wanders off for a hopeful look in his dish, sinks down and goes back to sleep. Maud is a different matter. It takes for ever for Georgia to persuade her that she's family, that they've known one another for thirty-five years, that she's Henry's wife, remember? Henry's widow, rather.

– Henry's *died*?

They go through all that again. Finally, she's allowed in through the back door, propped open with a stone. She sits down at the kitchen table, looks about her.

My God.

What was once a fearful muddle has become a hideous tip. Flies buzz about unwashed saucepans and open cans of dog food; wasps drown, hundreds of them, in a half-filled jar of sugar water on the sill. The sink is piled high, and stinking. Something else stinks too, of death and long decay.

SUE GEE

– Would you mind if I opened the window?

She leans across the sink and retches. The window has clearly been shut all summer: the sill swarms with ants, feeding on long-dead daddy-longlegs and much else. Silverfish flicker over the heaped-up draining board. Georgia pushes hard: there, it's open: she breathes in a lungful of air. Rich though it is with the scents of manure and silage, country smells of which she has always been fond, she is also reassailed by the rotting matter in the sink, and backs quickly away, her hand clapped to her mouth.

– Excuse me—

She runs from the kitchen, out to the lavatory in the hall. Here she is very sick, not least because of the state of things she finds. She washes her face, drinks down cold water, wondering, all at once, if it's safe: is Maud on the mains, or does her water come from some fearful tank in the yard, filled with dead birds; from a spring somewhere, gushing dumped chemicals through Maud's old lead pipes?

Too late now. It tastes OK. She comes out, beholds the hall. Yes, there has been a fire. Put out with a hell of a lot of water. It's damp underfoot, damp on the burned-black walls. It smells as only fire and water damage can make a place smell, when no one has lifted a finger to air and restore it all. The darkness, the airlessness, the dank stink of burned wet wood and plaster – all are overpowering. Georgia stands there, sick and empty, and tries to take it all in.

No one should be living here.

What is to be done?

Something is lying on the mat, on top of a heap of special offers. She goes to fetch it.

Ah.

Elderly Persons Care Pack in hand, she returns to the filthy kitchen.

– Do I know you? asks Maud, from her place at the heaped-up table.

194

Kep is sunning himself at the open door. He, of course, doesn't mind any of this, though if Maud goes on feeding him out of those flyblown cans he won't be around long anyway. (Might the RSPCA be useful now?)

Georgia moves a dozen things off a chair and sits down again. She takes a long deep breath.

How to begin?

A barmy and fruitless conversation ensues. Guilty though she feels, Georgia is not yet generous enough to invite Maud to stay with her in London. (Kep. The cats. This is one of the things she tells herself. He could go into kennels, of course, but even so, the thought of Maud in London is simply insupportable.) What, then?

– Maud.

– Have we met?

– Maud. I wonder if we could talk about . . . How are you managing these days?

– Very well indeed, thank you.

– Do you think you could do with a little help?

– Help? I have never needed help. She swipes at a fly. – If you need any further information, do talk to my cousin. Henry Hannaway. I believe he's in the Foreign Office. He manages all my affairs.

Oh, Christmas.

She tries again.

– Maud. Since Henry's not – not here at the moment, do you think you could talk to me?

– Certainly. What shall we talk about?

Maud, it is apparent, is subject to mood swings. This has always been the case, but it's now much more pronounced. One minute she's a roaring battleaxe, the next a pussycat. Sitting here now, in her hellhole of a kitchen, Georgia might, on the face of it, be taking tea in the drawing room with any sweet old girl. She still can get nowhere. Maud is very well, and very happy, thank you. How kind of you to ask. She needs no cleaner, cook, meals on wheels, or social worker. Moving anywhere at all is out of the question. There is nowhere else on earth that she would rather be.

Good God, she's singing. Strains of *My Fair Lady* waft down the years through Georgia's childhood and Maud's young days. Salad days, even.

– And where do you live, my dear?

– In London. I was married to Henry, remember.

– What happened? Did you divorce?

– No. He——

– Family break-up. So dreadfully sad. London, did you say? That explains it. Londoners always find the country difficult. They don't understand it, never have. Those of us who live here are up against it now. Listen to Us. We must Fight the Ban. If you knew what vicious creatures foxes are . . .

And she's off, broadcasting to the nation.

Georgia, after a while, gives up. She finds, after considerable searching, an apron and a pair of rubber gloves. There is a vast bottle of lurid washing-up liquid behind the dog biscuits. Torn black bin bags lie about in the woodshed. With windows open and the sun streaming in happily, she sets about it all. Maud has moved on to *West Side Story*. She's just met a girl called Maria.

From the window over the sink, Georgia can see the sheep, sleeping peacefully beneath the apple trees. Someone should be shearing them, should they not? Not today.

She goes into the village and returns with three kinds of disinfectant and a basket of provisions. She and Maud drink tea and eat half a fruit cake. By the end of it all she feels completely batty.

Then she goes home, with half a dozen new-laid eggs and the Elderly Persons Care Pack.

Ha bloody ha.

* * *

– Darling, I really need your help. We're all she's got.

Chloe listens (or so it seems). It all sounds really awful. Gosh. Poor Mum. Poor old Maud. Of course she'll help at some point, but the thing is that just at the moment, she's really, really busy. Sorry, Mum. Speak soon.

– Dido?

Dido sounds quite dreadful. She doesn't want to talk. All offers of help, and all concern, are implacably rebuffed. She'll be in touch soon, but she really can't talk about it now.

– How are *you*, Georgia?

– Fine, says Georgia. – Absolutely fine.

16

At last September comes. London, at the fag end of the summer holidays, has become a dustbowl of heat and boredom, but now (thank God) the playground gates are unlocked once more, and everyone's Back to School. New Woolworths lunch boxes, new trainers, new Miss. Ellie, whom Chloe has still not met, has gone up to Year 3, with her best friend Tara. And with the start of the new term comes the start-up once more of all those extra-curricular activities which so define the north London child: the After-School Club, music lessons, Kumon maths, dance class. Yes! Madeleine, Ellie's mother, has booked her into a lovely little class on Saturday mornings, at Lauderdale House on Highgate Hill. The arrangement is that she will drop her off there, and Jez will pick her up, taking her home for the weekend.

There are lots of children whose lives are like this now. And it's now that Chloe, sick with nerves and anticipation, is about to meet Ellie at last.

It's a fresh September morning, coming up for twelve. Chloe has spent the night with Jez, and the morning in cleaning and shopping. She has discovered that Ellie, when staying, sleeps in Jez's bed, while Jez stretches out on the sofa. Clean sheets, clean towel, and Chloe won't be staying tonight, then. Healthy cereal, organic milk, natural fruit-and-grain bars (what do unnatural ones look like?), an organic chicken, likewise fruit and veg and little pots of yoghurt.

– Could I get her something special, just from me?

– Sure. Why don't you get the juice?

Is juice special? She buys two small cartons of cranberry and apple, has one of them in her bag, now, nicely chilled, all ready for when Ellie comes out tired and thirsty.

Imagine doing this every Saturday! Imagine doing this for your own child!

Since we last saw Chloe, she has been to Matt and Sara's wedding. Amazingly, Jez came too: this gave her the most fantastic surge of adrenalin and hope. They stood together, guests of the bride in the Church of St James's, on Piccadilly, as Sara came floating down the aisle on the arm of her (very rich) stepfather. She wore a cream dress in which it was a certainty she was pregnant, but which looked dreamy and romantic enough for her mother not to mind.

It's ages and ages since Chloe (not to mention Matt and Sara) has stood in a church, but this is St James's, liberal to the last brass rubbing: they'll marry anyone, and often do. And a church wedding is so special, somehow: Chloe is in floods throughout.

At the Ritz reception (he is *very* rich) she introduces Jez to Matt and Sara's parents. She wants to be able to say: This is my fiancé (in the post-feminist twenty-first century all this stuff has come back, in Chloe's circle, if not Paula's) but of course she can't. Nor is he her partner. Not exactly. So:

– Hi. What a lovely wedding. This is Jez.

– Jez. How do you do?

– I'm good, thanks.

Hands are shaken, brief conversation made. The eyes of another generation flicker over him, but this is their own children's day, and they don't care, let's face it, who their children's friends are sleeping with. Soon, Chloe and Jez are back with their own crowd, who don't care either. There's a lot of champagne (a *lot*); they fall into a taxi to Charlotte Street (Edmund is out, rehearsing for the political thing) and go to bed. It's the best ever. Gosh, it's good.

– Jez?

– Mmm?

It's afterwards, he's falling asleep.

– Jez. (She's still drunk.) – Do you think – do you think we'll ever . . . But she can't bring herself to say it. Instead: – Will I ever meet Ellie? I'd so love to meet her.

– Mmm. Yeah. One day.

And now that day has come.

Leaves have fallen on to the flagstones inside the tall iron gates. The strains of a sad and then a happy piano come floating out from the dance class, with the sound of small feet jumping about. Chloe and Jez are wandering around in the hall, with other parents. (Do she and Jez look like proper parents? Do they?) They look at the heaps of leaflets: for yoga, poetry readings, creative writing classes, watercolour classes, recitals, private views. You could spend half your life here if you wanted. And they do Sunday lunch. The walls are hung with the work of a local artist: Recent Prints. Jez and Chloe give them the once-over. They're not holding hands, and they're not talking much: she senses he's as nervous as she is.

– Jez?

– Mmm?

– Nothing.

The clock on the wall shows a minute to twelve; the children come out at twelve and what with the shopping and cleaning—

– Come on! She'll kill me if I'm late.

Chloe knows he's not talking about Ellie. How would Madeleine know if they were late? Is she lurking outside, checking up? Or does she, on Sunday night, ask Ellie for a report?

The piano thunders out a triumphant final chord. Then the front doors are pushed open and in come two just-on-time parents.

Jeans, T-shirts, baby draped in a sling across his father. Jez glances towards them, then (rather quickly?) away. But:

– Hi, Jez! Haven't seen you for ages.

– Oh, hi. Hi, how are you? Hey, who's this? He smiles down at the baby.

– This is Fred.

Everyone's tired and smiling. Chloe hovers.

– Nice to see you again. How's Ellie?

– She's good. I'm just picking her up.

Chloe hovers a bit more.

– Is Madeleine here?

– Er, no. No, she's not.

Then Fred starts whimpering and New Man Dad starts rocking and patting. They move towards the garden. Is Matt really going to do all this, come November? Did Jez?

– Who are they?

– Oh, we knew them in the NCT group.

Chloe tries to imagine it all. Jez and Madeleine in the Tufnell Park NCT Group, all those years ago. How can he have had this whole other life without her? And now there's another baby. Fred. After a long long gap. Does Jez want another one, too? Does Ellie?

The door to the dance class opens. Out pour all the children. Who cares if he hasn't introduced her to the NCT? The only intro that matters today is amongst this throng of eight-year-olds in leotards and little skirts, carrying cool little rucksacks.

Gosh, how sweet. One of them looks a bit like Izzy. Well, she'd managed fine with Izzy, hadn't she? And Sam. Of course, she's known them all their lives, they're like family, but she's good with kids, isn't she? She'll be fine . . .

– Hi, Dad.

– Ellie!

He picks her up, he hugs her, swings her round. Chloe's heart goes into freefall.

– How was it?

– Good. I'm hungry.

– Me, too.

He puts Ellie down, looks round.

She's here, right here.

– This is Ellie, he tells her. – Ellie, this is my friend Chloe.

– Oh. Hi.

Ellie is older than her school photo. Well, she would be, wouldn't she? She's tallish, skinnyish, with a new-term haircut, very nice. She's self-possessed, she's London: only a couple of years older than Izzy, but on a different planet. Everything happens here, and not so much Little Grey Rabbit: it's all *Time Out*, KidsStuff, sleepovers, play schemes, city farms and single parents. Not that there aren't single parents in York, of course, but still: London children have a knowingness, an air. They're quickly streetwise – a term used by parents to indicate that they (children and parents) are pretty cool, but which masks a hideous anxiety.

Anyway, Ellie hasn't quite got to that stage yet, even if you sense that it won't be long. She holds her father's hand as they go out into the garden; she thanks Chloe for the cranberry and apple juice and Jez for the natural fruit-and-nut bar. Jez spreads his jacket on the grass, and they all sit down, like a family.

Now what?

A squirrel shows an interest in organic fruit and nut. Ducks sail over the lake, as ducks do; the vast bust of Karl Marx looms distantly beyond the trees. No one in the assembled party knows a very great deal about him, though Chloe has heard of him. Definitely. As they all get up and go for a little wander, she does what she does best.

– I love your rucksack.

– Thanks. It's old.

– We'll have to get you a new one, says Jez.

SUE GEE

Will we?

– I like old things. Where did you get your leotard?

– Mummy got it for me.

Oh. Right.

This isn't a brilliant scenario. It's one thing to do dressing up and nail parlours with a child whom (a) you've known intermittently since she was born, and who (b) has two perfect parents to return to. Your role, in this situation, is clear: grown-up playmate. Full stop. So everything's easy and fun. It's quite different trying to get to know someone (and make them like you) when there's a Whole Agenda waiting in the wings. Ellie has a mummy, and she doesn't need another. She has a daddy whose hand she's holding all the time. Like, all the time. Already, Chloe feels like a spare part, and they've only been going twenty minutes.

The doors of the restaurant are open to the terrace. Families are settling down inside: there's an inviting clatter and smells of this and that.

– I'm hungry.

– Let's have lunch.

In they all go. Gosh, it's packed. Jez should have booked a table: never mind, he'll know for next time. For now, they just about squeeze on to one where two old dears in specs and print frocks are tucking into pud. Their sunhats are on the spare seats, but no, they're not saving them for anyone: they move the hats on to their laps.

– Thanks.

They all sit down.

– You've been to dance class, one of them tells Ellie.

Ellie nods.

– And you? asks Chloe politely.

– Watercolours. Such a good tutor: we've been coming for years.

They beam at her, at Jez, at all of them, turning them into a family. With this, Chloe, studying the blackboard menu, allows

204

herself to dream. The place fills up some more; they talk about watercolours, waiting for a waitress. At last she comes. They order healthy vegetarian things, and Chloe asks for bread. She's starving.

Print frocks finish their pud and get up to go. They all agree they might meet again next week. Now there are two empty seats, and guess who comes to take them.

– Hi! We meet again!

– Oh, hi.

Fred is taken out of his sling and breastfed (by his mother). His sister, Rachel, who has of course also been to dance class, and who has known Ellie ever since the NCT Group all gave birth eight years ago (not all quite as naturally as they had imagined) perches on her father's lap. She's rather big to do this, but the place is heaving now. Everyone moves about a bit, squeezes up a bit. Ellie and Rachel aren't, it seems, mad about each other. Different schools. Now, they're supposed to be dance class friends. Ellie's eyes are glued to suckling Fred. Likewise Chloe's. Food (finally) arrives. Fred's mother changes breasts, and smiles enquiringly at Chloe.

– Tamsin.

– Chloe.

– Sorry, says Jez, picking up knife and fork. – I should've introduced you all.

You don't say.

– This is Chloe Hannaway.

– Hi. Hi, Chloe, I'm Steve.

An understanding New Man smile comes right across the table, just for her. Yuk.

– Chloe and I work together, says Jez, tucking in.

Oh, yeah?

For a moment, shaking tomato sauce over her vegetarian lasagne (to hell with it) Chloe is tempted to do a Georgia. Like, shock everyone. Get in touch with her inner viciousness. Tell them what she and Jez do when they're not working together. As if it isn't blindingly obvious. But there are children present. That's why, after all, she's here, after all this time.

What's got into her?

It was supposed to be so nice and cosy, and actually, it's like, really really *difficult*.

— It was all a bit *difficult*, she tells Edmund that evening. He's back from rehearsal, they're having supper, late. It's quite like old times: windows open on to the street, people out at tables on the pavement, crowded Saturday night chitchat down there, and an omelette and a glass of wine up here. Something nice on the telly to look forward to?

Edmund looks knackered.

— I haven't seen you in a hundred years, he tells her.

— I haven't seen *you*. How's it going?

— Good. It's going to be good.

— What's it about, again?

— If I've told you once—

— I know, I'm hopeless, sorry. Tell me again.

It's about 9/11. She forces herself to concentrate. It's about someone who doesn't believe that what happened happened quite as it seemed. Not by a long way. It's about someone dismissed as a conspiracy theorist, but who's asking important questions. Like: how come those two towers just collapsed on themselves like that, when hit right at the top? What do you mean? They crumpled, just crumpled, from within. Remember? What could cause that? You tell me. Not by being hit half a mile up at the top. So? So someone had planted explosives. Before the planes hit. Long before. Are you serious? Who? Who would do that? You tell me. Come and see the play.

— It's like 7/7, says Chloe, finally taking an interest. She reaches for an apple. — Now I come to think of it. How did the police find those credit cards, just like that? Amidst all that wreckage. I mean, if the carriage was such an inferno, how could plastic credit cards survive it, all neat and intact and just ready to find? And just happen to belong to the bombers. Were everyone else's credit cards lying about in the flames? Unmelted?

– Good question. You're waking up.

– Shut up.

Edmund makes herbal tea. He tells her that this is the first time she's talked about anything except men and clothes for as long as he can remember.

– Shut up. You don't know what it's like.

He looks at her.

– Not like this, you don't. It's all so *difficult*.

Down in her bag, her phone is ringing. She grabs it. That'll be him. It's voicemail: she listens.

– Chloe? Chloe, are you there?

Georgia's marvellous Oxford tones float through the evening air.

– No, says Chloe. – I'm not. She switches it off.

– Naughty.

– She'll be wanting me to do something about Maud. Remember her? I can't. I really can't. She begins to feel tearful. – Oh, Ed.

– Tell me what happened next. After the breastfeeding.

– If I ever have a baby, says Chloe (oh, please, please let me have a baby) – I will never, ever do that.

– What?

– Breastfeed in public.

– Of course you will.

– Well, I might. But not over *lunch*.

– You sound like your mother.

Chloe puts her head in her hands.

– She makes me feel so *guilty*.

– Family ties, says Edmund. – Responsibilities. Poor old Maud.

– Are you going to come down to Sussex and help me?

– Probably not. I'm in a play, remember? Go on. What happened after lunch?

– It just all went a bit pear-shaped.

They all say goodbye: breastfeeding Tamsin, New Man Steve, and Rachel.

– Bye, Ellie. See you next week.

Chloe can almost hear Ellie thinking: not if I see you first. She puts a colluding hand on her shoulder. Ellie moves away. Outside, she takes Jez's hand again. Jez has two hands, but the other does not take Chloe's. Nor does his arm go round her shoulders. She shouldn't mind: he's explained it all, in bed last night.

– You mustn't get upset if I'm not all over you tomorrow. First time, and all that. We'd better take it slowly, right?

– Sure. Of course.

And he's right: what child would want to see her father pawing someone who's not her mother? No matter how many times it's all been explained (has it?) that though her mother and father both love her very very much and always will, they just need to be apart from each other for a while, and they both have other friends, whom Ellie will meet one day . . .

It sucks. In Ellie's eyes, it must do.

So Chloe, who is of course an adult (in theory, anyway) completely understands that Jez doesn't touch her once, not even secretly, nor exchange a loving smile, nor give her a special look or anything.

Not once.

Off they all go to Hampstead Heath. That is, Parliament Hill. They're going to fly the kite which Jez has bought from the kite shop in Kentish Town and is now going to give to Ellie as a surprise. No, it's not her birthday. Does he often buy her things – quite big things, like kites? Sometimes, yeah. Is that a problem? This was last night, in bed. She backed off, sharpish.

So they're going to fly the kite and then have tea in the garden at Kenwood House.

    – Well, that sounds all right. What could go wrong with that?
    – Nothing. Well, not exactly.

Parliament Hill is thick with families, flying their kites on a Saturday afternoon. The September sky, filled with the last of the summer light before the clocks go back (or is it forward?) is full of things which don't look like kites at all: great black corrugated things which tug and pull like horses out of hell; spindly pale creatures with endless streamers; *Lord of the Rings* kites (don't ask); bird kites (now those are nice); box kites; bat (and Batman) kites; kites like polytunnels, multi-coloured and enormous, which make a horrid whistling sound—

They swoop, they dive, they fall to earth and are flung back up again, they tangle with one another (Sorry! Sorry about that! Don't cry, Zak, we'll fix it, OK? How many new men are there on Parliament Hill on a Saturday afternoon?) and they tangle in the trees. (I want it to come dow-own! Well, it won't. There's an unreconstructed mother or two out here.)

Now. When Chloe was little, she used to come here, with her father. There isn't a child in north London who hasn't been brought here to tug on the end of a string from time to time. Often (as in her case) they're brought by one parent while the other draws breath at the end of the endless working week. Thus Georgia, taking her time in Waitrose, or (thank you, Henry) reading her book in the garden, while Henry and Chloe stand on the very top of the hill and watch the sweet bobbing of their kite amongst the clouds.

Gosh, it was different, then. Chloe feels like her mother, contemplating the past from some lofty height while today's children race up and down with these hideous things.

She'd had a proper kite: a dear little thing in a proper kite shape, red and blue with a lovely long tail tied with bows. So pretty. And it *bobbed*, as kites are meant to do. It was a proper picture-book thing. A classic. (The blood of both Chloe's parents stirs in her veins as she recalls it.)

Where is it now? Please say Georgia's kept it. Dido would never get rid of anything her children cherished.

Jez is kneeling down on the grass, pulling his present out of his Ralph Lauren manbag. It's one of those kits where you have to slide in the bits of frame yourself, that's how he's managed to hide it.

– Bet you can't guess what this is.

– Bet I can!

Ellie is hopping up and down; she can hardly wait. And if presents can make up for things at home being less than perfect, here, when she opens it, and when she and Jez have together made it, is a very happy little girl.

Chloe watches. Chloe, nimble to her fingertips, a whiz with needle and thread, the most useful person in the world on any shoot (Necklace need threading? Give it to me. Broken strap on a strappy sandal? I'll do it) sits on the grass and watches. She wouldn't be able to make head nor tail of the diagram, but she wouldn't need to: like Jez, she can assemble anything. Something else they have in common: what a good pair they'd make; she knows it. But today: today is quality time for Ellie, and she doesn't interfere, just makes encouraging noises.

But when Ellie's own candy-striped kite goes up at last – a very nice one, it must be said, not sweet and old-fashioned like hers, but dinky – what a lump forms in her throat. It's not just because father and daughter are so close that she can't see an inch of room for her; not just because she longs, oh so longs, for a child of her own. It's because she sees another father and daughter, up here twenty-five years ago, getting on so well together, tugging the string of the kite together, chatting away. No one has yet found out that she's dyslexic. Nobody knows that Henry is going to die. The clouds are full and high and sunlit, her father is beside her, everything's easy, happy and good.

She's up off the grass now, standing up and shading her eyes against the sun. It's easy to hide the tears which come streaming down.

At least she hopes it is.

Then they go and have tea. Kenwood House (quite a long walk) is like a painting, creamy white against the sinking sun, and the garden is bathed in honeyed light. The grass on the approach is parched and pale; the roses are tired but still doing their stuff, and the lavender likewise. The hordes are here: there's a queue for the loos, a queue for the ice cream, the teas. Flies swim madly for shore in the metal dog bowl; spaniels and afghans lie panting in the shade.

Ellie is squirming a bit.

– I need the loo.

– So do I, says Chloe.

Now this is something they can do together. Even Jez can't follow his daughter into the Ladies. So what usually happens? He waits outside, he tells her, right outside. Sometimes emerging women report him to the police. They laugh for the first time all day. Then he goes to queue in the restaurant; they'll try to get a garden table when they come out.

Chloe and Ellie stand and wait. Doors bang, water pours, air dryers blast through everything. North London women come and go; Ellie's beginning to hop.

– I'm getting desperate.

– Oh dear.

This feels like their first proper exchange all day.

Chloe sees a kindly-looking soul at the head of the queue.

– Excuse me. I'm sorry, but would you mind . . . ?

She can't say My daughter, or My little girl. She can't say My boyfriend's/partner's/lover's daughter. Can she? So she nods towards Ellie, makes a gesture. The woman turns, sees Ellie, holding on.

– Your little girl? Sure, go ahead.

In goes Ellie, and, as someone else comes out, in goes Chloe beside her. They pee companionably.

– Better now? she asks, as they wave their wet hands about beneath the dryer. Ellie nods. They walk out into the sun together.

A dear little Westie is drinking from the dog bowl. He has a black button nose and cheerful air. Ellie stops to pat him. He gives her a lick.

– I wish *we* had a dog.

– You do live quite near the Heath, says Chloe carefully, as they go round to the garden.

– Mummy says we can't. She's too busy.

– Do you have a cat?

Ellie shakes her head. – She's allergic.

– What a shame. We have two cats at home. Abyssinians. Great big softies.

Ellie smiles. They crunch over the gravel, avoiding pushchairs, old people, more dogs. The garden, from where they scan it, looks absolutely packed.

– Over there? In that corner?

They make their way over the flagstones, and yes, there's a couple of places on a table with a sunshade. Lovely. An old boy in a Panama is saving a seat for his wife. He doesn't mind at all if they join them. They sink into sun-warmed chairs.

Ellie puts her head on the table. – I'm really tired.

– You walked such a long way. After all that dancing. Ah, here's Dad. Now, where's he going to sit?

Ellie looks up. – I'll sit on his lap.

– Or mine?

No answer.

Jez is bearing their orders, and something else. There's a pot of Earl Grey, pastries glazed with apricots and grapes, a tinkling glass of iced orange juice with slices of lime on the edge, and – oh, wow! – a knickerbocker glory. A really fantastic one, with a million layers, swirls, colours, mountains of whipped cream and – of course – a cherry on the top.

He sets all this down just as the old boy's wife arrives with tea for two. Everyone smiles and settles down. Everyone tucks in. Ellie, even on Jez's lap, can hardly reach the top of the knickerbocker glory, but tiredness is forgotten as she tries. The old pair talk companionably. Watching them, drinking her tea, Chloe thinks: this is how my parents should have been. Walking and reading and talking into old age together: they'd have done it very well.

Poor Mum. Poor Dad (especially poor, poor Dad).

– Chloe?

– Yup.

– You OK?

– Sure.

She turns to look at him; their eyes, at last, meet above his daughter's head. Jez gives her a melting smile: she melts.

Oh, if only, if only . . .

Surely they can make it happen . . .

Then Ellie, covered in pink and white, looks up. She sees the melting, grown-up (sexy) smiles. Jez sees she sees. He kisses her.

– OK?

Silence.

– Ellie? What's up?

– I just wish Mummy was here.

– Oh dear. And then?

– And then, Chloe tells Edmund, as sizzle and laughter rise from Charlotte Street – then nobody said anything and the old boy and his wife gave one another a look, and Jez said to Ellie that she'd be seeing Mum tomorrow, wouldn't she, and Ellie said she knew. But all the light went out of her. Everything sort of collapsed.

– Oh dear, says Edmund again.

He's rolling a joint. Chloe eyes it longingly. She wasn't going to smoke again, not ever, not now she was (ha) getting ready to have a baby, but frankly—

– So then? He's licking the papers.

– So then the moment sort of passed, and we finished tea. And then we walked back over the Heath to the station, and by then everyone was, like, shattered – it was all too ambitious, I think, anyway – and then Jez and Ellie got the train to Willesden, and I just came back here. In a cab. I couldn't walk another step. And now, now I feel, I feel just awful, really low.

– Here.

He's lit up, he's inhaling, he's passing it across.

Yes, yes, yes. To hell with it. Oh, that's better.

– Do you think I should phone him?

– No.

– I think I should. She'll be asleep. I just want to make up, have a normal conversation.

– No. Let the dust settle. Let's go and watch the telly.

He takes the joint, takes a drag or two, passes it back. He goes over to the sitting-room bit, and presses the remote. Some crap comes on; he changes channels. More crap.

Chloe sits alone at the kitchen table, smoking. It's almost ten. She pictures their evening together, Jez and Ellie, as she has done over and over again since they said their cool goodbyes. (– Thanks, Jez, it's been lovely. A kiss on the cheek. – Bye, Ellie. Not a backward glance.) They'll have curled up together on the train, she'll have fallen asleep, he'll have had to half-carry her home. When they get to his flat, he runs her a bath, with lots of bubbles;

he offers her something healthy from the fridge, but she's too tired, and full up with lunch, and syrupy knickerbocker stuff (does Madeleine let her eat things like that? Like hell she does). So he tucks her up, and reads to her in bed. *Harry Potter* has been put there, all ready. Everything's snug. Then he kisses her good night, and pulls the blind down, against the evening light.

– Night, sweetheart.

– Don't go. Stay till I'm asleep.

He stays, sitting (lying?) beside her, holding her hand. He's thinking: of what? Of Madeleine? Of Chloe? Is he waiting till Ellie's fast asleep before he phones her? Surely she must be asleep by now.

Laughter comes from across the room. Edmund is getting comfy.

– Stop being maudlin.

– It's all your fault, she tells him. – You were the one who said Jez and I were suited.

– Sorry.

– Sorry's not good enough.

– Come and watch Jonathan Ross. And bring that joint while you're at it.

Slowly she gets to her feet. Gosh. The last time she was as stoned as this was at her party. That's when Jez kissed her. That's when it all began—

She fumbles in her bag for the phone. Ed sees her. Don't, he says again, and she gives up. She weaves her way across the room, sinks to the sofa. In moments, she's out for the count.

Edmund must have covered her up on the sofa, bundled a pillow under her head. She wakes in the small hours, from a dreadful dream. She's running after Jez, but her legs won't do it properly; it's one of those dreams when your limbs feel like lead, but it's really really important you get where you're going—

– Jez! Wait!

He turns round, and she sees he's carrying Ellie. She's drooping in his arms, all limp and pale—

– Jez!

But he turns away, and goes on walking.

After this, she doesn't sleep a wink.

17

Meanwhile, in the groves of the academy.

This isn't funny.

The first thing is, they've lost the bloody test results. Georgia had told her this happens in London, and so it has in York.

– You can't be serious.

– I'm so terribly sorry.

The registrar is a woman in her thirties. She's not unlike Kate: clever, attractive, responsible. And, as Kate would be, embarrassed. Dido has waited (alone; she hasn't even told Jeffrey she's here) for something over an hour for her appointment. The waiting room is full of anxious people: you don't generally come to Neurology unless there's some ghastly reason. She's tried to read her book, tried to do calming meditation breathing, tried (failed, failed) to stop thinking every single minute about Jeffrey, and everything (everything?) he's told her. Now she's sitting in this cubbyhole, watching Dr Bailey dial the clinic clerk.

– I have Mrs Sullivan with me. Could you pop in for a minute?

In she pops, straight out of school and chewing on a piece of gum. Dido wants to smack her. (Oh, where has her lifetime of good manners, kindness and tolerance suddenly gone?) The clerk is dispatched with Dido's file and instructions.

– CT, Haematology, EEG. OK? Give them all a ring.

– OK.

Out she goes, and the door swings to.

– Now, while we're waiting . . . Dr Bailey looks at Dido kindly. Dido's thinking: did I really have all those tests? Could I really have blanked out all of that?

– I don't think I had an EEG, she says slowly. – I think I'd remember that.

– Did Mr Fisher not send you for one?

Dido looks at her. – You tell me. Then: – I suppose you can't, now she's gone off with the file. Oh God, I don't know. Isn't an EEG that thing when they wire you up? I'm certain I didn't have one of those.

– OK, says Dr Bailey again. – Well, let's just wait and see. Now tell me: how have you been?

Dido gives a hollow laugh. – How long have you got?

The registrar (*so* like Kate) sits back in her chair. She takes her seriously.

– I'm listening.

Dido closes her eyes. She hears herself say those very words, over and over again, throughout her working life: to hot and bothered, stressed-out children; likewise their parents. To a stream of distraught people in a counselling room. For decades she has leaned back in her chair and given of her best. *I'm listening. Just take your time . . .*

Now, Dr Bailey says quietly: – You were referred here because you were having blackouts, I think. Dizzy spells. Is that right? Have you had any more since we saw you? Any more problems with co-ordination? I think you said you were dropping things.

Listening, still with her eyes shut, Dido thinks: this sounds serious. All in a list, it sounds grim. I'd better face it. She swallows.

– Mrs Sullivan?

She hears herself say, in a high strained voice: – I haven't been brilliant, to tell you the truth.

Then, as dozens and dozens of her clients have told her, moving towards the heart of things at last: – It's not just . . . all this.

– Go on.

– I did have a couple of blackouts on holiday – well, several, I suppose, and one was really bad. I sort of . . . collapsed. I did collapse. And that seemed to churn up something so sad from the past . . . She swallows. – We lost a baby. Years and years ago. But – she waves at the air – it isn't that I'm thinking about it now. It's just that something happened. A bolt from the blue. Oh God.

She hears a box of tissues being slid across the desk. And dammit, dammit, damn it all, she's in tears all over again.

– I'm so sorry . . .

– Please. Dr Bailey is kindness itself. – There's nothing to be sorry about. Better out than in . . .

– Oh God. Oh God . . .

There's a tap at the door.

– Excuse me. Dr Bailey gets up, and goes out.

Before the door has closed behind her, Dido hears:

– No one can't find no results.

The consultation ends with Dido having managed to keep her home life to herself (and thus some measure of dignity) and Dr Bailey promising to telephone her at home the minute the papers turn up. Probably this evening: she's sure they've just been misplaced. And she's so sorry.

– You go home and rest.

Dido, puffy-eyed and drained, nods weakly. Out she goes, on to the Withington Road. While she's waiting for the bus, gazing at a poster of some young lout tipping back a beer, she remembers, all at once, a poster the Samaritans used to use.

DO YOU DREAD GOING HOME?

How could this ever, ever, have come to be true of her?

* * *

University teaching, of course, has not yet begun, but September is always crammed with admin and preparation. Everyone's still trying to finish the research which the summer at last (at *last*) gives them time to work on: the conference paper, the article, the chapter, the whole bloody book. Bang. Everyone's torn away from all this the moment September comes, and summoned in for meetings: timetabling, Induction, academic group review, curriculum review: it goes on and on. Now (joy) there's a new learning framework to get to grips with.

Dido, who in the past would be back at school by now, has long been used to Jeffrey's return to the campus at this time, to his coming home to cloister himself in the study in a fevered attempt to finish the project in hand before teaching resumes. She's usually been so busy with her own return to work that she's barely noticed. They have passed like weary ships in the night, collapsing at the end of the week into renewed companionship. Or sleep. Mostly sleep.

Is this how it all began? With her being – dread phrase – Too Busy to Notice?

She has a lot more time to notice now.

Two days a week at Hand in Need. (– Hi, Dido, how were the Lakes? You OK? You look a bit . . .) Three days to fill as she pleases. Getting off the bus, walking slowly (oh, how slowly) home, Dido thinks back to the carefree retirement life she was having such a short time ago. The festival with Georgia. The book group to supper, a concert, a film, drinks here and there, a bit of babysitting, the pleasing prospect of the summer hols. Ha. Had she cherished that time as she should? Walking now towards her own street, scattered with the first fallen leaves (and, as always, litter, even here) Dido thinks we should all mark and cherish every single moment of our time on earth when it is running smoothly, is ordinary, interesting. Happy, even. It's nice to think that such a store will set you up, give you the strength to endure whatever life is quietly getting ready to sock you over the head with, to rock your boat for ever.

Well. It's true that she does have strength because of all those good times in the past: all the good health, the good friends and colleagues, the long and loving marriage and family life. All these things, all these people – they did indeed sustain her in the darkest hour of her life, such a long long time ago now. Especially Jeffrey. Jeffrey, sobbing his own heart out in Ella's empty room, could not have been kinder, stronger, more loving. He's always been a wonderful husband: she must hold on to that. She must (must she not?) be a good wife to him now.

But this—

Profumo, that name which defined a decade, died at a great age not long ago, after a lifetime devoted to repentance and good works. Amongst all the obituaries, all the reruns of the past, was the story of how his wife, a fine actress, a great woman in her own right, had reacted when he told her (over lunch in Venice) who he really was, what he'd done (not, by today's standards, anything so very dreadful).

– Darling. (She lifts her linen napkin to her lipsticked lips, puts it carefully down again. Light dances blindingly over the canal; around them, the restaurant conversation fades. Is this how it was?) – Darling. We must go back and face it at once.

Not many women like that any more.

Can Dido (should Dido?) be a woman like that?

She picks up two empty crisp packets and a discarded burger box. Someone's dustbin lid is open: in they go. She turns into her street: she's nearly home.

Of course, good solid person that she is, she's essentially well placed to deal with what she's having to deal with now. There are, for a start, any number of friends she could call on.

She doesn't want to call on any of them.

Not even Georgia. Not yet.

What she wants (don't we all?) is to turn the clock back.

What she wants is to have Jeffrey put his arms around her, draw her to him, let her lie against his dear beloved chest, and tell her that she's had the most terrible dream. That there's no one he's ever loved but her, no one he's ever wanted, no beautiful young woman (a Law student; of course; she would be) whom he's ever tried (many times) to take to bed: because he thought that's what she wanted too, because he couldn't (just could not) resist her. Dido wants him to tell her that what now feels like their once-sacred life together is not shadowed by this dark and dreadful thing; that he's not going to lose his job, be splashed all over every paper, have to face his friends, their friends, his children (grandchildren – oh, please let them not be bright enough to read the papers), be the target of a furious demonstration, shouted at by every woman on the campus, staff and students—

Is this what's going to happen?

If Kate, as a young medic, had been repeatedly harassed by some consultant in his sixties, had been telephoned, texted, followed, waited for, so she'd become nervy, unable to concentrate on her work, frightened, even: would Dido not have thought this exactly what should happen?

Yes.

Well. Disciplined, certainly. Hounded and humiliated? That depends.

On what?

She's exhausted. She opens their front gate and is utterly exhausted. Tonight, oh God, there's a drinks do on the Fountains campus. Another. Must she go? Keep up appearances, and go? Up the path, tugging at the last of the deadhead roses, automatically, as if everything was just as it used to be. If things were as they used to be, she'd be having lunch in the garden, reading the paper, having (why not?) a little lie-down with *The Archers*.

Now—

She is, in truth, in need of lunch. Into the hall: pick up the post, come after she left for her appointment. What hell does the post hold in store today? Only, thank God, a postcard from Alex (Morocco) and a Wine Society mailing. This doesn't mean, of course, that there wasn't something else, something horrible, taken into work by Jeffrey. But he's left the paper, as he quite often does, just taking the Sport bit into work, to read at lunch for the cricket. This does make things feel like the old days. The party tonight feels like the old days. But reading the paper: is this easy, everyday thing – looking at the headlines, turning the pages, settling down – soon to become, like everything else, something to dread? Not yet, perhaps: the hearing hasn't happened yet.

So Dido picks the paper up, takes it, with her lunch of soup and leftovers, into the garden; puts on her specs, and tries to concentrate. British soldiers killed in Afghanistan. (Why does the phrase 'early this morning' make it so much more awful?) Keira Knightley at a premiere. A basking shark off the coast of Cornwall. She finishes her soup, picks up the tabloid. Jeffrey has left it unopened, as so often: he's right, it's gone so far downhill. Still, sometimes something interesting. She turns the pages. Manbags. Modigliani. Health. Usually something about allergies (how did they all survive when they were young?) Today—

How do you know if you've got a brain tumour?

Everything around her – the birds, the mower in a distant garden, the radio in another – goes spinning away into utter silence.

She reads.
She knows.

223

18

If you want to get on with a man at a party, you have only to ask him about himself, his work, his interests outside work (if he has any), stand back and let him do the rest. This is as true of the twenty-first century as it was of the 1950s and, no doubt, antiquity.

Getting on is not, of course, the same as getting off. But those days are (probably) long gone for some of us, and certainly, tonight, for Dido, such a thing is not even on the radar.

None the less, she finds herself, this very evening, nodding and smiling at the School party, as one man after another describes the places he's been and the work he's done this summer. She's been here before, many times, literally and metaphorically: here, in this rather nice room, thrown open to the September sunset, so you can watch returning wildfowl land safely on the lake; and here, as a new term gets into gear, welcoming new School staff, new postgraduate students (Comparative Literature, History, Cultural Studies), and she pretending to listen to the doings of the great and good.

Even now, even after the terror of the afternoon, she's here. She's changed, she's put on pretty earrings, driven out of the city, and out on the Roman road across the vale. Amazing that Jeffrey still cycles all this way. Not in winter, of course, and not when it's really wet: then, like anyone else, he gets the car out. But usually, while many men of his age are overweight, and stuck behind the wheel,

225

he's spinning along out here. No wonder he's so fit. She can hardly remember a day's illness, apart from the usual colds. Mind you, apart from the usual colds, she herself has been fit as a fiddle for years.

How long has this thing been creeping up on her?

Dido drives through the vale. To the distant west, the Pennines. To the east, the Moors, the Wolds. Here and there a ruined castle or abbey, high on a hilltop, is silhouetted marvellously against the sinking sun, a sight which on an ordinary day would fill her with happiness. Now, it feels charged with dreadful significance, ancient splendour set against life's shocking fragility.

How long does she have left?

The pitched glass roofs of Fountains come into view. She slows, greets the porter in the lodge, drives through as the barrier rises. She parks in the staff car park, walks along the path towards the library building, which, on the top floor, houses the offices of Jeffrey and his colleagues. Shadows lengthen on the grass. It's been given a last cut, and its pungent scent hangs in the air as it did earlier this summer, on the evening when that text arrived, and she had her first funny turn. Smelling it now, she remembers standing at the bathroom window, watching Jeffrey haul the mower up and down the garden, praying (to whom?) that her life could remain unchanged: ordered, purposeful, contented.

Now she knows that her life – their life – has changed for ever.

But still: she's keeping the show on the road, because she must. As long as she can, she must. Three things have brought her here tonight:

1. A determination to be seen at Jeffrey's side before all hell breaks loose. He's been invited here: not everyone knows about it, then. Thank God. Let him be seen here with his wife beside him. And if (here some of Georgia filters through) she pretends that all is well, it might (it might) turn out to be so.

2. An inability to stay in an empty house with what she now knows about herself. The hospital knows it too, at last: nice Dr Bailey rang at teatime, said gently and carefully that they'd found the results, and would she mind coming in to discuss them. Dido said there was no need: she'd realised what it must be. But, Mrs Sullivan . . . I know, I know. Give me a day or two to take it in. I'll phone you. Dr Bailey took charge. She gave her an appointment. She gave her direct line.

3. Willpower. So far in her life, this has never failed her.

So in she has come, said nothing to Jeffrey about the day's events, walked with him over to the lakeside room, talking of very little, stood with him as he's greeted by old History mates, been greeted herself, got into conversation (if you can call it that). And then, as always happens at parties, she finds that she and Jeffrey have moved apart, that he's on one side of the room making a new Ph.D. student from Albania feel at home, and she's shifting from foot to foot as one man after another describes in numbing detail his teaching methodology, his paper on Milton's catachresis; on hermeneutics; his encounter in the south of France last month with someone who had known Somerset Maugham, on whom, as it happens, he's writing a book. To tell the truth, some of the women here aren't much better, telling her, as they do, all (all) about their work on écriture féminine, Sybille Bedford, Kristeva's transformations.

Dido has, in her time, read and enjoyed both Maugham and Bedford. She has heard of Kristeva through Paula, and she can guess what écriture féminine might be, though Georgia would be better at discussing it. Beyond this: she couldn't give a damn about a shred of it, nor about a single one of these crashing bores who talk more and more about themselves with every year that passes. There are people in Jeffrey's department whom she likes: where are they tonight? At one point, she finds herself attending Wimbledon: turning from left to right and back again, as two tall

SUE GEE

men converse above her. She moves away. Neither of them notices.
She's cornered by another.

 – Dido! How are you?
 – Fine, thanks. And you?

And he's off, and there's no stopping him, flowing seamlessly from the new learning framework to the number of
student applications this year to the Arts and Humanities Research
Board, to his recent meeting with a sub-committee of the
Higher Education Funding Council, and the paper he's written
on . . .

But here he's lost her.

In the old days, she and Jeffrey would have gone home from one
of these occasions chatting companionably about it all. She (a bit
drunk) would confess that she hadn't taken in a huge amount; he
(more than a bit) would tell her she was better company than the
whole room put together. They might stop off in a pub for supper,
just the two of them, drawing breath before the onslaught of the
term.

Now, what can keep her going, as this man goes on and on? By
her watch (surreptitiously glanced at) he has been talking without
pause for almost twenty minutes. Each time he draws breath it is
only to shimmy along to the next paragraph, using clever Great
Bores connectives like: The way it works, you see, is that . . . or: I
don't know if this ever happens to you, but . . .

Now – how did this happen? – he's moved on to his other great
interest. He's taken up working with glass. It's fascinating. He tells
her why. Another ten minutes go by. He presses into her hand an
invitation to a private view. A small group show in the Shambles,
opening next week.

 – Oh. How kind. She gazes at it. – I'm not sure if we're free . . .
 – Don't worry, don't worry. I just wanted to let you know what
I'm up to these days.
 – How kind, she says again, with the heaviest irony she can give

without sounding truly insulting. Then (she's had a glass or two) she hears herself saying, as he draws breath for the next paragraph:

– The day someone here wants to know what *I'm* up to these days I'll know things have really changed.

There's a moment's pause. He looks at her uncertainly.

– Have I been boring you?

– Not for a moment.

An interesting little exchange. Now, were Dido to be told that she was boring, she'd apologise profusely, go home and worry about it, trawl sleeplessly through other parties, worrying even more: is she always so dull? What can she do to liven herself up a bit? But here: great offence is taken; she is unquestionably in the wrong. Dr Sub-Committee looks at her coldly, with something like contempt.

– Excuse *me*.

And he turns away, makes his way through the throng towards the drinks, leaving her standing there like a lemon. Dido is filled with conflicting feelings: idiocy, confusion, deep irritation, guilt. Most of these are, of course, displacement feelings, distractions from the dark enormities looming over her life, but still: they're there.

Another woman might, at this point, knock back her glass, follow the sub-committee to the drinks, take another and throw it all over him. Bore. Boor. Take that. But Dido is not this kind of woman, never has been. And what she does, thinking rapidly several things at once (viz. she must not alienate a single person here: she and Jeffrey might need all of them; she hates scenes; rudeness is scarcely in her nature) is to go after him, find him, touch him on the arm.

– I'm so dreadfully sorry.

He turns to look at her. He's medium height, medium build, is going grey; wears glasses; a perfectly ordinary, not unpleasant member of that sub-group of the human race which is the male academic. She's (still) married to one of them; Jeffrey (where is he?) has talked about this chap, worked with him for years; he can't be all bad, and anyway–

– I'm not quite myself at the moment, she hears herself saying. – I'm sorry I was so rude.

– Please don't give it another thought.

– No, but really. Careful, careful: she must not spill the beans, must not. – It's just that a few things have happened this summer – rather awful things. (Careful!)

Now. Does he say gently that he's sorry to hear it; offer her the space to tell him, if she wants to, what these things might be?

You guessed it.

– To tell you the truth, I haven't had such a brilliant summer myself.

– Oh dear. Oh, I am sorry.

And she's off: in full listening mode once more.

And then, all at once, he becomes human. He, like her, is a bit drunk.

– I'm just droning on to keep my mind off the real things, he tells her.

Ah.

– Which are?

He drains his glass. Tomorrow he'll probably regret saying what he says now.

– My wife has left me. He gives a wry smile. – A story of our times. She's left me for another woman.

– Oh dear, says Dido again. – Oh, I am sorry.

And as she once more shifts about, listening (and glad, oh so relieved she has not spilled her own beans) it comes to her in a flash: this is what's wrong between Paula and Nick. Of course it is. How can she, after all these years of training and experience, not have seen it?

The question is: has Nick? The question is: should she tell him?

230

Then all at once, as she stands there listening, the room beginning to thin out a bit, the early evening light beyond the open doors dissolving into dusk, waterbirds quacking softly on the lake, it happens again: she's going to black out, she can feel it coming—

— Get me a chair.

— I'm sorry?

— Get Jeffrey.

Then she's clutching at this man's arm, breathing fast, fast.

— Help me. I'm ill——

— It's OK, it's OK, lean on me, you're OK——

She can hear the most horrible groan. It's hers. She crumples. Then she's gone.

When she comes to, she's on the carpet, a space all around her, Jeffrey kneeling beside her, the party a million miles away.

— Dido—

— Oh, Jeffrey—

Someone is bringing a glass of water: far above her, he takes it, offers it. He lifts her head to take a sip, he slips his jacket beneath her head; she sips, she tries to move, feels every limb like lead. And something else. Oh no.

She whispers it to him.

— What?

She whispers again. — I've wet myself. Oh God.

— It's OK, darling, I'm here, I'll look after you. Let's get you home.

Home. Home. My sanctuary. My life.

— Don't let people see.

— They won't. It doesn't matter.

— Can I help?

Far above, it's the boring chap whose wife has left him (whose heart is broken, she knows that now), whose arm she had clutched in such uncontrollable need and frailty and who now, in this ghastly situation, looks so nice: kind, responsible, useful.

– Do you want me to call a doctor?

Jeffrey's holding her hand. – Dido?

– No, no. You're very kind, but I'll be fine once I'm home.

– You're sure?

– Certain, thanks. I just need to—

He and Jeffrey help her to her feet. Shocked faces watch this from all round the room. One or two people make to come over. Then, as they leave, they go back to their drinks. Dusk has fallen; rain patters on to the lake.

They're home. She's in bed. So, at last, is Jeffrey. She's had a shower, had something to eat on a tray, feels better. Exhausted but better. This (at present) is how this illness goes. Jeffrey has wanted to call Kate. She hasn't let him. Time enough for everyone to go pale, to do all they can to help her. Poor Kate. Poor darling Nick. As if they haven't both enough to think about.

Piles of books lie unopened, on the lamplit bedside tables. Reading has been at the heart of both their lives since both were children, but neither, now, since the Lakes, can concentrate or find distraction. Each longs for the solace good books offer, but life is taking over from art, and Dido, with today's discovery, isn't sure if she'll find pleasure in reading, or anything else, ever again.

– Jeffrey?

– Yes?

His arm is round her, she's leaning once more on his chest. He's wearing ancient pyjamas, the ones which have been washed and ironed perhaps three hundred times, and are now such a gentle, washed-out blue. There's a button or two missing: who knows where they've disappeared to? In their busy lives they could have gone anywhere. Not so busy now. But if she shut her eyes and pretended, if she lay here in Jeffrey's arms as once she used to do, and pretended, then everything could (oh, please, please) be as it used to be.

– I love you, he tells her, stroking her hair, her face (but not, she notices, her mouth). – Dido? You do know I love you.

She does. He's said it over and over again since the Lakes. But he hasn't (how can he?) told her that he's never wanted another woman, never craved another, much (much) younger woman, never wanted her so deeply, longed for her so madly that he lost his head, put everything at risk—

– I love you too, she says. She does. She always has. Can they come through all of this? How can they survive it?

Summer is ending: it's dark outside. Someone, down in the street, is walking home: a gate is opened, then (how quiet it is) a door. A car goes by. Then, as at Fountains, it starts to rain.

Listening to that steady fall together: what sweet companionship is evoked in this. Or even: what romance.

– I've got something to tell you, she says.

Jeffrey closes his eyes. His hand goes to his mouth. God, he looks old.

– I'm listening.

She swallows. Can it really be true, what she's about to say?

– I've had the test results. This morning, while you were at work.

Now it's her turn to shock him to the core.

19

A utumn arrives. Two or three squirrels blow about the garden. Georgia watches them, drinking her breakfast coffee. She's started putting nuts out for the birds again, remembering how Henry used to love them. This brings both sadness and comfort. Guess who gets there first. She needs to buy a squirrel-proof feeder, but there are more pressing things to be getting on with: she can barely remember a time when she was not in constant touch with Social Services. She's about to speak to them now.

Since that first, disturbing visit, she's been down to Sussex several times, finding things worse and worse on each occasion. Of course: if you are old, with galloping dementia, living alone in the depths of nowhere, with only your dog to keep an eye, how can things get better? The place is filthy. Ugh. Georgia, not without considerable effort, found at last a cleaner, a nice woman living on Partridge Common, only five miles away. Her previous employer, an elderly widowed doctor, had not long died: she was looking for work, had a car, understood that people get a bit funny, sometimes, as they get older, when they live alone. Oh, what a relief.

Maud will not admit her to the house.

Georgia arranged, with Social Services, for Meals on Wheels to call. Maud is losing weight. Who knows what happens to the shepherd's pie which Georgia prepares in London, brings down, and puts in the fridge? (Actually, she can guess.) Meals on Wheels pitch up at top speed, flying, as always, from house to house, with their little foil dishes of meat and two veg and apple crumble. Maud snatches the dishes at the kitchen door, sets them down on the crawling kitchen floor. Kep loves them (likewise the shepherd's pie). It's hopeless.

Georgia (weary, weary now) has long talks with Joan Starkey. Joan's Elderly Persons Care Pack is rather running out of steam. She has tried, once again, to visit, this time with a colleague, but with the same result.

– If she won't let us in, my love, there's really not a lot we can do.

Georgia snaps at her. She is not Joan Starkey's love. Please. And what is supposed to happen now?

Well. If Maud attended the hospital in Horsham, she could be assessed, given a proper diagnosis. Could Georgia make an appointment? Of course she could. And get Maud to the clinic, at the right time on the right day? That's a different story.

If Maud could be got to the hospital, and get an assessment, they could arrange for her to attend a very nice day centre. A special bus could collect her twice a week (they'd like to take her every day, of course, but the Trust is in some financial difficulties) driving her and other demented old bats through the autumnal countryside to town. She'd be given, in the day centre, a personal Care and Activity Plan. Which would involve what? Basket making. Board games. Interactive cognitive this and that. Sometimes people really pick up, with all this stimulation.

It's worth a try. Anything's worth a try.

Georgia goes down for the night. She takes her own bedclothes, sleeps on the sofa, gets up at six to prepare Maud for the day.

– Where did you say we were going?

– Glyndebourne.

– That sounds fun! Have we a picnic?

Clearly, in her long-gone youth, Maud did get out and about. Happy times. What went wrong? Who knows? But this, clearly, is one of her good days: she's co-operative, benevolent, even, until they actually stagger towards the car. What about Kep? He can stay here, Maud, he'll sleep, he'll be fine. You'll see him when we come home.

– I'm not leaving him.

– Maud, please. We can't take him to the hospital.

– Hospital? I thought we were going to the opera.

Oh, bloody hell.

They never got there.

Now, Georgia spends hours on the internet, researching care homes. They all sound like hotels: wildly expensive, four-course meals three times a day, little drinks dos, hairdressers, recitals, bridge . . .

How could Maud possibly fit in to one of these?

The soothing strains of *Desert Island Discs* come floating through the kitchen. It must be Friday, then. The end of the week. Chloe can't, surely, be working this weekend. She'll have to start pulling her weight. She'll have to. Now: what to do? Phone Joan Starkey, discuss a home or two. Phone the home or two, arrange a visit. Phone Chloe, tonight, and tell her that this has gone on long enough: Georgia's approaching the end of her rope.

And meanwhile, through all of this, there's been Dido to worry about. Not a peep. Not a chirrup. Georgia has never, ever, been one to intrude – in truth, like Dido, she's been far too busy all her life to think of intruding on anyone – but this silence is beyond a joke. It's not a joke at all. She phones: gets the answerphone. She's stopped leaving messages. She writes, gets a two-line card: *All (sort of) well. I promise I'll be in touch soon.*

But she isn't.

This is bleak. But whatever's wrong, there's nothing, without invitation, that Georgia can do about it. She finishes her coffee, turns off those mournful gulls. (It's someone who's made a fortune in vacuum cleaners: today, she cannot rustle up an interest.) She sits at the kitchen table, and dials Social Services, a number she now knows by heart, but for whose response she has to summon

SUE GEE

every ounce of energy and patience (getting thinner with every
passing day).

— Thank you for calling Social Services. Please note that calls
may be monitored for quality and training purposes. If you want
to speak to the Youth Offending Team, please press One . . .

If you want to top yourself, please hold.

Modern times. Who needs them?

Chloe and Jez are on a shoot. So are about a million other people.
This isn't an ordinary occasion, some catalogue in a rented studio,
some makeover kitchen shop or new collection for Homebase.
Forget all that. This is the most amazing house she's ever been in,
owned by someone so rich that they use it but two or three times
a year. When they're in London. The rest of the time they're in
Tokyo, Dubai, New York, Rome. They have homes in every single
one of these places. They have a yacht. Nobody knows who they
are, or how they got to be *so* rich, but the agency gave Chloe to
understand all this when she made the booking, and the insurance,
just for this single day, is four times her annual salary. Well, almost.

They're using this just amazing place as the setting for a five-page
feature in *Tank*. The clothes are Stefano Pilati, for YSL. The Russian
model is more expensive than the insurance. This is the biggest job
that Chloe's ever, ever done, and she's spent weeks thinking of
nothing else. That's when she's not thinking about Jez. That's, like,
all the time. Sometimes she feels as if her head will burst.

Today, she rose at five. This is not an hour she's used to seeing,
not from this end, anyway. Being up all night clubbing and falling
into bed at dawn is one thing (not that she's ever been a *huge*
clubber). Having sex all night is another (not that there's been a
huge amount of that lately, in fact not half enough. How's she
going to get pregnant if they don't even do it? Why aren't they
doing it? This is something else to worry about. Meanwhile, she's
still on the pill, just waiting for the word, and worrying about

238

breast cancer. In fact, she's worried all the time about something, and if she can manage to laugh about that with Edmund it's only because this shoot is dominating her whole *life* at the moment, leaving little time for all the rest of it. Which is just as well).

So. She staggered out of bed at five, showered, poured a black coffee and a million vitamin pills down her throat, took half an hour to decide what to wear, changing three times and ending up where she started, with pumps and different earrings, ticked off everything (twice) in her Filofax, picked up all her bags, tried to open the front door with her teeth, put the bags down again and finally, finally, got out of the house. Edmund slept through all of this, and not (she's certain) by himself. Someone has pitched up at the rehearsal rooms (or is it Heal's? Ed's still working there part time; he's got to). He comes in late at night. (Who is he? Wait and see. Just as long as you're happy. Thanks. How're you and Jez these days? Oh, Edmund . . . Sorry, I've got to go.)

Black cab through the black London streets. The clocks have gone back (she's sure it's back) and it's cold and there's no one about. She and the driver chat away. He's been to this place before, it turns out: it's rented quite a lot for shoots and things. Hearing this, her stomach does a nosedive. They're supposed to be really *original* for this feature: don't say everyone's bored to death by it before they've even started. Don't worry, he tells her, as they cross Regent's Park, it's big enough to do a dozen shoots and still have rooms which no one's ever heard of.

The last stars sprinkle the sky; it seems to be only them in the world, spinning smoothly along the silken tarmac. She's feeling just the tiniest bit sick with nerves, and lets the window down. Cold air blows in: that's better. Then:

– Hear that?

– What *is* it?

– Wolves, innit?

Of course: they're near the Zoo. Gosh. Wolves. Scary.

But the Zoo (if you like zoos, if you're not worried, like Sara, about animal rights and things) is a great place, of which she has happy childhood memories. She and her parents saw a baby elephant there: he was really sweet. Thinking of this, of his tufty little head and amazing eyelashes, makes her think of Ellie. Wouldn't it be great if she could bring her here? Just the two of them, really getting on. It also, for some reason, makes her think of Nick, to whom she's given barely a moment's thought since the summer. She can just see him, somehow, with a baby elephant.

Then her thoughts go back to Ellie. Even now, even on the way to this really important thing at work, she just can't help worrying about it.

She's only seen her twice since the dance class day. Once, she and Jez took her swimming, on a Saturday afternoon. They went to the lido in Gospel Oak: a bit late in the year, and frankly too cold for outdoor bathing. Shivers and gooseflesh and wanting Jez, not Chloe, to snuggle her up in a towel. They took her to see *Harry Potter* and the something or other at the Barbican Children's Film Club. That wasn't too bad: a fun movie, tea afterwards, looking out over the terrace, feeding the carp in the pools. But it's all been out, out, out – always something special and treaty, always a bit of a strain. There's no cosy home time, making things, dressing up, eating beans on toast and watching a video together, none of that. Not once have she, Jez and Ellie been in his flat at the same time. And she tries not to think about the conversation they had after the dance class weekend, when Ellie went back to stay the night and she went home to have a nightmare.

– How was it? Did you have a good time together?

Monday evening: he's come to meet her after work.

They're in a café in Camden, not far from the office. He stirs his latte. It doesn't need *that* much stirring.

– Jez?

He puts the spoon down.

– To tell you the truth, she wet the bed.

– Oh. Oh dear. Does she – has she – is this—

This does not sound good at all.

– She hasn't done it for years. Unless – unless there's something at home I don't know about.

He looks, she has to face it, pretty miserable. Poor Jez. Gosh, it must be difficult. But they'll get through this patch, of course they will. She covers his hand with hers. He gives a half-smile, and a great big sigh.

– Want to talk?

He shakes his head. – Not really.

– Shall we go home?

He moves his hand away. – To tell you the truth . . . He's started to use this phrase a lot, she's noticed. Is there (she just won't think about it) some great big horrible truth he's trying to tell her? – To tell you the truth, I'm pretty shattered. I need a bit of space tonight. Is that OK?

– Sure. She swallows. – Sure, of course it is. You go home and have a good night's sleep.

And he does, and she doesn't, but next time they meet he's really lovely. Then they try again with Ellie, the Lido, the Barbican, but it's still not really right with her, she can't pretend.

– She doesn't like me.

– Course she does.

They're in bed together. Willesden trains rattle past the window. It's getting chilly, the central heating on, everything snug.

– She just needs to take her time, that's all. It's only natural.

Of course. Of course it is. She can't imagine how kids cope with this kind of thing at all, not really, but everyone says they do.

– Jez?

– Mmm?

– Tell me about . . . about you and Madeleine. Please. I really need to know. Tell me what went wrong.

241

He's looking up at the ceiling; he moves a bit, puts his arm behind his head. It's like one of those old sixties movies when you can't show people in bed together, or if you do they mustn't touch, mustn't show an inch of skin. He gives a great big sigh. He's starting to sigh a *lot*.

– We were really getting on each other's nerves. She felt I was working too much, out too much, not pulling my weight with Ellie, not giving either of them enough. She said we were drifting apart so much we might as well be living apart.

Chloe listens. This happens, she knows it does, she grew up with and went to school with lots of people whose parents split. It's just that hers didn't: they really did, like, enjoy each other. Ed has always said she doesn't know how lucky she is in that department. Not so lucky now, with her father gone. What would he make of Jez? Go on, think about it: what would he be telling her she should do? But it's no good going down that path, for she knows that Henry simply wouldn't want her to be in this situation at all, and she is, she is, right up to the neck.

– But, Jez—

– Mmm?

– I mean . . . I mean I don't want to pry or anything, it's none of my business, of course, but when you and Madeleine first met, when you got together, were you really in love?

She wants him to tell her, No, not really, that's why it's all gone wrong. She wants him to say that she's the only one he's ever felt like this about, that when Ellie settles down he'll make the break properly with Madeleine, and then—

But he says: – Of course we were. We were mad about each other. Why else would we get married?

They've crossed the canal, and left the Outer Circle. Now they're looking at what people call world-class property. This is it: she's a world-class stylist now.

The taxi pulls up, the meter ticks as she gets out with all her clobber.

– Want a hand up the steps?

– Please.

She gives him (just so she knows what it feels like) a world-class tip.

– Nice one. Thanks, love. Hope it all goes well.

And he's climbing back in the cab, with a cheery wave. For a moment she stands beneath the portico, watching him spin away again, as the sky begins to lighten above the huge, almost leafless trees, and the first people begin their morning run. It's beautiful. Imagine living like this. She wouldn't want to, of course, she'd hate to be with really rich people all the time, they're so pleased with themselves, but just for a little while, perhaps, just to see what it's like. Wait a minute. Didn't the 101 Dalmatians all live here? Must be some nice people around, then.

Wolves howl across the canal. The taxi is almost out of sight, just the red back lights glinting in the dawn. She could have booked him for the return, of course, but – please, please – she'll be going home with Jez after this, won't she, and that could be at any time. She'll just have to wait and see.

And she turns, and rings the world-class doorbell (white china, set deep within the wall). It rings, the purest, strongest sound of any doorbell she's ever heard. Then the world-class door (oak, with a million coats of black gloss, hung with the heaviest Georgian brass that money can buy) swings slowly open. A smiling Filipino person stands there.

Deep breath. Here we go.

– Hi! I'm Chloe.

Of course, Joan Starkey is telling Georgia, some of these places are better than others.

– Of course, says Georgia, keeping an eye on the garden. A

squirrel is swinging madly from the peanuts. Tristan, below, is watching it with interest. – That's why I'm phoning you, she tells Joan. (– Please call me Joan, Georgia. May I call you Georgia? – No.) – To get the lowdown.

– Well, now. She can sound just like Lynda Snell. – If we begin with The Grove . . .

Georgia runs a finger down her list, leafs through her printouts. Got it. This is the one with a visiting naturopath. Why not an astrologer, while we're at it? But it seems to be this, at a thousand pounds a minute, or something so grim she wouldn't put a dog in there. (God, a dog. What's going to happen to Kep?)

– Go on, she says. – I'm listening.

Now almost everyone's here, and it's all just *mad*. Coffee gets going, down in the kitchen. It's vast, goes on for ever, looks, as kitchens do these days, like a hospital. Wall-to-wall stainless steel. Island in the middle as big as an operating table. Not a tin or jar in sight. Not a crumb. An orchid on the windowsill. Filipino persons serve the coffee, the lighting people are here, trampling about upstairs with their cables and stuff; Dot and Carrie are here (both of them!) the model's agent rings to confirm she's on her way, the Fashion Ed is here. She looks terrifying. There's a work experience person with her. She looks terrified. Makeup is here, with even more bags than Chloe. Jez is here.

Chloe's heart goes flip-flop. It's two days since she's seen him. This is a big big day for him too, she knows it. You can pretend to be cool, but this is serious moolah, and he needs it, still paying half the mortgage and the rent on his flat. And it's not just the money: this is status, this is being talked about, this is the big one.

– Hi.

– Hi, Chloe.

Isn't it a funny thing? Your name can sound the most intimate thing in the world on another's lips. And yet sometimes, when it's

244

used like this, it feels all wrong, and distant: like he needs to use her name, like he doesn't know her very well, and has just come upon her, in this great big place. He should be just saying Hi. He should be giving her a special look. OK, they're at work, they're not going to get into a clinch or anything, are they, but still – that kiss on the cheek could be given to anyone.

He looks, of course, fantastic. All hung about with cameras and that RL bag, a complete pro. She watches him take his cup of coffee, smiling at the Filipino person as if she's the nicest thing he's seen all week, greeting everyone. The doorbell goes again. The model's agent has arrived. So has the model.

Oh. My. God.

From Russia with love and just about anything else you can think of.

She's *gorgeous*. Everyone goes sort of quiet.

Very tall, big-boned, but with not an ounce of extra flesh, scraped-back dark hair soon to be revealed as a mane, a mass, a glory. Slav cheekbones, mouth from heaven, eyes to drown in, immaculate eyebrows raised, every now and then, in polite and intelligent enquiry.

Chloe has seen her in *Harper's* and *Vogue*. But to see her in the flesh. To be *working* with her. And the agent's said that this goddess (Irina) has a first degree in economics from the University of St Petersburg, and is using her modelling fees to fund her postgraduate studies at the London Business School.

Chloe can't think of a single thing to say. Not one. Every woman in the room, every woman in London, is put in the shade by this glorious creature, and today she must, must she not, have her Russian almond eyes only for Jez.

– OK, everyone, upstairs.

Dot and Carrie are marshalling the troops. They all troop up there.

The drawing room is like a ship.

* * *

Of course, Joan is telling Georgia, we could try one more time. We could get carers in there, once a week.

– What would they do?

– Wash her. Bath her. Put her in clean clothes and give her breakfast.

Sounds marvellous.

– She'll never let them.

– She might. They're very good, some of these people. Sometimes they really bond.

OK, that's it, tea's in the kitchen, thanks everyone, you've been brilliant. Irina: you're a star. I hope we have the pleasure of working with you again one day.

– Thank you. I should like that very much.

– Chloe: well done. It all looked terrific.

– Thanks, Dot.

It's only five o'clock in the afternoon, but she's shattered. *Shattered.* She's been up for twelve hours but it feels like twenty-four, and it's so dark outside it feels like the middle of the night. Winter shoots are always killers, that's why people go to Pacific islands and stuff. But there's something about a Russian in London, in this breathtaking interior – the floor-to-ceiling windows with their Georgian panes, the fireplaces at either end of the room, about a mile apart, the sweeping swags of curtain and simply all this *space* – that makes Pacific islands look like tat. The look they've got today sets off clothes so expensive you can only dream, but you want that look, you want it. And now, thank God, it's done and dusted, and she's drinking tea in the kitchen, with a splitting headache, before she packs everything away: the Evidenza watch (£2,180) the Vuitton bag (don't ask) the YSL bag (likewise) the glasses, the cafetière, the silver candlesticks, Doulton china; on and on it goes. Just imagine if someone broke into the flat while all this was in there. Imagine.

Anyway, they haven't. And she's leaning up against a stainless-steel unit, knocking back a couple of Nurofen (naughty) and a couple of extra multivits with her Earl Grey tea. She's standing because kitchens like these never have anywhere you can actually *sit*, and she's half listening to all the chat around her and mostly keeping her eye on the door through which Jez must surely enter any minute now. (He hasn't gone off in a taxi with Irina, has he? What man could resist her? But he wouldn't, would he?)

He didn't. He hasn't. He's here.

— Hi. She raises her teacup.

— Hi. He's taking his tea from a Filipino person, and a chocolate biscuit, looking round for somewhere to sit, then coming over to stand next to her. They've hardly spoken a word all day: not while he was shooting, obviously, but not over lunch, either: one minute he was here and the next he'd gone off for a walk in the park. It's freezing out there, she knows it is, but he needs to clear his head. She watches him from the drawing-room window, crossing the canal bridge, walking beneath the trees, all hunched up against the cold, like that old Dylan LP, only she's not there to be arm in arm, she's in here, not wanted as fresh-air companion at all. Now he's on his mobile, taking a call. Who from? Stop it! He needs some time to himself. So does she (sort of). Now he's turned a corner, now he's out of sight. It doesn't *matter*. They'll make up for it tonight.

— Hi, she says again, and reaches to give him a kiss. — You were brilliant. Isn't she amazing? Irina?

He nods, rubbing his stubbly face.

— I've never worked with anyone like her. She hardly needs directing at all; you only have to murmur.

— Mmm. Chloe gazes into her tea. Around them, everyone's beginning to peel away, putting their cups down, picking up their things, calling out goodbye.

— What do you want to do? she asks him, linking her arm in his.
— I've got to get all this stuff back, but then I'm free. Do you want

to come to mine? Or shall I come over to yours? Shall we eat out, or are you too tired? I could cook, I'm happy to cook . . .

Somewhere deep inside, as she goes prattling on like this, she can hear a voice. It's Edmund's, telling her to cool it. Shut up, she tells him. What does he know? He got her into this and now (bet you any money) he's about to lose his own head over some streak of nothing. He won't be so cool and clever then.

– Jez? What do you think?

– Um, well, actually, to tell you the truth, I've said I'll go home for supper.

????

– Sorry?

He's reaching for another tea, as Ms Filipino goes by.

– Thanks. Thanks so much.

– Jez? What do you mean?

How long does it take, to stir in a couple of sugar lumps?

– Madeleine rang me. At lunch time. She just said . . . she just said Ellie was missing me, and would I go home tonight?

– But . . . but I thought—

– Sorry. He turns and finally looks at her. – Sorry, Chloe, I couldn't say no. He leans forward, kisses her lightly on the lips. – Don't be cross, we'll do something nice tomorrow.

– Will we?

– Sure. Sure we will. He looks at his watch, downs scalding hot tea in moments. – I'd better go. I'll call you.

– Tonight? (SHUT UP, EDMUND.)

– I'll try. Tomorrow for sure. Bye, now.

And he's gone, leaving her standing there in the almost empty kitchen, poleaxed.

Home for supper. *Home.*

– You like more tea?

– What? Oh, no, no thanks. I must be going.

The stairs up from the kitchen go on for ever, likewise those to the first-floor drawing room. She's been running up and down them all day, full of nervous energy and excitement, hardly even noticing. Now, it's as much as she can do to put one foot in front of another. She reaches the first floor, gathers up her stuff. She'll have to get a cab: she reaches into her bag for her mobile, but blow me, it's starting to ring.

That'll be him! He's ringing to say he's changed his mind!

– Hi!

– Chloe? Chloe, it's Matt. Where are you?

– Matt? I'm on a shoot in Regent's Park, just finishing. Where are *you*?

– In the hospital. In UCH.

Has anyone, ever, ever, sounded so radiantly happy and alive?

– What? But I thought—

– It was early, Sara started this morning, two weeks early, but everything's fine. Oh, Chloe, she wanted you to be the first to know, after our parents, I mean ... He's mumbling, stumbling over his words. – It's a girl, it's a girl! She's the most beautiful thing I've ever seen in my life, you've got to come and see her.

– Now?

He's laughing.

– Not now. Sara's pretty shattered.

– I bet. (Bet what? What does she know about giving birth? What will she ever, ever know about it?)

– Tomorrow, Matt's saying. – You've got to come tomorrow.

– Of course I will, tell me the ward. Oh, Matt ...

All of a sudden, she's in floods.

– Chloe? I know how you feel, I've been crying myself, it's so fantastic—

– Give me the ward, she says again, and then, through her tears, – I've got to go. See you tomorrow. Tell Sara – tell Sara she's brilliant. Give her lots and lots of love, OK?

She flicks off the phone, and she cries and cries.

When she's finished, she gathers up her stuff again, and goes slowly down the stairs, leaving the beautiful empty space behind. Ms Filipino sees her out, with a lovely smile. Chloe stands on the steps and looks out over the winter park. Traffic spins round it, stars hang above it, she feels as small as anything, standing there beneath the world-class portico. Not a taxi in sight; she'll have to call one. And as she's searching in her bag again (why doesn't it have a proper mobile *pouch*, for God's sake) it starts to ring.

Oh, thank heaven, thank heaven, she knew he wouldn't really do this. They can go to the hospital tomorrow together, and when he sees Sara's tiny tiny baby—

– Hello?

– Chloe.

You wouldn't think a single stomach could do so many different things in the space of twenty seconds.

– Mum. Hi.

– Where are you?

– I'm in Regent's Park, and listen, Mum, I'm really shattered, sorry, can I call you back?

– No, says Georgia firmly. (She sounds, like, really *ratty*.) – No, you can't. I'm sorry, Chloe, but this has got to stop.

She's in the back of a taxi, they're driving through the park. Friday night traffic: not so much whizzing now. Chloe leans against the seat, gazes out at the distant mosque, the darkened grass, the rich and hardy runners on the paths beneath the lamps. They're coming up to the Zoo: the magical aviary, the mountain goats, the prowling, howling wolves.

They're quiet now: a pity. She could give them something to howl about.

20

No one will leave Maud alone. No one will let her be. How can they? She does still have good days, but not many. The place is going to rack and ruin, and it's not only she who is suffering from neglect. What about the sheep? What about poor old Agnes and Heidi, in need of pastures new? Who has sheared their shaggy old coats, so thick, so hot, so maggoty round the tail? Who's going to move them out of the orchard, into the sloping back field? Its long lush strands have sustained them (just) through the summer as they nibble and tug at whatever pokes through the rusting wire. Windfalls have helped, but too many windfalls can give dreadful gas, and if you remember your Thomas Hardy you'll know what that means. Now, everything is a mass of weeds and thistles, all gone to seed and dying down. Agnes and Heidi should soon be having hay, and winter feed. Who's going to buy in the hay bales, store them in the collapsing barn, order in the bags of sheep nuts?

Answer to all this: no one.

What about the hens? Hens can scratch about for ever, and there's been plenty to keep them going, what with the maggots, the grubs, the drifting seeds. Now it's late autumn, and they, like the sheep, need thinking about. All the lovely old leftovers – potatoes, porridge, burned baked beans, Georgia's shepherd's pie and Meals on Wheels' cauliflower cheese and blackberry crumble – when Kep's not wolfing them, and when Maud remembers to put them out, you've never seen anything like it, as those birds come racing down. Hens can really *run*. Often, however, she doesn't. Late autumn, and they've stopped laying. Uncollected eggs from the summer are going bad in the henhouse and in the nettle beds. What a waste. Autumn turns towards winter, and Mr Fox is back. In truth, he's never been far away, conditions being just perfect, thank you, for picking off first Harriet, then Jemima. Maud's nights have been disturbed by fearful squawking, shrieking, even. (Foxes aren't nice, however soft and sweet the face which gazes at you from the back of a London bus.) Her mornings are blighted by wild scatterings of feathers, limp, uneaten bodies, torn-off heads.

Maud, in her Wellington boots and nightgown (where is her dressing gown? It's freezing) stares out at desolation. On good days, as darkness falls, she shuts the hens up. On bad days, she forgets. One frosty night, Mr Fox brings a (female) friend. Between them, they tear to pieces every single one. This is one problem solved, of course (who's going to look after those moulting birds?) but in the most dreadful way.

And Kep?

Kep is putting on pounds, what with meat and two veg, the cauliflower cheese, decapitated hens, etc. He's getting slow from lack of exercise. Maud can't get about as she did: she's really beginning to lose mobility. It's not just memory which dementia eats away: it's the ability to put one foot in front of another. No more striding down the lanes, watching (oh, happy, disappearing days) the swallows skim the air before her; no more winter walks over the fields, checking on this and that in her moth-eaten old tweed coat. On a good day, she makes it out to the yard, and out to the orchard, to see the sheep. But even then, by the time she gets back to the house she's often forgotten where she's been, certainly doesn't remember to phone the vet, or tell Georgia to phone the vet when she comes down on a visit. (Most of the time, when Georgia comes, Maud hasn't a clue who she is.) She spends a huge amount of time just sitting, sometimes with the wireless on, and sometimes the Television, though she can make neither head nor tail of it now.

Kep lies at her feet. He's fat, he's not as young as he was, not by a long way. He's getting arthritic, and the extra weight's not helping. And – this is awful – he's going blind. He can't see the flies that in the old days he'd have snapped at unerringly as they buzzed by. He can always find his dish, but sometimes the effort of getting up the stairs to his basket is just too much. He flops on the mat in the kitchen and he stays there, while Maud goes creaking up to bed. Sometimes she notices. Not always.

Kep, in short, is not the dog he was.

Meanwhile, as Kep grows old and blind, as sheep grow sick and hens are horribly slaughtered, as Maud goes unstoppably downhill, Georgia lies awake filled with guilt and worry. She is a Londoner to her bones, likewise a cat person. What does she know about running a farm? About sheep and sheepdogs? Her concerns have been all for Maud, and somehow poor old Agnes and Heidi (not to mention Harriet, et al.) have not been given proper thought. And Green Lane Farm is so far out of the way of things, in that deep deep lane, that no neighbouring farmer has thought about them either. It's all agribusiness and polytunnels now, all Sun Valley lorries, thundering through the countryside with their million crates of living birds stacked up (and up and up). Who's going to notice a funny old place like this? A rotting old, stinking old, dangerously derelict place like this?

Who's going to care for Maud?

Georgia is doing her best. Short of packing her bags and going down to live there, something which (sorry) she simply cannot contemplate, she is doing her very best.

Needless to say, in a situation such as this (pretty impossible, let's face it) best isn't good enough.

* * *

Georgia has sat down with Maud and told her that a very nice woman (or possibly two) will be coming to help get her up, get her breakfast, tidy the place up a bit. It's a good day, and Maud doesn't seem to mind the idea. It sounds like Claridge's!

Georgia explains she's getting a spare key cut, just in case Maud isn't quite well enough to let the nice carers in. (Just in case she goes ballistic.) She has many (many) misgivings about all this, but what else is to be done?

So she gets a key cut in Petworth, drives to the Social Services office and delivers it to Joan (don't you worry about it any more, my love) Starkey. She drives back to London, filled with relief and anxiety.

They can only try.

Chloe is visiting Sara, Matt and The Baby. She's told them at work she'll be in a bit late. Everyone tells her to send them all their love.

Sara's bed is like Kew Gardens, a mass of hothouse roses, glorious out-of-season scented things picked by exploited African women and flown into London in a cool cool cabin. Chloe, choosing the most fantastic flowers she can afford – long-stemmed roses, lizzianthus, all in pink and cream – knows from Georgia that she should only be buying things in season (flowers, mangetout, topped-and-tailed green beans – away with all that evil supermarket stuff). But this is for a *baby*. You can't take holly and hellebores to a *baby*, and though those Chinese lanterns are really stylish they somehow just don't do it. Not for this.

Into the hospital she goes, into the ward, almost invisible behind the mass of flowers, the Cellophane, the palest baby-pink tissue, loveliest ribbons. And there is Sara, already in a greenhouse, cards stacked six deep upon the locker and she so pale and tired upon the pillows but also looking so so happy. And so *different*, somehow. And there in the transparent crib beside her, wearing only a scrap of snow-white vest and nappy (gosh, it's warm in here) is the smallest, sweetest, tiniest—

– Oh, Sara! Look at her, *look* at her.

– I know.

The most exquisite, tiny but so perfect little everything – those nails, those tiny folded feet . . .

– What are you going to call her?

– Daisy. Daisy Sara.

Of course. Whatever else could she be called? It's a bit retro, a bit hippy, but she's a Daisy to the last soft hair on her head. And to give your baby your *own name*, to have this tiny, darling baby version of yourself—

– Oh, Sara.

– I know.

– Where's Matt?

– He's just gone for a coffee. He'll be back in a minute.

– How are you?

– Fine, fine. Yesterday was a bit difficult, but now she's beginning to latch on.

– ?

There follows an extensive description of The Birth (– you wouldn't *believe* the pain) and an initiation into the mysteries of breastfeeding, latching on, colostrum (??) feeding on demand (versus Gina Ford) exhaustion (already) and Going Home. Probably tomorrow.

And here is Matt, also looking different: so uncool, so smiley. They kiss, he admires the flowers (briefly), he bends over the crib. Chloe plucks up all her courage.

– Could I – just for a moment – would you mind . . . ?

– Sure. Of course.

The smallest, warmest, sleepiest, most beautiful little bundle is carefully wrapped in a lacy shawl by her father (gosh, Matt!) and laid in the crook of her arm. Chloe can hardly breathe. She gazes down, she strokes with a finger the sweetest curve of cheek, the downy hair. The shawl is rather thick: when *she* has a baby (oh, please, *please*) the shawl will be like a *cobweb*.

Daisy stirs, she whimpers. Sara holds out her arms. Very very carefully, Chloe hands her over. And as Daisy (eventually) latches on, and Matt and Sara both gaze down upon her, Chloe looks about the ward, at all the other cribs and flowers and mothers, at the winter morning sun palely lighting everything through tall dusty windows, at the nurses, who all look about ten years younger than she is.

It's a different world in here.

Was this the ward she was born in? She must ask her mother. And she sits there, trying to imagine Georgia, thirty-one years ago, holding and feeding her, with Henry visiting, all quiet and kind and fantastically happy.

Daisy is suckling away. Chloe is pretty much a spare part. No one has asked about Jez, to whom she has not spoken for twenty-four miserable hours. No one asks when Ed's play is going to open, or how things are at work. (Russian models? Regent's Park? Forget it.) No one suggests that she might like (!!) to be a godmother. The fabulous flowers are still at the end of the bed, resting on all the charts and things.

— I'll just go and get a vase.

— What? Oh, right, thanks.

Off she goes, directed by a nurse to the sluice, where hideous metal things stand ready to kill dead the most beautiful arrangement. She hunts about, finds a tall cracked glass one at the back. The next ten minutes are spent cutting, plunging, snipping, taking out and putting in again, etc., until the whole thing really does look the business. Gosh. She carries it carefully back to Sara's bed. Now what? Where are they to go?

— Um, Sara.

Sara looks up, warm and flushed. Daisy's on the other side now, and Matt's taking a photograph.

– Oh, Chloe, they're lovely, thank you so much. Can you just squeeze them in somewhere?

She squeezes them in, just. Cards fall on to the floor and bed; she puts them back again. Then: – I'd better be going to work.

– OK. Thanks again. I'll ring you when we get home. Once we're settled.

– Great.

And they kiss, and Chloe drinks in the sweet warm milky baby smell, and Matt takes a photo of them both. He says his parents will be here any minute, and Chloe says give them her love and then she tells them both how clever they are, and how really beautiful Daisy is, so *adorable*—

Then she goes.

Oh, what feelings fill her, as she walks past all those babies. And right at the end of ward is a nursery where they stay when their mothers need to sleep. (When *she* has a baby she won't let it leave her side for a single minute.) She stands at the window and gazes in. They're all so different: some of them are enormous, after Daisy, really huge: imagine trying to give birth to that one over there! (Caesareans must be really brilliant.) Some are sound asleep, some starting to cry, one or two just being good as gold, lying there awake and sucking on a tiny fist. (That's what hers will be like.)

But one of them is really going for it now, really yelling. And someone is coming up behind her: Chloe turns to see a woman in her thirties, wearing an interesting dressing gown, hair a bit all over the place, pale and tired-looking. She gives Chloe a wan smile, then pushes open the nursery door. In she goes, and over to the crib where Bawler is letting rip. For a moment she stands by his side, and Chloe can somehow sense that she's steeling herself, taking a deep breath before she does her stuff. Then she's lifting him out (surely it must be a him) and taking him to a plastic chair in the corner. She sits down stiffly, like she's really sore, opens her nice dressing gown, and her pyjama top, and the baby's head is going like mad and he's red in the face and screaming until he latches on, at last, and begins to suck for England. Gosh.

His mother looks up, sees Chloe watching them. Again, she gives a wan tired smile, and something about her reminds Chloe of Georgia: a clever, interesting face, an older mother, someone whose life is about to really change. Chloe smiles back. On the other side of the glass, she feels herself on the other side of the world: young, free (who cares? who wants to be free?) with all this longed-for baby-world so far ahead, so out of reach, so (it seems) impossible.

She shuts her eyes, feeling the biggest lump in her throat. When she opens them, the tired nice mother is bending over her baby, stroking his head. He looks in seventh heaven. Chloe walks slowly out of the ward, and down the stairs.

After the warmth of the ward, the outside world is freezing. People in winter coats walk past, briskly dodging the pigeons; an ambulance is wailing through the traffic on Tottenham Court Road. As she stands on the hospital steps, getting out her mobile, a taxi pulls up before the entrance. Out gets a chap in a hurry, with one hand fumbling in his pocket and lifting out a weekend bag with the other. Out gets a hugely pregnant woman. The driver's paid, they start to climb the steps and Chloe moves out of the way. Then the woman suddenly stops, and doubles up, and stands there gasping.

– Breathe! Breathe!

Her chap is whiter than she is, looking wildly at the glass doors and trying to take her arm.

– Don't touch me!

– Sorry, sorry . . .

Chloe steps up. – Can I help? Do you want me to get a nurse or anything?

– Please!

She's back inside in a flash, running to the porter's desk, explaining. He's seen it all before, he calmly dials a number. The couple stagger in, and she sinks to a plastic chair, groaning. People come and go, Chloe hovers, and at last a nurse appears.

– Hello, my love, not to worry, we'll soon have you up on the ward.

– I'm going to have it! I'm going to have it now!

Chloe stands transfixed. Is she really really going to see an actual *birth*? Heads are turning as people come and go, and the poor woman is really yelling now, her partner white and sweating and the nurse bashing out a number on her pager thing.

– Could we have a stretcher, please? Down in reception. As fast as you can.

In moments, it comes gliding along, pushed by an African porter.

– Here we are now, up you get, that's it, good girl—

– Get off me!

Heaving and groaning and banging about. Whizzing along to the lift. Here it comes. In they go. And in moments all is quiet again, the drama taking place a long long way away.

Chloe finds her knees are trembling. Really shaking. She takes a deep breath (Breathe! Breathe!) and fishes out her bottle of water. Oh, my God. Oh, that's better. OK, now, off we go.

Outside, still dithery, she leans against the railings, digs out her mobile again. She's got to talk to him, she's got to tell him about it all, she's got to *see* him. She keys in his number; she stands there in the cold.

But it isn't even on voicemail: there's no sexy *Hi. This is Jez*, only that deadly flat female robot: *The number you are calling is not available. Please try later.*

She can't even leave him a message. Where is he? Why has he switched off?

She doesn't want to think about the answer. And she rings them at work, says she's on her way, and yes, she's fine, and Sara's baby's lovely, and all that stuff. Then she turns and walks slowly slowly towards the tube. The wind is whipping along the Euston Road; she pulls her coat about her and turns the collar up.

Oh God. Oh God.

And tonight she must go home for supper.

– Chloe. You look dreadful.

– Thanks.

– Sorry, but you do. What's been going on?

– Nothing. Well, not exactly. Sara's had her baby, she's sweet. I did this big shoot yesterday. Where are the cats? Oh, hi, Tristan, I didn't see you! Come and give me a hug.

Georgia has not been given a hug. She's been given a peck on the cheek and a bottle of Jacob's Creek. Chloe is thin, edgy, has dark circles under her eyes. She sinks into Henry's old chair by the fire (Georgia has taken to having a fire every evening, to raise her spirits) and scoops Tristan on to her lap. She buries her face in his fur, in what is clearly not just affection but an avoidance strategy. Do Not Ask Me Questions is written all over her.

Georgia doesn't. She has already opened a bottle of rather good Bordeaux, allowing it to breathe before serving the winter-warming casserole the scent of whose mushroom, wine and garlic sauce is now wafting through from the kitchen. She pours Chloe a glass, puts it into her hand.

– Thanks. Cheers. Oh, that's just hit the spot. What a lovely fire. How are you, Mum?

– Worried on every possible front, says Georgia, settling into her own chair.

– About?

– How long have you got?

Chloe returns the wry smile. She's thawing out a bit. There's a little sound at the door and Isolde pads in. She makes for the fire, stretches elaborately out on the rug. Both admire her. It begins to feel (almost) like old times.

– Something smells fantastic. Go on, Mum: I suppose it's Maud.

Georgia knows that Chloe's interest is in part deflection: you talk, and I don't have to. But of course it's Maud. And Dido, from whom she hasn't heard for a truly disquieting time. There have been moments (in between Maud) when she's wondered if the impossible has happened, and their friendship ended. Is that possible? Could it, ever? What did those tests reveal? Why isn't Dido telling her? She lies awake, wondering what to do. Then she goes back to Maud. And Chloe, now on her second glass.

– I'm listening, she says, with an enormous yawn.

When did she last get a good night's sleep? But Georgia will not press her, and instead she begins to describe it all: the decline and deterioration of property and person, the trips to and fro, the fox and hens (– Mum! That's awful), the sad old sheep, poor Kep, the fire, the Social Services, the Day Centre (ha!), the keys, the glimmer of hope, but general ghastliness.

– The thing is, she concludes – if this day-care arrangement doesn't work, we'll have to get her into a home.

– She won't go, though, will she?

– She'll have to.

– What are you going to do? How're you going to make her?

– I don't know. But I'm really beginning to need some help. I know you're up to your eyes, darling, but do you think – one weekend or two – you could possibly look at a few places?

– I suppose so. Yes, sure. Chloe gazes into the fire. There's a whole world in there: caves and mountains and fairy-tale things. That's what she used to think when she was little. Fairy tales. If only. Is she supposed to spend her weekends looking at old people's homes? Is this what life holds for her now?

– I just can't do it all by myself, says Georgia quietly, and this sentiment is so unheard of that Chloe is stopped in her sad little tracks. Poor Mum: she must be really low.

– Of course I'll help, she says, two glasses of wine now well and truly making themselves felt. – Can we have supper now?

Supper is cosy. Supper is very, very good. Chloe feels a bit like Toad, in *The Wind in the Willows*: revived in prison by hot buttered toast; revived after open-air adventures by a gypsy stew. Say what you like about salads and health foods: there's nothing liked baked potatoes and a casserole to make a girl feel human.

– Mum? Which ward was I born on? In UCH. Can you remember?

Georgia tries. The truth is that she can't. She can remember (indelibly) the name of the ward in Barts where Henry had his chemo. But the place where Chloe came into the world?

– Do you know, I can't think of it, she says. – Why do you ask?

– Oh, it doesn't matter. It's just that I went to see Sara's baby this morning, and it made me think of things. You know. You and Dad. Me.

She finishes off a potato skin, smothered in yummy sauce. Fancy not remembering where you had your only child. Would Sara, too, after years of juggling work and bringing up Daisy, look back one day in the middle of the twenty-first century and be unable to think of the place of all that happiness? Or perhaps Georgia hadn't been so happy. Chloe's pretty drunk, now. Perhaps she'd never been really wanted, perhaps it was only Dad who'd loved her. Like, really loved.

– Chloe?

– Sorry, Mum.

But she can't help it: she's in floods.

– Oh, darling.

Georgia gets up. She comes over, puts her arms round her, strokes her hair.

– Poor Chloe. You're having a bit of a difficult time?

– Not really, no more than you. Oh, Mum . . .

– I know. I know.

Does she? How could she? How could anyone who'd had that lovely long marriage, that lovely husband – oh, poor, poor Dad – who'd married so young and been so clever and everything – how could they possibly understand what it was like to want someone so badly, to want a baby of her very own so badly?

The kitchen is warm and snug and lamplit. The cats are flat out by the fire. It's horribly nice to be home.

– Do you want to stay the night?

She doesn't, but she does.

Maud wakes with a violent start. It's the middle of the night. The light is on (forget cosy bedside lamps, we're talking a naked fly-blown bulb drooping from the ceiling). Someone is standing beside her bed.

– Good morning, my love. Time to get you up.

Maud, hair all awry and dentures in a glass on the floor, clutches the covers.

– Who the hell are you?

– My name's Betty, dear. I'm from Social Services.

– Get out!

– Now, now.

– Call up my dog! Kep! Kep!

Where is he? Why is he not here?

– Kep!

– Don't you fret, my love. Here he comes.

Betty the carer is wonderful with confused old people, and very good with dogs. She has a son who shows at Crufts (beagles). She has already quietened Kep down in the kitchen, and here he is now, moving slowly up the stairs, untrimmed claws clicking across the lino. His nose goes into Maud's outstretched hand; she seizes his collar.

– See them off, boy! Attack!

– Now, now, dear, don't get overheated.

And Kep, though he gives a token burst of barking, is no match for impassive Betty. She's seen it all before, and her confident soothing tones soon calm him down. Maud is a different matter.

– Get your hands off me! Get out! Get out!

Betty, large, capable and kind, explains that it's seven o'clock, that she's come to give Maud a nice warm bath, get her into clean clothes and take her downstairs for breakfast. She's sorry if she frightened her, reminds her that she has a key, and says they'll soon get to know one another. She turns back the covers: the holey counterpane, ancient eiderdown, motheaten blankets and greying sheet, all in a heap and muddle.

– Up we get.

Strong hands turn Maud carefully towards the edge of the mattress. That's the plan. But Maud, though she has dreadful shuffling days, has not for nothing walked all her life over hill and dale. Deep down, though her muscles are wasting, she's as strong as a horse. It is, furthermore, amazing what one can do when roused. And as nice kind Betty's arms go round her from the front – That's it, good girl – Maud kicks her in the stomach with the force of a mule.

– I'm calling the POLICE!

Betty staggers back, doubled up and gasping. Maud advances towards her, arms upraised and Kep beside her.

– The POLICE! Get out of my house! Be gone, be gone!

And Kep is all at once a guard dog once again. He's stirred by the violence, stirred by the frantic note in the voice of his mistress, and by the general extraordinariness of the situation (no one, in his lifetime, has ever, ever been in Maud's bedroom). All his youth and vigour courses once more through his ageing veins, and he leaps towards poor Betty, now stumbling to the door.

Slam!

– Good riddance!

Betty clutches at the banister, still gasping.

Maud, panting but victorious, takes herself back to bed. Kep (likewise) makes for his basket. Soon, in the familiar squalor of the bedroom, all is still.

Outside, when Betty finally reaches her car, the last few stars and a thin old moon, like a junk shop dinner plate, are fading above the fields. She sits in her nice safe driving seat (locking the door) and she calls her team leader on her mobile. No one will be there yet, but she has to make her point. She's not coming back to Green Lane Farm. Ever. Full stop. End of story.

It isn't, of course.

Later that morning, when Chloe has breakfasted, and left for work, Georgia receives a phone call.

It's not the one she's been expecting. That one, from Joan MyLove Starkey, comes just before lunch. (We've had a bit of bother, my love, we'll have to think again.) By this time, Georgia's concern for Maud has been utterly eclipsed.

She's turfing Tristan off Chloe's unmade bed when the phone rings. Here we go. She crosses the landing to her own bedroom to answer it. Rain clouds are gathering darkly at the window: Chloe (no umbrella, of course) will be absolutely soaked.

– Hello?

– Georgia.

– Dido! My God, I'm glad to hear you.

– I know. I'm sorry.

– How are you?

– Are you sitting down?

21

Brain tumours aren't always malignant. They put you at dreadful risk, but they don't always kill you. As with so much else in your body, if (oh, magic if) they are caught in time, you have a reasonable chance of recovery. Of picking up your life again; being happy, even.

All this is explained to Dido by her neurosurgeon. She concentrates with all her being upon what this chap is telling her. He's reassuringly clever-looking (thin nose, bright eyes, nice specs) and he doesn't patronise. Dido knows women who've been made to feel idiots by confident loud men in hospitals – it still goes on. But this isn't one of them; this is the kind of person she and Jeffrey might have met and liked at a dinner party, in the days when such things were a part of their lives. (Will they ever, ever, be so again?)

So she listens, and has all her questions answered, as clouds sail serenely past the window and Jeffrey makes notes, as she's asked him to.

– Thank you so much.

– Not at all. I'll see you on the ward before the op. And the anaesthetist will come up as well, of course.

– Oh, good. That's nice.

What is she talking about? How can it be nice to wait quaking on a ward for visits from such people? But old habits die hard, and as they all get to their feet and shake hands they might almost be saying goodbye at a party – save for the look of kind concern the consultant gives them both; save for the anteroom outside, where some pretty sick people are waiting.

– Did you take all that in? asks Jeffrey, as they make their way down the endless corridor.

– Sort of. Not really.

He pats the notebook in his pocket.

– I've got it all in here.

And at home they go through it all over again, picking out all the hopeful, positive bits, all the good chances. Kate comes to supper, and she, like the clever consultant, is full of reassurance. Dido listens attentively once more.

It doesn't make the slightest difference.

She's mortally afraid.

That night, in bed, with Jeffrey asleep (is he really?) beside her, she gazes into the darkness, and she tries to face it all.

She can make out, just, the tiny phosphorescent points of light on the dial of the alarm clock: that little ring of hours which seems tonight so precious, as the hands creep round. Ordinary though it is, cheap, even, just a little black travel clock bought years and years ago, it seems tonight to hold all that makes us human: life framed within the vastness of the world, given order, sequence, purpose; and, in that ring of light, a gleam of hope.

For years the clock has got them up, sent them out to the bathroom, down to the kitchen, out of the front door to their busy busy lives. It has presided here over sex (though not for far too long); over children waking in the night; over tears and sleeplessness; over the long dark hours of sleep.

What long dark hours lie waiting for her now?

Listening to Jeffrey's restless breathing beside her, to the almost soundless ticking of the clock, Dido looks ahead to her operation, and back across her life. She thinks: I've had all life's great experiences. I've been in love, I've had my children (although I lost my Ella), my grandchildren; I've done work I value, travelled (if not hugely), read (enormously), had marvellous friends. What more could a future grant me now? Should I not be able, now, to be thankful for all I've had, and let the light go out?

She tries. She can't.

She turns over. Now the streetlight through the curtains shows her the heap of all those books beside the bed. Hard to say which, in their full lives, have been the more important: books or people. They have flowed into one another, for all of them: she and Jeffrey, Georgia and Henry – each, in different ways, has had reading at the heart of everything, touching and defining everything, a ceaseless inner life so rich it's hard to say where life and literature begin and end.

What comfort can reading bring her now? All that modern fiction: what does it have to say?

Henry read, almost to the end: so Georgia told her. The Russians, mostly. What was he thinking, as he reached for his book, his specs, and turned Tolstoy's pages? Was he seeking to lose or find himself?

Dido turns over once again. Beside her, Jeffrey stirs and shifts; then he turns over too. Now she's facing his back, a position in which for years they've gone to sleep: her arms round him, or his round her, if they're facing the other way. Warm, comforting, sexless (not always) and secure.

Now everything is fraught with danger, and it's not, of course, only the great last things which are keeping Dido awake, so long into the night. It's not just an operation she (they) must face, but Jeffrey's hearing.

The operation is on Thursday morning. She goes in on Wednesday afternoon, The hearing, unbelievably, is on the following Monday. Who knows what state Dido will be in that day? Will she not need Jeffrey beside her? Can he not change the date?

SUE GEE

He cannot. Already, it's been postponed from late September (get it all over, before term starts) not once, but twice. First Jeffrey's union representative – male, from another faculty – had it adjourned on a technicality. Dido cannot imagine that a liberal academic, albeit male, could take anything but the dimmest view of Jeffrey's (alleged) behaviour. None the less, the duty of this man is to stand by his colleague, at least at this stage, and he played for time. Teaching resumed, another date was set.

During those long long weeks, Jeffrey was as tense as Dido has ever seen him: conducting his classes, chairing meetings, drafting papers – he missed nothing, but he looked like death. And by then, of course, she'd told him about her test results. By then she was having more tests: lots. And blackouts: quite a few.

The date of the hearing approached. Then the Dean, who must be present, went down with flu (a lot of it about). Meanwhile, the young Law student at the heart of this dreadful business, the lovely young woman over whom Jeffrey lost his head, had written to the Vice Chancellor. A copy of her letter was forwarded to Jeffrey. He showed it to Dido: he shows her everything now. Humiliating for him, and shocking for her.

I was phoned, I was texted, I was emailed and besieged with letters. I was followed. I was approached before class, after class. I would find him waiting outside my house at night. I was begged for sex . . .

They read these appalling lines sitting side by side on the sofa. The fire was lit, the curtains drawn, they'd had supper. Anyone coming upon the scene would think it the most ordinary, most pleasantly domestic moment.

Dido scanned the page. Vile. She read it again, properly. She could not speak.

– It sounds worse than it was, said Jeffrey slowly. He was ashen.

270

– It sounds much much worse.

    – But she hasn't made it all up? She's not a fantasist?

    – No.

    – Some of this is what really happened?

    – Yes.

Those little words, and everything they meant, filled every corner of the room. Dido put her head in her hands.

    – How long? she asked at last. – Jeffrey? She turned to look at him. He was leaning back against the sofa, his hands up to his mouth: that old gesture which used to indicate only that he was thinking, concentrating, working something out. Now, what used to be one or two fingers put to his lips, had become hands white to the knuckle, clamped across his face. He looked hunted. Trapped.

    Then they were both in tears.

    – Tell me, tell me . . .

And he told her. How a lunch-time glance across the canteen last autumn stayed with him all afternoon: that fall of long dark hair, those brows, that flicker of interest. How he saw her again, two days later, as he came out of a lecture hall and she, with friends, went in. A fleeting smile, and he fell. It happens. Dido knows it happens: she's been listening to such things for years. It just hadn't happened to her, that's all. Or if it had – and of course, over thirty years of marriage, she'd met men she liked the look of – it had been put aside, discounted. A glimmer of interest, a moment or two spent wondering, then back to work, to normal, to the everyday press of things.

    But Jeffrey: Jeffrey became obsessed. And told her nothing. And got deeper and deeper.

    At length she asked him, when both were quite exhausted: – Was it really all one-sided? Did she not feel for you? Not encourage you?

    She was thinking of that text, in early summer. Of that disquieting, disturbing little line:

Can U get away tonite?

Was that the sentiment of a woman being harassed? Trying to get away?

And she told him of that moment in his study, that quiet, sunlit moment amongst his books and papers: leaving his post on the desk, hearing the text come through, breaking a lifetime's rule of respect for other people's privacy.

And he told her that at first it seemed this young student felt the same: how they met for drinks, went for walks, exchanged one long passionate kiss. And then she said it had better stop, and he could not accept it. That was when everything changed. That's when it became as this letter described, though she made it sound so terrible.

– Was it not terrible? For her?

– Perhaps. Yes. I suppose it was.

The fire had gone down. It was raining. That steady sound accompanied, once more, a moment of crisis and disclosure.

– And do you still feel . . . ?

There was a long silence. The rain fell on and on. Then Jeffrey groaned.

– I don't know what I feel.

How did they get through all those dreadful days?

By keeping themselves to themselves. By closing the door.

Dido has had to tell them at work that she won't be in for a while. She has had to tell them why. Everyone's been kind and concerned: flowers from Caro, lots of cards, unending offers of help: to cook, to clean, to shop, to plan. She has thanked them all: she's sure they'll manage, but it's so good to know – really, thank you. What she hasn't said is that this is only the half of it. Of Jeffrey's situation she has not breathed a word. So much for openness; so much for disclosure, and the healing power of talk. Forget it. What's needed now is silence, secrecy, the curtains drawn.

* * *

Sometimes Dido, so sociable and outgoing all her life, has felt like one of those people you read about in the papers: said by the neighbours to be ever so quiet, keeping himself to himself, a bit of a loner, really. Hardly knew he was there. Until he went out with an axe, or a nail bomb. Or met three friends at Luton. She realises that the kind of appalled disbelief which neighbours feel in such circumstances is what everyone who knows them – friends, colleagues, and yes, neighbours – would feel if Jeffrey's behaviour ever came to light.

She battens down the hatches even further. No one, not even Georgia, must know. Until this week, when she cracked at last, and phoned her. Georgia's stunned silence haunts her still.

What about the children? Surely they must be told. You can't let your grown-up children be the last to know. Can you? Oh God. Are their careers and lives to be blighted by having Jeffrey as a father?

Kate and Nick were invited over: no, don't bring Leo, darling, he can look after the children; no, darling, I'd rather Paula wasn't here this time – no, no, it's nothing against her, nothing like that, it's just—

Kate and Nick turned up for supper, looking tense and drawn. They knew about Dido: wasn't this enough? Now what?

It took (it seemed) for ever for Jeffrey to tell them. Then, after two stiff drinks, he did.

There was a shocked and dreadful silence. Dido saw her children look at one another across the room in horror. Then they rallied. They offered, dear generous people that they were, to help in any way they could. These things happen: they both knew the ways of the world (Nick was less convincing, here). They understood, of course they did. So long as Mum was OK . . .

But this was their own father. Of whom no one would ever dream . . .

Their words tailed away. By nine, they'd gone.

* * *

Dido tosses and turns. The hearing looms. The operation looms.

She tries again to rationalise her fear. She makes herself think: I'm not here any more. It's as simple as that. Nothing to be afraid of.

But Dido is no Buddhist, and she can't find this calm acceptance.

In truth, can anyone?

You might be wondering how Dido can possibly be sharing a bed with Jeffrey now. Sharing the house, even. This second question is quickly dealt with: few can afford to up sticks and move out just like that, when trouble comes. If they could, no doubt a good few marriages long past their sell-by date would be brought to a merciful conclusion. Without funds to rent some marvellous bolt hole, the option is to land on friends and family, a situation which can be fraught, once the first few days have passed. There remain two possibilities: changing the locks and getting an injunction; or fleeing to a woman's refuge. But this is in the territory of domestic violence, and real danger. Dido is not, thank God, in such a situation. She is, however, ill, and in illness most of us long for our own bed. As for sharing it with Jeffrey . . .

Does she not feel rage, humiliation, a desire for revenge? For total separation? Might she not, at least, be sleeping in another bedroom, or insisting that Jeffrey does so?

She might. She has indeed felt some of these hideous things, or did when he first told her. But Dido is not a raging or a vengeful person: these impulses are not really in her nature. She is a worker, a conciliator and a realist; she is essentially loving and kind. And pretty strong. There is also the question of forgiveness, not a word you hear a huge amount these days – like guilt, which you never hear at all, except to be told you must not feel it.

So cynical has our age become that the idea of a woman

forgiving such behaviour as Jeffrey has confessed to connotes only the poor wife of some ghastly MP, a poor brave smiling creature standing by a selfish lying bastard to whom she should long ago have given the boot. But Jeffrey is not such a man, and Dido knows it: like her (and some MPs, no doubt) he is essentially decent and hard-working, not to say sensitive, loving, generous. He is in the deepest shit, with everything to lose: career, income, status, colleagues, friends and future. Is he to lose his wife of thirty-odd years as well?

The more they talk, the more she listens, the more Dido is determined to face it out beside him. She's hurt, she's anxious, but she does understand, and does forgive. Their closeness in this hour of need makes both feel a loving tenderness and concern so deep that their long familiar marriage enters a new phase: it truly feels that only death can part them.

Chloe and Jez are going to the theatre. At last, after weeks of rehearsal, not to mention years of treading the boards at Heal's, Ed is on the London stage once more. The venue, you may recall, is the Tricycle, a fine north London theatre, which stages important political drama. Neither Chloe nor Jez has ever been there, which says much for their general disengagement from the major events of our time, since it is within walking distance of the studio where they are quite often to be found. Georgia and Henry, on the other hand, when not in their Friends of the National seats on the South Bank, or their Friends of the Almeida seats in Islington, used from time to time to venture up there. Once or twice they invited Chloe, but she was busy. They saw the play about Stephen Lawrence; a very good two-hander about (among other things) life on a Brixton street, and the play about Iraq. This was, in fact, the last they saw together, so it has a particular poignancy for Georgia to know that Chloe's flatmate, a young man she's never been quite sure about, is appearing at the Tricycle now, in a three-week run. Everyone's hoping it will transfer to the West End.

– I'll ring the Cartwrights, she says on the phone to Chloe. – I'm sure they'd be interested.

– Great. I'm sorry about the first night, Mum, it's just that—

– Don't worry, darling, I quite understand.

What Georgia has been given to understand is that the whole house is sold out for the thrilling first night, not a seat to be had and no chance of a cancellation. She knows this must be nonsense; that Chloe, through Ed, could easily have got her a ticket when booking opened and she received her comp. There must be a reason for this fib (as she chooses to think of it, blatant lie being too harsh to contemplate about her own daughter) and she guesses that Chloe is attending this occasion with the married man who seems to be making her so unhappy. Chloe is clearly still not prepared to discuss, let alone introduce him. In any case, Georgia has at present so many things to worry about that Chloe's situation has had to go on the back burner, while trips to the theatre, no matter how meaningful the play, seem something of a frivolity.

Maud goes from bad to worse. Chloe has promised (*promised*) to help with the hunt for a suitable Home. Georgia has already been down to look at one: a place with all the appearance of a comfortable hotel. There are lovely grounds, a lake.

– Does she wander, dear?

– I beg your pardon?

– Your auntie. Does she wander?

– Miss Hannaway is not my aunt, but my late husband's second cousin.

Georgia delivered this line with all the hauteur of which Maud herself once was capable.

– Sorry, dear. It's just that with the lake – we can't have wanderers.

– Miss Hannaway has been used to walking miles a day. I

should think it entirely possible that without supervision she might walk straight through those French windows and out to the lake and drown. So might any demented person. The place is clearly quite unsuitable. I have wasted my time.

And with that she was gone. Slam. Off to Green Lane Farm to cook a nourishing little lunch, clean everything in sight and change the sheets.

This cannot go on. She is the only person Maud will admit to the house, and it's more of a battle on each occasion.

– Get off my land!

– Oh, shut up, you old fool.

It has come to this.

Henry, if you could see me now.

Perhaps he can. Anything, these days, seems possible. And Georgia's exasperation, down in Sussex, is fuelled by her terrible anxiety about events in York. As she drives back to London, through leafless lanes and empty ploughland, she is haunted by the thought of Dido in hospital, shaven and shorn and facing (perhaps) the end. She is troubled by extraordinary fantasies about Jeffrey – so strong, so sure, so deeply married, so entirely fallen, now, from all these certainties. Sexual harassment: low, shabby, vile. Georgia knows, of course, that the phrase can be used by the vengeful and self-seeking to sully a pat on the shoulder. But this, Dido has told her, is not such a case: Jeffrey did not, he swears, have sexual relations with this woman, but, as with Clinton, something certainly went on.

It could be worse. He could have been revealed to be grooming little girls (or boys) on the internet, or visiting prostitutes, or having a second family all these years, for whom he is now abandoning the first. There's always something worse. But as she contemplates all of these scenarios, dismissing each as impossibly out of character, Georgia, driving through darkened villages, is forced to accept that the man she has known, liked and admired all her life, Henry's closest friend, has indeed acted quite out of character, has concealed and deceived and broken trust. That this does not make him a monster; that he must have been tormented; that he is now loving and contrite and caring; and that, above all, as Dido so stoically put it, These Things Happen – none of this escapes her. It is still most deeply shocking.

And as Georgia considers and recoils from all of it, she is troubled still further by thoughts which lie closer to home. If strong and upright Jeffrey could keep something so dark and hidden, then might even Henry— She slams the shutter down. Impossible to contemplate, unworthy even to consider. She will not consider it for another moment.

She's out on the motorway, picking up speed, the radio on and the car filled all at once – oh joy – with Bach cantatas. But as faster cars speed past her and headlights glare, Georgia cannot turn her mind so easily from a darkened country lane, a summer moon, a kiss upon the cheek, and then another, a hand upon her arm. For a moment, a familiar gesture of farewell had been charged with sexual tension; for a moment, decades of friendship fell away. Had Jeffrey made a single move she would have responded: this is the dreadful truth. Dido and Henry would have been forgotten: all that mattered would have been two craving mouths, two people flooded with desire and longing.

Is this what lay behind Jeffrey's boorish behaviour over lunch, a few days later? Was he trying to provoke her in another way, to reveal a side of her long kept repressed and hidden? What he provoked was fury: had that been her displaced desire and regret? Her shame?

Lorries are thundering by; Bach's beauty and order sound all around her. She thinks: but Jeffrey was then – he must have been – tormented by anxiety, trying to fend off what he knew was coming, trying to keep the family show on the road and pretend that all was normal when in fact he was (was he?) still dreaming, still hoping, still longing and sleepless and approaching desperation. That was why he was drinking; he didn't give a damn, not really, where my future lay, he was just turning the heat away from his own misery.

The truth is, Georgia, that the sexual tension you felt in that moonlit moment was all in your own mind. Jeffrey's mind, all holiday, was on someone else entirely.

She drives on, drives faster, turning up the volume, seeking in music's passion all which now seems lost to her in life.

Chloe and Jez are having a drink in the Tricycle bar, ten minutes before curtain up. It's the first time they've been to the theatre together and the first time, in fact, that they've seen each other at all since Regent's Park, except for work. The glamorous Russian pics are done: he's brought them into the office and they've all gone ooh and ah. Dot says he's brilliant. Jez smiles modestly, the work experience person (another one) makes tea for everyone and blushes when he thanks her. Chloe tries out cropping this and that, with enormous concentration. Phones ring, emails pile up: it's just a normal day in the office, except that normal days have come to mean Happy Hour with everyone and then going back to Jez's flat for sex and supper, or he coming over to hers for the same. Now he's packing up his stuff, hoiking his bag on to his elegant shoulder, saying goodbye to everyone and see you later.

'Later', in Georgia's lexicon, implies that something has been arranged, that there is a particular time and place where people will meet again. In Chloe's world this is not the case at all: 'later' has come to replace 'soon', and is now a loose and sloppy word that could mean anything: ten minutes, tomorrow, one day if you're lucky. What does it mean today?

– Jez?

He turns and smiles at her. Does she imagine it, or is he looking shifty?

– Um, Jez?

He glances at his watch.

– Are you . . . are we . . .?

– I'm picking up Ellie from school today. His hand is on the door. – I'll call you tonight, OK?

– OK. Sure.

And she turns back to the bloody office, and he goes clattering down the stairs. Hope he trips. Hope someone's left a banana skin, and he trips and—

But such thoughts lead only to affecting scenes in which Jez lies prone upon the pavement, ambulance sirens wail and she devotes the rest of her life to caring for him.

Even Chloe, though she has tears in her eyes, knows that this is all nonsense. She goes home, rather the worse for wear after Happy Hour with the work experience person (nice enough), opens a bottle, drinks a lot of it, rings a few people, rustles up some pasta, rings a few more and finally succumbs to a hot bath swimming in essential this and that. Her phone goes just as she's sinking in: she grabs it from the laundry basket. It's him.

– Hi, Jez.

– Hi. Hi, how are you?

He sounds almost like his sexy old self: warm, with an undertone of purr.

– I'm fine, I'm in the bath.

– Oh, yeah?

Now he sounds really interested. Chloe sinks deeper into fragrant pools of Tranquillity Rose, Energising Lavender Balance, Vitality Essence and Seaweed Scrub. (She was really pretty drunk when she ran the taps.)

– Why don't you come over?

– I've got Ellie with me.

– Oh. Right.

That's the end of that, then.

– It seems an awfully long time since—

– I know. I'm sorry.

He's sorry! Thank God for that.

– Do you want to – um – do you want to talk about it?

– Not just at the moment, to be honest.

– Is she awake?

– No, but . . .

– It's OK.

She understands, of course she does. You don't go talking about sex and Relationships when your daughter of eight is asleep in the next room. Not if you're a decent sort of person, which he is, of course, he's a fantastic father, just fantastic, which is why she—

– I went to see Sara's baby, she tells him, turning on the hot water with her pretty toes, just like they do in old movies, bubbles all piled up to the neck and everyone wearing lipstick.

– Oh, yeah?

Something in Chloe gives a little cringe. You don't say Oh, yeah? about a newborn baby. You just don't, somehow. She knows this is Georgia speaking, but well, sometimes she has a point. Anyway, you can't stop loving someone just because they say Oh yeah, can you? And she does love him, so so much, and she knows that if he actually *saw* the baby it would be completely different, he'd be all tender and—

– She's really lovely. Exquisite. They've called her Daisy Sara; they're doing really well. I think they've all gone home now, I've tried them a couple of times but the answerphone's always on, I expect they're really up to their eyes, you are with a new baby, aren't you? And do you know what, Jez? Someone almost gave birth in the hospital *hall*, everyone was, like, really *rushing* her to the delivery room. And I kept thinking about you, and about us and everything, and I mean I know you can't talk now, but can we talk soon? About everything? Jez?

– Yeah, yeah, sure we can. Hang on a minute, I think she's woken up.

Oh God.

There's a pause, quite a long one, in which Chloe swishes about, trying to get the measure of the Seaweed Scrub, which isn't meant to be in the bath at all, and is really scratchy, just when she's trying to relax—

– Hi. Listen, I've got to go, sorry, she's had a bad dream, I think. I'll call you tomorrow, OK?

– You know it's the play on Wednesday, don't you?

– The play.

– Ed's play. The 9/11 thing. Wednesday's the first night, remember?

Surely he hasn't forgotten that. She got an extra comp specially, put off Georgia and everything.

– Sure, sure, sorry. Why don't we meet there? It's at the Tricycle, right?

And here they are, sitting on stools at the bar with first-night buzz all round them, trying to spot the critics. This is fun! And she's determined (a) to give Ed all the support in the world, even if the play is really awful (he's been in some pretty weird things in the past), and (b) to be really nice and understanding with Jez, so he doesn't feel threatened or anything, doesn't feel she's coming on too strong. Did she come on too strong about Sara's baby? Thinking about it, she thinks she did. After all, how easy can it be, trying to have a relationship when you've got a really demanding job, and a little girl to look after, and two households to support, and an ex-wife phoning you at work?

She is ex, isn't she? She will be ex, won't she?

Stop it! Just be nice and cool and happy, and everything will come right. And she chinks her margarita glass against his and lets him talk: about work, about Ellie (preparing for SATs and all hyped-up), about where he got his shoes (Hoofs) and that really nice grey sweater (Gap, where else?) until suddenly the bell's going and she feels all at once really *sick* with nerves, as if she, not Ed, were waiting behind the curtain while everyone goes in.

– Come on!

And in they go, buying a programme and settling down and seeing Ed's name in the cast list and his *Spotlight* photo at the back with a list of all his credits. Blimey. Reading this, you'd think the boy was never out of work. 'Has appeared in' can mean anything, of course. Never mind. He's got this great part now, something really serious, and it feels so cool to be here, she doesn't know why she doesn't come to the theatre more often.

Then the lights go down, and she reaches for Jez's hand. He takes it. Everything's going to be all right.

The play is pretty weird, and pretty scary. It opens with a huge back-projection of the twin towers falling, in utter silence, and though Chloe, like everyone, has seen those clips a million times before, sitting here in the darkness it's like, really sinister.

It's shown again, and then a voice that makes her jump out of her skin says somewhere: – Are you watching?

That's Ed!

– Are you really watching? Can you see how those towers come down? Look again. Do you think that aircraft could bring them down like that? So neatly? Does anyone here remember Ronan Point?

Chloe has never heard of Ronan Point, but there was something in the programme notes, with a picture of the corner of a tower block crumbling to the ground. She'd thought it was one of the WTC towers, that's what the play's about, isn't it, but no.

– Ronan Point came down in 1968 because of a gas explosion. What do you think brought down the World Trade Center towers on 9/11? Aircraft crashing into them, almost at the top? Or was there something else as well? Look again.

And everyone looks, as the towers crumble, floor upon floor upon floor, like packs of cards, and flames and smoke billow into the blue blue New York sky. Then all at once there's a soundtrack, really loud, and on the screen are the terrible scenes they've all seen before but which will never lose their impact: people down on the street yelling and screaming, running for their lives, looking back in terror.

Cut. They're all in darkness. Chloe is squeezing Jez's hand so hard it hurts them both: they disentangle. Then the stage is lit by a single spot, and into it steps Ed. He's holding a clipboard and a mike. When he speaks quietly into it, he doesn't sound like Ed at all.

– I'm here to ask questions: of you, and of the American government. 1. In 2005 the Windsor Building in Madrid was destroyed by fire, yet the steel frame stayed standing. How come the twin towers crumpled as they did? 2. In the nine months prior to 9/11 the standard US military procedures to intercept hijacked aircraft were operated more than sixty times. So how is it that those planes flew on and on for almost two hours? Why weren't they intercepted? 3. It takes 2.4 minutes to scramble fighter aircraft from the Andrews Air Force Base in Washington DC in the event of a hijack. So how is it that on 9/11 it took one and a half hours, by which time the Pentagon was in flames?

– I'm not alone in asking questions like these, Ed continues, walking along the stage. – People all around the world, including serious American academics, have been asking them now for a long time. One of these people, close to home, is the MP Michael Meacher. Another is David Shayler, ex-MI5, as you know. There are no satisfactory answers: not in the 9/11 Commission Report, not in any testimonies or reports about that day. But if truth and democracy mean anything at all, we have to keep on asking.

Up go the lights on the stage, and there's Bush, in a schoolroom, having something whispered in his ear. It's one of the most famous pictures in the world: even Chloe can identify this scene.

– Mr President, Ed demands. – Can you spare a minute? I'm from a British newspaper. Could you explain why the FBI failed to investigate and arrest four of the 9/11 hijackers when they were given their names by Mossad a month before? When Mossad had warned that a huge terrorist operation was being planned? Could you explain why, when CNN was breaking the story of the first plane at 8.48 on 9/11, you were not told until you had settled down in the classroom of a school in Florida ten minutes later?

And so it goes on, and on, and on, without an interval. It gets in all the major players – Bush, Rice, Rumsfeld, the heads of the CIA and FBI, the authors of the 9/11 Commission Report and a gathering crowd of people on the street: firefighters, witnesses, relatives of the dead.

The play asks, over and over, extraordinary questions. Like: did US officials have advance information about 9/11? Did they obstruct investigations before the attacks? Did they have reasons for letting them happen? Were they complicit? More than that: were explosives planted at the foot of the twin towers before the planes were hijacked? The play links the Bush and Bin Laden families. It asks why, when intelligence was given about his whereabouts, Bin Laden was not captured months before. And so on and so on and so on.

Chloe doesn't know a thing about any of this. Some of it sounds completely mad. And yet: not one convincing answer is given.

And when the play's technique of question and evasion has begun to grow repetitive (even, dare she think it, boring) in comes a subplot to keep you on the edge of your seat. Ed, dismissed at first as a crackpot conspiracy theorist, begins to be seen as a dangerous political activist. He's stalked, his flat is bugged, he's threatened. The play ends with his violent arrest in the middle of the night, the seizing of his computer, and then a courtroom scene. Now Ed is in the dock, now he's the one being questioned and accused. And sentenced. And led away, in handcuffs. By the time this happens, Chloe is in tears. There's a silence, then thunderous applause.

Then it's the first-night party. Exclusive or what? Chloe, used to seeing Ed wandering about the flat in his dressing gown, unpacking the shopping or draping his washing over the fire escape (what would they do without it?) now finds herself gazing at him across a crush of people like he's a *star*. They're down in the greenroom, packed to the gills with the hip, the cool, the seriously clever. There are pictures all round the walls of intense-looking actors, and stills from this production, with Ed shouting at Bush, and Rumsfeld shouting at Ed. And there's a great big mirror, which makes the party look twice as big, and everyone's trying to look as if they're not looking at themselves in it, though everyone of course is doing just that. Digital cameras are flashing everywhere, you can hardly hear yourself speak, and two or three young women in micro black skirts are weaving through it all with trays of fizz and canapés.

Ed looks shattered and high as a kite, all at the same time, and he's hugging and kissing everyone in that luvvie way but he's also become – you can just tell, somehow – a really serious actor. Everyone's asking him and the director lots of stuff: she's sure that must be the *Time Out* critic, he just looks as if he couldn't be anyone else, and there's – gosh – that woman from the *Observer* whose pic she's seen when reading the Sundays with Georgia. Not that she's done that for a while. What on earth would her mother make of all this? She can just hear her, see her, looking down her nose. Internet conspiracy stuff. OK, clever clogs, what answers do *you* have to all those questions?

– Jez? Did you think it was all loopy?

– I don't know what to think. He drains his glass, takes another from a passing tray. – Bush is a moron, we all know that, but blowing up your own people? I don't think so.

– Nor me. But it really made me think.

That seems to be about it. Neither of them is sufficiently well informed to continue the discussion as it deserves, and as they go on for a bit saying how meaningful it was, and how well acted, and then begin to discuss the lighting (Jez has plenty of views on this) Chloe finds herself thinking: if Dad were here, he'd have lots to say. He'd be able to fill me in on everything, he'd tell me if he thought it was pie in the sky, but I think he'd take it seriously. Thoughts of her father lead, of course, to further thoughts about her mother, who would be far less tolerant but have plenty of clever views. If Chloe were here with Georgia and her friends she'd be feeling (as usual) a bit of an idiot, but she'd also be learning something. And if it was really nice people, like the Sullivans, she wouldn't feel so much of an ignoramus (unless it was Kate). Jeffrey would be giving all the history background, and Dido would be discussing the script, and talking about other new plays, and Nick – Nick would be with Paula.

Anyway, poor Dido's really ill now, having an operation any minute, and something else is going on up there, she's sure of it: Georgia's gone all mute and peculiar about it.

Anyway, why's she thinking about all of them, all of a sudden, while she's here with Jez?

– I'm so glad you came, she tells him, and he smiles.

– Me too. I never really go to stuff like this.

Across the room, Ed's posing for his pictures. There's a big cast dinner party after this. He's said they can go, but she knows what it'll be like: more of the same, and she and Jez a bit out of it, like now. And anyway, they need to *talk*.

– Jez? Where shall we eat? Are you coming back to mine, or shall I, um, come back to yours?

He's glancing at his watch. – The thing is, I've got to be up really early. I'm on a shoot. In Chelsea.

– For?

– Prada. For *GQ*.

– Gosh, Jez, that's fantastic. You're doing so well now. When did that come through?

– A month back. I thought I'd told you.

– No. No, I don't think so. Anyway, what do you want to do? About – about food and stuff. I suppose the thing is: it'd be quicker for you to come to mine, wouldn't it, if you've got to get to Chelsea early. Why don't I treat you to supper at Nina's? We never go there and it's just down the road. What do you think? I feel like going somewhere really nice, don't you? And they've got that lovely little quiet room at the back, so we can talk.

She can hear herself, on two (three?) glasses of fizz, beginning to go on; she can feel she's beginning to crowd him, but the thing about fizz is that it makes you pretty reckless. And come *on!* This is Ed's first night, it's special, and if they're not going to the cast party then she wants to have her own celebration, to feel all special and happy herself, and—

– Jez?

– The thing is, I'd have to pick up all my stuff from the flat.

– OK. Let's go back there then. Shall we get a cab? I'm beginning to feel a bit—

She is, too. And as she puts her glass back on a passing tray, and takes (to hell with it) another, she catches sight of herself in the mirror, in her little black dress and faux-fur jacket, and Ed's black seed pearls, which have always made her feel the most lovely mix of chic and sexy. She's had her hair cut (Vidal's, this morning) and she's wearing loads and loads of lash-thickener (not, though she says herself, that she really needs to). Does she look like Audrey Hepburn? Just a bit? Or – God forbid – like Liza Minnelli?

Chloe puts her glass back down on that tray before you can say jackrabbit. If she goes on drinking like this she'll start to look really *raddled*. Liza Minnelli must be sixty.

– Jez? Shall we get a cab, then?

He looks down into his glass. – Like I say, I've got to get up really early.

Across the room, Ed has his arm round a skinny young man who she knows is the New One. Perhaps it is The One. They look so happy.

And suddenly, the words tripping over themselves, she's saying to Jez: – Oh, give me the brushoff, then. Again. Excuse me—

And she's making her way through the crowd, fluttering her extra-thick eyelashes at the *Time Out* critic, who raises a cool (but not uninterested) eyebrow, and reaching Ed at last to hug him and tell him he was really really brilliant. And it's a fantastic play. Really important. And at the end, she was in floods.

– I knew you would be. By the way, this is Simon.

– Hi, Simon!

– Hi.

He's kissing her on the cheek though they've never met before, but this is what everyone does now, especially when they're gay, and especially on a night like this. You just want to kiss absolutely everyone.

– Where's Jez?

– He's just over there. She turns. No, he isn't. Her stomach does a violent nosedive. – He was standing right there . . .

– Well, I expect he's just gone to the loo. Don't look so—

– I'm not.

But she is, she is, she feels all at once quite frantic.

– Sure you don't want to come out to dinner?

– No, no, thanks. But have a fantastic evening. She flashes a smile at Simon, gives Ed a kiss. – I'll see you tomorrow, I've just got to . . .

And she's pushing her way through everyone again, saying she's sorry, sorry, excuse me, thanks, thanks . . .

– Hi. You again.

It's the *Time Out* guy, and he's interested, she can tell, but this is not the moment, and she brushes past, saying sorry all over again, many times, until she's reached the door, and is out in a corridor, looking wildly about her for the Gents but knowing, just knowing, that that's not where he is, and she runs up the stairs and through the bar, all shut now and dimly lit, and out to the foyer, hung with those stills from the play, and down to the guy on the door.

– Good night now.

– Good night!

And she's through the glass doors and out on the Kilburn High Road, looking frantically up and down, and there he is. Just getting into a taxi.

– Jez! Jez, wait!

But the Kilburn High Road is noisy at the best of times, and it's noisy now, everyone spilling out of the pubs and burger bars, and she stands there waving helplessly as the taxi comes speeding past. Jez hasn't heard her. Jez hasn't seen her. The traffic lights are green, and he's gone, gone, gone.

Chloe jumps into the very next taxi (oh, thank God!) telling the driver: – Follow that cab! She leans forward, tapping on the window. – See the one I mean?

– I see it. Done a bunk, has he? Pretty girl like you?

Chloe slams the window to. She leans back in her seat and dives into her bag. Got it! And guess what: he's on voicemail.

– Jez. Jez, it's me. Listen, I'm so so sorry, that was so insensitive of me, I know how much pressure you're under, I was just a bit drunk, I think. Anyway, I'm coming over, I'm in a cab behind you, OK? And I can't wait to see you, and show you how sorry I am. Lots and *lots* of love.

She leans back again, keeping those tail lights right in view. Of course, it doesn't matter if they lose them, all she has to do is give the driver the address: there must be lots of ways of getting across to Willesden.

Hang on a minute. It's surely not *this* way. She might be dyslexic, but even she can tell if they're turning towards Tufnell Park. Even she can tell if they're turning into a deeply residential street down which no taxi would be going unless to drop someone off. Like, take someone home.

– Excuse me! Excuse me, but can you slow right down?

– Stalking, are we?

– Do you want a tip?

– All right, all right.

And he slows, and ahead she can see Jez's taxi pulling up, outside a v. v. nice flat-fronted house, with creeper, and lights on, and—

– Stop!

– Keep your hair on.

But he pulls up at a decent distance, not too close, but not so far that she can't see Jez getting out, feeling in his pocket, paying the driver and glancing up towards the house.

His house.

Their house.

Frozen, Chloe sits there, as the meter ticks and Jez clicks open the gate and walks up the garden path. She can see his head and shoulders. She can't see if he's ringing the bell or getting his keys out, but she can see, in a moment or two, the rectangle of light as the front door opens, and the way he hesitates, as if not sure he's welcome. And then he goes inside.

22

I
t's the night before the op. Dido's surgeon and his anaesthetist have both been up to see her: one before supper, one after. Supper is by now academic: one of those dread 'Nil by mouth' signs hangs above her bed, and in any case she couldn't eat a thing. Both medics have been again kind and reassuring, the anaesthetist a frighteningly young woman who after Dido's first astonishment struck her as both sensitive and clever, a pleasing combination you don't find that often. They discuss her previous operations (none, since her tonsillectomy in 1957) and reactions to anaesthesia.

Dido remembers a horrid rubber mask, and the sickening smell of ether. Having to breathe it in, when all you wanted to do was push it all away.

– I expect things have changed since then.

– They certainly have.

They laugh (well, smile) at the old joke about feeling a little prick.

– And when you come round it should be quite gentle and calm.

– No being sick? Well, that's something.

Nurses (they're still called nurses) are moving up and down the ward with evening medication. Why it can't be called medicine, as for time immemorial, is something Dido has never understood. Kate's explained that medicine implies liquid, while pills on the whole are pills. 'Medication' embraces both. Not that anyone swallows medicine any more, except cough mixture, perhaps, and even that seems to be in pill or powders now. Not that Dido has taken more than a couple of paracetomol for as long as she can remember.

– I've always been so *fit*.

– You look fit. You look fit and strong.

– Not pale and anxious?

They smile at one another. Dido being Dido, she's soon listening to the details of the flat the anaesthetist is buying with her partner.

– Another anaesthetist?

– Yes, as it happens.

Dido starts to laugh.

– Is that so funny?

– No, of course not. It just makes me think of Flanders and Swann.

Needless to say, young Jenny has never heard of these two, and by the time Dido's explained, and sung a little snatch of *I'm a Gnu* she's forgotten all about the op. (Well, almost.)

– I wish all our patients were like you, says the nurse, come to check her chart.

– What was that you were singing?

Dido sings it again. She has to explain what a gnu is, and by the time she's done this (not that she's a huge authority) it's not quite as funny as it was. The nurse (Kerry) takes her blood pressure and goes on her way. Dido picks up her book and waits for Jeffrey to arrive.

In the end, after much deliberation, she brought in *The Wind in the Willows*. What she needs is comfort, and comfort, in modern fiction, is perhaps in short supply. It's back to the books of her childhood, back to:

Once beyond the village, where the cottages ceased abruptly, on either side of the road they could smell through the darkness the friendly fields again; and they braced themselves for the last long stretch, the home stretch, the stretch that we know is bound to end, some time, in the rattle of the door-latch, the sudden firelight . . .

Dido reads this passage over and over again: partly because it delights her, partly because, even so, she can't really take it in. Not even Mole and Ratty can distract her now. She shuts her eyes, suddenly exhausted. Trolleys bang about, phones ring, nurses shriek with laughter. Hospitals are so *noisy*. Will it be like this tomorrow? (Will she live through tomorrow? That's the main thing.)

– Dido. Here I am.

She opens her eyes to see Jeffrey beside her. He looks as pale as she feels, but he's bearing long-stemmed roses, cream and yellow, out of season and unethical, but oh, so lovely.

– How are you?

– Fine, fine. They're beautiful, thank you so much. Tell me what's going on.

Jeffrey lays the roses carefully on the bed table. He kisses her, sits down in the chair beside her, takes her hand. She turns to look at him. God, he looks old, she thinks again. Old and unutterably weary. Like her. How have they come to this?

– Everything's OK, he says, and though of course it isn't, they're both on the edge of a precipice, they talk in civilised fashion about his day (a seminar, a meeting) and her admission here.

– What's the food like?

She indicates the sign above the bed. – What about you? Have you eaten?

– I'll have something when I get back.

– Promise? You've got to keep your strength up.

– I know. He leans back in the chair, he shuts his eyes. For a little while, neither speaks: they just hold hands, and the noise of the ward (all those other patients and their visitors, the drama of all those lives only feet away, and everyone trying their best to keep sane and cheerful) sounds all around them.

– Well, now, says Dido at last. – What do we have to say to one another? Just in case.

Jeffrey opens his eyes, he looks at her, he raises her hand to his lips.

He says slowly: – I have always loved you. Even though I've been so . . . so hideously off the rails.

– I know. And I you. Always. And if . . . if I don't come through—

– You will, you will.

– But if I don't. You never know. Just make sure the children know how much I love them.

– How could they fail to know that?

– You know what I mean. And Izzy and Sam. And don't brood. Don't let anyone brood, or be gloomy. I'll be OK.

– What do you mean?

– Well, says Dido. – Either death really is the end, in which case I shall know nothing about it, and nobody need worry, or there's something more, in which case – she falters – in which case, I suppose I might see Ella.

– Oh, Dido . . .

– But I don't think I will, she says, struggling to pull herself together. – I think I'll just go out like a light, and—

– Dido, darling. Please. Please.

She breathes deeply, steadies herself.

– Sorry. Sorry.

– You don't have to be sorry, it's just—

– I know.

And she breathes again, and smiles at him, and they talk of other things, though this is the only thing that matters. She tells him, after a while about the gnu, and that cheers both of them. They go through all the old Flanders and Swann songs they love, dwelling upon the armadillo, falling in love with a tank on Salisbury Plain, and the one about the convolvulus and the honey-suckle whose love was doomed from the start because one climbed anti-clockwise and the other . . . Which, finally, reminds Dido that there's something which, what with one thing and another, she's failed to tell Jeffrey, all this time.

– I think Paula's gay.

– What?

– It came to me, all at once, at that party where I had a blackout. That chap who was trying to be helpful – his wife left him for another woman.

– How on earth do you know that?

– Oh, Jeffrey. How do you think? Anyway, I realised, then. About Paula. I can't think how we can all have been so blind. But I think she's repressing it all, and I suppose perhaps in some strange unconscious way we've all gone along with it. Do you think?

How nice it is, to be talking about someone else's problems for once. Jeffrey considers. Yes, he thinks she's right. Poor Paula. What it is to keep things hidden. (He should know.) Even from yourself. Poor old Nick: has he guessed? Should one of them tell him?

– Well, says Dido. – It won't be me for a while, will it? And don't you think you've got enough on your plate?

They agree he has. And now it's really dark outside, and wintry, and Dido, all at once, is again so tired she can't talk for another moment. They kiss. They hold hands tighter than tight.

– I'll see you very very soon. I'll be thinking of you every single minute.

– And I you. Good luck. Oh, Jeffrey. Good luck on Monday.

He nods, he smiles. And then he's walking slowly down the ward and turning at the door to raise his hand, in the understated gesture she's always loved. And then he's gone.

Dido leans back against the pillows. The scent from the roses, brought out by the warmth of the ward, drifts up towards her. She must get them put in water. And she lies there, thinking of things both great and small. Dying. Flowers being given a drink.

Chloe is sobbing her heart out. Poor Chloe. She knew it was coming, but you always go on hoping, don't you? When you're in love – which she was, she was. Even when it's as plain as the nose on your face that this isn't right, this isn't working, this is going nowhere fast, and should never have been begun. And it just hurts and *hurts*.

Where is she, in this vale of tears? In Charlotte Street with Edmund, fresh from his (rather mixed) reviews and being sweet and understanding? No. Ed is girding his loins for the second week, and though he's sympathetic, he's not giving her his fullest attention. Is she at home with Georgia, telling her everything at last, and being comforted? No! She's thirty-one; she's not going to be running home: partly because it's a pride thing; partly because Georgia is so anxious about Dido's op that she can't give proper attention to much else; but mostly because she (Georgia) has kindly but firmly dispatched Chloe on a mission.

Chloe is sobbing her heart out in that refuge from the world which so usefully shields the broken-hearted: the car. Amazing how you can drive and cry at the same time. No one can see you, no one can get at you; above all, no one can hear. You can turn up the radio full blast and *howl*. She's in Georgia's nice clean car, with its Thermos and travel rug and hardback road map; she's been insured for the weekend; she's driving round rural Sussex on a Sunday afternoon, looking at demented old people's care homes. It has, as she had dreaded, come to this.

Poor Chloe. So far, she's visited somewhere whose aspect was so gloomy that she refused, on principle, even to ring the bell. Maud may not care what the place looks like, or what it looks on to, but

Chloe is not going to have any relative of hers living in a pebble-dash house on a main road, with Leyland cypress, UPVC windows, a hideous porch full of cacti and a Christmas tree with flashing lights. (It's still November, for God's sake.) And the telly on all the time. It is: she could see it, from the path: a horrid dark dayroom with everyone sitting round in polyester cardigans looking drugged out of their skulls. It's a taste thing, a snob thing, but too bad. She hasn't spent her whole working life caring about appearances for them not to matter now. Who would come and visit Maud in such a place? Not her, that's a certainty: life is depressing enough. Sorry.

The next on Georgia's list sounds lovely. Honeysuckle Rest. And it's certainly an improvement on the *leylandii* (not a name Chloe can spell, but she's seen enough gardening programmes to know what they are, and why everyone hates them). It's winter, so the honeysuckle by the front door is cut back hard, but the house is nice: double-fronted Edwardian, with proper painted windows and a calm and roomy air. On this cloudy afternoon there are lamps on inside – nice soft ones, and no blaring telly. (Not that Chloe doesn't love a good old movie on a Sunday afternoon, it's just the idea of it being on all the time, with nobody taking it in.) She rings the bell, she's admitted by a kindly middle-aged helper in an overall, she's taken to see the proprietor.

Gosh, people are weird. Nice though this place seems to be, who would actually *choose* to run an old people's home? When, as proves to be the case, they have young children. She supposes they make lots and lots of money, but imagine: having to be quiet all the time, and polite all the time, and bringing friends home after school and having, like, twenty grannies? Anyway, she's given a tour (nice big clean kitchen, cosy sitting room with everyone looking quite happy – Hello, dear! – and knitting and things; nice bedsitting rooms – Excuse me, Doris, can I show this young lady your room? That's a nice photo: is that your grandson? – and so on). She's given a cup of tea and a piece of home-made Victoria sponge, and then the proprietor sits her down in his office and asks for a few details. If he notices her swollen red eyes and general misery, he's kind enough not to give a hint; no silly questions about has she got a cold. Just:

— How old is your aunt?

— Not my aunt. She's a sort of cousin. Second once removed, or something. Gosh. I'm not sure. How old she is, I mean. I suppose she's well into her seventies.

— And tell me a bit about her.

This proves fatal. Not for nothing has Chloe been listening all these months to Georgia's long descriptions of Maud's sad decline. And today, she's so upset and miserable that (how unusual) she's not really thinking, as she chats away.

Out it all comes: Maud's eccentricities, and a period in a mental hospital (ages ago, mind you). The farm going to rack and ruin; Maud's galloping dementia, her inability to recognise or remember; her cussedness, her refusal to let anyone except poor Georgia near her, the fire, the general filth, the violence. Violence? Yes, she kicked a poor care worker right in the stomach, apparently, and she's refused to go there again. (Too late, Chloe realises she should be playing this right, right down, like not mentioning it at all.)

Anyway, she concludes, as brightly as she's capable of, today: — This place seems really lovely. I'm sure she'd be really happy here.

The proprietor shakes his head. He's not so sure. This is, as she can see, a small quiet place whose residents aren't really used to, well, to people like her cousin. And as for the question of kicking . . . It sounds, to be frank, as if this old lady would be much better off in a place specialising in mental health. He does not say illness; no one ever does, these days. People aren't ill any more, they have health issues. Mental health issues.

— Like where? asks Chloe, putting down her tea cup and feeling faintly insulted. Of course poor Maud is bats, she always has been, but to have her actually *refused*, when this place seems just the ticket. It's horrid. Another rejection. And she feels too, as if something's rubbing off on her, like having a mad relative puts you sort of outside the frame. She feels outside everything already.

The proprietor of Honeysuckle Rest is telling her there are any number of places where her aunt – sorry, cousin – might be happy. Happy and well cared for. He gets out a list from his desk. Chloe runs her eyes down the page.

– We don't want her, you know, put away.

– Of course not. Of course you don't. Some of these places are very very good. Some of them have just a proportion of residents with dementia—

– Why don't you?

She's feeling cross and belligerent. Here's what seems to be the perfect place, and they won't have her. Poor Maud. Poor Chloe. Tears fill her eyes.

– I'm sorry, my dear, I know it must be a dreadful worry for you.

But he's on his feet, and he's not going to give an inch. Out they go, to the spacious hall with its flowered carpet and the soothing sounds of supper from the kitchen. Wouldn't Maud settle here? Wouldn't she calm down and be nice? (But what about Kep? She keeps forgetting him.) She asks to use the loo, then off she goes, out into the darkening afternoon. Oh, bloody hell. Now what?

Now she's on the last lap, sobbing again, driving deep into the countryside in search of Kingsland Hall. Georgia has spoken to them on the phone: it's a big place, apparently, but perhaps Maud would like that, looking out on to Sussex acres, being able (on good days) to go for walks. Perhaps she could have Kep there? Do they take pets? Does anyone? Will he, too, have to go into a home? Some rescue place, from where he won't be rescued? The thought of him, all cooped up and waiting, all anxious and bewildered, and barking in his cage, upsets Chloe so much that she has to stop the car. She pulls into the verge and she cries and cries. Why is everything so horrible? Poor Maud, all turned away. Poor Kep, who'll think that no one loves him, poor Dido, with such a dreadful operation, poor poor Dad – it's cruel, it's cruel.

And how could Jez – how *could* he – without explaining, without even *talking* about it – after all that fantastic sex – how could he? What will become of her now? How is she going to go on *living*?

At last she stops. She dries her eyes, she blows her nose, she drinks half a pint of mineral water and puts six drops of Rescue Remedy on her tongue. It's just brandy, she hears Georgia saying impatiently, it's just brandy in a lot of nonsense. Whatever, it helps. She must have gone through three bottles since that dreadful night. Now, then, where's the sodding map?

You might wonder how Georgia could have sent Chloe out into the Sussex countryside on a winter afternoon with only a map to guide her. Maps, as you will realise, have never been Chloe's strong point, and it's quite a long time since she's been behind a wheel, let alone tried to find somewhere she's never heard of. Would it not have been much more sensible for them to go together, Chloe driving, Georgia reading the map, both of them sharing this piece of family business in companionable fashion? It would – but Georgia doesn't want to leave the house. If anything happens to Dido, and she's not there to take the call . . . Furthermore, she is sick of it all: kindness and reason are at present not uppermost in her mind. All she can think is that it's time Chloe pulled her weight, even if she is unhappy. (Georgia does not know, of course, just how unhappy.) Enough wool-gathering over a married man. Time to grow up.

Poor Georgia. She must be feeling low to think so coldly.

Poor Chloe, parked at the side of a country lane, and struggling to see which way up lies Petworth. Or was it Midhurst?

OK. Here we are. I think that's it.

She pulls out, she drives on, she turns the volume up. And wouldn't you know it? Here on Jazz FM (she's had to retune Georgia's radio) is a vintage show, and here is Billie Holiday, with the saddest song ever written. The last time she heard it she was giving her birthday party, all dressed up and getting off with Jez. Couldn't it have told her, that mournful, haunting voice, that it would end in tears?

She can't cry any more: she's all washed up, dried up, a wreck. She drives on, to Kingsland bloody Hall, and not since her father died can she remember feeling as terrible as this.

And that was different.

At last, after two or three false turns, she finds it, directed by a woman out walking her dog. Chloe turns up another lane, sees a sign, finds herself approaching tall, distinguished gates. They're open; there's a lodge. There's a light on: it looks quite snug. On she goes, up a smooth smooth road, bordered on either side by fields. There's livestock ahead: Maud would like that. At first, in the approaching dusk, she thinks it's just horses. Or cattle; she's not really looking. Then she has to slow at a cattle grid, and then she does look, and she gets the fright of her life.

What's *that*?

What's that, towering up by the grid in the gloom? What's that great long neck and weird mad hairy face—

Oh God, there's a lot of them, crowding towards the car.

Llamas. The place is a llama farm.

It's supposed to be a fucking old people's home!

How can you run an old people's home as well as a llama farm? It's weird, it's mad, it's horrible. And as she drives on (she can do nothing else) they all crowd closer and then one pulls back his lips and *spits*. Right at the windscreen.

That's it. That's IT. She's going home.

But she can't turn round, not without having them all around her, so she drives on, slowly at first and then, as they bound away (not before spitting at the tail lights) she increases her speed, seeing the Hall ahead, and lights, and silhouettes of people. So she pulls up, checking behind her, but they can't get past the grid, and gets out, rings the bell, and is admitted.

Oh dear God.

A hundred old people are shuffling in a queue all through the hall towards the dining room. Some are on Zimmers, and some are on sticks and some have helpers, helping. But they all look ancient, crumbling, frail, in pain, and the line goes on and on, and no one's talking. And someone, somewhere upstairs in this appalling place, is wailing. Wailing: no other word to describe it.

Chloe has never seen or heard anything so sad and pitiful and awful in all her life.

– Can I help?

Yet another kindly middle-aged person is approaching her. Chloe shakes her head. She backs away. She flees.

She gets through the llamas, shaking like a leaf, and she cries all the way back to London, getting lost twice. She returns the car to Georgia in a dreadful state. Grief. Rage. Exhaustion. Hunger. Not to say starvation.

Georgia has a Sunday-night chicken roasting nicely in the oven. She's stricken by Chloe's demeanour. She makes tea, runs a piping hot bath, laced with very expensive rose geranium oil. She puts a glass in her daughter's hand.

They settle down to supper, and at last they talk. About everything.

Dido has come through the op. She's white, she's shaven, she's thin as a rake, but she's through. The staff in intensive care are like angels. In two days, she's back on the ward.

Jeffrey is there all day every day. Kate and Nick come for an hour each. Georgia's phoned the ward twice. She's sent roses.

Everyone's shaken beyond belief. But Dido is through. And it is, as expected, benign. She will recover.

And now, first thing on Monday morning, it's time for Jeffrey's hearing.

The hearing is to be held in a part of the campus he rarely visits: no teaching rooms, no lecture theatres, no examination halls, no lab or library. No refectory. And thus few academics and few students wandering about: how tactful. This is an admin building, populated by registrars, secretaries (they do still exist, if under other names), organisers of scholarships, European funding and years abroad. That sort of thing. The last time he was here was to talk through an appeal about a class of degree with one of the registrars, and that was – well, he can't remember. With email, everyone's joined up nicely: no need to set forth across a windswept campus every time you need to thrash things out.

An appeal, however, cannot be held on email. There are some things that have to be thrashed out behind closed doors.

It's twenty past nine. He walks through swing doors, and down an endless corridor, looking for the room. People come and go, unlocking their offices, greeting one another, making coffee, turning on the photocopier. Ordinary, everyday things, which keep us all on track. There are posters on the walls, of foreign universities: Rome, the Sorbonne, Chicago. He's given papers in Chicago, chaired a furious debate in Paris. There are posters offering postgraduate degrees, and the faces of one or two great figures of his teaching life, his passion, gaze out as he walks past: Luther; Wolsey; Mary, Queen of Scots. He has spent decades with all of them, at different times; he's lived through a revolution in his subject (few 'great figures' now), he's taught perhaps two thousand students, published countless papers, edited half a dozen collections, published three books of his own. If his working life in recent years has begun to be strangled by bureaucracy he still wouldn't change it for any other. He loves his job, he loves this university, he had hoped to end his time here with a bit of a publication flourish.

Now . . .

He looks at his watch. He needs a pee. Where's the Gents? (No one, on any campus now, talks about Ladies and Gents, but there's something down to earth and reassuring, on this sickeningly uncertain day, about using the word now.)

– Excuse me . . .

A chap a bit like Leo directs him to a turning.

– Thanks. And Room 164? Thanks.

Inside the washroom, he sees himself in the mirror. Christ. He looks a hundred. No wonder she—

Inside a cubicle, he's suddenly throwing up. Tears start from his eyes as he gasps and heaves. There's hardly anything there: he couldn't manage breakfast, and with Dido in hospital he's barely eaten for days. With Dido in hospital, this morning's events have felt meaningless, unreal. There's been only her white and sunken face, her bandaged head, all those machines. There's been only the moment when she opened her eyes, dark and frightened, then gave him a flickering smile.

– My love. My very own.

He sat there and sat there. Monday lay in another universe. Now it's come.

He gets to his feet, he goes out and washes, he gulps down water. Come on, for Christ's sake, it's not an execution.

And he goes out, checking his watch, walks on down the corridor, and finds the room. He knows who'll be in there. He knocks. He waits.

– Good morning, Professor Sullivan. Take a seat.

– Thank you.

There are five of them in this featureless room, seated round a blond-wood table. He notices a door to another room; a clock on the wall. Then he focuses on the Dean, seated at the far end of the table. To his left, a senior female academic (Applied Mathematics) from another School, whom Jeffrey knows only by name. Another woman, in her early forties, whom he recognises: a student counsellor: someone like Dido, perhaps, but with less style. There's the union rep (Cultural Studies) on the other side, to whom he spoke briefly on the phone last night, after getting back from the hospital. (This is a pretty difficult time for you, I gather. Yes, you could say that.)

And her.

He nods to everyone, sits down. Her presence obliterates everything: the people round the table; the papers and jug of water; his life until this moment. Everything that's happened. (Dido, forgive me.) That fall of slippery dark hair, the sudden severity of her clothes (he can't take them in, but he thinks she's in a suit); the fact that she's against the light, in profile: she seems outlined by a ring of fire. He can't bear to look at her – he dare not look at her – but the impact of seeing her again is like being winded. They haven't spoken for weeks. Months. There has been only her accusation; her reported threats; that dreadful letter.

He followed me, he waited for me, he begged for sex . . .

The memory of their last meeting sears him.

I want you, I want you. Please, please . . .

When does unrequited passion turn into sexual harassment?

That's what this hearing will decide.

– Professor Sullivan, you know why you are here. A serious charge of professional misconduct has been brought against you. Ms Newman alleges, as you know, that you propositioned her, and that when you were rejected, you subjected her to a sustained campaign of harassment. Sexual harassment. Now, then. We have two things to consider.

Jeffrey's personal file is before the Dean; dull blue card, thick with papers. He knows what's in there: every application for promotion: Lecturer to Senior Lecturer, Reader to (eight years ago) Professor. The notes of all his interviews in support of every one. Assessments of his teaching. The details of his salary. His annual appraisals: excellent, on the whole. He's been involved in many promotion interviews himself; he's conducted countless such appraisals. He knows that what's in that file is the evidence of the most solid career. But now, on the top, are the copies of her letters: to the Dean, bringing the initial charge; to the Vice Chancellor, written as she grew impatient, waiting for this day.

He texted me, he emailed me . . . I would find him waiting outside my house at night . . .

– The first thing we need to consider is, I think, quickly dealt with. The Dean has his hand upon the file. – The question of propriety. You know, of course, the boundaries of professional life. No member of academic staff should be – how shall I put it? – consorting with a student. This is entirely inappropriate behaviour, threatening the whole fabric of university life. However, Ms Newman is an adult. For a member of staff to have a relationship with a student is not unheard of, nor is it a crime. If that member of staff is married . . . if I may say so, Professor Sullivan, it would not be conduct I would expect of you. There's a cough; then he continues. – But as I say, such impropriety would not, in itself, bring us all here today. He looks round the table. – Are we all agreed that Professor Sullivan's initial – shall we say, advances – lie outside the interests of this hearing?

There are nods. Cultural Studies. Applied Mathematics. Then she speaks.

– I would not be wasting everyone's time, nor my own time, if that were all it was.

She's an ice queen, the Snow Queen, clear and cold and strong. In all the thousands of students he's taught and known, he's never known anyone like her. When he first saw her, when they were first getting to know one another, she seemed so alive, so open. Now–

– Indeed. The Dean is opening the file. – Now, then. Professor Sullivan, Ms Newman has alleged that when she wished to terminate what had been a very brief relationship, you refused to accept it. She claims that you began to follow her, to besiege her with letters and texts and emails and requests for meetings; to, as I think she puts it, he consults the file – to lie in wait for her: outside class, outside her house. She claims that she grew frightened, and that her studies suffered as a result. She claims that she was unable to sleep, that she began to fear she would never be free of you.

He stops. – Ms Newman? Am I representing you correctly?

She nods.

– And do you still stand by these accusations?

– Yes.

– Is there anything you wish to add?

– Not at the moment.

There's a brief pause. The Dean looks round the table. – We proceed?

There are murmurs of assent. – Well, then, Professor Sullivan, perhaps you would like to – account for yourself.

He cannot speak.

For weeks he has rehearsed this moment. Sometimes, he's thought: if Henry were alive, I'd be talking this through with him. Would I not? At other times he's known he wouldn't – that there's no one amongst all his friends (most of whom are colleagues), not even Henry, in whom he would confide.

In truth, the only person he trusts is Dido. And strong as she is, human as she is, he's not going to tell her everything. How can he? How can he tell her how deeply he was consumed? Obsessed? How he's haunted, still, by the memory of a touch, the deepest kiss? And anyway, Dido is ill, she's ill, she's stricken with what could have been the gravest thing. And anyway – he loves her still; he has, as he tells her, always loved her. He's protecting her, is he not, as well as himself, in keeping some things back.

So he has lain awake, has gone for endless walks alone; has conducted this interview (once or twice aloud) while driving. He has written pages, and torn them up again. And sometimes, in his wildest fantasies, he's allowed himself to hope. He has played out scenes wherein, in front of everyone, he says he did it all for love. He apologises, from the bottom of his heart, and she melts. She melts, and afterwards they meet . . .

Yes. He has allowed himself to think like this. It's the last gasp of a drowning man, but it's there: until Dido's revelation he still allowed himself to dream. Then, when Dido told him what had befallen her, everything fell away; he did, at last, come to.

And now—

Now, in front of everyone, he's seeing her again. Not accidentally glimpsing her in corridor or canteen, not climbing the stairs in the library and realising that yes, that's her voice, two stacks away – these things have happened, in the last two months, and each time the world has stood quite still. But now – they are in the same room, now she's only feet away. And dear God, even now, he feels that lurch of recognition: you are someone I have always, always wanted. And I want you still.

Dido's ashen face swims up before him.

– Professor Sullivan?

Jeffrey hasn't shaken with nerves since he gave his first lectures here, over thirty years ago. He's shaking now, his knees knocking together and his hands trembling upon the blond-wood table. He clasps them together, but he knows they've seen. He clears his throat.

– I – have behaved very foolishly. What has been said of me – it sounds appalling. It is, I confess, appalling.

– You admit that everything Ms Newman says is true?

– No. Yes. But not as much, that is to say – it sounds like a campaign, it sounds relentless. My memory is . . . my memory is that I wrote perhaps three or four letters. Some emails. A few texts . . .

– Excuse me. The applied mathematician has something to say; the Dean gives a nod; she leans forward. – Would you say, Professor Sullivan, that these communications were of a pornographic nature?

He swallows. He's blushing now, to the roots of his balding hair.

– No. No, I wouldn't describe them like that.

– Erotic?

– Well, yes.

There's a little sound.

– Ms Newman?

She opens a file before her: he glances across, and his hands go up to his mouth. She's printed out every single one.

– May I? she asks the room.

Everyone is very quiet. Then Jeffrey's rep asks if this is really necessary.

In the Dean's moment of hesitation she says: – It's proof. It's evidence.

And she begins to read.

I think of you every moment, I dream of us being together. I long to lie with you beneath me, I long to . . .

It goes on. His head in his hands.

– Thank you, Ms Newman. The Dean intervenes. – I think we all understand the nature of this material. We can return to it if necessary. Professor Sullivan, you acknowledge that you are the author of such communications?

He straightens up; he clears his throat.

– Yes.

– And as to the question of . . . following. Of – as Ms Newman puts it – lying in wait, is this something you also acknowledge?

He takes a deep breath. – Yes, though put like that . . . Of course I did not intend to alarm, or frighten. I did not think of it as lying in wait—

– What you thought, or intended, is not at issue. Do you acknowledge that you waited for Ms Newman, and accosted her, on university premises?

– I would not describe it as accosting.

– Did you follow her home? Did you wait for her outside her house?

– Once.

– At night?

– One evening, yes.

There's a silence. Then the Dean makes a gesture to the table. He asks if anyone else has anything to ask. Or to add. Jeffrey sees her glance across at the student counsellor. This woman could be Dido, though she's a good twenty years younger. She could be Kate. He shuts his eyes. He waits. The counsellor clears her throat.

– Ms Newman has asked me to be here today. She has asked me to testify to the deep distress which Professor Sullivan's behaviour caused her. As her counsellor I can certainly testify to that. Ms Newman came to see me in considerable turmoil, and I continued to see her for some weeks.

And the counsellor goes on to describe all the symptoms of anxiety and depression: the sleeplessness, the loss of appetite, the loss of concentration. Above all: the fear.

Jeffrey listens; they all listen, as the clock on the wall behind the Dean ticks quietly on, and one or two heads go past the window, though the slatted blinds mean no one can properly look inside and see who's in here. He's pouring sweat; it feels as if this has been going on for ever. At last this account is ended. People reach for glasses of water, cough, shift in their seats. He reaches for his own glass, filled by his rep, who does not look at him.

– Thanks. He drains it, sets it down.

– Professor Sullivan. You have been accused of very serious misconduct. What do you wish to say?

Another deep deep breath. Then:

– That I am very sorry. That I acted foolishly, shamefully. But I had no intention of frightening or alarming Ms Newman. Ever.

In his fantasies of the hearing, he'd addressed her directly: now, this feels impossible. – For all the distress I caused her, I can only offer the most heartfelt apology. And nothing like this will ever happen again. I give my word.

Another silence. Then:

– Thank you. Now perhaps . . .

Ms Newman is asked to leave: a secretary comes to show her out while the panel consider.

And the Dean indicates the door Jeffrey noticed, when he first came in. He's invited to go through, and wait.

This place is as soulless as the last. Dull grey carpet, wall clock, standard-issue coffee table and a couple of low chairs. There are a few leaflets pinned to a board, which he glances at: old Erasmus scholarship things, and some stuff about student loans. The window's shut, and it's very stuffy: he fumbles to open the casement, and sits down. The slatted blinds rattle softly in the stir of air; voices drift through – a couple of caretakers, and someone's sweeping leaves. He sits down, completely drained, and lets these sounds, and the winter morning air, wash over him.

He can hear nothing through the door, can only imagine what everyone is saying. But now he knows something deeply, once and for all. Whatever the outcome of today, he must never set eyes on this young woman again.

He must never catch sight of her, as she walks across the campus. Never brush past her in the corridor. Never see her across the refectory, or in the library, climbing the stairs to the Law shelves. Never run the risk of glimpsing her as she gets on to the student bus, as he cycles home.

Whatever she meant to him, in whatever way she moved him,

and however – yes, even now, after everything – she moves him still, this is the end of the road. Even if it means uprooting everything.

Never again.

He feels an unutterable relief.

– Professor Sullivan? Will you come through?

He's been in here over twenty minutes. He's grown chilled, the sweat drying on his skin; he's got up to close the window once again, then paced about, watching the clock. Now the moment's come.

He takes his seat before them.

And what, after all, did he really expect? Did he really imagine that after thirty years without a mark against him; after decades of fine teaching, and valuable research; after the devising of this and that new programme, attracting fine calibre students from America, Malaysia, all over the EU, enchancing the reputation of School and university, in this country and abroad; after all applications for funding, the steering of this and that committee, the stepping in at the last minute to cover (for weeks) a colleague's illness; after all the years and years of listening to students, as tutor and as pastoral tutor – students in debt, in love, in trouble with drugs, and with the landlord – all of that, and the writing of references, encouraging letters . . .

Did he really imagine that they would throw him out?

It's over.

Everything that's been said today is on his file and always will remain there. He's formally cautioned, formally reprimanded. He's told that if anything remotely like this ever happens again . . .

But it's over.

– Thank you. Thank you very much.

Papers are gathered up. No one looks at him, as he turns to go.

* * *

When he gets to the hospital, Dido isn't there. For a moment, seeing her empty bed, he feels sick with fear. Then they tell him she's in X-ray, and he sits and waits, falling asleep in the chair beside her bed. He wakes at a sound, to see her being wheeled back by a porter, a nurse alongside, steering a drip.

– Dido. He stumbles to his feet, moves aside while they get her – gently, gently – back into bed. She leans back on the pillows, very white. He takes her hand; she gives him a weak little smile.

– How did it go?

– OK. He feels relief steal through him, once again. – OK. She squeezes his hand. – Tell me.

– Later. You look so tired. After lunch.

– No. Now.

He leans over and kisses her. Then he sits down beside her again, and tells her (almost) everything.

That night, he sleeps better than he has for months. He's phoned the children, heard the flood of relief in Nick's voice, the happiness in Kate's. – That's fantastic, Dad. Well done. They agree they'll meet on the ward tomorrow, see Dido, then all go out for a meal.

In the morning, he makes a proper breakfast, skims the headlines, phones the ward, says he'll be in at lunch time: no teaching this afternoon, and everyone understands he's putting Dido above every meeting he can. He takes a class, gives two tutorials. It feels almost normal again: back in the swing, with it all behind him. As he cycles away from the campus, through the vale, and back to the winter city, Christmas lights glint everywhere, and lots of trees are up. He padlocks the bike in the hospital rack; goes up to the ward. There's a tree here too, at the nurses' station. And now there are curtains round her bed; a nurse tells him the consultant's on his round. Why doesn't he wait in the day room?

So he goes in there, finding it empty, and makes a coffee at the machine, and settles down to read the paper properly.

Terrorist plots. A missing child. The discovery of a painting in an attic, said to be by Rembrandt. He turns the pages, sees his own face gazing out at him.

DISTINGUISHED PROFESSOR IN SEX SCANDAL
A young law student told last night how she had been subject to a sustained campaign of sexual harassment ... Although Professor Jeffrey Sullivan was yesterday formally cleared of misconduct, he confessed to having behaved 'appallingly' ...

She's done it.

23

Christmas approaches: that happy season when everyone gets together and everything (quite often) falls apart.

It's *Christmas*, isn't it? Surely they can meet for a drink? And, like, talk?

Not a good idea.

They meet in a bar in Soho. Out of both their territories – and Chloe will never set foot in Tufnell Park again. Ever. She gets there bang on time. It's packed. Heaving. Everyone looks super-cool, and though she's taken hours to choose what to wear, and looks, even Ed says so, pretty slinky, no one takes a blind bit of notice as she pushes through.

– Excuse me – sorry – thanks . . .

Nowhere to be seen. She should have arrived a casual half-hour late, of course she should. But then he might have thought she wasn't coming, and have gone before she got here.

Like she might, if he doesn't show up soon. It's horrible, being on your own in a place like this. Especially if everything's Over. It's different if you're waiting for someone when you're in a rock-solid relationship.

What's that, when it's at home?

Chloe goes up to the bar. She orders a whisky mac, not exactly the coolest drink in the world but wintry, Christmassy, strong. (Will her breath taste of whisky, if he wants to kiss her? Will he want to kiss her? Surely she's looking good enough to kiss. And if that happens – her stomach is full of every kind of butterfly – then surely he'll just realise, won't he, that he can never let her go?)

Oh, Chloe, Chloe.

She drinks, she stands there, watching the door. Trying to look as if she hasn't been stood up. (He wouldn't do that, would he? Jez? You wouldn't, would you?) The door swings open. People come, people go. That's a really nice Christmas tree: why doesn't she just go over and look at that?

She's studying all the camp little fairies when he's right behind her.

– Hi. Sorry I'm late.

She leaps six feet in the air.

– Gosh. Hi! I didn't see you.

They kiss on both cheeks. Of course that's what they'll do: they're friends now, aren't they?

Like hell they are.

What fool ever told you that friendship follows passion like the night the day?

He gets a drink. There's nowhere to sit, so they stand there in the crush, and of course they can barely hear themselves speak.

– How are you?

– I'm good. Busy. And you?

– Oh, pretty busy.

Now what?

They talk (after a fashion, given that they have to keep shouting – God, there are a few things she'd like to shout) about everything except what matters. Work. Shoots. Features. He looks completely gorgeous, as he always has. Who's going to ask the dread question first?

– What are you doing for Christmas?

What does he think? Having a great time, just fantastic, all on her own again, dropped like a stone, and not a clue what to do except:

318

– Oh, I expect I'll be with my mother.

How pathetic is that? Thirty-one and Christmas with your *mother*.

– That's nice.

No it bloody isn't.

– No it isn't.

He smiles. Like, properly, as if he understands. Like, he's human. Oh, Jez, Jez.

– What about you? (OK, they're moving towards it now, they've got to.)

He looks into his glass. Funny how people do that. What does he think he's going to find?

– Oh. I guess I'll be at home.

As if it's just any old place. As if he hasn't broken her heart, and turned everything upside down and, like, ruined her life.

– How's Ellie?

– Oh. She's good. She's really good.

A tiny murmur from Georgia sounds in Chloe's ear. Good? Why do people say good, now? What happened to fine? If you say a child is good, doesn't it mean they're behaving?

Oh, never mind, what does it matter?

– Jez—

– Like another drink?

– Sure. Thanks.

He takes her glass, and their hands brush one another's. Oh, please, please . . .

– What are you drinking?

– Whisky mac.

He laughs. – My granddad used to like that.

Oh, thanks. Thanks a lot.

Two people are getting up to leave, at a nearby table: two gay guys in leather and earrings who look like the world is at their feet. Lucky them. She calls after Jez, – I'll be over here! And he nods, and she sits down at the tiny table with its naff (but ironic, so that's OK) little Christmas tree in a pot. Its lights wink on and off. It's the kind of thing which, if you were happy, would make you feel even happier. She flashes the gay guys a bright little smile, and one of them smiles back so warmly that she thinks, as you do quite often with gay men, that deep down they really fancy you. They don't.

Jez comes back. They settle down, if you can call it that. Now there's nowhere he can go, and nowhere else he can look, except at her. Also, they can hear a bit better.

– Jez.

– Yeah?

– Do you want to talk?

Chloe, dear Chloe. Men never want to do that.

He looks into his glass again, so uncomfortable that all at once she feels (gosh) that she has the upper hand.

– I'm not going to get heavy or anything.

Are you sure?

He knocks back his drink.

He says: – Look, I'm really sorry.

Isn't language funny? Isn't it funny (Georgia's here again) how just a single word can change an entire *meaning*? 'I'm really sorry' sounds quite, well, heartfelt. Add on that 'Look' and it's all defensive, layered with Leave me alone, and It wasn't my fault.

Yes it bloody was.

And out it all comes, with two large whiskies inside her, like, unstoppable. That he was *married*. OK, separated, but not like, really separated. He was about as separated as an egg within its shell. (How did she think of that one?) And she's never, ever, been involved with a married man before, and what did he think he was *doing*, getting all her hopes up and then just, like, *dropping* her. Without even being a man enough (she's really getting into her stride, now) to talk it through? Just – withdrawing. Edging away. Hoping she'll get the message. How cowardly is that?

He looks dreadful.

Good.

Then suddenly something's happening in the bar. Through all the noise come—

Carols. Some charity thing. Shaking a money box and singing *O, Little Town of Bethlehem*.

Chloe bursts into tears.

– Look, I'm really sorry.

And now he sounds as if he really means it, now he's covering her hand with his, and being really nice. He *is* nice; she would never (never) have got involved with him if he hadn't been, essentially, a decent guy. This is what makes it even worse. Oh, if only, if only – couldn't they just somehow sort it out?

No.

– You're really gorgeous, he tells her. At least he's doing something right, at least he's not leaving her feeling like she's got two heads or something. – And it was really good. It? Which bit in particular? As if she doesn't know. – But in the end—

– I know, I know, I'm sorry.

– Don't be sorry. You're right: I should never have started it. Just couldn't stop myself – fancied you for years. Still do.

Naughty. Naughty. Cruel, even, raising a girl's hopes.

Chloe dries her eyes, and smiles. Sort of.

The carol singers are on *Hark the Herald* – not one you could ever cry to, somehow. The collecting tin's coming round, shaken by a young guy in specs and a Father Christmas hat. Children in Care. They each put in a fiver.

Then they go.

Out in the street, he asks if she wants to go on the tube with him. She can't think of anything she wants to do less. She wants to go out for a really nice meal with him, and then to bed.

– No, thanks. I – I think I'll walk.

– OK. And he stands there smiling down at her, and gives her

a kiss on the lips. Just a very small one. – Thanks, he tells her. –
Thanks for everything. Happy Christmas.

– Happy Christmas, Jez.

And each of them turns away, though in truth they're both
headed in the same direction, but she turns right towards Greek
Street, and he walks on to the tube.

He hasn't told her they're trying for a baby. For that, we can be
grateful.

And how are things in York? It's a beautiful old city, made even
lovelier by Christmas lights reflected in the river, really nice shops
full of pretty things, fabulous music in the Minster. In other years,
Dido and Jeffrey would have been listening to Bach and Handel
there, taking all the family, introducing Sam and Izzy to the greater
things in life.

What might they be?

This year, Dido's not going anywhere, except home from
hospital. Jeffrey's collected her, bringing her home to a tree,
candles, holly in jugs and corners, heaps of logs by the fire. No one
could be trying harder, and no one could mean it more. Everyone
(are you sure?) will be coming for Christmas lunch and the most
enormous (organic) turkey has been ordered. Wine Society cases
stand in the hall: goodness. Do you really think we're going to
drink all that? Well. It'll come in for the New Year, won't it? I
suppose so. If we get that far.

She sits by the blazing fire, wearing a woolly hat on her shaven
head, and opens all their Christmas cards.

What a signifier *those* are.

They always get hundreds, but this year – does she imagine it,
or are there not quite as many? Does she imagine it, or are they all
going on about her illness and recovery, wishing her a *really* good
New Year, but not, somehow, alluding to . . .

What's in the papers one day is gone the next. It was a great story, run by pretty well everything, including (of course) the *Yorkshire Post*. The *Guardian*, *The Times*, the *Indie* and the *Telegraph*. The *Mail*. For a couple of days, they really went to town. (*Professor Sullivan's wife is in hospital, recovering from major surgery* . . . Just how much of a complete shit can you be made to seem? *Their daughter, a well-respected local GP, was not available for comment . . .*)

It was hideous. For a few days, it was a nightmare. Yes, there were local reporters on the doorstep. And even at the hospital, waiting in the foyer. A photographer jumped out from behind the Christmas tree, catching Jeffrey swearing at one of them, and looking like a pretty nasty piece of work.

Hideous.

But then . . . Great stories have their moments. But a week is a long long time in journalism, and great though it was while it lasted (crusty professor, sexy and clever young woman) it faded, as such things do. No interesting complications, no more scandal to be uncovered (not that they didn't try), no minister to fall because of it, nothing more to say. Soon (though it felt like for ever) it was gone.

But of course—

Does he imagine it, or do people avoid him as he walks along his corridor, up to his door with his name upon it? When he photocopies the last handouts of the season (even professors do photocopying now) do people who used to stop and chat give a little smile, and walk on by? Is the School Office, usually so jolly, especially at Christmas, paper chains everywhere, and everyone in Father Christmas hats – does he imagine it, or is it rather quiet when he pops in to book his last leave of the year, or borrow some Blu-Tack? (Even professors put up their own notices, now.)

Not everyone, of course.

There was a flood of sympathetic emails from his own department. He went for a couple of drinks, and was told just to ride it out, it would blow over, and no one would think the worse of him.

Are you sure?

Even in universities, populated (supposedly) by the sensitive, the liberal, the people who know What Students Can Be Like, and have had some pretty sticky moments themselves, in their time—

There's no smoke without fire.

And the truth is: there was a fire.

Whichever way you look at it, something certainly went on.

Thank God it's the Christmas break. His last class over (and he's been lucky, he knows, not to have been locked in a lecture hall, besieged by chanting students) he dumps all his stuff on his desk, switches off his computer and locks the door.

Home.

It's cold. He's driving now. As he unlocks the car in the car park, he glances up, and sees her.

No he doesn't. He thought it was her, walking fast towards the bus stop, but it isn't. His knees are trembling as he starts up the engine and drives away.

Home. When he unlocks the front door and hears Dido calling, he gives thanks (to whom?) for everything he has.

Meanwhile, in a rented flat, on the other side of the city.

Not many Christmas decorations up here. There never have been: Paula hates Christmas. Some people do. Try as he might, it's always really difficult. Trying to explain at home why she might not be there (Darling, don't worry, we understand), looking each year for a new excuse: a chapter, a sick aunt, a filthy cold she doesn't want anyone to catch. All that. Usually, she does come in the end. She sort of does her stuff. Nice presents (usually books). But God: trying to get her to really *enjoy* it, especially with Izzy and Sam, when she's just not into children, never will be, not in the way you need to be, at Christmas. Sometimes it's better than others. Sometimes they've had a good time. Charades: no one is better, or quicker, at guessing. But trying to get her to do a turn herself, or to play Monopoly without looking as if there's a nasty smell, somewhere. It's only a *game*. OK, he knows there's no such thing as Only; that everything, every single thing, has a political implication, and of course Monopoly is all about capitalist greed, and he supposes you could say, yes, that it teaches children all the wrong things, but—

It's *Christmas*.

Every year he thinks: Thank God it's over. It's only a few days a year, we'll be fine now. But every year it comes round again. Like now. And it's not as if this year has been exactly brilliant. Poor Mum. Poor old Dad. Who would ever have imagined . . .

As for him and Paula . . .

He's in the sitting room, at the table by the window, wrapping the children's presents. He's got a long piece of Sellotape between his teeth, and it's sticking to the wrong bit of paper, and then, as he tries to unpeel it, it all rolls up on itself, and is completely useless. Damn. He flicks it away, and tries again.

– Nick.

He looks up, sees her face, knows just what she's going to say. That she can't face coming, she's really sorry. That she thinks she'll just stay here and work. Great. He picks up the Sellotape again, finds the end has stuck back on the roll. Try as he might, he just can't find the join.

– Nick.

– Yup?

It's getting dark, and all at once there's a little leap in the boiler, as the timer reaches five o'clock. Flames rise, the heating's coming on. All day, they work in coats and sweaters, saving every penny. Five o'clock is a highlight: he can feel the room grow warm. And he's mastered the Sellotape, though really they need one of those dispenser things, the sort of thing that people buy when they know they'll be wrapping stuff year after year. Like, when things feel permanent. He uses his teeth again. There. Done it.

– Do you think you could stop that for a minute?

He stops, he looks at her: standing in the doorway to the kitchen, a good woollen scarf around her neck (a present from Dido, last Christmas, and really useful) and a sweater round her shoulders, on top of another. She must be cold. Does he imagine it, or is she really pale?

– You OK?

She shuts her eyes, leans against the doorjamb, opens them again, comes across, sits down on the sofa.

– I've got something to say.

And now her tone has his entire attention.

This is it.

She takes a long time to tell him, and in the middle she starts to cry.

– Paula . . .

She cries so rarely, he wishes she'd cry more; it would make things more human, somehow. He gets up, goes over, puts his hand on hers.

– Come on. It's OK. You can tell me.

– I can't.

Then she does.

How could he have been so blind?

What about Kate and Leo, that seemingly perfect couple? How are they getting on, this Christmastide? How, still reeling from the double whammy that Kate's parents have given them, are they coping: with the horrible phone calls from the press, national and local; with the visits to Dido, now she's home, the listening, the comforting (Dido and Jeffrey both, for the first time ever, rather in need of that) on top of all the surgeries, the old people going down with pneumonia and the young unvaccinated breaking out in killer spots? How are they coping with Christmas shopping (for Dido, too – No, really, Mum, it's fine), Christmas overdoses, the fall off a ladder while putting up the tree lights (Leo, but luckily nothing broken), the cooking, the wrapping, the Christmas play (Sam) and Christmas concert (Izzy), which they must, simply must, pitch up for (and wouldn't, in any case, miss for the world). What about arranging childcare, now it's the Christmas holidays? The locums at the surgeries, so they can swap shifts, and make it all as nice at home as they possibly can? What about the party? They always have a party. If they don't have one this year, it'll look as if they're ashamed of something, hiding something, won't it? Everyone – everyone – has seen the story.

Kate and Leo don't give a fig what anyone thinks. Good for them. They know that giving a party, this year, is just one bridge too far, and everyone understands that they're spending all their spare time with Dido. If they don't, if they think it's a cover, well, who needs friends like that?

They do go out to a party, a really good one, given by their closest friends, and come home late to a nice warm house full of Christmas cards (only one or two fewer than usual). Leo runs the babysitter home. Kate checks on the children and goes downstairs to tidy up a bit. She gives herself a moment on the sofa: by the time Leo's back, she's fast asleep there. He sits down beside her, puts his arm round her shoulders, falls asleep too.

The truth is, this is a marriage which seems like it's really working. Not to say happy. Tired but happy. It looks like it's going to last.

As if, says Georgia wearily, hauling in the tree. *As if* it's going to last, not *like*. Like goes with nouns: He looked like a wet weekend. She looked just like her sister. Got it? The little phrase *as if* seems to have dropped off the planet, except when used on its own, with heavy irony. She isn't talking about Kate and Leo's marriage lasting. Not a bit of it; she's talking about that long lost thing: a knowledge of English grammar. *As if* accompanies a verb: it looks *as if* it's really working. It looks *as if* it's going to last.

Doesn't anyone know anything any more?

She lies the tree down in the hall, picks up her (late) post and goes to put the kettle on. Of course, language is an evolving thing, she thinks, as she feeds the cats. (Special treats for Christmas coming up, wrapped by Chloe and – not long now – tucked beneath the tree. Catnip! They go mad every year.) Language, like everything else, is changing all the time.

Not always for the better.

Oh, to hell with it. Even Radio 4 says 'like' these days. Even on the News. Sometimes she thinks she'll write a letter, but then she can't be bothered. Too much else to worry about. She takes her tea to the sitting room, sits by the unlit fire. She'll light it at six, with a drink; routine is what saves you, as you get older. She opens her Christmas cards. Lots. Thank God for friendship.

This is the second Christmas without Henry. Why do people think it gets easier, the longer it goes on? How do widows without children survive? Tonight, she'll be decorating the tree with Chloe. That will be fun.

What's going to happen to Paula? She doesn't know – except that she'll finish her thesis. She's certain of that.

Nick watches, as she packs all her things, a few days later, and gets ready to say goodbye. She's going home to Durham, where her parents, getting on now, will be so glad to see her. In the New Year she'll come back here, find somewhere else to live. Perhaps she and Nick will see one another. One day, perhaps they'll be friends. She closes the last suitcase, zips the last bag, looks round. That's it.

– Bye, Nick.

– Bye, Paula.

They can't meet one another's eyes. Then he steps forward; then they hug. They're closer than for a long long time: closer, perhaps, than they have ever been, now everything is told at last. He pulls her to him, he kisses her cheek. For a moment—

But no. This is how it has to be.

Downstairs, the minicab she's called is hooting. They move apart, he helps her with her bags, all the way down the stairs. The hall is full of the usual discarded junk mail which no one, in a house full of rented flats, ever does anything about. It's pretty bleak. He pulls the door open, carries everything down to the cab, helps her and the driver to sling it all into the boot.

– Look after yourself.

– Thanks. And you.

Then she turns quickly away, and he sees that her eyes are full of tears. In she gets, and he closes the door. It's freezing.

She's leaning forward to talk to the driver; he starts the engine.

– Bye! Nick raises his hand, and stands there until she's out of sight.

Betty the carer – kicked violently in the stomach; winded; refusing to go back – is persuaded to have one last go.

– Felt like a blimming horse, that kick.

They understand. Of course they do. She's been so wonderful, all these years, they don't know what they'd have done without her. Of course, if she won't go back, she won't. But could she just think about it? If someone went with her (Tonya, perhaps) might she try? There's no one like Betty: if she can't help Maud, no one can.

– Oh, all right, then.

Off she goes with Tonya (divorced, three children). They've worked together for years; they make a good team. They'll give it a go. This time, she won't be frightened. They reschedule one or two of their regulars: poor old Mr Matthews (dialysis twice a week) and poor old Miss Pennell (ulcerated leg, two cats) are roused for their bath and breakfast at the crack of dawn. Right, then. Now for mad old – what was her name again? No one, for some reason, can keep hold of Hannaway. Mad old Maud.

That all these old bods can stay on in their flats and bungalows and rotting farms, instead of sitting round the telly all day in plastic chairs in care homes, or lie unvisited in geriatric wards for months on end, is something of which the Care Team is justifiably proud. They're not in it for the money. They do it because they really care. Betty's own mother, etc. Tonya's auntie. They've seen what it's like to be old and frail, over and over again. How they long to see Maud fresh and clean and smiling, eating up her meals on wheels and going to the Day Centre.

So up they pitch, at a quarter to nine on a cold December morning, all ready to do their best.

– Blimey.

– I know.

You'd never know it was Christmas, here. The house looks so shut up and derelict, you'd never guess anyone was living here at all. Then a dog barks, deep within the house, as they park the car (Tonya's) and walk up the long path to the door. Do they imagine it, or does a curtain twitch upstairs?

Woof woof.

– He's a soft old thing really. We have to go round the back.

Betty gets the keys out, but Maud has long since forgotten about things like locks, and keys, and night time. In they go. Woof woof! He hadn't the strength to climb the stairs, last night.

– Morning, boy! Remember me? Have a biscuit.

Tonya is looking about her.

– Blimey, she says again, and then: – Are you sure she's still here?

– Course. I expect she's waiting for us.

She certainly is. Maud has been waiting for some time, for this very moment.

In the good old days – that was, in her happy days, her best days, when the farm was running well and she was more properly in charge – Maud used to go out from time to time to stride across the fields and pot a rabbit. Off she went, Kep at her heels: racing after the kill and trotting home with her, limp little body dangling from his jaws.

Things have gone a long long way downhill since then, and it's an aeon since the gun (her father's) has been brought up from the cellar, cleaned and loaded. Somehow, she never thought of it, when Mr Fox came round.

She's thought about it since. Oh, yes.

Isn't memory a funny thing? As your mind goes, you can hardly remember your own name. Yet things you haven't done for years: somehow, when needed, they all come nicely back.

Maud, in the wake of Betty's visit, remembered something. She went down to the filthy old cellar with Kep (Woof *woof!* He felt quite young again, on this adventure) and she brought up her father's rifle. It's old and cold and rusty, but she knows just what to do. Not for nothing did she spend her childhood watching her father (someone whom Henry, as a boy, had liked a lot) cleaning and polishing and loading, trying out the catch. Not for nothing did she do the same, for years. She used to be a bloody good shot.

Out come the rags from the gun box. It feels like yesterday, as she cleans it up, and oils it (an ancient can is leaking on to the rags). Then she loads it. There are six cartridges in a little box beneath those rags: as she slips one down the barrel, she feels more herself than she has done for months.

– Come on, Kep.

Up the stairs they go together. She pulls back the bedclothes and she tucks in the gun, over on the side, by the wall, so it won't fall out. Then she goes downstairs again, and forgets all about it. Georgia, too tired to change the bedclothes on her last visit before Christmas (what does she imagine Maud will do, this Christmas, all alone? Oh, thank God for Betty) knows nothing about it. Now and then, of a winter's night, Maud feels the long cold barrel against her mottled legs, and wonders what it's doing there.

Now she remembers.

They stand at the foot of the stairs.

– Hello, dear! You've got visitors!

Up they go, past the damp and peeling paper and over the rotting carpet, along the dusty landing to Maud's bedroom door. Slowly, slowly, Kep comes up behind them.

Knock knock.

– Can we come in?

Silence.

– Look, the dog's come up.

– He'll have to be put down, won't he, if she goes into a home. Sad, isn't it?

– I'd take him in, but with the beagles—

– Poor old fellow. Still, he's old.

Maud, in her bed, is shaking. Out she gets.

– Hello, dear? Are you awake? It's Betty, remember me?

– I can hear her. Come on, in we go.

In they go.

The bed is empty, and at first they don't see her.

Then they do.

She's up against the window on the far side of the room. The curtains are still drawn, so it's shadowy in here, and she's against what light there is, but they see her all right: toothless, mad eyes glinting, grey hair sticking up all round her head, pointing a gun straight at them.

For a second, there's a silence, as they take it in. Then they scream, and scramble for the door. But Kep's come up behind them, and he blocks their way.

– Kep! Bring them down! Attack! Attack!

He sees the gun and he's on to them in a flash. He's old, but he's a gun dog, trained to obey every command, and he leaps up, barking as he's never barked in his life, and seizes Betty's arm. She screams again, as Tonya bolts for the door, and then the gun goes off.

Tonya, on the landing, is punching 999 into her mobile, shaking so hard she can hardly stand. The gun goes off again, and there's a dreadful sound. Out staggers Betty, screaming, clutching her arm. Somehow, they make it down the stairs. She's pouring blood, but they make it to the car.

– Is it fire, police or ambulance?

– Ambulance! Quick! Quick! And the police! There's a madwoman here and my friend is bleeding.

Tonya rips off her coat, rips off her overall, binds it as hard as she can round Betty's arm, all her old nursing training coming back. Somehow, she finds the strength to drive away.

Sirens. Police and ambulance, racing through the lanes.

Upstairs, in her dusty old bedroom, Maud is slumped over the body of her dearest friend in the world. He wasn't meant to die at all. Not ever.

Maud is sectioned. This is vile. It's vile, but what else can anyone possibly do? She's taken away in an ambulance by four strong men and women: restrained, injected, locked away.

Georgia almost faints when she hears the news. She's giving a little drinks party: the Milners, the Cartwrights, people from Birkbeck, people from the street. She didn't give one last year, she couldn't face it, can still hardly bear to think about last Christmas, but now—

Now the tree is up, and the house is full of people, wine mulling away on the stove and everything looking festive and cheerful. Lovely to have everyone here again, and Chloe is doing her stuff, and helping. She's brought her flatmate, Edmund, and though Georgia's still not quite sure about him (or that play) he's certainly useful now, going round with a jug, and the bowls of—

The phone is ringing.

– I'll get it! Then: – Mum? It's the Social Services. They sound a bit—

In York, the Sullivans have a gentle but very happy Christmas, everyone together. Well, almost everyone. No Paula? No. No, she's . . . well, actually, we've split up. Nick! It's OK. Really. I'll tell you about it after Christmas. Anyone want a drink?

Dido's best present (apart from being alive) comes from Chloe. It's a little striped silk hat, to wear when she's reading in bed. She can't do very much of that at the moment: her eyes still aren't quite right, since the op, and she mustn't strain them, though her consultant says they should get back to almost normal. They'd better. In the meantime, the hat is the most beautiful thing she's ever seen: bands of gold, emerald, crimson, Prussian blue. It suits her perfectly: clever, clever Chloe. It comes wrapped in tissue paper, and with lots and lots of love.

In London, Georgia and Chloe do their very best. They go to midnight mass on Christmas Eve, as they've always done. Both of them cry, as *Once in Royal David's City* sounds in that pure high note through the crowds of people, but then, who doesn't? I'm crying now, just writing about it. On Christmas morning they open their presents and watch the cats go mad.

Then, after a light lunch, they both drive down to Sussex.

24

– Chloe? Hi. Hi. It's – um – it's Nick.

– Nick! Hi, how are you? Happy New Year! How's everyone?

All the decorations are down, and the flat is pretty well back to normal. She hadn't the strength to give a party, but in the end she was glad that Edmund got it together. What is New Year's Eve, without a party? They all did all the usual things, everyone kissing and hugging round the telly as the hour struck, and she (to hell with it) got plastered. Now she's sobering up a bit, back to work, and thinking: now what?

– I rang to thank you for your fantastic present for Mum. The hat. She really loves it.

– Gosh, thanks, Nick. I'm so glad. She's written to me, actually. (Don't say that, or he'll feel all useless. Too late now.)

– Has she? Well, I just wanted to sort of . . . you know . . . get in touch.

– Thanks. It's really lovely to hear you.

(It is.)

– How was your Christmas?

– You haven't heard? About Maud?

– Maud?

She reminds him, she tells him all about it. No, he didn't know, for Georgia, thinking, quite rightly, that the Sullivans have all had quite enough on their plate, has decided not to tell Dido yet. Not until things have calmed down a bit. If they ever do. Maud is still in hospital.

— It's *awful*. And the worst thing was — well, I shouldn't say that, but it really upset me — her dog got shot. By mistake. Of course, it would've been much worse if the carer had been killed or something, but—

He understands. He's always loved dogs. (And cats.) It sounds dreadful.

— Anyway, Nick, how are you getting on? How's the Ph.D.? Thought of a title yet?

— Er, no. Not yet. It's going OK, I suppose. The thing is, I need to come down to London, to do some research.

Oh, yes?

— And I was wondering . . .

They meet in a restaurant near the British Library. You might think that King's Cross, still going through its Eurostar development and an utter mess, would not be the most promising place in the world for this meeting, but you'd be wrong. Georgia has been to a silver wedding party at a place tucked away in a Georgian back street. Quite a revelation. She happens to mention it to Chloe. Once it was a warehouse, but now . . .

— Hi!

He's there before her, standing in the plate-glass doorway, wearing a really nice winter coat and scarf, and inside it looks, like, really twinkly.

— Hi, Chloe. Good to see you.

They kiss on both cheeks; they go inside.

— What shall we have?

Not, What would you like? But we. Already, even over the menu, it's clear what's going to happen.

Let's face it they've known one another all their lives.

Let's face it, they were made for one another.

Coming out of the restaurant, into the cold, she says it's *freezing*, and he puts his arm around her, and then just pulls her into him, and both, as they kiss, (and kiss and kiss, all out on the street, who cares) feel properly alive for the first time in – well, in Nick's case, years and years. As for Chloe: next morning she knows what real love really feels like. So does he.

And their news makes everyone so so happy.

In York, Dido and Jeffrey are over the moon. A spring wedding? (Why wait? Why wait another minute?) How simply lovely.

Dido and Georgia are on the phone, arranging for her to come up for a visit. Dido's taking things very gently still, but she'd love to see her. A real tonic. Dear Georgia, you must be so pleased. We're thrilled. With such a joyful event in view, Georgia thinks she can risk telling Dido about events with Maud. Then she decides that she won't. Not yet. It's still too awful.

You might think that the future for Maud is too sad and bleak to contemplate. For quite a long time, it looks like that. Charges are brought against her, but soon dropped: she's not fit to appear in court and of course the verdict will be While of Unsound Mind.

Georgia has written a long letter to Betty, apologising from the bottom of her heart. She offers compensation. It's a bit out of order, but Betty takes it. Slowly, she gets better. Thank God for that. Tonya's off with stress. No wonder. But in the end – brave women – both go back to work.

Georgia goes down to visit her. God, it's grim. Maud is drugged up to the eyeballs, doesn't know her, can't remember anything of what happened, looks about a hundred. She eats, and is putting on too much weight, without proper exercise. She sleeps (too much). It looks as though she'll end her days like this. Let it come soon. Don't let her go dragging on for years.

But then—

There's a lot of research going on into dementia now. It's not (not nearly) funded in the way that cancer research is funded, but then nothing is, though dementia probably lies in wait for most of us. However, some clever and imaginative researchers have people like Maud in view. You could call them truly original thinkers. Inspired, even.

Two clever people are driving down to Sussex. Musical instruments are in the car: a banjo, a drum, percussion. As it happens, one of them is doing research in York, but that's neither here nor there, though it does rather nicely bring everything together.

At the hospital, on their prearranged visit, they have a long discussion about which patients might most benefit from what they want to do. Three or four are mentioned. Fine. What about someone who seems intractable? A real challenge. Someone you'd never imagine could connect with the world again . . .

It takes months. First, they have to get Maud off some of the drugs, and she goes completely haywire until they get it right. But then – they give it a go. They sit with her and talk, and get to know her. Then they start playing a bit, to see how she reacts. A nice tune on the banjo, a bit of drumming. No doubt about it, Maud is interested. They give her percussion things to try: she shakes a tambourine. She shakes it again.

– What about this?

They offer the triangle and stick. They tinkle away on it first, and at those high clear sounds her eyes light up, just a bit, enough for them to keep at it. But it's too much for her to strike the thing herself: unless she can hold it by its thread, it just sounds dull. She flings it away. They give her a go on the drum. She bangs away. Then it's time to go.

Next week comes.

– Hello, Maud. How are you today?

Can't get a word out of her. Not a dickybird. Must be a bad day.

– Why don't we give her the banjo?

One of them (Ben) strums away for a bit. Then he hands it over. Maud is sitting in her chair, in the room the hospital has set aside for these sessions. A light spring wind is tossing the trees about outside the window. Afternoon sun streams in. Maud takes the banjo, and runs her fingers over it. She does it again. She smiles.

– Maud? Want to tell us a story? We can set it to music. Would you like that?

It takes months. But there's no doubt about it: it's working. Maud, with that banjo, is happy. She sits, she strums, she (sort of) sings for hours. At first, no one can tell what she's going on about, but after a while, as she sings the lines over and over again, they piece a story together.

It all has a kind of a country and western feel to it: we're not talking Woody Guthrie, but it certainly has a shape, a form. They start recording: they play it back. This she really likes. They watch her listen, like the dog with His Master's Voice, on that lovely old label. They edit. They splice. When they play it to the Director of the Hospital Trust, he has tears in his eyes. When they organise a concert, Maud is the last to make an appearance. It's not on a stage, of course, just a room: everything safe and familiar, with people in a circle. Staff. Other patients. Relatives. This means Georgia, Chloe and Nick. Guess who's in floods, at the end.

Maud, with Ben and Sally, shuffles into the centre. She sits down; they give her the banjo. They turn on the tape, so she can hear herself, and (sort of) sing along. After a while, unbelievably, she does.

– Get up in the morning/Go out with my dog/with my dog/through the fields, through the fields/down the lane, down the lane/over the hills/over the hills/over the hills and far away . . .

25

G eorgia is up in Henry's study. It's spring, and she's tidying up a bit. She's cleaning (with her cleaning lady) the whole of the house. You can't have a wedding party in a house that's less than spotless: she can't, anyway. What is it going to be like, seeing her only daughter married, without her husband beside her? A part of her is so happy; a part of her dreads it. And for a long time there was the question: who, now Henry is gone, will give Chloe away? Of course, she and Nick could have chosen to have a register office wedding, as (not like) both their parents had done. But how could Chloe have passed up the chance of The Dress? Sorry, Mum, you don't mind, do you? It's just— I know, darling. And Nick? He'd get married in a combine harvester, if he thought that's what Chloe wanted. But in truth: deep down, he's always wanted to get married in church. Can't put his finger on why, exactly, but it just feels right.

Now, then. The big question. Could Jeffrey give away his future daughter-in-law?

No. No, surely not. All too much. Probably against the law, anyway.

But Henry was Jeffrey's oldest friend. It makes much more sense than an uncle in Canada whom Chloe hardly sees. And Chloe has always been so fond . . . And he of her.

Could he? Would he like to?

He can't think of a single thing in the world he'd like more.

Right. It's settled then. (Over champagne, in York.)

341

* * *

It's a long time since Georgia has been up here. She's still not going to clear things out; as far as she's concerned, it can all stay like this for ever. No one's going to come up here, anyway, at the party. Dido and Jeffrey will be in the spare room; Leo and Kate and the children in a hotel. (Izzy is going to be bridesmaid: now she and Chloe can really go to town. And Sam, of course, will be pageboy.) Georgia is treating the family to the London hotel in the same way she's paying for the wedding: with the insurance policy which Henry took out to pay for just this occasion. Was there nothing he didn't think of, plan for? Hope for?

Georgia sits at his desk with her head in her hands.

How can he not be here, to see Chloe married?

Oh, will he never come back? Surely now, after two whole years . . .

Surely it's time.

After a while, she gets going again. She brushes down his jacket on the hook behind the door, she brushes the cat hairs off his chair, she dusts the bookshelves, and the photographs: Chloe, aged about six, holding the string of a kite on Parliament Hill, looking up and up. Georgia and Henry, snapped by Chloe in the Lakes, squinting into the sun, with sheep on the fells behind them. Georgia, reading in the garden. As she takes this one down, something falls out from behind: a letter.

Do you open other people's letters? Even those of your dead husband?

But she knows who it's from: there's no one else who writes like this. She wouldn't mind, would she? And Henry would understand. She looks at the date on the postmark. Autumn, three years ago. Henry had had his diagnosis. Just. She slips out the single page.

Darling Dad,
     This is just to tel you that I love you more than enything on erth . . .

It's a while before Georgia starts tidying up again. She dusts Henry's computer, and his desk. She blows dust off all the heaps of paper: the files of policy papers, briefing papers, minutes, submissions to the Minister. All that, and his unpublished book, the life of the great-great-uncle who went to govern a long-gone African province, and never came back. What happened to him? Who, now, cares at all?

The thing about Henry (one of the things) was that he could really write. If he put his mind to a biography, he'd do it really well, make it the kind of thing you'd really want to read, however unfashionable the subject. She pulls out the file of the second draft, and blows the dust off. The window is open to the fresh spring air. This was always a lovely room. Being up here brings back all her sadness, but being up here, after all this time, reconnects her with everything which, to both of them, has always mattered. Books. Writing. Quietude.

In the spring of 1861, a young man set sail for an African province which no one remembers now . . .

She settles down. Time passes.

She looks at her watch. Heavens (as Dido would say). She must get on. And she stands up, slips the file back into its place. It's awkward, and one or two pages fall out.
     What's this?
     A quotation, written in Henry's fountain pen. Written when? She reads, and she knows. When else would it be?

Human kind cannot bear very much reality . . .

Eliot's line has lived within her for as long as she can remember. She's taught *Four Quartets* more times than she cares to think. She and Henry once read them together, long before Chloe was born. Was this the line which came back to him, when he knew?

Oh, Henry, Henry, Henry.

How could this have happened to you? To *you?*

There's another loose page, with lines scratched out, rewritten, several times. This isn't a quotation, this is something Henry's written himself, trying out this and that, crossing out, then finally settling on two brief lines. He never told her he was writing a poem. Perhaps, as illness overtook him, he forgot.

What is the meaning of my life and death
The arc from the first to the last breath—

The last great question. Georgia sits at the desk. She cannot move. It's as if he is here, as if he's speaking to her, from a long long way away.

– Henry? Darling?

But there is, of course, no answer. There's only a piece of paper, lifting in the air at the open window; only a paper, soundlessly rising and falling in the air at the open window.

Acknowledgements

Extract from *The Brothers Karamazov* by Fyodor Dostoyevsky, translated with an introduction by David Magarshack (Penguin Classics, 1958), copyright © David Magarshack 1958, reproduced by permission of Penguin Books Ltd.

Lines from 'Burnt Norton' by T. S. Eliot (*Collected Poems 1909–1962*) are reproduced by permission of Faber and Faber Ltd.

Extract from *My Childhood* by Maxim Gorky, translated with an introduction by Ronald Wilks (Penguin Classics, 1996), copyright © Ronald Wilks 1966, reproduced by permission of Penguin Books Ltd.

Quotations from Logan Pearsall Smith are reproduced by kind permission of The London Library.

Extract from *Little Grey Rabbit Makes Lace* by Alison Uttley reprinted by permission of HarperCollins Publishers Ltd © Alison Uttley 1950.

You can buy any of these other **Review** titles from
your bookshop or *direct from the publisher*.

FREE P&P AND UK DELIVERY
(Overseas and Ireland £3.50 per book)

The Mysteries of Glass	Sue Gee	£7.99
The Hours of the Night	Sue Gee	£7.99
The Ingenious Edgar Jones	Elizabeth Garner	£7.99
Villa Serena	Domenica de Rosa	£7.99
Wives of the East Wind	Liu Hong	£7.99
The Vanishing Act of Esme Lennox	Maggie O'Farrell	£7.99
Red River	Lalita Tademy	£7.99
Last Seen Leaving	Kelly Braffet	£7.99
Symphony	Jude Morgan	£7.99

TO ORDER SIMPLY CALL THIS NUMBER

01235 400 414

or visit our website: www.headline.co.uk

Prices and availability subject to change without notice.